OF
THE
BLOOD

USA TODAY BESTSELLING AUTHOR

CAMEO RENAE

OF THE BLOOD

1

HEIR OF BLOOD AND FIRE

CAMEO RENAE

MORE BY CAMEO RENAE

TALBRINTH

To Incendia

CRIMSON COVE

SANGERIAN SEA

CARPATHIA

t Port

of the blood

To Ewelina – my friend and beta reader – for loving this story so much,
and cheering me on (pushing me) to finish the next.

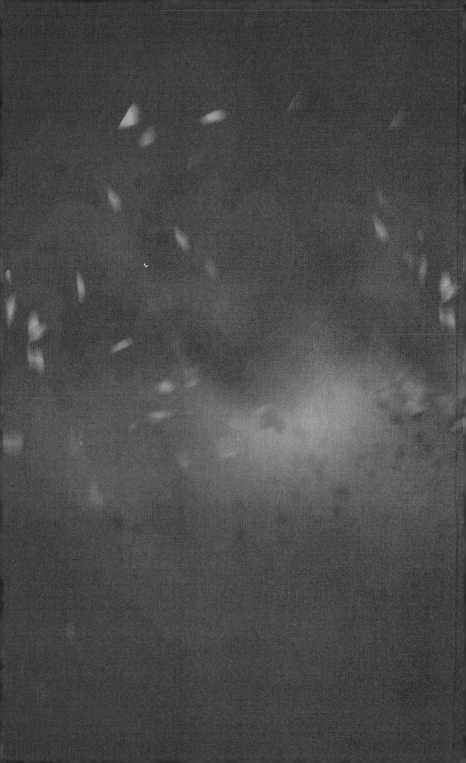

CHAPTER ONE

I pleaded for death. Prayed it would come swiftly and end the agonizing pain consuming my body. Yet, at the corners of my dimmed eyes, a shadowed figure remained at my bedside, whispering lies of promise that this suffering would soon end. But the misery was ever powerful, destroying all illusions of hope, enfolding me in a cocoon of flame and darkness.

Was this how my life would end? Was I going to die on my eighteenth birthday?

Six hours earlier…

"Finished," Brynna informed. "Gods, I'm good." Long lashes flickered over baby-blue eyes as she regarded her work. "You have to let me make you up more often."

With an internal sigh, I drew in a heavy breath. "No thanks. My skin prefers to breathe."

"I'll wager you twenty gold skrag you'll have looks from

all the guys tonight." The glint in her eyes and widening smile caused me to smirk.

"Not interested. You can keep your skrag *and* your guys."

I had to remember that Brynna was doing this for me, for my eighteenth birthday, although I'd only desired the company of my best friend and a peaceful, simple dinner. But Brynna was far from simple. She was taking full advantage of the fact our parents were overseas for the next few weeks, sailing to the country of Hale to trade and barter mined reserves at Merchant Port.

"Whatever," she said, snickering. "But that's why you have me. My objective in life is to snap you out of your shell, Calla Caldwell." She straightened her back and crossed her arms over her chest. "I'm serious. Look at yourself. Go on." Her hand signaled toward the mirror, urging me to look. "There will be boys here tonight. Very *handsome* and suitable boys." She thrust her palm up an inch from smacking my nose. "And before you protest, just remember you're eighteen now, and the only guy you've ever had any interest in might as well be a figure in one of your romance novels. A fabrication of your imagination."

"He is not," I mumbled.

"Are you kidding me?" I was afraid she'd lose her eyes as they rolled clear to the back of her head. "Your crush is nine years older than you and in the military. Your dad hired him to educate you in self-defense when you were *ten*.

It's been years since you've seen him. Not to mention, the obsession was one-sided." She let out a pathetic sigh. "It's time to wake up and slip your toes into new pools, Cal."

I bit my tongue. I wasn't going to bicker with her. For one, she was correct. As usual. Yes, I'd had a childhood infatuation with my self-defense mentor. And yes, I continued to use him as an excuse to evade any committed relationship, because the truth was . . . I didn't want one. I'd witnessed the amount of effort that went into relationships—via Brynna—and I wasn't ready to tie any part of my life to someone else. I preferred to live on my own terms. At least for a bit longer.

Rising, I ran my fingertips across the birthday garment she'd purchased for me from a small boutique in town—a modest, yet exquisite, pastel pink dress with ivory roses stitched into the bodice. The bottom was flowy, settling just above my knees. She'd styled my long chestnut hair half-up and half-down, with a braided crown around a small bun.

Drawing in a heavy breath, I swiveled and peered into the mirror. Brynna had an extraordinary means of altering me from plain to almost regal. My face was glowing, cheeks dusted in pink, and lips glossed. My golden eyes looked much more pronounced outlined in kohl, and she'd even curled my lashes.

"So, what do you think?" Brynna asked.

She slipped on a floor-length, blue silk gown, which hugged her hourglass figure perfectly. Her silky blonde hair was curled over her shoulders, and her makeup made her look like a figurine, finished with ruby red lips. Around her neck, she wore a golden, heart-shaped pendant with a swan engraved on the top. The swan's eye was a small diamond, a present given by her parents on her sixteenth birthday, and she wore it every day.

I twisted backward and wrapped her in a hug. "Thank you," I whispered. "For everything. But seriously, you shouldn't have."

"Hey," she exhaled, hugging me back. "You'll enjoy yourself tonight. That's an *order*. Your best friend threw this party for you because she loves you."

"I love you too," I sighed.

The doorbell chimed, causing Brynna to squeal. "They're here!" She clasped her fingers around my wrist and tugged me down the stairs.

About fifty guests showed up. Most I didn't care for, and at least a dozen I didn't know. Brynna had assured me it would be modest, but word had spread like wildfire. The youth in Southport were always looking for a reason to party, especially when alcohol was involved. And most knew Brynna's parents were affluent and had an ample supply.

A couple of visitors said hello and wished me a happy birthday, but the majority didn't know who I was or even cared. I smiled as I maneuvered through the bodies, trying to intermingle and be cordial. But as usual, I found it awkward associating with others my age. I never felt like I fit in, and they never really cared to include me.

Although Brynna's home was spacious, I still felt heated and claustrophobic. There were too many bodies inside.

Air. I needed fresh, cool air.

A few of the boys addressed me as I made my way toward the back door, but I quickly claimed I needed to meet someone outside. *Lies.* I just hoped Brynna wasn't within hearing distance. If she were, I'd never hear the end of it.

Hurrying towards the exit, I felt the stares and heard unguarded whispers. Those who recognized me were stunned to see the bashful girl—who usually had her face buried in a book—all made up. Tonight, they were calling me *pretty.* But it was just a mask, courtesy of Brynna.

Brynna noticed my attempt to sneak out the back and threw me an unsettled glance. I returned a smile and a thumbs up, letting her know I was fine. Throwing this party—or any party in general—is what made her happy. She loved entertaining guests and was damn good at it. So, if she was happy, I'd be too. For her. She deserved that much.

Once outside, I discovered reprieve in a shadowed corner just beyond the pool. I stood still, inhaling the balmy salt breeze, gazing up at the moon and watching its luminous light dance across the Argent Sea. I could have stood here all night, alone, with this remarkable view and would have been content.

Peeking back at the crowd, I realized no one even cared that I'd disappeared. I spotted Brynna and smiled, watching how easily she maneuvered through the crowd, a bit envious of how comfortable her exchanges were with others.

Brynna and I had been best friends since birth and were raised together. Not only were we born two months apart—she was older—but our parents were best friends and business partners.

We lived in Southport, a modest coastal town in the country of Sartha—the largest producer of mineral reserves on the continent of Talbrinth. Our fathers owned two of the largest mines, which yielded silver, copper, and gold.

It had taken a few years and a considerable amount of assistance from the communities to bring the mines back up and running after the Great War. But our fathers employed hundreds in Sartha during the process.

Brynna lived in a grand, two-story home on a ridge overlooking the Argent Sea. It was magnificent and lavish, the furnishings extravagant. Her mother spared no expense on the decor, loving to barter and trade at Merchant Port, particularly with merchants from Baelfast who were wealthy in textiles. They'd recently built a pool made with exquisite mosaics, which is another reason why Brynna wanted to throw the party. To show it off.

My parents were much more reserved with their wealth. My father knew there were still many struggling to get back on their feet after the Great War, so we lived in a modest single-level home that didn't attract scrutiny . . . at least from the outside. But inside, my mother exhibited tapestries, art, and furnishings that would rival any palace.

I sucked in a deep breath and let my head fall back, gazing up at the eggplant-colored sky filled with sparkling stars. It never ceased to amaze me how glorious and infinite the sky was, and how insignificant I felt standing beneath it.

As the party crawled on, I found a bench nearby and for the next few hours, perched alone, watching the crowd mingle for my birthday. I could tell a great deal about an individual from observing them—those who were born leaders, those who were followers, and those who'd had way too much to drink.

The party would be ending shortly anyway because of Sartha's new curfew. Ever since Sartha's new ruler, Lord Braddock, came into leadership, any youth under the age of nineteen captured on the roads after the bells tolled at midnight would be thrown in a prison cell where they would spend the night on a cold, stone floor. Stories had spread that the cells were filthy, and rat infested. So very few disobeyed.

As I rose to my feet, I felt lightheaded. My limbs were suddenly weak and weighted, and my body heated. Taking a few steps backward, I leaned against the cool rock wall behind me. The air became so heavy I could barely breathe.

What the hell was wrong with me?

Something inside, deep down in my core, felt as if it was being pulled by an unseen string. A string attached to — I froze in place as my gaze settled across the pool on a pair of azure eyes affixed to the most gorgeous guy I'd ever seen. He was tall, at least six-two, maybe in his mid-twenties. Strands of raven hair feathered across his chiseled face. He wore a crisp, black button-down shirt—a few of the top buttons left undone—and black slacks which caressed his muscular contours.

Good gods. *Where did he come from?* He looked as if

he'd stepped right out of a dream.

Voices murmured and people pushed outside to where he was standing. It seemed everybody was trying to figure out who this handsome stranger was and where he'd come from. He was obviously out of his element, failing miserably at blending in.

My heart was racing, a cold sweat blanketed my body. All within the time he'd arrived.

It didn't look like he was associated with anybody here, and it made me wonder if he was from our town of Southport, or Sartha for that matter. I'd never seen him before. He had the face of someone I wouldn't easily forget . . . rich, no doubt, apparent from his attire and stately demeanor.

And now, he was the life of my party.

A few of the girls flung themselves into his pathway as he wandered by, seeking to get his attention. But I observed from afar, from my private, shadowed place, marveling at the way he carried himself with a formal reserve.

I caught a cluster of girls moving toward Brynna, likely to question her. Their lustful eyes raked over the newcomer from head to toe, but as Brynna glanced in his direction, her eyes narrowed, and she shook her head. She didn't know who he was either.

He was cordial, his smile melting the young women around him. But he continued to keep himself at a distance.

What was he doing here?

But those eyes—those deep, azure eyes—kept finding their way to my dimmed corner. To *me.* And every time our eyes met, for a few breathless moments, I swore I heard a slight voice which seemed to cover the distance between us saying, "I see you, Calla. I've come for you."

It was foolish to think such absurd thoughts. I shook my head, struggling to snap from whatever bewitching spell he'd cast over me. But every time he glanced over to where I stood, I found myself slipping further, tangling into whatever mysterious, enchanted web he was weaving.

I watched a few guys drag their intoxicated dates inside, away from the newcomer, and I didn't blame them. If I were them, I would have done the same.

Then, out of the blue, the stranger strode in my direction, his hands tucked casually into his pockets. Each step so smooth, so measured, it was as if he was sliding over air.

All eyes outside were affixed on him. There was something about him, something regal and commanding in the way he moved, completely postured with each lengthy stride.

My breath stopped as he halted a foot away from me. I was mesmerized by the way the moonlight shimmered over the sharp contours of his face. And those eyes —

"Happy Birthday, Calla," he uttered in a deep, elegant tone. Dipping his head, he presented me with a smile that warmed my insides.

Gasps erupted, and I could feel the heavy stares of girls who had vied for his attention. Brynna was standing in the crowd with wide eyes, mouth agape, hands crossed over her heart. As her eyes caught mine, she smiled.

Before I could say a word, the stranger leaned over and pressed his cold lips against my cheek, making my insides quiver. I was falling apart, unhinging at the seams. All over a guy? That was *not* my thing.

"H—how do you know me?" Those were the first words to exit my mouth, and I immediately wanted to take them back. But I knew everyone within hearing distance was just as anxious to hear his reply.

Ignoring my question, an incredibly sexy grin spread across his full lips. He reached down and slipped his large hand around mine, swallowing my fingers whole. "Come. I'd like to speak with you."

The world dissolved and pooled beneath my feet. Every sound muted, bodies faded, and the only two who remained were this beautiful stranger and me. Without another word, he led me past the guests and into the house.

"Calla!" Brynna shouted from behind.

The stranger halted and we both turned to face her. But he was the one who spoke. "Don't worry. Calla is safe with me. I'd just like to speak with her alone for a moment. If that's all right?" The sincerity in his darkened eyes and in his gentle voice seemed to melt Brynna's apprehension . . . and mine.

Brynna, as if in a trance of her own, glanced at me and nodded. "Okay. But let me know if you need anything." I nodded back before the stranger proceeded to lead me up the stairs, as if he knew the place.

Entering one of the rooms, he clicked the door shut

behind him, keeping the lights off.

I stepped away from his overpowering presence and stood in the heart of Brynna's spare bedroom, my feet fixed to the floor. My eyes were frozen on this fiercely beautiful man, powerless to look away, even if I'd wanted to. Moonlight spilled through the window, gilding his sharpened features and statuesque frame.

"You're a vision. Even more beautiful than I imagined," he finally spoke, his eyes appraising every inch of me. There was a darkness which seemed to emanate from him, and I swore I felt it coiling around me in a cool caress.

Shaking my head, I struggled to free myself from whatever fog had entered my mind.

"H-how do you know me?"

He hesitated, carefully regarding my question. "Are you frightened of me?" It wasn't an answer, but his tone was smooth, gentle.

"No," I replied much too easily. But I wasn't afraid of him. I felt . . . *safe*, somehow.

His purplish-blue eyes seemed to be glowing, and an almost feral smile raised on the edges of his lips. Lips I envisioned against mine.

Well defined arms crossed over a broad chest as he leaned against the door, one foot casually crossing over the other. "Tonight, is about you, Calla. And I'll remain here, fixed to this spot, unless . . ." His head inclined to the side with a lopsided grin. "Unless you want me to come closer."

If it were possible, my heart thumped louder inside my

chest. My unspoken answer was yes, but it terrified me to say it out loud. I'd never been so carefree or reckless in all my life, never one to throw caution to the wind. But there was something about him. Something mysterious and intriguing. Something every part of me was attracted to. Maybe it was lust, but whatever it was, he had me fully wrapped in it.

Brynna had boasted about her one-night flings. No attachments. Just a single night of fun that was forgotten the next day. If she could manage it, why couldn't I? It was my birthday after all, and I was now an adult.

But . . .

"Why me?" I repeated. "When you could've had any one of those girls downstairs." It was a sincere question of which I expected an honest answer.

His eyes darkened with an obvious want. "I didn't come for *any* girl, Calla. I came for *you*."

Butterflies whirled inside my belly, but he still didn't answer my question. "Why?"

His eyes flashed, assessing me. Gods, he was gorgeous.

"We are somehow connected, you and I." He seemed as if he was going to take a step forward, but he stopped, remaining in place. "I don't understand it myself, but I feel tied to you," he crooned, his gaze narrowed. "You feel it too, don't you?"

"I—" I hesitated. I did feel something between us but wasn't sure what *it* was. There was an undeniable physical attraction and having him so close caused every cell in my body to hum. But I wasn't about to admit that to a stranger .

. . no matter how attractive he was. For all I knew, he could have been a pervert or a murderer. But as the thought crossed my mind, I didn't sense he was either. "I'm not certain what I feel."

His smile grew and with it a need pulsed heavily inside me, melting my core, awakening my deprived desires.

"Just say the word," he purred. His voice was low and dripping with seduction, quietly waiting until I recovered my voice. "Tell me to come or tell me to leave. I will willingly do either. The choice is yours."

In my mind, I considered the risks. All the risks. But hell, it was my birthday, and I *was* technically an adult. Besides, he was giving me a choice, and I wasn't under any influence of alcohol, although around him I felt like it. And I wasn't being pushed to do anything I didn't want to.

My choice.

I peered deep into those darkened eyes and offered him a nod, tossing my conscience to the wind.

"Come."

CHAPTER TWO

In a split second, he was inches away, splaying his palm over the middle of my chest, leaning forward as if seeking my heartbeat. Closing his eyes, a grin unfurled on his full lips. "Can you hear it? It sings for me."

Good gods.

In one sudden move—so fast it caused my head to whirl—I was in his arms, my back pressed against the far wall, his body tight against mine. His breath was sweet, his lips drifting precariously close to mine. "Tell me you feel it, Calla. The link between us."

All I could do was nod because all speech was failing me.

His scent was delicious. A wild mix of blends I couldn't describe. Maybe a touch of earth and wind and spice, but also a hint of something sweet. Perhaps it was all those elements combined and melded together. A perfect blend.

"Calla," he breathed. "I'm going to kiss you."

I wanted him to kiss me.

With a nod of approval, he pressed a tender kiss to my lips.

Slow, soft, thoughtful. Not rough or wild. And that kiss took my breath away. It made my brain numb and sent tingles surging through my entire body. But I wanted more. Craved more. I opened my mouth to him, letting him deepen the kiss. And he moaned in approval.

His mouth ravaged mine, this time unrestrained. Our mouths and tongues moved like they were meant to be together. A primal need was drawing us closer. His kiss was so deep, so passionate, that I started swimming in that sea of starlight I'd been admiring moments ago.

I wanted him, like I'd never wanted anyone or anything before, and that awareness both frightened and thrilled me.

His cold hands trailed down my collar and over my shoulders, but his lingering touch felt like fire, setting my skin ablaze. There was electricity around us, between us, through us. If his arms weren't folded around me, holding me up, my knees would have buckled.

While I had some common sense left, I drew away from his kiss.

"Who are you?" I breathed. This was something I needed to know before things went any further.

His forehead relaxed against mine, his breath heavy. "A dark knight come to protect you. A knight who can pleasure you beyond anything you've ever imagined."

I abruptly forgot my question and didn't care. Those soft-spoken words added fuel to the already roaring fire inside me.

He leaned back, his azure gaze capturing mine. "But you have to want me too."

His voice was pure seduction, like a balm instantly soothing my insecurities. How could he do that? This man had placed me under a spell so powerful, I wasn't capable of breaking free. My body craved more. More of him. Desperate for whatever he could give me.

"Do you want me, Calla?" His words resounded through my very core.

"Yes," I returned in a breathless whisper.

I was suddenly on the bed, his powerful frame hovering above me.

"I'd never harm you," he breathed.

I don't know why he said it, but I believed him.

He paused, those alluring eyes studying mine. No one had ever looked at me the way he was looking at me. He'd enchanted me, and I knew after tonight, I'd never be the same.

His name. I was about to ask his name when his lips crashed against mine. This time with a powerful, primal possessiveness that made me gasp and clutch his shoulders.

My mind was gone. Lost to reason. Lost to this stranger with a handsome face I most definitely felt a connection with.

He tugged off his shirt and flung it to the floor, the darkness swallowing it up. I ran my palms down his back and felt nothing but solid muscle. His tongue swirled on my neck, making my fingers clasp him tighter.

He stiffened.

Everything stopped as he drew back from me, his expression one of bewilderment.

What happened?

Regret and insecurity oozed into me.

"What's wrong?" I asked. His eyes shifted to my left hand.

Clasping my wrist, he examined the silver purity ring on my finger. And just like that, the moment came to a plunging, icy stop.

His eyes scrutinized me. A curious look emblazed within them. "Are you a virgin?"

I yanked my hand from his grip. Embarrassment heating my cheeks. "What if I am?"

Everyone knew I was the virtuous granddaughter of a clergy. The girl who wore a purity ring and vowed to remain pure until the day I married. I was seven back then, and it sounded like a wonderful plan. But I'd grown up since, and now, the glittering silver ring shackled to my finger was strangling me.

His eyes softened. An affectionate smile blossomed on his full lips. "It doesn't change anything, Calla."

I knew nothing about him, yet he knew my name and spoke it like he'd known me for a lifetime.

I was never one to attract attention from the opposite

sex. Not like this, and especially not by someone like him . . . otherworldly beautiful who exuded a strong, masculine energy.

Caressing the sides of my face, he pressed another gentle kiss to my lips, my stress melting into a puddle. He continued planting kisses down my throat and across my collarbone until . . .

A searing pain stung my shoulder. I wailed, shoving his shoulders back, but he was like stone, unmoving.

Suddenly, his beautiful face was in front of mine, hovering inches above me. I gasped in dismay as crimson liquid dripped from two sharp incisors protruding from his blood-smeared lips. Shrieking, my cry was cut off by his mouth plunging down over mine. His lips were wet, a coppery taste coated my tongue. Blood. My blood.

He bit me. The bastard bit me.

The world around me started whirling. My body weakened as darkness slithered into the corners of my eyes, threatening to fill them entirely.

I struggled to force him off, but my arms were fastened beneath the power of his heavy grip.

"I'm sorry, Calla," he sighed, his cool breath nuzzling my ear. "I had no other option. And soon, you will understand why."

"Get the hell away from me," I cried. Anger and confusion erupted inside of me like a violent river. I couldn't breathe. I couldn't think. And I was losing consciousness.

"Go away!" I wailed again as darkness embraced me.

I woke to Brynna and a few other girls standing over me. Brynna was shaking my shoulders and calling my name. Concern swelled within her blue eyes and crumpled on her brow.

Blinking, I took in my surroundings and finally remembered where I was. And still groggy, the inquiries began. Questions I couldn't answer. Questions hammering my skull . . . pounding, pounding, pounding until I couldn't take it anymore.

They all demanded to know who the newcomer was, and where he went. They wanted details on what took place between us while we were alone.

"Please. Not now," I whined, massaging my closed eyes with the palms of my hands.

Brynna rose, telling the others that I needed rest and to be alone, then showed them out of the room. I heard her tell her goodbyes, and not long after, she returned with a glass of water and handed it to me. I gulped it down.

"Do you need me to send for a physician?" she asked, carefully examining me.

"Gods no. I'm fine," I exhaled, pushing a finger to my temple, hoping it would release a bit of the building pressure. "I'm just a little woozy and tired."

"Did—did he drug you?" she asked softly.

I shook my head, causing it to throb even more. "No."

But realization crashed into me like a stone wall. *He* was real. *He* had been here.

"Who was he?" she asked.

I let out a heavy groan. "I don't know."

"You didn't get his name?"

"No."

She let out a sharp sigh. "Well, he clearly knew you. He knew your name and knew it was your birthday. But I didn't invite him, and no one else has ever seen him before either."

There was nothing I could say. I truly knew nothing about him, and it made me feel entirely pitiful.

Fear coiled around me, slithering into my mind as I visualized the mysterious stranger with those penetrating azure eyes and sharp incisors stained with my blood.

I warred against the growing pressure tightening my chest. "I need to go home."

Brynna nodded and helped me gather my things before fetching the carriage to take me home. She traveled with me. The clatter of hooves and wooden wheels against the cobbled street didn't help the pulsing pain in my skull.

I needed to be alone. I needed to get home and sift through my night.

A few months ago, my parents had given me the cottage which sat on the edge of our land, overlooking the Argent Sea.

On most days, I'd relax out on the stoop, curled up with

a novel, listening to the wind rustling through the surrounding oak and sycamore trees. The birds would sing their lively tunes, while the waves of the sea crashed against the rocks below. To me, it was the most peaceful place in Sartha. It was my safe place. My sanctuary.

When we finally reached my home, I leaned over and enclosed Brynna in a hug.

"You know where to find me if you need anything, right?" she questioned. Settling her palms on my shoulders, her eyes scrutinized me. "Are you positive you don't want to stay at my place tonight?"

I shook my head. "No. But thank you again. The party was one I'll never forget." I forced a smile and she beamed back.

As I opened the carriage door, she grasped my arm. "Wait!"

Brynna dug through her handbag and shoved a small, white box into my hand. "Happy birthday, Calla."

I let out an exhale, shaking my head. "Brynna, you threw me a party and bought me a dress. You didn't have to buy me a gift too."

She shrugged. "You know me. I was in town the other day, and some relentless force drew me into this antique shop. As I wandered around, something just happened to jump out at me, imploring me to buy it. So, I did." She wiggled her fingers at the present, her face radiating with a wide smile. "Go ahead, open it."

I removed the small white ribbon and lifted the lid. Inside was a silver chain that held a pretty, circular pendant—about an inch in diameter—also fringed in silver. Around the edges of the circle were strange markings, rune's maybe, and inset at the very center was the most exquisite, sparkling gem. A rich azure—the exact hue of the stranger's eyes.

Goosebumps prickled my skin as I picked up the pendant.

"Well? Do you like it?" Brynna asked, her eyes twinkling, anticipating my response.

"I love it." Leaning over, I wrapped her in another hug. "You're too good to me."

"I knew you didn't want the party, so this is my *thank you* for entertaining me. And, since you declined to stay over, I guess I'll go visit Claude for the next couple days." She threw me a wink and a mischievous grin.

Claude Bentham was Brynna's present companion. He resided about a half hour away on the outskirts of Southport, where he had his own flat, and worked as an apprentice in his father's blacksmith shop. They met when Claude made a delivery to their home. Brynna said they connected immediately, and it seemed to be reciprocal. Claude was handsome, and although he was the son of a blacksmith, he was quite intelligent.

I growled at her. "Please, be safe."

"You know me." A devilish grin widened on her lips.

"Exactly. Which is why I mentioned it."

Her laughter filled the carriage. "Go on. Get comfortable.

Grab one of your romance novels and enjoy the rest of your birthday."

"I will." I hugged her one last time, watching and waving until her carriage disappeared down the darkened road.

My brain was still throbbing and my body weak as I strolled down the stone passageway to my cottage. I could hear the waves crashing against the rocks beyond the cliff.

I'd spent countless nights gazing out at the dim horizon, fantasizing of what existed beyond. But not tonight. Tonight, I needed to curl up in bed under my warm blankets and sleep.

After drawing a hot bath, I paused in front of the mirror, the night's events replaying in my mind. My fingers skimmed the area where I was bitten. I leaned toward the mirror, searching for marks. There was nothing but smooth skin. Not a blemish or bruise in sight.

I knew it was real, though. I felt it. Saw the blood dripping from the stranger's elongated teeth. I could also recall, in vivid detail, the sharp contours of his face, the way he walked and carried himself, and those unforgettable, soul-piercing eyes that had captured me completely.

The most disconcerting part was that he knew me, yet I still—after being more intimate with him than anyone else *ever*—knew nothing about him. Not where he lived and clearly not a name or even an initial. He'd somehow managed to dodge all my questions. And my over-zealous libido and fogged brain didn't help me.

After my bath, I slipped into my bedgown and snuggled

up with my blanket and favorite book. It wasn't long before waves of nausea and cold chills struck me. I grabbed a bucket and placed it next to my bedside, just in case.

My head was pulsing and every muscle in my body throbbed. Throbbed so severely, it had me coiling up into a ball. Soon, my insides started to heat, like someone had lit a torch inside of me.

I could scarcely move. The pain and searing of my insides caused a veil of darkness to linger at the fringes of my eyes.

I was losing consciousness, helpless, and there was no one around who could help me.

With my heart palpitating and breath quickening, I could only consider one terrifying conclusion. I was going to die, and no one would discover me until I was a decayed and smelly corpse.

As the night crawled on, dark and invisible tentacles coiled around me, pulling me down, down, down into a scorching hell.

Flashes of the stranger's face pulsed in front of me. His deep cobalt eyes. His smile stained with crimson.

My blood.

The fever was making me delusional. Through the unending nightmare—in between blacking out and barely gaining consciousness—I swore there was someone with me. A shadowed figure at my bedside.

I felt a cold compress against my forehead and a feathered touch sweep across my cheek. I even felt a hand had grip mine through the agony and heard a voice whispering comfort . . . saying this hell would soon pass.

But the suffering was too powerful, destroying all illusions of hope, enveloping me in a cocoon of flame and darkness.

There was no respite, and no knowing when it would end. I lost all track of time. Countless hours, days . . . who knew how long my cries went unheard as the blaze ravaged me.

I prayed to the gods to let it end. Even pleaded for death.

Then, all at once, it stopped.

Gasping, soaked with perspiration, I struggled to move, but was paralyzed. Every cell inside of me was spent, weakened to the edge of failure.

The darkness was again threatening to devour me whole. But this time, it offered no suffering. It was serene and calm, greeting me with open arms. Death had finally come for me. And I embraced it.

CHAPTER THREE

My aching eyelids drifted open, and much to my dismay, I was still alive. The drapes were drawn shut, and the lamp on my nightstand was lit. Peering down, I noticed my bedgown was changed, and the blankets were fresh and clean, neatly tucked in around me. Someone had been here. Someone had changed my clothes and bedding. If they did, they saw me nude.

The thought sent a shudder up my spine.

The dark figure in my nightmare . . . were they real? Or had my parents returned? I wasn't certain how long I was unconscious. The days and nights had fused together. I didn't even know what time it was.

Glancing to my side, I spotted a single red rose at the base of my lamp. Next to it lay an ornate golden flask with an envelope leaning against it, my name handwritten in script on its front.

I moved, relieved I was no longer paralyzed, but my body was still frail and quivering. Pushing myself to a sitting position, I reached for the envelope, my feeble fingers scarcely able to grasp it.

The back was sealed with crimson wax, impressed with a decorative crest of a shield, a sword and dragon. I snapped the seal in half and slipped out the piece of parchment.

Then it struck me. That familiar and indescribable scent of earth and wind and spice. I brought it to my nose and inhaled—that perfect blend.

My fingers trembled as I carefully unfolded the note and held it toward the light. The message was penned in the most exquisite handwriting—script with decorative swirls and curves—looking more like art than a letter. I inhaled again and began to read.

Dearest Calla,

I must apologize for not properly introducing myself at your celebration, but time was my adversary. I realize you have many questions, and I vow to answer them in greater detail when we meet again. First, I must apologize for the bite, but let me explain.

My name is Trystan Vladu. I am a representative of one of the seven vampire clans on this continent. Your grandfather, Nicolae Corvus, was born a Dhampyr—a half-breed—or at least we are led to believe this. There isn't enough information on him, but we were advised, through a recent decree, that he has been charged with the murder of a Prince of Morbeth. We are unsure if this is a fact, but as of now, your entire family has been marked and is in grave danger. They've dispatched hunters to come for you, and their orders are for the arrest and execution—the complete elimination—of Nicolae's entire bloodline.

I realize this sounds like lunacy, but I am urging you to trust me.

Representatives of our clan have produced names of your family members and an address of where you reside. As soon as I saw your name, I felt a profound connection—like nothing I'd ever felt before. I knew I had to save you.

The only way I could, with such limited time restraint, was to claim you.

When I bit you, part of my essence was delivered into you. It's what started your transformation. For the past three days, your mortal body was dying, and like a Phoenix rising from the ashes, you've been reborn and given an immortal body. Another attempt to keep you alive.

The liquid in the flask contains my blood. If you consume it, our blood bond will be secured, and the rival clan cannot touch you. Any attempts to harm the bonded of a pureblood will immediately dissolve the centuries-old treaty between kingdoms, and war will swiftly befall them.

But I am allowing you the option.

If you choose me, I will make certain you and your household will be protected and well-tended to for the rest of your lives. However, if you do not choose me, I cannot make *any assurances.*

Your decision must be made with urgency. The enemy has already been dispatched, and tonight when the moon is full, they will come for you.

If you choose not to consume from the flask, I beseech you to run. Leave your home as soon as the sun sets and never let the light of day touch your skin. Travel to the Moonlight Tavern, where I will have someone waiting for you, regardless of your decision. They will help answer any questions you have and will take you to a protected location until I can meet with you once again.

Until then, be safe,
Trystan Vladu

My body was trembling. There were two words—*you died*—that slammed me, causing my adrenaline to pulse with anxiety.

But I wasn't dead.

Was I truly reborn as an immortal like he said? A *vampire?*

A wave of panic had me hyperventilating. I sucked air deeply into my lungs, then slowly blew it out, attempting to settle my frazzled nerves.

Vampire.

Vampires were fables. Fantasy. They were the ominous creatures who resided between the pages of my novels. Terrifying, evil monsters who fed off mortal blood. They couldn't likely live in my world. *Could they?*

A vision of Trystan's teeth, his sharp incisors dripping

with *my* blood, warned me otherwise.

I read the note a few more times, still skeptical. But deep inside, at the back of my mind, was that still small voice saying, *"What if it is true?"*

Was my biological grandfather truly a Dhampyr? I'd heard tales of them. Half breeds of mortals and the blood-sucking monsters. It was preposterous. But what if it *was* real? What if my grandfather was still alive and had murdered someone?

My parents told me my grandfather had passed before my father was born. If he was still alive, he'd never tried to contact his family to let us know. And now, the bastard had cursed us all to death.

That was only one of my concerns. The greatest now was . . . how the hell was I supposed to tell my parents? I already knew what would happen if I told them. My parents were well recognized and highly respected in our country of Sartha. They were also rational and analytical. To have a crazed daughter declaring she was a vampire, and that her deceased grandfather was still alive and had murdered a vampire prince, wouldn't be favorable. That, and the fact we would soon be hunted by the deceased prince's country. It was outrageous. They'd find a means to keep me quiet.

Which is why I was grateful they were on a merchant ship, sailing to Hale. For now, I wouldn't have to explain this crazed situation.

Would *anyone* believe I'd been bitten by a vampire who wanted to save me from a rival clan's execution? Did *I* believe that inside of the golden flask sitting on my nightstand was Trystan's blood, and if I drank it, I would be bound to him?

Maybe it was real. Maybe it wasn't. Maybe I was dead, and this was purgatory or even hell. Or perhaps it was all just a dream and I was still caught up in it.

But the anguish and misery I'd encountered over the previous days were all too real.

Had it only been *three* days? It seemed endless.

The whispers. The fevered hallucinations. The shadowed figure assisting me. The letter.

The only answer was that Trystan *was* here.

Goosebumps prickled my skin as I glanced over to the nightstand where the single red rose and golden flask sat gleaming under the lamplight. The rose was perfect, a deep blood-red with a strong, delightful fragrance.

I reached for the flask, taking the heavy object in my hand, inspecting it closer. By the weight and the gems set into it, it must have been valuable. In the center of the flask was the same crest as on the wax stamp. The shield was outlined in what looked like diamonds and rubies. A gold sword was faced downward, hilt to tip, and set in silver was an intricate dragon with wings outspread at its center, its tail coiled and pointed at the end. The interior of the shield was polished onyx. I ran my fingers over the exquisite details. This flask alone must have been worth a fortune.

My fingers quivered as I unscrewed the cap and brought it to my nose. My mouth watered, my pulse raced. My breathing hastened, and the world around me began to whirl. Suddenly, there was an unusual movement inside my mouth. I gasped as my eye teeth elongated, becoming razor sharp. My tongue flicked against one of them, piercing it, causing it to bleed.

I reached for the small hand mirror in my nightstand drawer and held it in front of me.

Gods be damned. I had fangs. Fangs!

These new incisors made it quite apparent I was no longer mortal. I was one of them. A monster. *Gods above!*

At least I didn't look too dreadful. I still looked the same, aside from the dark creases surrounding my eyes. Feeling faint, I set the mirror down. The flask was still clutched securely in my other hand, filled with blood that my entire body craved.

"Trystan." As soon as I whispered his name, tingles surged through my body.

I raised the flask to my nose and the potent odor of copper and iron struck me. My hands quivered, and it took everything inside me to hold back the unseen force pressing the flask toward my mouth, demanding me to sip. Every cell inside my body echoed the desire.

No, my mind hollered. *Don't do it. You'll be bound forever.*

I hurriedly screwed the cap back on, securing it shut, and set it on the nightstand. My treacherous body was battling with itself to open it back up and take a sip.

Trystan claimed he was giving me an option, but he lied. When he'd bit me, he sealed my fate, transforming me into something else. Something non-human. Something nightmarish. Something that craved blood.

From this moment on, *I* was going to determine what became of my life, whether right or wrong. Alive or dead. It was my decision and mine alone. Right now, I wasn't going to be bound to anyone. Let alone someone I didn't even know.

But those two words kept ringing like a resounding gong in my mind. *You died.* And Trystan was the cause of my death. But he was also the cause of my rebirth and immortality. If that was even the truth.

I dragged my feeble and shaking body out of bed and shuffled to a set of clothes folded on my dresser which consisted of black pants, a black tunic, and a black, hooded, knee-length cloak. They were brand new, the material soft. My gut twisted, wondering if Trystan was the one who had put them there.

Letting out a heavy sigh, I hurriedly put on the all-black attire. They'd probably chosen black to help me meld in with the darkness to avoid capture.

A new pair of black boots were also set next to my dresser. Sliding my feet into them, they were an exact fit. Someone had gone through the trouble of getting everything sized precisely, and not only that, they were the most comfortable footwear I'd ever worn.

Stepping up to the mirror, I examined myself. The girl staring back was still me, but different. Changed, but not entirely. My skin looked soft and unblemished, but I still looked fatigued.

My hair was silken, and my golden eyes were considerably pronounced, practically glowing, and everything around me looked more vibrant and intricate than I ever remembered it before.

I shuffled toward the window in my modest living space. I didn't even know what time it was. It was around noon because the sun was full and brilliant, spilling in from a split in the curtain.

Maybe it was my over-inquisitiveness, but I had to know if the sun was my enemy. I gradually drew back a section of the drapery and slipped my hand into the narrow beam of light streaming through the window.

Nothing.

Then my skin started bubbling before bursting into flame.

A terrified scream ripped from my throat as I darted to the washroom and shoved my hand under the spigot. Cool water doused the flames but searing pain and festering charred flesh remained. My skin smoked and hissed under the water, but the pain gradually eased. In a few moments, the pain was totally gone.

Blood and pieces of charred flesh fell off and washed down the drain as I continued to keep my hand under the flow. When I finally turned off the water and lifted my hand, I gasped, gawking at the entirely new skin. What the hell? There was only one explanation.

I am a vampire. A gods damned vampire.

This discovery also brandished a massive red flag. If this was true, then hunters were coming for me and my family. And I only had a few hours to figure out how to get my new vampire ass to safety.

Would Trystan send someone to the Moonlight Tavern to meet me? As frightening as it seemed, his offer was the only option I had at this moment. There was nowhere I could think of to run, except Brynna's, and there was no way I was putting her in danger.

I paced the entire cottage at least a hundred times, waiting for the sun to set, wondering how my world would change once I stepped outside the door. If I could, I would have holed myself up in this cottage and wait it out. But this place was far from a fortress. It was small and easily accessible. *And* completely destructible. If anybody was coming for me, I would be captured in no time.

Captured. It sounded so ludicrous, but I wasn't going to wait here and find out if it was true or not.

I wanted to take my horse, Shadow, but the thought of leaving him behind, especially at the vulgar Moonlight Tavern, made me ditch that plan.

Shadow was my non-mortal best friend, a present given to me by my father on my tenth birthday. He was a Friesian, with a sleek black coat, thick mane, and long tail. He was magnificent, powerful yet agile, and extremely careful with me on his back.

When my parents were abroad on business and I was left alone, Shadow would carry me to secret places on deserted shores where he would graze, and I would spend hours reading and relaxing.

No, I wouldn't risk taking him. Shadow was too important to me. The stable boy would take care of him while

I was gone. And hopefully this dilemma could be over, and everything would return to normal.

Wait. Who was I kidding? My life would never be normal again. Good gods, I had fangs and was deathly allergic to the sun.

From the split in the drapery, I watched the sun's rays gradually inch across the floor. Tick. Tock. Tick Tock. It seemed like an eternity until it faded altogether.

As the last trace of light vanished, my apprehension grew. I snatched the pack I'd filled and opened the door. A burst of chilled wind accompanied me as I rushed out into the night. The pack on my back bore a few items: a change of clothes, a couple day's rations, a bag of gold skrag I'd been saving, and Trystan's flask. I wasn't certain why I took the flask, but I'd persuaded myself it was because it was valuable, and I didn't want it to be stolen.

Filling my lungs with the icy air was invigorating. My senses were on full alert, and I paused as my eyes adapted to the darkness. Everything around me was alive and humming. The world seemed more appealing—the brilliant hues of fallen leaves, the whispers of wind through the trees, and the earthy aromas of the surrounding landscape. Details I hadn't recognized before. Beautiful scenery I'd taken for granted.

Feeling awkwardly slow and weak, I realized I hadn't eaten in days, and I had a sinking suspicion I knew what my body needed. I'd resisted the thirst as soon as I'd opened the flask, and I knew from this day forward, there would be an endless battle raging inside me.

All the stories I'd read about vampires weren't exaggerating. The thirst was real. But the thought of consuming blood made my gut churn.

After walking the five miles, much quicker than expected, I finally reached the Moonlight Tavern.

Standing outside the olive, paint-flecked door, I cringed. The heavy smell of urine stung my nostrils and I started to second guess myself. This place was a rowdy pigsty filled with drunken patrons and nightly brawls. A place my parents instructed me to steer far away from. I doubted I'd even get through the front door without anyone noticing me.

After a cursory glance of the area, I was surprised to find there was no guard. But I supposed they didn't need one. No youth in their right mind would show up at a place like this. I just hoped that Trystan kept his word and had someone waiting for me.

Gathering my courage, I stepped up to the door and pushed it open.

Darkness enveloped the hallway, and the only sign of patronage was the raucous laughter and obscenities thrown from intoxicated men socializing deep in the tavern's underbelly. After a few shallow breaths, I made my way across the sticky wooden floor. The smell of urine mingled with other vile manly odors smacked me in the face.

Sneaking past the toilet rooms, I prayed repeatedly to the gods that Trystan remained true to his word. I was placing my complete confidence in him—someone I didn't even know. And that terrified the crap out of me.

Building up enough courage, I rounded the corner. Lingering in the shadows, I scoured the room. Wooden tables and chairs were crowded to the brim with drunken men. A few of them had women splayed over their laps. One had her skirt dragged up way too high, and a man's grimy hands receding even further, her hips swaying back and forth across his thigh.

Was this a brothel?

What the hell had I gotten myself into?

I kept tight to the wall, trying to stay concealed along the dark edges, searching the inside to find someone, anyone, who looked respectable enough to be my rescuer. And it didn't take long to discover him. A young man sitting at the bar, well-suited and handsome, looked quite out of place. He twisted to me and smiled, so I took that as a signal and promptly made my way over, sitting on the vacant stool beside him.

"Hey," I greeted, anticipating he would immediately get us the hell out of here.

"W-what brings you to this pigsty, lovely?" His speech was slurred, his eyes bloodshot and droopy.

My conscience waved a massive red flag before smacking it upside my head. *Good gods.* This guy was *not* my contact. And now I'd opened myself up to the rest of the drunken riffraff. I could practically feel their lustful eyes raking down my back.

"I'm meeting someone," I returned.

The barkeeper, a towering man with a bald head and tattoos running down his neck and arms, paused in front of me. "Aren't you a little young to be in here, darlin'?" he asked. "I could get in a lot of trouble serving alcohol to a youth."

"I'm not here for drinks. I'm here to meet someone," I reiterated, trying to suppress my inner trembling. Gods be damned. What was I supposed to do now?

"Who would ask you to meet them in a shithole like this?" the barkeeper queried, shaking his head.

"I don't know," I sighed. "I was just thinking the same thing."

He produced a half-witted grin, shrugged, then grunted at a man a few stools down, who was pounding his empty glass on the counter, demanding another brew.

Heavy footsteps pounded across the wooden floor until they came to a sudden halt directly behind me. I caught a whiff of strong body odor and practically got drunk off the alcohol emanating from whoever it was. If I still had a heart, I imagined it would be bursting through my rib cage and running far, far away.

Damn Trystan. And damn me for believing him.

"Hey, precious." A firm hand clutched my shoulder, forcing me to turn around. "You're new here. You lookin' for a good time?"

I'd read that new vampires had super strength, but I wasn't about to test that assumption, because three burly, bearded men stood behind me. Their heavy, wasted eyes bore looks of lust and ill intentions.

"No. I'm waiting for a friend. A *male* friend who should be here any minute," I responded boldly. "I was just about to head outside and check."

They snorted, calling my bluff.

I turned to scoot off the stool, but the man's grip tightened on my shoulder, holding me in place. I'd learned self-defense when I was younger but feeling weak and powerless, along with being hemmed in by these broad and extremely drunk men . . . it was of no use.

"Hey, Bart, why don't you let the young lady go?" the barkeeper suggested, drying a newly washed glass.

"Stay outta this. Unless you want trouble," Bart slurred, scowling at him.

The bartender murmured and stepped away. *The bastard walked away!* Leaving me alone with these assholes. Even the young man seated next to me had magically disappeared. Cowardly bastard.

"We want you to stick around, precious." Spittle flew from Bart's mouth onto my face. I held my breath, swallowing down the impulse to heave. His breath, a blend of alcohol and whatever food he'd just eaten, violated my nostrils, causing me to gag. "We'll show you a good time, I promise." He grabbed his crotch to confirm his point, forcing my entire body to shudder in disgust.

Stepping into this place was a terrible mistake. Trystan had lied to me. *Bastard.* But it was complete foolishness on my part to put my confidence in someone I didn't know. And I was naïve enough to show up without a weapon.

"I just need to leave," I said, attempting to free myself from the man's steel grip. But I felt very weak. I hadn't eaten anything in days.

"You can't leave," Bart slurred. "I want to give you a tour of my personal room."

"Hey, jackass!" A powerful voice hollered from behind the men. "The young woman is with me." All three men wrenched their heads toward the voice, their broad girth blocking any visual contact with my would-be protector. "I advise you to let her go before someone gets hurt."

"Who the hell are you?" Bart spit his words, his steel grip remaining on my shoulder.

"I'm her personal guard, and if you don't get your fetid, filthy palm off her, I'll snap it into pieces."

My *personal guard?*

The three men burst into laughter. Then Bart threatened the mysterious man.

"I'd like to see you try."

As the last word escaped Bart's mouth, the room fell deathly silent. Suddenly it swelled with the sound of snapping bones. Within the span of a breath, the two men with Bart were curled on the floor, wailing and writhing in agony. Bart instantly released my shoulder, and with a few more snaps, collapsed to his knees, clutching limp, displaced fingers. His screams sounded like that of an injured hog.

"Let's ditch this joint," a gentle voice murmured in my ear. Cool breath swept against my neck, causing me to twist back.

A handsome young man, who appeared not much older than me, extended his hand to me. He was around six-feet tall, with the deepest turquoise eyes. Eyes that looked like the sea on a bright summer's day. Jet-black hair was clean cut and drawn back, but there were a few misplaced strands which had spilled over his sharp-featured, unblemished face. He was attired in black trousers and a black tunic. The belt slung around his midriff held two sharp daggers, one on each side, protected under a long black coat. Even with layers of clothes on, I could tell he was muscular.

He reminded me of Trystan, enough that it made me wonder if they were related.

Without a second thought, I clutched his hand and he promptly led me out the door and into Whisper Forest. I inhaled the clean air, savoring it.

He hauled me along with him, quietly weaving through the dense spruce, alder, and birch trees.

All I could think was . . . Trystan wasn't a liar. He'd kept his word.

CHAPTER FOUR

My hero and I moved in silence for a few miles before he finally halted and faced me. He had to have been a vampire because he was unnaturally beautiful, just like Trystan.

"My name is Kylan. Trystan sent me. I'm sorry I was late." His melodic tone had a slight accent I couldn't place.

"Thank you. It's fine. I mean, I'm fine, so it's . . . fine." Gods, I sounded like a fool, stumbling through my words. But a grin raised on his perfect lips. "Where are we going?"

"To a secure place, where you'll meet the rest of the team."

I sucked in an abrupt breath. "Trystan sent a *team*?"

"Yes. His personal cadre." I detected a slight furrow in his brow, and his tone made him sound almost disappointed. Maybe he didn't agree with Trystan assigning them to help me. Perhaps he didn't want to be here either.

"What's a cadre?" It wasn't a word I was familiar with.

He hesitated, his eyes scouring the woods, observing, sniffing. When it seemed to be clear, he explained. "We are members of his personal cell, trained assassins dedicated to protecting the Vladu family at all costs."

Whoa. That was a load to take in. "If you're trained to protect his family, then why are you here?"

A sneer. "Because I am adhering to Trystan's direct order. Please don't judge his actions too hastily, Miss Caldwell. He is trying his best to keep you and your family safe, but his hands are somewhat tied without the blood bond."

I crossed my arms over my chest. "You know about the blood bond?"

He spun and faced me entirely, eyes narrowing.

"We know everything that concerns Trystan and his household. Everyone within the Vladu coven knows about the bond. There is nothing hidden, especially something as serious as a blood bond, and I am here because rescuing you is his main priority."

"Why would I be a priority?" I sighed.

"Because Trystan is our prince; therefore, if you choose to seal the bond with him, you will become our princess."

A prince? I choked on my next breath. "Wait. What? I assumed the reason Trystan had all these resources and a personal cadre was that his family was wealthy. He said he was a pureblood, but he never mentioned anything about being a prince."

Kylan's head cocked to the side. Amusement danced in

those turquoise eyes. "Would it have made a difference if he did?"

"Yes. I mean . . . no," I paused, considering what I honestly thought. "I wouldn't have sealed the bond, if that's what you're asking." I shook my head. "I—I don't know your prince. He was the one who pursued me. Then he *bit* me. I had no choice in the matter." I exhaled, rubbing my throbbing temples. "I can't . . . I won't be bound to someone I don't know anything about or make such a reckless decision that will influence the rest of my life. This is a huge deal to me. Something that can't be rushed."

He nodded. "Fair enough. I do understand your dilemma. But I'll have you know . . . Trystan has never made such an impetuous decision; especially regarding something as serious as a blood bond. You have no idea how many women would die to be in your position."

I sighed, recalling the night of my birthday party. I'd watched the girls contending for his attention, hurling themselves at him. But he was a vampire, and I was certain his charms and persuasion were considerably greater being a prince.

"Trystan is free to choose any woman he wishes. I won't bind him to me just because he chose to save my life. Don't mistake me. I'm grateful. Incredibly grateful. But being bound to someone for that purpose alone . . ." I hesitated, overwhelmed. "I *just* turned eighteen a few days ago. I'd like to live life on my own terms for a while."

"You are the first woman who has ever refused our prince." He shook his head and repressed a smile. "But admit it. Being bit by a handsome vampire prince was quite a birthday gift."

Was he serious right now?

I fisted my palms, my nails digging into my flesh. Anger heated my face.

"Your prince's *gift* killed me. Literally killed me. I died slowly and painfully. My body felt like it was thrust into an inferno for three gods damned days. *Three days*!"

He snickered. And it made me want to reach out and claw his perfect face.

He stopped and raised his hands in front of him. "Listen, I get what you're saying, but just remember, you'll always have an out. All the running could stop if you consider his offer."

I scowled at him. "It sounds as if you're trying to sell me on bonding with your prince."

Leaning back against a tree, he crossed his arms over his chest. "I'm simply providing you with some facts. Being a princess is not such a terrible thing. And securing the blood bond could relieve us of senseless complications."

"Like what?" I huffed.

"Like war and possible death."

I shrugged, but inside my belly knotted. "It seems that in this new world, war is inevitable, and death is imminent." Yes, war and death were some significant obstacles, but I was prepared to fight and remain on the run to be free.

He resumed walking, so I followed.

I cleared my throat. "If you are truly who you claim you are—a skilled assassin to the king and his household—then I shouldn't have anything to worry about, right?"

Kylan flashed a dashing grin. "Right."

My temples started to throb so severely my eyes were seeing dark spots.

Kylan took hold of my arm, stopping me. "Are you okay?"

"I'm fine," I sighed. But I wasn't. I felt like I was going to pass out. "I suppose I'm just overwhelmed. Three days ago, I was a mortal, and today I woke up a vampire. I was left a letter ordering me to run for my life and then provided a flask of blood from a vampire prince. On top of that, I was nearly molested in a disgusting tavern by some old, smelly drunks. Other than that . . ." I shrugged, presenting him with a large, cheesy grin. "Everything's just fantastic."

Kylan's brow crumpled, his head tilted back with a bellowing laugh. "I'm pleased to see you have a good sense of humor. Most newborns are wickedly moody."

Kylan was charming and handsome in every respect, making my stomach twist with butterflies. If Trystan hadn't bitten me, I wondered if — "Could I ask you a question about the bond?"

"Anything," he replied.

"Trystan said he claimed me by biting me."

"Yes."

"What if I refused him? Could I be claimed by someone else? Do I have a choice?"

His brilliant turquoise eyes examined my face, appearing to analyze my words carefully. "You will always have a choice, Calla. Trystan would never force you. But if you choose to bond with another, it could never be with anyone within his kingdom. Trystan has already marked you, and once a pureblood prince marks his mate, it is law that no one from that same coven can claim them. If they do . . . let's just say, it won't end well."

I stopped abruptly, forcing him to stop too. "Wait, wait, wait. Did you say *mate*?"

"To mark or claim an individual is a serious matter, especially by royalty. But it is not our position to dispute our prince. In all honesty, his father did not take too kindly to the news."

My head was spiraling. Not only from discovering who Trystan truly was and what he did, but also thinking about what his father—a vampire king—felt about his son's impulsive choices. I wondered if Trystan informed him about his trip to Sartha, to claim a girl he'd never met, but felt a connection with. A connection from seeing my name on a sheet of paper. The same girl whose grandfather was the assumed murderer of another vampire prince. I didn't blame the king one bit for having negative feelings toward me. I was a nobody. But I still required an answer.

"When you said it wouldn't end well . . . what did you mean, precisely?"

"Execution," he answered firmly. "Of both parties.

Usually beheading."

"Oh." I swallowed the knot in my throat.

Mental note: *Don't get attached to Kylan.*

I could tell I was drawing on his nerves, but I had a thousand questions racing through my mind. If I didn't get some of them out of my head, it would probably explode. "What about someone outside of the Vladu coven?"

He exhaled loudly, a wary expression in his eyes. "If you decline to tie the bond with Trystan, anyone outside of his kingdom or coven can claim you. But I should caution you. Although the grass may appear greener elsewhere, most of it is dangerous to tread upon."

"Thanks. I'll keep that in mind."

Kylan picked up his pace, probably wishing he could lose me at some point, but I followed closely, trying my best to keep up and keep quiet.

I didn't need anyone anyhow. I'd survived eighteen years without a bond. Not to mention, I was *not* princess material. Trystan's father would probably prefer he bonded to royalty, anyway. I didn't wish to be tied to a crown, or laws, or people I didn't even know or identify with. Being attached to royalty usually had tiresome burdens and obligations connected to it. At least that's what I thought. I truly had no idea.

Besides, my parents would go mad if they found out I'd made out with a gorgeous vampire on my birthday who bit me and claimed me as his mate. And then they'd murder me if they ever found out I went to the Midnight Tavern and was now running around in Whisper Woods with another handsome immortal.

I cleared my throat, but the bothered expression on Kylan's face informed me now wasn't the time to ask any further questions. We were in the midst of Whisper Woods, known for its terrors and hauntings. No mortal in their right mind would ever enter these woods after dark. Not after the countless tales reported about the horrors that lurked within. Which is why I remained close to Kylan, so close I even bumped into him a few times. But he was like stone, unmoving, and continued pressing on. It made me wonder how many damsels in distress he'd rescued before me. Maybe one too many.

After some time, Kylan finally turned to me. "We have a secure place about a half-mile away. If you can keep up, we could get there promptly without running into trouble," he said, offering me a smirk. "Not that I couldn't take care of any threat myself."

"Of course," I agreed. "I can keep up." After walking for a few minutes, I finally broke the silence. "So, this rival kingdom, are they positive it was my grandfather who killed their prince?"

He didn't pause or look at me, but answered, "They wouldn't have issued the order had it not been confirmed."

I was still struggling to wrap my brain around the fact there was a major family secret withheld from me. Did my parents know about my grandfather and what he was? Did they honestly believe he was dead, or was it hearsay? "I was informed my grandfather passed before my father was born. I've never met him and don't even know what he looks like. And now I'm being hunted because of him."

"I'm sorry," he said gently.

"Is there anything we can do to stop it?"

He finally passed a glimpse in my direction. "Trystan has sought counsel with his father. I'm confident he'll dispatch a team to investigate."

"I don't understand why Trystan is bothering to save me. I mean, none of this applies to him or his kingdom."

Kylan shrugged. "There are some things Trystan does that cannot be explained. But know this . . . everything he does is done with a great amount of thought and consideration." He glanced at me with an indecipherable expression. "If I share something with you, please don't take offense."

I raised my hands. "No offense will be taken."

He swung back to me. "None of us—those in his cadre— understand why he is so determined to keep you alive. Or why he would dispatch us away from his kingdom to find and protect you." He shook his head, combing his fingers through his thick onyx hair. "But that was his order, and we are never to challenge it, especially in his presence. We just do as we are charged."

I wasn't the only one questioning Trystan's motives. For his own cadre to be doubting, increased my confusion. "Trust me. I know how you feel and don't blame you. I'm still struggling to make sense of it all myself."

He gave a curt nod, then proceeded again, snaking through the darkened woods as if he knew the twisted tangle by heart.

I caught up to him and had a few more questions. "Do you know who's hunting me?"

"The kingdom of Morbeth," he responded.

"Morbeth?" Everybody in Talbrinth knew Morbeth was the country that initiated the Great War. I was a child when the war began. Leaders across Talbrinth were executed, and thousands of innocents were massacred, all because Morbeth, a country who wished to increase their territory, waged a merciless and bloody war in hopes of conquering the entire continent.

They failed. But in their wake, disease and plagues ran rampant and trade had all but ceased, causing food and water to become scarce and costly commodities. Most were struggling, doing whatever necessary to survive.

For a time, the law had become nothing more than what was left in a man's heart. And most hearts proved to be cruel and evil, even against those they'd once befriended. But it wasn't long before new rulers emerged, seeking to eradicate their territories of disease and disorder—drawing strength from their militaries to restore law and order, doling out swift punishments to those who resisted. These new leaders shared one common purpose, to rebuild their countries as swiftly as possible.

No one truly knew how these leaders were appointed. Whispers claimed they were figureheads—that puppet masters existed in the background, tugging on their strings.

So many lives were lost, and although Morbeth had one of the greatest and strongest militaries on the continent, they withdrew behind their wicked Red Wall. Rumors had spread that all inhabitants in Morbeth had become captives of their own country, powerless to escape. Those who tried were charged with treason and promptly executed.

The thought sent an icy shiver down my spine, knowing this was the same country hunting my family.

Kylan halted and sniffed the air. When it was clear, he moved on. We must have been close. "How many immortal kingdoms are there?" I queried.

"Seven," he replied. "Each country in Talbrinth has its own kingdom and is ruled by a Vampire King. Because the Vladu clan is one of those seven, we were also delivered the Death Decree."

"Why would Morbeth send it to the rest of the kingdoms?"

"Because if any of those kingdoms decided to harbor your grandfather, a war would come swiftly to them."

"Wow, that's—"

My words were cut short as the world around me spun. I gasped for breath, reaching forward, expecting to grab hold of Kylan, but instead, plunged into an endless darkness.

CHAPTER FIVE

My eyes flickered open. I was lying on the ground with Kylan's turquoise eyes looming over me, worry engraved intensely on his brow.

"Drink. Now," he ordered, placing a flask to my mouth.

"No!" I shoved it away. "I don't want to be bonded."

"Don't be a fool. You need to feed. This blood carries no ties to it. I promise." He held up a black plastic flask in front of my face. "I'm sorry I didn't give it to you sooner. You're quite weak from your transformation and need to feed."

He held the opening of the flask to my lips. As soon as I detected the scent of blood, the thirst grasped hold of me. Every cell in my body demanded me to drink, and I knew if I didn't, it would revolt. It was terrifyingly powerful.

Sharp incisors lengthened, piercing my lip. I cursed, but the sting didn't last long.

The ravenous thirst burned deep, numbing my conscience.

I was turning into a bloodthirsty monster, and right now, there was nothing I could do to stop it. My body trembled, perspiration trickled down my brow. The essence of the blood beckoned, pulling me into its clutches.

"Drink. I promise you'll feel better once you have," Kylan advised, putting a hand under my back, raising me slightly.

Tipping the flask to my lips, a slight trickle of blood touched my tongue. It was the pleasantest taste imaginable. Blissful, even. My tongue, my mouth, my body, cried out for more.

That was all it took. I seized the vial from his hand and poured the contents down my throat. I could hear Kylan's faint voice, but the hunger had taken over. All my senses were submissive to the will and desire of the all-consuming thirst, numbing everything else around me.

When the contents were emptied, I closed my eyes and let the bottle slip from my fingers. I was high, every part of me buzzing and tingling. The blood coursing through my veins was waking my cells from slumber.

My muscles were no longer tired but felt stronger than ever. Energy filled my limbs and stimulated my brain, like an electrical current jolting everything back to life. The feeling was indescribable. I felt revitalized, my strength restored.

When I opened my eyes, Kylan stared at me, shaking his head. Giving a half smirk, he took a handkerchief from his back pocket and gently wiped my mouth. "You're going to have to learn to control the thirst. If you let it take over, it could lead to your downfall."

Embarrassment heated my face when I realized what I'd done. My tunic was cold and wet, and as I peered down, I found trails of blood down my chest. Thank heavens my tunic was black, or I would have died of shame.

"I'm sorry," I apologized. "I don't know what happened to me. I—I couldn't stop."

The power of the thirst was frightening. I never wanted to fall prey to that wild and violent desire or feel that weak or helpless again. There had to be a way to bridle it.

"Don't apologize." He hesitated, his eyes softening. "It happens to all the newly transformed. It takes time to learn to control the thirst."

I sighed, still feeling the heat in my cheeks. "What kind of blood was it? Was it animal or human?"

"We survive off human blood. Animal blood never satisfies the thirst, and most of it makes us sick. You could consume it, if it were a life or death situation, but we need human blood to survive. The fresher the blood, the more potent it is, and the stronger it makes us."

I shuttered, realizing what his words meant. "I just drank *human* blood?"

Kylan stood and gave me his hand. "Don't worry. This blood was freely offered. It was a legitimate and consenting transaction; one of the many businesses Trystan's family runs."

My eyes widened. "People willingly give them blood?"

"Yes. Why not? Trystan's father has a sagacious eye for business. If mortals are willing to donate blood in the name of medicine, then we don't have to hunt unnecessarily or seduce our victims to get it. Besides, they get paid well for it. It's a win-win for both sides concerned."

I grabbed hold of his hand and he hauled me to my feet. Then, one word, which should have remained in my brain, slid from my lips. "Seduce?"

Kylan gave me a look that had my cheeks warming. A look that didn't need words. A look that told me I should already *know* . . . because it was how Trystan got me into Brynna's spare room that night and into this present mess.

"Humans are easily seduced," he explained. "Their minds are easy to penetrate. The trouble arises once one of us latches onto a mortal to feed. The touch, the smell, the hunger, are all intensified. It's considerably stronger than what you've just encountered, and often harder to break free from once you've attached onto a living, breathing being. Our Kingdom is opposed to latching because of the casualties that can arise, especially with those who are newly transformed. Thus, the blood donations."

So, Trystan's family weren't ruthless monsters after all.

I dared to ask. "Where is Trystan now?"

"He has returned home to organize meetings and is likely getting ready to travel." He spun to me. "He won't rest until he gets answers."

I still wanted to find out why. Why would he jeopardize so much for me?

"Where is his home?"

"Carpathia," he answered.

"Carpathia?" The country was recognized for its wealth and rich, fertile soil. Although Carpathia was a part of the continent of Talbrinth, it was detached, an island roughly half the size of the continent and furthest away from Sartha. "If he resides in Carpathia, then what was he doing in Sartha?"

Kylan exhaled a sigh. "He came for you."

"Don't you think that's kind of creepy?"

"Creepy?" His eyes narrowed on me. His face serious. "He traveled here to save your life."

"Precisely. A prince who lives on the opposite side of Talbrinth, *across* the Sangerian Sea, on a rich, independent island, comes to protect a mortal girl he knows nothing about but feels an attachment to by seeing her name. You don't think that's just a bit creepy?"

He paused. "Trystan has made quite a few decisions based on pure intuition, and so far, he's never been wrong. We've come to trust his decisions, even if we don't understand them. And to answer your question . . . no. Crazy, yes. But not creepy."

"Fine." I guess he was entitled to his own opinion, and I shouldn't have expected anything less. Kylan was probably Trystan's best friend and confidant, and I highly doubted he would ever badmouth him or his kingdom, especially since he was chosen to protect him.

"Are you a pureblood?" I asked.

"So many questions when we should be silent," he scowled. "But no, I am not a pureblood. Trystan sired me. And that, Calla, is a tale for another day. For now, we must move swiftly and quietly." He exaggerated the word quietly.

I nodded, accepting it was his nicest way of ordering me to shut up.

Weaving through closely knit trees, Kylan led us toward a monticule, its face composed of jagged rock. I wasn't sure what the plan was because when we arrived, he casually walked alongside the rocky ridge, trailing his fingers over the stones.

"Are we lost?"

"No." Frustration edged his voice. "I'm waiting."

"For what?"

He halted at a formation of rocks which started to swirl right before my eyes, giving the appearance of liquid. Letting out a strong puff of air, Kylan grumbled. "It's about time." Then he stepped directly into the center of the liquid rock and disappeared. *Poof!* Gone.

What the hell? I took a step closer when a hand shot out and seized my arm, making me yelp.

"Shh—" Kylan's head popped out with a grin tugging at his lips. "It's safe. I promise." He stretched his hand toward me, but I pushed it aside and stepped through the rock by myself.

That simple step—through a magic portal—landed me inside a dark, stone cavern. My feet crunched on gravel and the odor of smoke lingered in the air.

"Come. I'll introduce you to the others." Kylan took a few steps, then paused, and rotated. His eyes found mine. "I'm sorry for startling you."

"It's fine," I replied, keeping my expression neutral. There was no reason to be upset with him. He'd rescued me from the disgusting men at the tavern and offered me blood when I needed it.

He nodded, then strode away, satisfied with my response.

Following him further into the cavern, a lambent light flickered against the back of the cave wall. A low murmur of voices had nerves settling in the pit of my gut. These men were the king's personal guards, here on orders to protect me—a babysitting assignment—and not of their own will. Kylan had already admitted they didn't understand why Trystan had sent them for me, and I wondered if they despised me for it.

As we followed the cave, which twisted to the right, I spotted four bodies settled around a small fire. Three males and one female. Kylan cleared his throat, and when they turned their attention to us, I found myself sliding behind him.

How was I expected to act?

The first male—the biggest and tallest—stood and approached us, and I instantly felt two inches tall compared to his six-foot, five-inch frame. One of his biceps alone was the size of my head. His hair was the color of raven's wings, drawn back behind his neck. His skin was darkly tanned, his features sharp and menacing. He was frightening in every aspect, especially with the three scars marring his left cheek, which extended down his neck, disappearing under his black tunic.

Kylan stood between us, his hand gesturing to the giant towering a foot away from us. I was fixed in place, reminding myself to breathe and not pass out.

"Calla, this is Brone, the biggest and meanest bonehead you'll ever meet."

Brone growled and gave him an intense gaze that had my insides trembling. An . . . *I'll shred you to pieces if you keep it up* look. I cringed, but Kylan casually laughed it off, slapping the man's boulder of a shoulder.

Brone's intimidating gaze shifted to me and—heavens above—I stopped breathing. As he held out his massive hand to me, my limbs went weak. He could probably take off my head with one flick of his sausage-sized fingers.

Glancing at Kylan, he gave me no assistance except a terse nod and a lopsided smirk.

Damn him. He was reveling in this way too much. And was probably making me pay for having to come and rescue me.

"Don't worry, Calla," Kylan murmured, casually crossing his arms over his chest. "Brone's bark is much worse than his bite."

Brone's piercing eyes settled on Kylan again, his lips curling in a ferocious sneer. "That's because you've been fortunate enough to escape it." His attention swung back to me with his arm still extended, so I provided him with my quivering hand and a tightlipped smile.

His rough and calloused fingers swallowed mine whole, but his grip remained delicate.

"It's a pleasure to meet you, Calla," he declared in a rich baritone voice, with a bow of his head.

When his head lifted, I couldn't help but peer into his deep, obsidian eyes. He appeared to be in his late twenties, in mortal years. For all I knew, he could have been hundreds of years old. *Hundreds.* That thought alone sent my mind reeling.

The giant studied my face, then he smiled. His smile wasn't scary, but warm and sweet. It transformed his features and gave me a glimpse of what lay beneath the rough exterior. I caught a glimmer of tenderness and wondered how many he'd revealed it to. Then, to my complete surprise, he raised my fingers up to his lips, which were soft—a complete contradiction to the rest of his rough exterior—and kissed them.

"It's nice to meet you, Brone," I replied softly.

Brone leaned forward and murmured in my ear. "Let me know if these bastards cause you trouble. I'll take care of them."

I swallowed the massive knot in my throat before responding, "Thanks."

As Brone walked away, the other two males stood and made their way over. It was evident they weren't thrilled to see me, and I didn't blame them.

The first one had dark mahogany eyes and dark brown hair—half drawn up in a bun, while the rest hung down past his shoulders.

"Calla, it is a pleasure to meet you." He bowed at the waist in front of me. "My name is Feng," he said with a strong, foreign accent. He had to have come from Asiatica, an eastern continent noted for gold and fine silks. His attire was the same color as the others but tailored differently. Feng's tunic was longer, falling mid-calf, with a red and gold belt secured around his waistline. He was around six-foot, slender yet muscular, and carried himself with refined elegance, which I could only describe as a warrior's grace.

"Nice to meet you, Feng." I tipped my head to him. Kylan chuckled, but Feng gave me an approving smile that seemed to ease the tangles of anxiety in my belly.

As Feng stepped back, the next male stepped forward with eyes as gray as a stormy day. I'd never seen eyes that color before and stared much longer than I should have. But the twinkling in those eyes said he didn't mind. He also stood around six-foot tall with sun-kissed skin and sculpted features. Muscles flexed under his long black coat, while golden-brown hair was clean cut on the sides and tousled on top, adding to his dashing look.

"Andrés, at your service," he said with a glint in his eyes, bowing shallowly at the waist.

I'd heard his accent before—deep and velvety—from a man who'd sailed from Almeria to trade with my father.

He presented me with his hand, and I received it. Then, he tenderly pressed a kiss against my fingers, causing my cheeks to warm. His grayish eyes met mine, along with the deepest dimples I'd ever seen.

How had Trystan managed to secure such beautiful assassins from other continents to be part of his personal cadre?

The girl, who stood right behind him, heaved a sigh and all but shoved Andrés to the side before thrusting her hand out to me. As soon as I touched her, she jerked back, like I'd shocked her. Opening and closing her fingers, she glared at Kylan.

"What is it?" Kylan asked, taking a cautious step closer.

I stood still, realizing this girl didn't like me. She made no attempt to disguise her emotions or expressions. She was around my age, and a few inches shorter. Her hair was wild—the color of fire—and she wore it in a loose braid down her back. Stray strands fell around her pale, freckled, heart-shaped face. Her eyes were the color of jade, her lips full and pink.

"She has power, but not like anything I've encountered before." Her bewildered eyes settled on me.

"She's a newborn," Kylan replied simply. "She will possess significant power during the early stages."

"Perhaps." Her manicured brow rose. "Or, perhaps she's hiding something."

Hiding something? I was itching to test out those significant powers Kylan mentioned on this girl who looked like she wanted to drive a wooden stake through my heart. But I didn't feel stronger. Maybe it was because I was still extremely weak from the transformation.

"I have nothing to hide," I finally spoke. "And it wasn't my idea to come here. I was a mortal until your boss bit me and turned me into this bloodsucking monster." I quickly held up my hands and glanced at Kylan with a worried expression. "No offense."

A mischievous smile tugged on the girl's lips. "I like her."

Kylan groaned as the girl stepped forward and held out her hand to me again. "I'm Melaina." She sniffed the air between us and her freckled nose scrunched up. "Did you feed before you arrived?" I swallowed my growing humiliation. "I didn't mean to offend you earlier. Come," she ordered, seizing my wrist, tugging me toward the fire. "You can get cleaned up over here."

We sat on boulders placed around the fire. "Sit. Relax. I'm certain you've suffered a few hellish days," Melaina said, taking a seat across from me. She picked up a large pack from her side, sifted through it, and drew out a rag. She then unscrewed a flask and poured some water on it before tossing it to me. "Keep it."

Through the fire and smoke, she grinned. But I could tell that behind the grin was something lethal. Something hidden that made Trystan hire her to protect me.

"Thanks," I said, rubbing my neck and chest, the rag turning a brilliant crimson.

I searched through my pack and grabbed one of the few spare shirts I'd packed. Pulling my arms inside the bloodied one, I slipped my clean top over my head and started manipulating the wet one off. In moments, I'd made the transition and tucked the bloodstained tunic into the rag, rolled it up tightly and placed it in my bag.

Feeling cleaner, I peered at Melaina. Through the fire, her eyes set on me, brow pulling tight.

"I can see why Trystan chose you," she finally said as the others joined us around the fire.

I shook my head. "I don't know what you mean." I wasn't sure if she was being polite or rude.

"It's the first time Trystan has ever claimed anyone," Andrés replied with his dimpled grin. "And he's at the top of the royalty's most eligible list."

Melaina's head snapped to Andrés, giving him a death stare that caused the hair on my neck to stand erect. Her finger directed at me, but her eyes glowered at him and then turned on each of the others.

"What Trystan did to her was wrong," she roared. "She should have been given a choice. I mean, good goddess! He took her mortality without her permission."

"Watch your words, Melaina," Kylan replied calmly, throwing her a frigid glare.

She snorted at him, crossing her arms over her chest. "I'm free to say whatever I want. He employed *me*, remember? And he is *not* my prince. I have no loyalty to him."

Melaina's temper was just as fiery as her hair. Through the flames and smoke, her jade eyes found mine again. "If these guys give you trouble, feel free to come to me. I have a means of keeping them in line."

I nodded, wondering . . . "Are you part of Trystan's cadre?"

Melaina choked on a snort. "Goddess, no. I'm just a witch, employed for my awesome magical skills to keep you alive."

"Witch?" I gasped. First, vampires. Now a witch?

"Yep. I'm the one who warded this cavern and placed an invisibility spell on the entrance. No one can enter here without my permission."

"She may look like a delicate thing," Brone said from his spot next to Melaina, "but she's one of the most powerful witches in Talbrinth."

Melaina shrugged, but then nodded. So, I had to add . . . "Are you a vampire too?"

"Me? Vampire?" Melaina snarled as if I'd cursed at her. Her eyes skimmed over the guys, then her head bent back as she let out a sharp-pitched laugh. "I am one hundred percent human. I eat real food and will eventually die of old age, and would have it no other way. And if any bloodsucker tries to bite me," her eyes prowled the group again, "I'll make them *suffer* . . . before I change them into some shit feeding, belly crawling animal."

The four assassins remained silent, but I could see fire stirring in Brone's eyes as he sharpened his dagger, extra slowly, with a flat stone he'd plucked off the ground. I wondered if he'd stick the witch with it.

I caught Feng and Andrés glancing at each other with

smirks on their faces, but Kylan's expression remained one of boredom.

"So," I said hastily, trying to diffuse the rising tension. "Is there some awesome getaway plan, or are we staying in this cave until things blow over?"

Brone ignored me, continuing to whet his dagger. Andrés kept his gaze on the fire as if he were mesmerized by the dancing flames, while Feng drew Asiatic symbols in the dirt with a stick.

"We are awaiting Trystan's orders," Kylan finally answered. "And we will remain here until we receive them."

Great. Trystan, who was supposedly thousands of miles away. "How can you get orders from him if he's still in Carpathia?"

"I can channel him," Melaina replied. "Before we left Carpathia, I linked myself to him. It's the easiest way to connect." She stirred a small pot that had been simmering over the fire. The pleasant aroma of meat and spices wafted to my nose, making my mouth water. "You're welcome to have some if you'd like, but it'll make you sick."

"Sick? Why?" My stomach rumbled at the temptation.

"No offense," she said, rolling her eyes, "but you're different now. If you ingest regular food, you'll vomit. It's all part of your new immortal package." Her voice had a bite to it that stung me. "Most new bloodsuckers can't resist the scent of mortal food, especially with your heightened sense of smell. Those who are weak, engorge, and later find themselves puking their guts out. It's part of the curse."

"It's about how one regards it," Feng spoke, finishing a symbol in the dirt.

Melaina shrugged her shoulders before spooning some broth and raising it to her lips. When she sipped, her eyes closed and she let out a subdued moan. "I can't say that I blame any bloodsucker who does partake of solid food, though. The taste of it is a luxury compared to that disgusting bodily fluid you all drink to survive. How can anyone live off one food source forever? That would suck. Literally."

Feng raised his mahogany eyes to mine and smiled. "After some time, you'll become desensitized to mortal fare. Once you do, you'll find that you will appreciate and enjoy life for what it's worth. Yes, being immortal has its blemishes, but so does being mortal. It's in how one regards his or her own journey. To see beyond the gilded masks man has created . . . the commodities and frills which devalue the raw beauty of life and nature and everything it has to offer. Things that truly matter."

I offered Feng a sweet smile, grateful that he'd thrown me some wise words of instruction and encouragement. Because, fact was, I wasn't mortal anymore. I would have to learn to survive off blood for the rest of my life. But I was hopeful, because they were here, proving it could be done.

"Feng," Melaina purred, placing a hand over her heart. "You have such a way with words."

"I'm a realist," he replied, shifting his attention back to

his symbols in the dirt.

"How long does it take? To no longer crave human food anymore?" I asked Feng while trying not to focus on the stew, which was invading my enhanced sense of smell.

"For me, it took about five years."

"Five years?" I practically choked on the words. I expected maybe a few months . . . but years? Heavens above! The thought made me want to punch Trystan in the throat.

All of them laughed, and it made my blood simmer.

"In immortal years, it's nothing but a breath," Kylan added. "Besides, everyone is different. You could adapt a lot sooner."

I bit my tongue because I didn't want anything else I said to be dissected.

"I'm going to rest," Brone said, standing and stretching his extra-large frame. He snatched his pack, quickly scanned the cavern, then headed for a spot at the far-left edge.

"I thought vampires didn't need sleep." It was in one of the books I'd read.

Kylan chuckled. "We require just as much sleep as mortals do. Sleep helps our bodies to repair and rejuvenate."

"Oh." I swallowed hard, wondering how many of the tales I'd read gave incorrect information.

Feng also stood without speaking a word, but angled toward me, giving me a modest bow and smile before he seized his pack. He claimed a small alcove on the opposite side of the cave from Brone. After smoothing out the ground, he set a small blanket down before plucking out a small piece of wood from his satchel, along with a small, sharpened blade. His mahogany eyes were narrowed and fixated, twisting the wood in his fingers. Then he started carving it. I was curious as to what Feng envisioned that lump of wood to be. Time would tell . . . if I survived until then.

"Want some?" Melaina asked, reaching toward me with a small bowl of stew.

"No, thank you," I sighed. "I don't feel like being sick, and I don't think anyone in here needs to hear me puking all night."

She drew the bowl back and set it in her lap. "I understand . . . and I'm pretty sure everyone else in this cave is grateful for your decision."

"I'm exceptionally thankful." Brone's low voice reverberated against the far side as he set his tattered blanket between a few huge boulders. "It's a wretched sound, especially when one is tired." He plunked down, then laid back, tucking his arms behind his head and closed his eyes.

Brone was someone I'd want on my side if I were ever in a bind. Just his mere presence — his towering, massive frame corded with muscles—exuded power. He looked like a warrior who had slaughtered countless enemies in battle.

"You should get some sleep too," Kylan suggested, combing a hand through his thick raven hair. His eyes captured mine and my stomach fluttered. "Your body is still adapting to becoming immortal. You'll require a lot of rest over these next few days."

"When will she start training?" Andrés asked.

Kylan gathered his things and threw his sack over his shoulder. "She'll need to master the basics as soon as she's up for it. Nothing too arduous."

"She knows nothing?" Brone questioned, his head rising.

I cleared my throat, letting them know I was still sitting there, listening. "I know how to defend myself if that's what you're asking. I was trained by a soldier."

"A mortal soldier," Brone mocked with a cynical grin.

I took offense. "Yes, a mortal. And he is *highly* skilled in warfare."

Grant Willbrow was nine years my senior. He was tall, tanned, handsome, and well educated in war and weaponry. His father was a miner who was employed by my father. When my father made mention, he wanted me to learn self-defense, the elder Mr. Willbrow suggested his son.

Having wealth in Sartha, with still so many poor, came with a price. Many thieves robbed and even killed over a few gold skrag. So, my father wanted me to learn to defend myself and made sure I always carried a small, sharp dagger with me.

For a full year, after my tenth birthday, Grant came a few days a week and taught me every self-defense strategy he learned. He even showed me where it would be best to strike a man if I were ever attacked. I hadn't been strong enough to knock anyone out, but I could hurt them well enough for a chance to flee a dangerous situation.

As the year progressed, I'd found it increasingly difficult to concentrate on my movements while staring into Grant's beautiful chestnut eyes. But he never showed any interest in me. I was just a child back then. Brynna was right. It was a one-sided infatuation.

Brone's brow raised. "Tomorrow, we shall see how well of a trainer your human was."

"I suppose you will," I puffed.

Melaina shook her head and snickered. "I can't wait to see that."

"You know, witch," Brone said carefully from his space, eyes closed. "There might be some things you could learn too. What would happen if your magic is suppressed? You should consider training with her."

I was awaiting a sarcastic remark from Melaina, but her response startled me. And probably all the others.

"I'll consider it," she answered.

CHAPTER SIX

The vampires prepared their beds in key areas around the cave as an added security measure should anyone enter. But with Melaina's ward and glamour over the entrance, I was confident we would be safe for the night and could sleep peacefully.

Melaina and I made our beds near the fire. The ground was solid and rocky, so I did my best to clear my area of any rocks that would make for a miserable sleep. I spread out my blanket and used my pack for a pillow. Melaina did the same on her side, grumbling out-loud the entire time.

"I thought we'd at least have a bed, you know, being employed by the wealthy Prince of Carpathia and all. A smelly, dank, dirty cave amid Whisper Woods was the last place I expected we'd bunk down," she whined.

"This is the best we could do with short notice," Kylan said dryly. "Once we hear from Trystan, we'll move on."

"He owes me big time," she mumbled under her breath,

causing me to bite back a laugh.

I was grateful she was here. If it had only been me and the assassins, I would've felt uncomfortable. Watching her toss and turn and grumble, helped to keep my mind occupied and gave me a sense of comfort, letting me know I wasn't alone in this situation, despite our present conditions.

Once Melaina settled and the cave grew quiet, my attention turned to the fire. I was mesmerized by the way the tendrils of flame and smoke twirled like an endless dance. A warm and elegant dance which slowly lulled me to sleep.

I dreamed I was standing on a balcony made of white marble. On either side of me, alabaster columns rose from the floor and touched the ceiling. Each one had a dragon intricately carved along its entire length. Their maws were opened wide, revealing sharp teeth. Feet were curved with tapering claws, and long, scaled tails coiled all the way to the bottom. But as impressive as the dragon carvings were, it was the view beyond those columns that took my breath away.

To the east, the first golden rays of dawn stretched and kissed the land below, nudging its inhabitants to wake from their slumber. I was on a mountainside, overlooking the greenest rolling hills flecked with lush oak and pine trees. Between them, a river hurriedly flowed through its course, and beyond that, the same golden rays glistened and danced across a boundless sea.

I inhaled the crisp, fresh air which smelled of morning dew and fresh pine.

A glass table with a lone chair slid under it rested near the edge of the railing, facing the view. I drifted over to it, my bare feet padding against the icy marble floor. Pulling out the chair, I sat, gazing out at the magnificent masterpiece laid out before me. Wherever this was . . . it was paradise.

Footsteps behind me had me spinning back to find Trystan leaning against one of the alabaster columns, arms leisurely crossed over his chest, eyes fixed on the eastern sky.

Good gods, he was even more attractive than I'd remembered. His sheer presence exuded grace and power.

He was wearing a dark gray shirt, the top-half unbuttoned, exposing a tattoo I couldn't entirely see, and it piqued my interest. Azure eyes, flecked with gold, seized mine, forcing my breath to hitch.

"It's good to see you, Calla." Trystan's tone was tender and smooth like honey, but his eyes looked tired.

My body wanted to rise and move toward him, but my mind refused to let me budge. Instead, I folded my arms over my chest.

"I'm mad at you," I managed to say, but my words didn't have as much sting as I'd intended.

"And justly so," he replied with a heavy sigh. "I'm terribly sorry things happened in the manner they did. If I'd had more time to prepare more thoroughly, matters might have turned out differently. But, as I expressed before, time was my adversary." He moved from the column and took a few strides toward me. "I don't blame you for being upset. But claiming you was the only way I could think of to save you."

"You could have given me a choice."

He shrugged his broad shoulders. "Would you have believed me?"

"Probably not," I sighed. "I'm still having a tough time accepting it all."

Behind him, white gossamer curtains blew carelessly in the breeze from an opened door, and beyond that was a grand open room where I spotted a massive, lush bed and a fireplace with a small sitting area. The details of this dream were so elaborate, much more than any other dream I'd had.

"Is this place real?"

A lopsided grin grew on his perfect lips. "As real as you want it to be."

"How is this even possible?"

"When I bit you, your blood became a part of me, and in turn, my essence was left inside of you. We now have a partial blood bond which allows you to visit me while you sleep."

His explanation sounded oddly erotic, and it made me wonder . . . "Do all the others you've bitten have dreams like this?"

A mischievous glimmer flickered in his eyes. "No." He hesitated momentarily before clarifying. "Each bite a pureblood gives, is done with a specific purpose. Whether for pleasure, to feed, or to sire. But I've never sired anyone who wasn't in need or didn't wish to be reborn." Sadness swam in his eyes. "The intention I had when I bit you was for a vastly different purpose than all the others. It was—"

The expression on his face showed great regret and sorrow. He looked exhausted, and from what the others had said, it was because he was trying to save me and my family. I still couldn't understand or begin to wrap my brain around why.

"You thought I was going to drink from the flask, didn't you?" I said softly.

His attention averted toward the west, his eyes distant. "I had hoped."

The answer made my heart compress. "So, unless I consume your blood in the flask, everything you did . . . finding me, biting me, and making me turn into *this*," I gestured to myself, "it was all for nothing. Right?"

His deep gaze found mine. "No. Not for me," he replied with a wistful grin. "In the end, I'll always know I tried to rescue the girl, even if she didn't want to be rescued."

I soaked in his words. In his soul, he genuinely wanted to save me. But I still had so many questions and fears.

I rested against the railing, taking in the view. "Where is this place?"

"My home in Carpathia."

I twisted to him; a gleam of pride lit his eyes.

Home? I leaned further and peered down. Heaven's

above, this was a *castle*. A real castle. In the distance I spotted an imposing, black iron gate, with a cobbled pathway that led to the castle's entrance below. "You live in a castle?"

He gave another tired grin, his eyes studying mine. "Yes."

I shook my head in complete awe. "Are you the only one here?"

"In your dream, yes. But there are a number of attendants, guards, and others employed who reside here." His grin tugged a bit higher. "One of these days, when you arrive, I'll give you a formal tour."

There had been a moment when I wanted to lash out at him, to confess how upset I was for all that he'd put me through. But I couldn't find it within myself to do so. Instead, I responded, "I'd like that. Thank you."

His smile widened as his eyes roamed the countryside. "This could be ours one day," he uttered carefully, gently. "If you ever decide . . ."

To choose *it*. To choose *him*.

"I still don't understand why you're doing this for me. Why would you give so much attention to and put so much effort into someone you don't even know? What if I'm a terrible person who could create trouble for you and your family?"

He studied my face, his head bending slightly forward. "Because my heart tells me otherwise."

I sighed, letting out a mild giggle. "So, Vampire princes have hearts?"

He shrugged. "On very rare occasions."

There was another pause as we gazed deeply into each other's eyes.

Watching the golden light illuminate the masculine features of his face made something deep inside me stir. His hair was in disarray as if he hadn't slept in days, and if it were at all possible, caused him to look even more handsome. I despised him for that. Despised that he made me question my decision, even in the slightest bit.

But I wouldn't let it cost me my freedom. I needed to make a decision because it was right, and not because I was under pressure. And I didn't want him to regret his decision, either. He said he bit me because it was the only way he could think of to save me. That told me he had no other choice, or option, at the time. And I wasn't going to hold him to that.

I gazed back at the ascending sun, its golden warmth illuminating my skin. "The sun is out. Why aren't we bursting into fire?"

His laughter resounded through my chest. "For one, purebloods are able to live in the daylight. And, as for you," he purred, "this is but a dream. The sun cannot affect you here."

I peered toward the horizon, taking in the entire splendor of the risen sun. To be able to see the sunrise, even in a dream, was just as wonderful as the actual thing. Maybe this was a way to have the best of both worlds. But this way also came with a catch. *Trystan.*

I wasn't going to lie. It wasn't a bad catch, and I *was* physically attracted to him. But I wasn't going to throw my life away for a handsome face. This wasn't a decision I could make on an impulse and take back later. No, *this* decision would change the rest of my life. And his.

There were still so many unanswered questions flooding my mind. The biggest of which was not knowing if any of his claims about my grandfather or the rival clan hunting to execute my family were legitimate. How could I truly trust him when I didn't have any confirmation? I wasn't one to blindly follow anyone without cause. To do so would be maniacal.

"Are there really vampires hunting my parents and me?" I questioned.

Trystan pushed off the railing and ambled toward me. My body went rigid, so he halted a few feet away, casually folding his hands behind his back. "I can show you if you wish. Show you the threat, to prove to you it is real."

"How?"

"Nyx," he replied. "My crow. She's my eyes when I cannot be in two places at once."

Crow? "I—I don't understand."

"She's not a normal crow," he noted with a glimmer in his eyes. "She's . . . magical. I can show you the threat through her eyes. I can allow you to see what is hunting for you, even now, as you sleep." He took another step closer, eliminating the distance between us. I could feel the cold from his body seeping through my skin, even in the dream. His head inclined slightly. "Would you like to see?"

There was only one answer. "Yes."

If this were true, it would be the answer I needed to the biggest question I possessed. I had to see it. Needed to know if there was truly a threat and a reason as to why I was hiding out in a cave with four vampire assassins and a witch.

Trystan gently caressed my face within his large calloused hands and lifted until I found those warm, azure eyes that looked even more striking up close. Sweet breath feathered across my face as he rested his forehead against mine.

Then he whispered, "Close your eyes, Calla. And *see*."

Moments after I shut my eyes, the darkness behind my eyelids started to flicker. Images flashed before me. A forest with countless trees. A rocky hillside. A narrow creek.

I'd become a witness, soaring high in the sky, seeing clearly through another pair of eyes. Crow's eyes. But this view could have been anywhere in Talbrinth. There were trees and hillsides all over the continent with terrain like this.

As if reading my thoughts, the bird banked left, and after a few moments, there was different scenery I instantly recognized. In the distance, I located the Moonlight Tavern— the reeking piss-hole Kylan had rescued me from earlier.

The bird banked left again, circling around, and soaring back over the Whisper Woods. Leveling off, just above the trees, it headed toward a rocky monticule near the edge of the wood. Landing on the branch of a towering oak, its eyes caught movement below.

In the dark, I located at least a dozen figures wearing black masks, attired in black, quietly weaving their way through the trees. Silver weapons glinted in their hands and at their sides.

The bird hopped down a few branches, and I soon picked up a conversation.

"They've been here," one declared, sniffing the air. "Looks like the girl has help. We discovered two sets of prints heading in that direction." He pointed toward the monticule where we were concealed inside . . . sleeping.

"They couldn't have gone far," another growled.

"I demand to know who is helping her. I want their head on a stake," a deep voice roared, sending a bone-chilling shiver down my spine. He must have been their commander.

"Do you expect they're heading to Hale?"

"Hale is a possibility. But they could just as well run to Baelfast. Lord Huxley has a reputation for taking in strays," the leader replied.

"The Prince of Carpathia has marked her," another deep voice responded.

"I don't give a damn who marked her. I'll deal with Prince Trystan in time. Right now, we need to find the girl. I want her alive and delivered to the castle. Anyone else in Nicolae's bloodline can die."

Trystan pulled away, breaking the connection. I blinked and landed back in the dream.

What the hell did that guy mean? He clearly hated

Nicolae enough that he demanded to erase his entire lineage. But why keep me alive?

Hot tears burned my eyes. "Why don't they just execute Nicolae and leave us alone?"

"I don't know," Trystan breathed. "We can't locate any record of Nicolae, except that he was raised by a servant in Northfall. After that, he just . . . disappeared."

What I'd just seen made matters even more complicated. I gazed into Trystan's glowing azure eyes, my breath ragged. "Your men and Melaina are in danger because of me."

"My men and the witch are more than capable of taking care of themselves. We must move you here, to Carpathia. It's the safest place for you to be right now."

"What about my parents? They're sailing to Hale . . . to Merchant Port."

"I've already dispatched some men to search for them and will let Melaina know as soon as I receive any news." He stepped away from me, but I grabbed hold of his hand, halting him.

"You don't have to do this for me. I can find a means to survive." *Lies.* I knew I wouldn't last long on my own. I'd heard what the men in the forest had said. They were hunting for me and would execute anyone helping me.

Trystan's eyes softened. "I wouldn't be doing this if I absolutely didn't believe that I needed to. My conscience, instinct, even my soul won't rest until you are safe."

There was no way for me to understand why he was

doing this, or to know what he was thinking.

"Thank you," I said and meant it. Those two words sounded so unimportant, but they were truly sincere.

"Be safe, Calla," he said, gripping my hands.

He stepped toward me, his scent wrapping around me. There was a current traveling between us, causing my entire body to hum. I froze, bracing for a kiss, but instead, he bent forward and pressed his lips to my forehead. That act left me breathless.

When he leaned back, his beautiful eyes found mine.

"I'll see you soon."

I woke to find Melaina sitting up and staring at me through the fire. "What were you dreaming about? You were fidgety and *moaning*. Please share." Her brow lifted, and a smile spread on her lips.

But inside, I was rattling with the knowledge I'd received. "It's . . . there are men outside hunting for me. And they're close," I replied.

The color leached from her face, her smile fading. "How do you know?"

I struggled to understand what had just happened. "Trystan showed me through his bird's eyes."

"Trystan?" Her jade eyes widened.

I needed to wake the others. "We have a partial bond

which allows us to connect while I sleep."

"Well, that explains the moaning," she chortled.

"Nothing happened," I replied. She didn't realize the severity of the situation. Men were outside. Coming to kill us.

"If you say so."

I was about to stand, but Kylan was already behind me, snapping on his armor. "You said there was a threat outside. How many?"

How did he hear me? He was on the complete opposite side of the cave.

"At least a dozen, from what I saw," I answered.

"Andrés. Feng. Brone." As quickly as Kylan spoke their names, they bolted up and started strapping on their armor and weapons, as if they already knew something was amiss. In a few minutes, they all stood in front of Kylan, ready and awaiting orders.

"They're here. At least a dozen," he reported.

Brone yawned, stretching his arms over his head. "Those bastards woke me from a deep sleep. Let me out to unleash my fury."

"No," Kylan replied, his face like stone. "We'll do this together."

"Wait, you guys can't go out there," I exhaled. "They outnumber you, at least three to one."

They all shifted their attention toward me. Brone chuckled, while Feng, Andrés, and Kylan grinned.

I wasn't sorry for what I'd said. I was genuinely concerned.

"You'll soon understand why we've been appointed by the King of Carpathia," Andrés said, sliding a sword into its sheath at his side. "We're his personal cadre for a reason."

I bit my tongue. Yes, I'd just met them, but these guys were here to protect me, and the thought of losing any one of them, on my account, caused my chest to ache. I didn't want anyone to die on my account, especially knowing they didn't agree with Trystan's order to save me in the first place.

"Don't worry about them," Melaina said, running a comb through her wild, red mane. "The only way they can die is if their heads are taken off." She placed another log on the fire, and I watched the sparks flitter upward. "It's nearly impossible to kill Brone," she continued. "His neck is broader than the trunk of a full-grown oak, and probably just as tough."

Brone let out a barking laugh. Andrés also laughed and slapped a hand on Brone's back. "She's got you there, brother."

I stood and faced them. "One of the men demanded the head of the person helping me," I declared to no one in particular.

A light flickered in Kylan's eyes. "Did they now?" He angled toward the others. "Sounds like a challenge to me."

"A challenge I'm more than happy to return," Brone said in his deep tone.

"How did you obtain this information?" Andrés questioned.

"Calla has a partial bond with Trystan," Kylan replied. "Because of it, she saw everything through Nyx's eyes."

Brone's brow furrowed, his onyx gaze locked on me. "There must be something extra special about her. Our prince has never displayed an interest in binding with anyone, especially outside of our kingdom. And *especially* not a mortal."

I sighed. "Trust me, there isn't anything special about me."

"There must be." Andrés stepped to the side of me and laid an arm across my shoulders. He was tall and smelled like a blend of leather and sweet spice. "You've seized the attention of our prince, which is not a simple feat."

I wasn't sure if I was being insulted. "I assure you, I did nothing to capture him. He was the one who came for me. I had no idea he existed until he showed up at my party."

Andrés patted his hand on my shoulder. "Well, whatever the reason, if you see Trystan again through the bond, give him a big, wet kiss for me."

I slid out from his touch and growled. "The next time you see him, you can do it yourself."

Brone barked out a laugh and slapped Andrés on the shoulder, so hard he had to take a few steps forward to regain his balance. "She's got you there, brother."

"Are you guys finished?" Kylan snapped. They all stood at attention. "Feng, you and I will go left. Brone, you go right. We'll go wide, quietly, and catch them off guard." His eyes swung to the massive brute. "Brone, I cannot emphasize the word *silently* enough."

Brone shrugged, and it was almost comical to see him taking orders.

"What about me?" Andrés asked, his hand clutching the hilt of his sharpened blade.

"I need you inside, directly behind the glamour," Kylan ordered. "If anything happens to slip through, you'll be responsible to take care of it."

Andrés closed his eyes and groaned. "Gods be damned. I guess I'm sitting this one out."

Brone turned to me with a wink. "The odds are four-to-one now, Calla. Care to bet against us?"

I shook my head. "Nope."

Brone let out another barking laugh. "That's good."

Truth was, Brone alone could probably take out half the men I saw. I would have loved to see them in action. Being the King's cadre, they must have had some major skills.

Kylan, Brone, and Andrés were clad in polished black leather armor and black boots. In the center of their chests was Trystan's crest—the shield, dragon, and sword. Their shoulders, breasts, and abdomens were protected with leather pieces riveted one over the other, the ends trimmed in silver metal. The cuffs around their thighs and forearms were also made of black leather, affixed in the same scale-like patterns.

Brone carried a giant mace in his right hand with a spiked metal head, stained black, while Kylan and Andrés had polished, double-edged swords around their midriffs and daggers strapped to their thighs.

Feng remained in his long leather tunic and pants, also wearing black leather vambraces around his forearms and shins. Each stamped with Trystan's crest. Two long, narrow blades were crisscrossed behind his back, and clutched in his fist was a tall black staff with golden symbols etched into it.

Fierce, black steel helmets were placed on their heads, concealing everything except their eyes, noses, and mouths.

Kylan strode toward the exit. "Let's move."

Melaina suddenly gasped, stumbling backward. She collapsed to her knees, her hands clutching the sides of her head. When she blinked, her jade eyes had turned completely white.

"Kylan!" I cried, stepping away from her. She looked possessed. Her alabaster eyes snapped directly on me.

Kylan ran back to us and dropped to his knees in front of her, grasping her arms.

"Melaina, what is it?"

Those ghostly-white eyes latched onto him. "Is Calla safe?" she inquired in a low tone that wasn't hers. Goosebumps raised across my skin. *It was Trystan's voice.*

"Yes. She's here and she's safe," Kylan replied.

"I need to speak with her. I just received information from my men regarding her parents." The tone of his voice caused acid in my stomach to rise.

Kylan turned his attention to me, signaling me to come. As I neared Melaina, he stood and backed away.

"I'm here," I responded, kneeling in front of the witch.

"Calla, my men found your parents' vessel. It was run aground about a mile from Peddlers Pass." He hesitated and I knew something was wrong.

"Tell me," I implored, preparing myself for whatever news he was about to give.

"Everyone on board was killed, except—"

He paused again. But I'd only heard two words. *Everyone.* And *killed.*

"Except what?" I breathed, gripping Melaina's shoulders tightly. The surrounding ground spiraled as her white eyes pierced mine.

"They couldn't locate your father's body."

My chest felt as if a hole had been punched straight through it. "My mother? What about my mother?" I shoved the words out before reality set in and I was incapable of speaking.

"I'm so sorry, Calla," his voice was soft, weary. "She was on board with the others."

No. I searched those alabaster eyes, struggling to grip the words he'd just delivered.

Dead. My mother was dead.

A heavy sob ripped from my chest. I dropped back onto the ground, my body folding into itself. I couldn't breathe. The pain was greater than any other I'd experienced. Even greater than the pain I'd suffered to become this monster.

Melaina's warm hand settled on my shoulder. "My men

are searching for your father. For now, we must believe he's still alive."

My mind was numb, and the hole in my chest growing wider.

Nicolae.

I despised him. I hated the man who was the cause of all of this. Whatever he did, whatever crime he committed, I held him responsible. He killed my mother and possibly my father. I wanted his head on a stake, as much as the enemy did.

My parents worked and traveled a lot for their business, but they provided me with everything I ever needed—food, shelter, an education. I knew my parents loved me, more than anything, and I hoped they knew how much I loved them too.

I made a pledge to train hard and learn everything I could from these assassins. From this day forward, retribution would be my drive. I would avenge my mother. I would move out from the shadowy corner I'd been standing in for too long. I was ready to fight for them. Even if it meant dying.

CHAPTER SEVEN

I barely heard the orders Trystan gave Kylan to take me to Carpathia.

Carpathia was at least three thousand miles from Sartha, through treacherous terrain. On top of that, we'd have to sail across the deadly Sangerian Sea to get there.

Stories passed down through the generations said the sea was cursed. Countless ships and entire crews had vanished on the Sangerian Sea, without a trace, never to be seen or heard of again. Whispers claimed the sea was alive and hungry, lying in wait for its victims. When the seas were calm and all was quiet, and when the men least expected it, the sea would wake and devour them whole. No one knew what truly took place because no one survived.

But there was one other option to get to Carpathia. To go the long way around and brave the Lonely Ocean, which also had equally horrifying tales of its own.

I despised the water and I hated sailing on it. Seasickness plagued me as soon as I set foot on a ship. That, along with the stories, was reason enough for me to stay in Sartha on solid ground. I never sailed beyond the Argent Sea. The furthest I'd ever been was to Merchant Port with my parents on their trades.

When the assassins left, I was a sobbing mess. I heard Andrés tell Melaina he'd be near the entrance if we needed anything.

Melaina stayed next to me, her hand stroking my hair as I lay curled by the fire. "Don't worry. You'll be okay," she whispered.

But I wasn't going to be okay. My mother was gone. She was never going to come back. And I didn't have a chance to say goodbye.

"I also lost my mother when I was young," Melaina said softly. "The last thing I remember was her giving me a kiss on the cheek and telling me to be good while she went out to gather herbs in the forest. It was a beautiful summers day. The sun was shining, and I was playing outside. But when the sun set and she never returned, my aunt and grandmother sent men to search for her. They found her body lying in the forest. She'd been abused and murdered." She paused. I glanced up at her wiping a tear that slipped down her cheek. "We never found the killer. He's still out there. But one day I'll find the man who did it. I'll make him suffer, like he did to her."

"I'm so sorry, Melaina," I breathed. She shook her head.

We both stared at each other. Without words, we shared our agony and grief. With a sad grin, Melaina's lips started to move, but I could scarcely hear what she was saying. In moments, my eyes became heavy, head numb, and body tingly. Before I could curse her for placing a spell on me, darkness overtook me.

I dreamed I was soaring in the clouds high above the sea. Swooping down, I sighted my father's ship, run aground in a rocky cove. I knew it was his ship because *Calla* was painted on both the port and starboard sides.

My eyes fixed on the lifeless bodies sprawled out over the deck. The wooden slats beneath them were painted crimson with their blood. As I flew closer over the carnage, my stomach heaved.

These were people I knew. People who'd worked closely with my father, who had visited our home, talked and laughed with us, dined with us, who we'd befriended. The pain in my chest—an immeasurable, encompassing sadness—crashed over me, engulfing me in sorrow.

Then, I located the Whyte's—Brynna's parents—lying next to each other, hand-in-hand. Blood smeared across the deck, about fifteen yards away, showed me that in his last moments, Brynna's father had dragged himself across the deck to be with his wife. To die with her.

Then my eyes latched onto a figure. It was *her*. *My mother.* She was lying near the bow of the ship with her auburn eyes opened wide, staring into the brilliant sky. She looked so peaceful, as still as the sea on a windless night. Around her head, in the shape of a halo, was a pool of blood.

I wasn't prepared for it. Wasn't prepared for her death. I would never get to see my mother again, or hear her voice, even to scold me. Death was forever, and I hadn't even had the chance to say goodbye. *I hadn't said goodbye.*

It felt as if my heart was shattering, over and over, into irreparable fragments. The sight of her lifeless body crushed me thoroughly. Every cell within my body travailed, throbbing with a grief I'd never encountered before. A pain so sharp and radiating it felt as though my chest was going to burst.

"No!" I wailed, shooting up out of the nightmare. Deep, violent sobs burst from inside me. I was soaked in sweat, my head and chest throbbing.

"Calla, are you okay?" Kylan asked, heading over to me.

"I—I saw them. The bodies. On the ship." I could barely choke out the words through my heaving sobs. I struggled to compose myself so I could speak. "My mom. She was . . . she was there." I gasped for air. I couldn't breathe. Another set of heavy sobs tore from me. "Why would Trystan do that? Why would he show me?"

Kylan sighed and shook his head. His eyes moving to the others who looked equally confused as he was. "I'm deeply sorry, Calla. I don't know why." He kneeled next to me, his palm lying tenderly on my back.

The last words my mother had said to me were . . . *Be good, darling. We'll celebrate your birthday when we return.*

We'll see you in a few weeks.

I couldn't hold the tears and uncontrollable sobs. "My best friend . . . her parents . . . they're dead too. Is she in danger?"

Kylan paused and glanced at the others. They didn't respond, just remained there, silent and somber. "We don't know how much the enemy knows about you, so we can't make assumptions about your friend just yet. Right now, the enemy's focus is entirely on your grandfather and his bloodline."

I inhaled a sharp breath and tried to collect myself. "He's not my grandfather! He's a murderous bastard, responsible for all those innocent deaths." Tears streamed down my face. My chest heaved and ached, and although I wasn't certain if my heart was dead, it felt very much alive.

"I don't blame you," Melaina added. "I would disown the bastard too."

I tried to wipe the tears spilling down my cheeks. "I need to be sure my friend Brynna is safe. I can't leave Sartha until I know. She has no other relatives, and when she finds out about her parents, she'll come looking for me. She'll assume I'm dead too. And what happens if they find her?" The thought of her alone, finding out her parents were dead, and I was missing? "I'll never forgive myself, or Trystan, if anything happens to her. She's all I have left." Another loud sob ripped from me.

"I'll send a message to Trystan," Kylan said, his eyes

softening. "And there is still hope that your father is alive. They could have taken him to Morbeth, knowing he is Nicolae's kin. Trystan's father has spies throughout Talbrinth. If they see or hear anything, they'll let him know."

I'd heard of the wealth of Carpathia and of its mortal ruler, Lord Astor. But I'd never heard mention of a vampire kingdom, or the Vladu clan.

Everyone remained silent, allowing me my space while I composed myself and was ready to communicate without crying.

"Why don't humans know vampires exist?" I finally asked.

Kylan, perching next to me, set a few dried branches onto the fading fire. "The vampire kingdoms are concealed from the mortal race. They've been heavily warded with strong glamours to keep them invisible to mortal eyes. Only vampires and mages can see through the veils. And of course, those who serve within the vampire kingdoms."

"How long have they been on Talbrinth?" I recalled Kylan telling me there were seven vampire kingdoms in Talbrinth, one located in each country.

"Since the beginning," Kylan answered. The others made their way back to their beds to settle back down. Probably not wanting to be involved in this discussion. "They were established centuries before mortals settled the land."

"Do the Lords of each country know about the vampires?"

"Yes, because each mortal Lord was appointed by an

immortal King."

The thought was startling. To know there were immortal beings who'd been residing in Talbrinth from the beginning, ruling, and watching us from their large, hidden kingdoms. *They were the puppet masters.* It all made sense now. No one had known how the mortal rulers came into power so quickly, but it was because they had wealthy, immortal backup.

Kylan continued, "When the Great War broke out, causing devastation and ruin, the vampires watched and waited. When it was done, they stepped in to help rebuild and reestablish their regions, while remaining silent and invisible."

"Why didn't they do anything to stop the Great War?"

Kylan shrugged his shoulders and sighed. "Man possesses a free will. When they wage war against one another, we don't interfere."

"And vampires don't wage war?"

"With cause, vampires will go to war. And right now, Trystan is working at all costs to avert such a war."

It was all so overwhelming, and the agony in my chest wasn't going away.

"Hey, get some rest," Kylan said. "At first light, we'll leave and make our way toward Carpathia."

"What about the sun?" I saw and felt what a small ray of light did to my hand.

"We'll be protected under thick robes and cowls while remaining under the canopy of trees as long as the forest allows."

The thought of walking miles in the dank wood, under a thick, hooded cloak, didn't sound like a pleasant way to travel. "How long did it take for you to get to me?"

"So many questions," he exhaled, a lopsided grin tugging on his mouth. "We left Carpathia seven days ago."

"A week?" Good gods. This rescue had been set in motion days before I'd even met Trystan. And it again proved he had planned it all out, while I'd remained clueless. "I just have to know that my best friend is safe."

"As I said, I'll speak with Trystan," Kylan said softly. "But if she's not blood-related to you, she shouldn't be in any danger."

I hoped Kylan was right. "So, what happened to the threat outside?"

"They were disposed of," he answered promptly, then his eyes went distant. "Except one. He was remarkably fast and wielded magic."

"Magic? Vampires have magic?"

"Only purebloods," he stated, putting another log onto the fire. "But few possess magic like the one that got away. He must have been the Prince of Morbeth—the brother of the one your grandfather murdered."

I stared into Kylan's tired, turquoise eyes. "Does Trystan have magic too?"

He grinned. "He does, and he is immensely powerful. All purebloods are. But they are careful to whom they reveal their magic, for it can be used against them. Even I, after all these years of working for Trystan, don't know the full measure of his magic." He pushed up to his feet. "try to get some rest. The more you rest, the faster your strength will return."

I had one more question. "What kind of power do newborns have?"

A gleam flickered in those turquoise eyes. "It differs. Tomorrow, we'll put you to the test."

Lying back down, I closed my eyes, but couldn't sleep. I said a silent prayer to the gods above for my parents. That they would embrace my mother and welcome her into the next realm. I also prayed they would keep my father safe . . . wherever he was.

A gentle nudge roused me from my sleep. I blinked a few times until my eyes focused on Melaina a few feet away.

"Wake up. It's almost time to leave."

"What time is it?" I yawned, stretching my stiff limbs.

"The sun hasn't risen yet, but I just made contact with Trystan. The Prince of Morbeth *was* here last night. He's furious that his mission failed and is presently assembling another unit. They should be making their way toward us now."

"Wait." My head started reeling. "He traveled to Morbeth and back in a few hours? How is that even possible?"

"Purebloods have magical abilities. And for all we

know, the Prince of Morbeth could have had an army waiting nearby."

"If an army is coming, what should we do?" I could feel my panic rising.

"Don't worry about that right now," she replied coolly, pulling her satchel over her shoulder. She moved until she stood in front of me. "I thought you should know, I gave Trystan hell about showing you what happened on your parent's ship last night. He swore it wasn't him and truly feels like shit. I must admit . . . I do believe his sincerity. He thinks maybe you and Nyx have a connection like they do, because of the partial bond. And he also thinks that because your thoughts were on your parents, Nyx took it upon herself to show you." Melaina shrugged, then whispered some words, and waved her hand over the fire and it instantly went out. No hot coals and no lingering smoke. "Let's go," she said.

Kylan and the others were already up, packed, and dressed in their fighting leathers.

I hauled myself up, my muscles ached, but the pain in my chest was much worse. *My mother.* I'd never get to see her beautiful face again or hear her sing in the mornings while she made breakfast. She couldn't carry a tune but, gods love her, she would belt out her songs, anyway. I needed to get her body and give her a proper burial. Maybe Trystan could help with that.

Kylan made his way from a distant part of the cave toward me. "How are you holding up?"

I shrugged. "As good as I can be, after finding out my mother is dead, and that my father has been possibly taken captive by hunters who want to execute him. Do you think they'll use him to draw Nicolae out from hiding?" I blew out a frustrated breath. "I have a feeling Nicolae couldn't give a shit about what happens to him—or me, for that matter."

"No one has much information about Nicolae or even if he's still in Talbrinth," Kylan replied. "For all we know, he could have run and is on another continent."

"What's our plan then?" I asked Kylan.

"Our plans have changed. We're to head north toward Havendale, where we will meet Trystan."

"Trystan will be in Havendale?" My insides twisted at the prospect of meeting him again. Havendale was Baelfast's largest town. It was also where Lord Huxley, the ruler of Baelfast, lived.

He gave a wary expression. "It seems he wants to ensure your safety. He also wants to speak to the King of Baelfast in hopes he has further answers about Nicolae, and hopefully, the whereabouts of your father." Kylan handed me a leather belt with a sheath on its side. "Here, put this on."

I did as he said. Then he held up a white cloth with a dagger lying on top. It looked ancient. Its hilt was made of a white stone with two symbols carved into it, embedded with gold.

"Those are runes." Melaina stood next to me and pointed to each of the symbols. "This first one means guidance and the second . . . accuracy." She stepped even closer, her right palm skimming the air above it but not touching it. "This blade is old. I can sense its magic. It's a rare relic," she spoke mostly to herself.

"It's Trystan's," Feng replied. "It was his father's, passed down through the generations." He sheathed two freshly sharpened swords to his back. "I've never known him to be without that dagger at his side. I'm astonished he let it go."

I swallowed hard and picked up the dagger. As soon as my fingers folded around its shaft, electricity jolted me. I gasped, releasing the blade, and watched it fall and hit the ground.

We all stood in a circle around the relic, witnessing the gold runes glow bright red.

"I'm sorry," I breathed, wondering if I should back away or pick it up. "I didn't mean to drop it."

Melaina's jade eyes narrowed on me. "You do have magic inside you. Strong magic. I felt it the first time I touched you, and now," she pointed to the dagger, "this relic has affirmed it."

"I—I don't have magic. I've never felt or sensed anything out of the ordinary. No magic. No power. Not even a spark until now.

Melaina shook her head. "One of your ancestors had to have been a witch or had considerable power."

That couldn't be true. "Neither of my parents have magic."

"Sometimes magic can skip a generation or two. It seeks out those deserving of its power," Melaina explained. "Do you know anything about your grandparents?"

"My grandparents on my mother's side were mortals who lived and died in Aquaris. My grandfather was a fisherman and my granny was a seamstress. They were simple people who lived modest lives. There was nothing unusual about them."

"What about Nicolae and his wife?" Melaina's arms crisscrossed over her chest.

"Until a few days ago, I didn't even know Nicolae was alive, let alone know anything about his wife . . . if he even had one. My father has no record of his birth parents. Shortly after he was born, he was left on the steps of an old parish in Sartha. The minister and his wife—my grandparents—took him in and raised him as their own."

Melaina cast a glance at Kylan, then back at me. "Well, there is clearly magic in your blood. The only way to know for sure is to find your origins."

"Good luck," I murmured. "If Nicolae is killed, all hopes of obtaining any information will die with him. I don't think anyone knows what he looks like."

"Except the Prince of Morbeth," Kylan replied. "He must have information on him."

Melaina took a stride toward me. "If I had anything that belonged to Nicolae, I could attempt a locating spell."

"We have nothing," I groaned. "Nothing but a death decree."

"What about her blood?" Brone asked. "If they are kin, Nicolae's blood flows through her."

"Using blood is complicated. It not only carries his DNA, but everyone else in her lineage . . . on both sides. That can make the location spell overly complex."

"Wouldn't it only locate someone alive? Everyone, except for me, Nicolae, and hopefully my father is all that's left. At least that I know of."

Melaina shrugged, her brow furrowed as if she were contemplating it. "We can try, but it takes time, and I'll require a few supplies."

"What do you need?" Kylan asked.

Melaina's freckled brow crumpled. "Water and a quiet, dark corner of the cave."

She then drew a black cloth from her pack and started to unfold it. Wrapped inside were four candles in varied colors that were previously used. She strode to a far edge of the cave and began to clear the ground. She then asked me to help her gather larger stones and create a circle.

I did as she said, and when the circle was complete, Melaina said a prayer to cleanse the space before setting the candles inside. She explained the green candle, representing earth, was set toward the north. The yellow, air, was set east. The red, representing fire, was placed south, and blue, water, to the west.

In the center of the circle, facing the green candle, she set a book down on the ground, then spread the black material over the top. "This will be my altar," she said.

On top of the altar, she placed the bowl she filled with water. To the side of the bowl, she set a sharp knife, a small empty bowl, a piece of parchment, a white feather quill, and a white tapered candle. Before she started, she made it clear that everyone needed to remain silent—her gaze narrowing on Brone. Brone growled at the witch, but she ignored him and carried on.

Melaina motioned to me. "Calla, I want you inside the circle with me."

"I—I don't know if that's a good idea." I remained in place, not sure I was the best person for this. "I don't want to mess it up."

She gave an assuring smile that made her face appear softer. "You won't. All I need you to do is focus on Nicolae."

I nodded. "I can do that."

Focusing on Nicolae was simple. He hadn't left my mind since I was told he existed and that my family was being hunted because of him. I needed to find him. I needed answers. And then I wanted him dead.

CHAPTER EIGHT

Melaina led me inside the circle to my spot next to the altar. I sat still and silent while she moved around the outer perimeter, lighting each of the candles. Returning to the center, Melaina raised her arms in the air and called upon the energies of each element, shifting to each direction as she did.

She was cleansing the circle, keeping evil spirits out, while evoking each of the elements, guardians, and deities to aid her in her cause. I concentrated on her voice, let her words sink down inside of me.

As she completed the circle, I witnessed a bluish-white light emanating from her fingertips, like sparks of electricity. There was a tingling energy buzzing in the air. The stones around the circle began glowing, finishing the ritual, enclosing us in.

Melaina spoke again, her words directed to her goddess, seeking for guidance. When she finished, she sat next to me and grabbed hold of my hand. With her empty hand, she picked up the blade and slipped the sharp tip across my palm, creating a narrow incision. I flinched but refused to make a noise, per her orders. Melaina then guided my hand, twisting it over the bowl and collecting the blood.

When the blood stopped dripping, she let go. Looking at my palm, I saw the incision was almost completely healed. Melaina took the feather quill, dipped the tip into the bowl of blood, and on the piece of parchment wrote out the name *Nicolae Corvus*. It was strange to see his name. To think this man, who I thought was dead since before I was born, could be alive and we were now in search of him.

When she was finished, she folded the parchment in half, and half again, while speaking another prayer. A prayer invoking the deities to help her locate the individual whose name she'd written in blood. Then she held a corner of the folded parchment over the flame.

As it burned, the surrounding air thickened. Melaina leaned forward, gazing into the bowl of water, and I found myself leaning closer.

Inside the bowl, images flickered. A face, fuzzy at first, gradually became clearer. I wanted to cry out, to say something, but I remained silent and still as Melaina had warned.

The image was of my father. He was alive, curled on the ground in a fetal position, darkness enveloping him. There was nothing I could see around him but grass, twigs, and leaves. His head suddenly popped up, face dirty, hair matted.

His golden eyes, just like mine, held an expression I'd never seen on my father before. It was the expression of *fear.*

His head jerked to the left, then to the right. His body stilled before he bound up and ran away. He was running for his life.

I tensed and felt Melaina squeeze my hand.

The image of my father dissipated, and another flickered to life. It was the face of a girl who looked around my age, with golden hair. But her eyes. Her eyes were different colors. One was emerald and the other sapphire. I'd never seen this girl before. I was sure of it. But as I tried to examine her features, her image faded and another emerged.

Familiar golden irises with flecks of auburn came into view. Eyes so identical to my father's . . . to my own.

Was this Nicolae?

He looked young. Maybe in his early thirties, with shoulder-length hair. He was handsome, though. I could see the resemblance between him and my father.

The man was on his knees, on a well-maintained grassy area hemmed in by large beautiful trees laden with lavender blossoms. He leaned forward, scooping water into cupped hands, drawing it to his lips and drinking.

He strode back toward a tent, not far away, where a campfire was burning. As he reached his encampment, he waved his hand in the air and it all vanished. Instantly. It was as if he wasn't there.

Melaina's bowl of water became black, with nothing further to reveal. I remained quiet as she whispered another prayer, drawing the energy of the elements back into her, offering thanks to those who had aided her to complete the ritual.

When she was done, we rose and kicked the stones away from the circle. I presumed it was so that no one would realize a witch performed a séance. Kylan and the others had moved out of sight, but I could hear their hushed voices.

"Did you see?" Melaina asked, discarding the water from the dish and putting it back into her sack, along with the candles and the blade.

I'd been waiting for her to give me a signal that it was okay to speak.

"Yes," I responded softly. "The first man was my father." My eyes heated with tears again. "He's alive, and I've never seen him so frightened." My words broke out in a sob.

"Hey," Melaina said, taking a step toward me. "I'm sure your father can handle himself. Right now, the attention has shifted toward you. They are sending warriors here because Roehl knows you're getting support from Trystan, and his over-inflated ego won't allow him to lose." I nodded, hoping she was correct. "Do you know who the girl with the colorful eyes was?"

"No," I shook my head. "That was the first time I've ever seen her."

"To appear like she did, she has to be closely related to you."

"I honestly don't know her. I've never seen her before. My parents had no siblings, so I don't have any relatives. But who knows? It seems my life isn't as simple as I expected."

"Yeah, well, you didn't know Nicolae was alive until a few days ago. Maybe he had other relationships."

I nodded, struggling to steady my nerves and settle my emotions. "That third face, it was Nicolae." I spoke softly. I knew it was him. Everything inside me confirmed it.

"I presume so." She flung her satchel over her shoulder. "He's a handsome witch."

"A witch?" I choked, and she nodded. "I thought only females were witches."

"It doesn't matter. Male or female, they are both referred to as witches. It's obvious Nicolae is powerful and well-experienced," she added. "To make an entire camp disappear with a flick of his hand shows maturity—years of training." Her eyes narrowed on mine. "He's clearly the link to your power."

"But I don't have any power."

Her brows crumpled. "You've never had strange things happen that you can't explain?"

I thought about it. "Besides Trystan biting me, making me change into a vampire? No."

"Well, I felt it. Maybe your magic has been dormant and for some reason will be released at a specific time." She shrugged. "You definitely have something, especially if your grandfather is that powerful."

"You must be just as capable," I uttered. "You glamoured this cave, like he did his camp."

"Not with such ease. Even as powerful as I am, I cannot

cast a glamour so quickly. Not with a flip of my wrist."

Footsteps crunched in our area. "Did it work? Did you see anything?" Kylan asked, moving around the corner. He'd probably overheard us with his keen vampire hearing, but he acted as if he didn't know anything.

"My father is still alive. He's running, but they're after him." I replied. "I think he might be somewhere in Whisper Woods."

Melaina responded. "If his ship ran aground near Hale, he is surely in Whisper Woods. But he could be anywhere, maybe even heading in the opposite direction."

"We have to find him," I pleaded, shifting to Kylan. "He's the only family I have left. He's out there alone, and I've never seen him so frightened."

Kylan paused, his worried brow turning back to Brone and Feng, who were standing behind him.

"It's your call," Andrés said.

Kylan turned to Melaina. "Did you see a landmark?"

She shook her head. "It was too dark. The only thing we could see were trees. He's definitely in the woods."

I wanted, more than anything, to leave and look for him, but without a landmark or something we could use to identify his location, it would be like searching for a shadow in the pitch black.

"If he's smart," Brone spoke, "he'd head north. There are safe places inside the town of Havendale. The Lord of Baelfast is generous when it comes to his people. It possesses many places to hide or even disappear if you wanted to."

"I also agree we should head north," Kylan said. "Trystan will be in Baelfast, and we'll have a better chance of locating your father with his help. To survive, we must stay ahead of the enemy."

As much as I wanted to go looking for my father, I knew the likelihoods of finding him was virtually impossible, given how incredibly large the Whisper Woods were. Hopefully, he could stay hidden. I had to believe that. Maybe he could make it to Baelfast. Or even head in the opposite direction toward Aquaris, or even to Northfall. My father had many friends and business acquaintances in those territories. And as much as I didn't want to leave him, Kylan was right. We needed to move north, immediately. I needed to get out of these woods. They were claustrophobic.

"We also saw Nicolae," I added.

Kylan quickly glanced to Melaina, and she nodded in confirmation.

"Do you have a location on him?"

"He could be anywhere," Melaina sighed, shaking her head. "But one thing vexes me. You said he was a Dhampyr, right?"

"That's what the decree said," Kylan answered. "Why?"

Her eyes went distant, arms crossed over her breast. "I'm not entirely sure that's correct."

"Explain," Kylan said. All the cadre's eyes were pinned on her.

"He has powerful magic. He glamoured his entire camp with a wave of his hand, which tells me he's not simply a vampire, but something else. Something magical. And he knows how to wield it."

"Witch?" Brone asked.

"Likely," she replied. "But there could be one more explanation."

"What?" Kylan and I asked at the same time.

"He's a pureblood and magic is his gift."

"Pureblood? It can't be," Andrés exclaimed from behind us while Melaina shrugged. "How?"

"When two purebloods come together—" Brone began.

Andrés cut him off. "I know how they're conceived," he growled, "but no one has ever heard of Nicolae Corvus. Every pureblooded vampire ever born is recorded in the royal registry. Nicolae's name is not there."

"How would you know?" Melaina challenged.

"Because it was one of the tasks Trystan assigned to me before we left Carpathia to travel here," Andrés stated.

My head became a whirlwind. "Does Trystan think Nicolae is a pureblood?"

He shook his head. "I don't know. But he likes to be thorough."

"Well, we can't confirm anything about Nicolae until we find him," Melaina cut in. "And that'll be the tricky part. Scrying can only show us fragments of the puzzle. With his magic, Nicolae can disappear, and it shows he's incredibly experienced at. It's possibly the reason no one knows or has any record of him."

"I don't know if it'll help, but I did recognize something,"

I replied. All eyes moved to me. "Nicolae was surrounded by a grove of jacaranda trees in rich bloom. He had a small encampment, set up on a clearing of grass that was groomed. There was a water source nearby, possibly a river or lake."

"Jacaranda trees flourish in the north," Feng noted. "On Talbrinth, most groves are in Northfall, but they are also on private land."

"I spent my childhood in Northfall," Brone spoke. "My parents would take me to the Enchanted Lake which was surrounded by beautiful jacaranda trees. My father would set up camp on a grassy area while he hunted. The lake there is filled with fish, and the wood beyond has lots of wild game. It's the perfect place for someone to hide out and survive."

"Do you know how to get to this area?" Kylan asked Brone.

"Yes, but the land is owned by the Kingdom of Northfall and run by the mortal, Lord Grayson. Only those of noble blood or those granted special permission can set foot there. Trespassers are severely punished."

"How did your family acquire those kinds of privileges?" Melaina puffed, her brow rising.

Giving her a narrowed, sidelong glance, Brone replied, "My father was commander of the King of Northfall's guard."

Melaina shrugged, but her expression revealed she was impressed. "Well if it's off-limits and he's using an invisibility spell, my assumption is he's there."

Feng took a few strides forward with a question in his eyes. "What I don't understand is why he would come out of hiding, after all this time, to execute a prince? Everyone knows that killing a royal means a direct execution, especially when that royal comes from the Kingdom of Morbeth—the one kingdom who takes pleasure in war and executions. I would like to know what his motivation was?"

Andrés said, "I've heard rumors the King of Morbeth is dying. But no one can confirm if it's accurate or not because their kingdom is so heavily guarded."

"Yes, especially behind their insufferable Red Wall," Brone muttered, shaking his head. "One has to wonder how news can travel past such a monstrosity."

"The same way it gets past you." Andreas laughed, whacking a palm on Brone's broad back. "It's highly unlikely . . . but possible."

Brone growled at him, exposing lengthened incisors. But Kylan chuckled again, affixing a black leather vambrace to his forearm. "Morbeth's walls were erected to keep their people in and all others out."

"I'm fine with that," Melaina declared. "Morbeth terrifies me. There is immense dark magic lingering behind that wicked Red Wall. And I, for one, will never set foot in that territory."

"What if you were awarded ample gold skrag to last a lifetime?" Brone questioned.

Melaina shrugged, her face an expression of boredom. "Maybe."

CHAPTER NINE

Kylan and Brone left the cave early to scout the surrounding area and make sure it was safe for us to leave. As soon as they returned and announced all clear, we departed the cave in single file, hastily retreating into the dark Whisper Woods. Melaina and I were instructed to remain in the middle of the group on our course through the tangle of dense woods.

My eyes adapted to the darkness rather quickly. My limbs were strong and agile, even at the fast pace we were moving. I inhaled the odors of the forest . . . the morning dew on the blades of grass and fallen leaves, the scent of moss, oak, and pine as we zigzagged our way through the labyrinth of thick trees. But there was a sound that troubled me. The sound of Melaina's ragged breathing. I could tell she was fatigued and winded, her heart thumping strong and fast against her ribcage, and I was amazed she'd held pace for this long.

Her face and cheeks were flustered, beads of perspiration

dripped down her brow and dotted on her freckled cheeks.

"Do you need to rest?" I whispered.

"No," she puffed. "I may be mortal, but I'm strong enough to bear my own load."

I realized it was her pride speaking, so I didn't push any further.

As we made our way further into the forest, I addressed Kylan. "Could we pause for just a few moments?"

"We shouldn't stop," he declared. "Why? What's wrong?"

"It's just . . ." I discretely tipped my head toward Melaina, hoping not to annoy her. "Not all of us are immortal."

Kylan held up a hand, and we all stopped.

Melaina pressed her back up against a tree, then sifted through her satchel, withdrawing a canteen. Her face was red and splotchy, dripping with sweat.

Brone stepped next to her. "If you're tired, I can carry you."

Melaina's eyes expanded, and she practically choked on her water. "Goddess, never! Just because I'm human doesn't mean I'm an invalid. I just need a few seconds to catch my breath."

"I didn't mean it as an insult," Brone said, tipping his head. "I was merely offering my help."

Her glaring eyes considered him for a few moments, then softened as she drew in another sharp breath and exhaled. "Thanks, but I don't need your help." She screwed the lid back on her canteen and stuck it back in her satchel before pushing off the tree. "Let's go."

I peered at Brone and shrugged. At least he offered. No one else did, and probably wouldn't have.

"She's a feisty one," he murmured, gently nudging my arm.

I snickered, glancing at the scarred but handsome brute at my side. "Too much for you to handle?"

He nodded. "I think I might have met my match."

We'd trekked through the woods, making our way north, toward Baelfast, pausing a few times for Melaina to rest and rehydrate. Kylan had a few extra canteens filled with blood, one of which he demanded me to consume.

This time I was determined to control the thirst. It was a tremendous challenge when I placed the container to my lips, and the scent of blood hit my nose. The thirst monster inside tried to burst free, but I somehow managed to contain it and consume the entire contents without spilling a drop.

When I handed the empty vessel to Kylan, he cocked his head to the side and grinned. "I'm impressed."

The looks from Brone, Andrés, and Feng also said they were equally impressed.

I smiled but didn't say a word. It took everything inside me to resist the overwhelming power of the blood flooding through my veins. But my willpower held steady. And I knew it stemmed from one thing. Humiliation. The thought of making a complete ass of myself in front of the others like I did with Kylan. But it did prove that I was stronger than the thirst.

We proceeded at a consistent pace, remaining in the darkest parts of the forest. But when the sun finally began to set, we were still deep within the Whisper Woods. I had no idea where we were, or how long we'd traveled, but it had to have been miles. We could have continued, but we had a mortal in our midst who looked like she was about to collapse at any given moment.

"We'll stop here for the night," Kylan said, pointing toward a small clearing between a few trees. The area inside the trees was about ten feet wide, so it would be tight.

Melaina drank some water before she began her wards and spells to cloak the area. After a few moments, Brone and Andrés stepped inside and disappeared.

"Kylan," Feng said, kneeling about ten yards away from the ward. We headed toward him.

On the ground was a massive paw print, larger than the size of my head. From the impression, it had long claws that sunk deep into the earth.

"What is it?" I breathed, my eyes scouring the area.

"There are beasts in these woods," Kylan replied.

"Shadow Hounds," Brone added, stepping out of the ward. "Dark beasts with eyes of fire that can shred a man in seconds."

My body shuddered. "How do you know this?"

Brone's fingers scraped against his scars, and it became evident. They weren't from battle, as I'd first thought. They were from a Shadow Hound.

A loud howl, which sounded miles away, shot a shiver up my spine.

Brone patted my back. "You should go inside the ward before the sun sets."

I didn't argue. But I did want to know how he ran into such a beast and survived. I suppose I'd have to wait for another time to hear that tale . . . if he wanted to share it.

Inside the ward, our sleeping situation was tight, but it was the only place in the forest nearby that had any kind of space. Melaina insisted on sleeping on one edge of the ward, declaring she was claustrophobic and couldn't sleep in between anyone. I took the spot next to her, with Brone on my other side and Feng next to him. Kylan took the narrow space above us, stretching out against the stump of a tree, while Andrés chose to lay horizontally at our feet.

"Brone, don't roll in your sleep tonight," Feng nearly pleaded. "I would like to live through the night, and I think Calla would too."

"If I do roll," Brone said in his rich baritone voice, "It won't be in Calla's direction." His eyes swept to mine, offering me a wink.

"Thanks," I said, returning a smile.

Brone rested his large hand on my shoulder. "It's

compensation for not accepting the witch's stew and retching all night."

"Ah—" I exhaled. "So, I guess this makes us even."

"It does. And because Feng has offered me nothing, if I do roll, it will be that way." He thumbed toward Feng.

"Oh, but I do have something to offer," Feng replied, drawing his blade and his carving block from his pack. The chunk of wood was starting to take shape. I could make out a head . . . maybe the head of a dragon? I still wasn't sure. It could have been a dog, for all I knew.

"You would give me one of your carvings?" Brone asked, his eyes wide.

"No," Feng replied. "If you roll in my direction, I will offer this blade to your side."

There was a moment of silence before Brone burst into laughter. Feng and Andrés joined him, and even Kylan couldn't help but smile.

As everyone settled down, Brone slipped off his right boot. Andrés popped up and started gagging, his eyes watering. "For the love of the gods, put your boots on. You'll kill us in our sleep."

Brone lifted his foot across his knee, then leaned over and sniffed his foot. His face scrunched. "I suppose it's not pleasant," he exhaled, then pulled his boot back on.

"When we reach Havendale, we can all take a bath," Kylan said.

I stretched my arms over my head. "How much longer before we make it there?"

"If we move fast, a day or two," he responded.

"Two days?" Melaina moaned, rubbing her back. "If that's the case, I might be willing to let Brone carry me."

Brone glanced over to me, his eyes wide. "The offer stands as long as we are on this mission."

Melaina nodded without any expression on her face, then rolled over to her side, away from us. I smiled at Brone, who returned a playful grin. I sensed that maybe he was fond of the witch who stood up to him. The one he claimed was his match.

"It's hot in here," Brone grumbled a few hours later. And he was right. The air in the ward was stagnant and stifled. There were too many bodies packed together.

"It is hot . . . and sticky," Andrés added, kicking off his blanket.

Melaina growled under her breath and sat up. She closed her eyes and thrust her arms upward. An ice-cold gust swept into the ward and whirled around us, ripping Feng and Brone's blankets off. Brone turned to me with the biggest smile I'd seen on him yet.

Melaina dropped her arms and plunked back down on her satchel, the breeze still blowing.

"Better?" she snipped.

"Much," Brone replied, inhaling the cool air. "Thanks."

A faint growl came from Melaina. "Good. Now let

me sleep."

In no time, with the remaining cool air, we all fell fast asleep.

I gazed up at a sky of starlight, the breeze whipping through my hair. I inhaled the refreshing breeze and caught a familiar scent—that perfect blend of earth and wind and spice.

"I'm dreaming again, aren't I?" I murmured.

"Yes," was the response.

I swung around to see Trystan leaning against the bow of a ship, arms crossed over his muscular chest, his hair tousled by the wind. I was lost, trapped in that tug of war happening within myself whenever he seemed to be around . . . even in my dreams.

"Where are we?"

"On my ship, heading to Baelfast. I'll be meeting with Lord Huxley tomorrow in hopes to discover information on your father and Nicolae."

"My father is alive," I said, stepping toward him. "Melaina found him using a location spell. He's scared and is running for his life, somewhere in the Whisper Woods." I couldn't hold back the emotions that spilled down my face.

In a flash, Trystan was in front of me. "Don't cry," he sighed, his thumbs wiping my tears.

Overwhelmed, I folded my arms around his neck and

buried my face into his chest. His steely arms wrapped around me, his cheek pressing against the top of my head. I felt so comfortable in his arms. Like it was the one place I was secure. "Don't worry, Calla. We'll find your father," he whispered.

His soft promise entered my ear and traveled to my soul. They were genuine, and although I didn't understand why, deep down, I knew I could trust him. I had no reason to doubt.

"I'm glad you trust me," Trystan breathed. "And my arms will always be accessible to you, should you ever need a place to feel secure."

I pulled back, looking deep into those beautiful azure eyes. My cheeks flushed with heat. He'd read my mind.

The blood bond.

"Don't ever feel embarrassed around me," he added, taking a step backward. "This blood bond is new for me too. I don't understand everything about it, but I cannot doubt the emotions pulling inside me. Believe me, I've tried to resist them because I won't push you to make a decision you aren't ready to make."

"Thank you." I was truly blessed that fate led him to me.

I turned my attention toward the sea, not able to look him in the eyes. Because every time I did, I felt myself falling for him. "Maybe one day, when things settle down, we'll get to know each other better . . . more intimately," I murmured.

Trystan stood next to me, setting his hand over mine. "I made a decision to claim you, Calla. And I will continue to wait until you decide whether you want to seal the bond."

I grinned, watching the darkened sea ahead. The breeze was steady, causing the ship to sail steadily through the water.

"I didn't get a chance to thank you for sending your cadre. I genuinely like them," I said, trying to break the silence.

He gave a side-eyed glance. "I'm glad. Are they treating you well?"

I nodded. "They are. They're exceptionally nice. Especially Brone."

Trystan turned to me with a narrowed glance. "Brone?"

"Yes, Brone. He's like a gigantic stuffed bear. He looks a bit rough on the surface, but inside, he's soft and sweet."

Trystan laughed. "Are you certain we're speaking about the same Brone?"

"Yes. Why?"

"Well, Brone has never been nice. Or soft. Or sweet, for that matter. Especially to anyone outside of the cadre. And anytime he's around women, he stiffens and turns into a mute."

This was news to me. "Well, he's been nothing but a gentleman. He even told me to come to him if any of the others act up. I also think he has a thing for the witch, Melaina. Their banter is quite amusing."

"Is it?" There was a mischievous glint in his eyes.

"Please don't tell him I told you," I said, twisting back to him. "He'd never forgive me."

Trystan held up his hands. "Your secret's safe with me." He shook his head again. "I can't believe that big old brute," Trystan whispered to himself.

"I'm actually sleeping next to that big old brute right now."

His smile immediately fled, and his brow crumpled. "You're what?"

I was about to laugh at his expression, when an intense pain in my gut had me folding over, gasping for air. Something was wrong. Very wrong.

I clutched Trystan's arms. "Help," I bellowed.

His eyes flew wide with panic. "Calla, what's wrong?" His strong arms drew me against him, holding me tight.

A mighty wind ripped around us, tearing me out of his grasp. It was immensely strong. So strong, our grips slipped.

"Trystan!" I wailed, right before I was sucked into the darkness.

My eyes jerked open, and I found myself lying on my back amid chaos. The ward was breached. Countless men in black had surrounded us, battling with Trystan's cadre. Melaina was screaming, being dragged by her leg into the forest.

Jumping to my feet, I snatched my pack and flung it on my back as Kylan yanked my arm, shoving me behind him, pinning me up against a tree.

"Stay here," he ordered. He didn't have to worry. I was already fixed to the spot with fear.

I immediately scanned my surroundings, trying to get my

bearings. All four assassins were fighting the enemies who looked like the same I'd seen earlier through Nyx's eyes . . . killers dressed in black, with masks on. There were too many of them. Dozens pressing in from all directions.

Andrés ran after Melaina. Her screams pierced the chilled night air.

"Calla." A whispered voice called inside my head, sending prickles over my skin. "Calla Caldwell." Frozen in place, I held my head straight ahead, because I didn't recognize the low, gravelly tone. The fact this mysterious voice knew my first and last name was frightening.

It was hard not to look, so I concentrated on the battle ahead.

Just in front of me, Brone yelled and swung his spiked mace, taking out three men at once. Their bodies flew backward with the brute force of his power. Blood splattered and bones fractured. The first one who caught the brunt of the blow, didn't move. His body lay mangled and bleeding on the ground. The other two wouldn't get up anytime soon.

Kylan had a double-edged sword in one fist. He was fast, skirting the swing of an enemy blade and ducking under another. He caught the forearm of an opponent, and in one swift movement, swung behind him, plunging his sword into the breast of another. With his grip still on the other, he withdrew his sword, whirled back around, and took off his head.

Feng's long staff was like an extension of him. An extra-long limb, which he handled with remarkable speed and ability. I watched him push a button and a blade slip out from the tip. The way he moved was like a dance, fluid and agile, though powerful, and destructive. His staff, applied to specific vulnerable spots on the head and neck, were deadly blows.

Watching these men in the heat of battle, I realized why Trystan's father had appointed them. I'd never seen anyone fight like them. Their enemies were falling as fast as they were running in.

Andrés had rescued Melaina. His arm was around her midriff, pulling her along, while the other gripped a sword, dispatching those attacking them.

"Calla." The voice called again.

I shouldn't have looked, should have resisted the impulse to see who was calling me, but I was weak.

My eyes settled on a dark figure stepping out of the shadows with luminous alabaster eyes.

I could sense this man had power. I could feel it radiating from him.

"If you wish to see your friend alive, come with me." I didn't see his mouth move, but it was as if he were standing right beside me, his voice speaking directly into my ear. "If you inform your companions, you will die."

I didn't move. I stayed pressed against the tree while Kylan, Brone, and Feng advanced toward the continual threat. The thought of Brynna in the enemy's hands—an enemy that murdered my mother and her parents—caused me to turn back toward the ominous stranger.

But had they truly captured her?

The man's head inclined to the side. "You seek confirmation." His left hand slipped into his dark overcoat pocket and withdrew something gripped in his fingers. With a snap, a glowing light in his right palm illuminated a heart-shaped, golden locket with a swan engraved on top. A swan with a diamond eye.

Gods damned. It was Brynna's.

"Come without struggle, and I'll take you to where she is."

He realized he had me. There was no way I'd jeopardize Brynna's life.

I turned my attention back to the assassins, quickly realizing most of the enemies who were pressing in weren't really fighting. They were distractions, sent to draw the attention of the cadre so the true enemy could get to me.

"Now," the silvery-eyed man warned, his palm extended.

With Brynna's life on the line, my hands were tied. I had no other option than to leave with him.

I took a few steps toward the white-eyed stranger when I heard Kylan roar, "Calla, no!" The expression in his turquoise eyes and on his face was one of complete dread. He lunged toward me, but it was too late.

As soon as my hand linked with the man, we were encompassed in a cloud of darkness. Wind tore around us, lifting us skyward, away from the others.

CHAPTER TEN

When we stopped, in what seemed like a minute later, we were no longer in the Whisper Woods. We were in a small room, ten by fifteen feet, where the walls and floors were made of stone. On one side was a small alcove with a primitive toilet—a pail with a wooden board set over it.

This wasn't a room. This was a cell.

"Where am I?" I questioned, shoving away from the man.

"Morbeth," he responded.

I struggled to calm my frayed nerves, but it was useless. "Where is my friend?"

"She is safe," he responded gently.

"You told me you'd take me to her!" I couldn't stop shaking, my mind reeling.

"I said I'd take you to where she is. She is here, in the palace."

"You bastard," I hissed.

"The prince will see you soon. If you act appropriately, he might let you out of here to see her."

Act appropriately? What the hell did that mean? If that meant surrendering to a man who sent his army to hunt for me and my parents because of what Nicolae did, I would *never* submit to him.

"Take me out of here," I wailed, swinging my fist at the man. But his body dissolved, as if he were mist, my hand shooting straight through him. When he became solid again, he stepped closer and clutched my wrist.

"It is not prudent to lash out when you have a price on your head. They are capable of evil you cannot fathom. Do not give them reason to use you as an example." His eyes were hard set and rigid, his words like lashes. But it seemed like he was trying to help me.

This man was older. Maybe in his fifties, with silvery hair and a weathered face. But I couldn't get over those eyes. Those alabaster eyes.

"Who are you?" I inquired, my voice quivering.

He released my wrist and stepped back, his eyes still narrowed on me. "My name is Erro. I was sent by Prince Roehl Tynan to retrieve you."

"How did we get to Morbeth so quickly?"

"I am a Wanderer," was his reply.

I'd heard tales of Wanderers. Magical people who controlled the wind and used it to travel. They appeared human but were far from mortal, and no one thought they still existed. Some claimed they were formed from magic and wind, and after experiencing it firsthand, I believed it.

"I've done nothing wrong. Please don't leave me here," I pleaded. "They'll kill me, just like they killed my mother."

"I'm sorry," he apologized, his tone softening. "I've sworn under an oath. A vow I cannot break. My family's life depends on it." His eyes met mine, his head cocked slightly to the side. "There is magic in you. But it is dormant. Concealed with stronger magic. Find a means to release it," he implored in a muffled tone, placing his warm palm on my arm. "It can keep you alive."

With a bow of his head, his body turned to mist. And just like that, he dissolved, leaving nothing but a burst of icy wind behind.

Weak, I dropped to the bitter, rough ground, my entire body trembling.

His words meant nothing to me. In my entire life, I'd never experience magic. Not a spark or flicker of any kind. And if I did have it—whatever it was—how the hell was I supposed to release it?

Worthless. It was all meaningless words, and I was useless, sitting in a dingy cell, captured like a rat in a cage.

Morbeth wasn't a place someone could easily break into, especially with their infamous Red Wall. Hell, it wasn't a place anybody in their right mind would even consider breaking into without regarding their lives. Even Melaina swore she wouldn't step into this territory.

Before Talbrinth's Great War, Morbeth had been in the process of raising their wall. After its completion, the Red Wall was named for the countless bodies and blood spilled around it during the war. No enemy could penetrate the wall, and all those who tried fell to Morbeth's army of archers and arrows. The soil around the wall, which claimed thousands of lives, was given the name Dead Man's Land. Even years afterward, the area was still desolate, bereft of life, and every living thing ceased to exist as if it were cursed. I had no doubt it was cursed, as was the entire region of Morbeth.

I searched for my pack, but it wasn't there. I remembered throwing it over my back when Kylan grabbed me. Erro must have taken it at some point without my knowledge. The dagger Kylan gave me—Trystan's dagger—was in it, and so was the flask. At this moment, the flask seemed like the only option. But it was gone.

The cell was dark and bleak, the air stagnant. I could practically smell the fear and loneliness mixed with excrement, blood, sweat, and tears from the countless prisoners once held here. It was a fetid smell that would permanently tarnish the walls of these cells.

I kicked the door several times, but it was made of solid wood and didn't budge. So much for super vampire strength.

I shouted from the narrow-barred window at the top, but my cries went unnoticed. It seemed the only sounds down here, wherever this was, were coming from me.

I wasn't sure what time it was, but I was exhausted. I curled up in a dry corner of the cell and closed my eyes, wishing to fall asleep and see Trystan . . . but sleep eluded me. There were too many questions in my mind, along with the strong, overwhelming anguish of the loss of my mother.

I lost track of time when a latch on the door clicked, and a smaller door on the bottom raised. A small tray slid inside before the door clicked shut.

"Wait!" I screamed, jumping to my feet and rushing to the door. "Wait! Come back." I pounded on the door, but the footsteps didn't stop and continued until I was left alone, in silence.

Gods damned bastards!

I crouched over and picked up the tray. On it were two small slices of stale bread that appeared as though they'd been sitting out for a few days. I picked up a cup of clear liquid and brought it to my nose, sniffing it. There was no odor. It must have been water.

If the Prince of Morbeth was in the Whisper Woods, he knew Trystan had claimed me, and that I was now one of them . . . a vampire. By bringing me water and bread, he clearly wanted me to suffer. How long was I to remain a prisoner? I knew the decree. They were going to execute me, and eventually my father. We were the last of Nicolae's bloodline . . . that's what I'd assumed.

The truth was, I wasn't sure of anything anymore.

I could only hope Erro wasn't assigned to locate my father. If there were other Wanderers out there like him, my father had no chance. There was no way he could run from the wind.

Erro had found me and was able to break through Melaina's wards, snatching me directly from Trystan's cadre. I hoped they were alright. The look Kylan gave me before I disappeared made my stomach ache. At least he knew I was taken and not lost somewhere in the woods. And he had to have known I would be taken to Morbeth. I hoped.

I exhaled heavily, pressing my back against the cold stone wall, slipping down it. Hugging my knees, the only thing I could do was wait.

It felt like an eternity before my next meal arrived and it was the same crap. Stale bread and water. My stomach felt like it was devouring itself from the inside out. I knew if I didn't get blood soon, I'd pass out. Which wouldn't be awful. Sleep was a much better option than having my mind awake with too many emotions and unanswered questions stirring.

Every time I closed my eyes, I hoped to see Trystan. But every time, that hope was shattered, replaced with recurring nightmares. Was the blood bond weak because I was weak?

With each passing moment, I found myself fading in and out. If I had Trystan's flask, I would have drunk from it.

Finally, after my eyes became so heavy they couldn't stay open, I welcomed sleep.

Darkness enveloped me, and as much as I searched, I couldn't see a light or detect a way out.

"Trystan?" I cried out, but there was no answer. "Trystan!"

I could hear movement around me, but couldn't see past the dense, pitch-black gloom. It sounded like there was something slithering on the ground around me.

"Who's there?" I wailed, hoping it wasn't a snake. Gods, I hated snakes.

There was no answer, but the movement was now behind me. Then to my side. And front. It was everywhere. I extended my arms, feeling, reaching for anything to grip onto. But there was nothing but empty space.

The darkness was vile. It was heavy and humid, making it hard to breathe.

I sensed I wasn't alone in this endless black chamber and could feel the weight of ominous eyes observing me.

Then something slithered across the floor and struck my foot. Screaming, I raced forward, slamming into something broad and solid. I whirled to run away, but powerful arms wrapped around me from behind. From the height and muscles, I knew he was male. My captor's scent was foreign, a blend of leather and maybe oak—a heady, woody fragrance.

It wasn't awful, but it wasn't anything like Trystan's.

"I've got you now," a low voice spoke into my ear, sending a shudder down my spine. "You don't have to fear the dark. I own the dark."

Fear gripped me, smothering me so I couldn't move or breathe. "I despise the dark," I replied, trying to fight from his hold. But those arms held me firm.

A sudden flicker in the dark soon shifted into a ball of light hovering in front of us. I struggled to twist back, to look at the face of the stranger holding me, but he gripped me tighter against his chest, keeping me steady.

"Let go of me!" I exclaimed, trying to free myself.

An evil laugh rumbled against my ear. "Soon," he breathed. "But right now, I have you exactly where I want you."

Terror filled every part of me. Who the hell was this bastard?

"It's such a pity you didn't take the handsome Carpathian prince's offer to seal the bond."

"Get away from me," I screamed, trying to push out of his grasp. But I couldn't budge. His arms were like steel.

Wake up. Wake up. Wake up. I needed to get out of this nightmare.

I snapped out of the dream, my wrists burning. I raised my arms to see thick steel manacles clamped around them, connected to heavy chains that were attached to the rock wall behind me.

Sucking in a breath, I caught a whiff of a strong scent lingering in the cell. The same as in my nightmare . . . leather and wood. Whoever was in my dream was here now.

It took a moment for my swollen eyes to adjust, but when they did, I gasped, looking at a tall figure standing at the far side of the cell. He was over six feet tall with muscular arms crisscrossed over a broad chest.

"So, you are Calla Caldwell—granddaughter of the savage and elusive Nicolae Corvus."

I twisted over onto my hands and knees and stood on unsteady legs. It took some effort, but I finally straightened, my bound wrists hanging heavy at my sides. I wouldn't show this bastard weakness, although I was a grand illustration of the word.

I scowled at him. "And you must be the murderous bastard. The Prince of Morbeth."

He gave a devilish grin. He looked a bit older than Trystan, maybe in his early thirties, with midnight hair that fell past his shoulders. But his eyes were unlike any I'd seen before. They were dark obsidian rimmed with crimson. Eyes of the devil.

"Yes, I am Roehl Tynan, Prince of Morbeth," he said, stepping out of the shadows.

I hated to admit it, but he was handsome, with sharp features. In those mysterious eyes, I could see something cunning, something evil writhing within. "You've been difficult to locate. You *and* your father. But lucky for me, I know the whereabouts of a few Wanderers. And I have no doubt your father will be accompanying us soon enough."

"Why are you doing this? We're innocent. We've done nothing to you," I roared, shoving against the shackles. If I weren't tied up, I would have lurched forward and punched the pompous expression off his face.

My trembling legs were threatening to give by the second, but I held my ground. "Whatever Nicolae did to you is *not* our issue. I've never even met him. He left my father on the doorstep of a parish, and I was told he was dead way before I was born. So, why are we being hunted for someone we don't know or couldn't care less about?"

His head inclined slightly to the side. "It's complicated."

I could feel the heat building inside me. "Complicated?" I stepped as close to him as the shackles would allow. "You murdered my mother and many more innocent lives!"

"I didn't mean for your mother to be killed. All those on the ship were collateral damage. If your father hadn't made such a huge fuss and come voluntarily, they would all still be alive."

"You bastard!" I wailed. I lurched at him, swinging, but he seized my wrist.

In a blink, Roehl pushed my back against the rough wall behind me, pinning me up against it with a force that slammed the air from my lungs. His eyes went completely black.

"I'm not the bastard," he replied through gritted teeth. "Nicolae is."

I fought him with everything I had, but he was too powerful. Looking into my eyes, he simply spoke the word, "Stop," and my body froze. I couldn't move a muscle.

He'd cast a spell on me.

Another sly smirk, and Roehl took a step back. From his pocket he removed an object, then brought it up between his fingers, shaking it a few inches from my face. It was an ornate, golden flask with Trystan's crest on its front. My body ached at the sight, and he recognized it. The bastard was tormenting me.

His darkened eyes tightened. "You should have taken his offer and sealed the bond. Then things would have turned out much differently." He slowly began to unscrew the cap. "If you did seal the bond, I would be holding a prince's mate prisoner, and that, my dear Calla, would not be beneficial to me or my kingdom." Sniffing the blood inside the flask, his nose crumpled, like the smell was repulsive. But I caught the scent, and my entire body craved it.

One sip. That's all it would take to seal the bond with Trystan. One sip and this could all be over. It was so close, but utterly unattainable in his grasp. I knew there was no way he'd let me touch the flask now.

"It's a shame, really, what your stubbornness to remain free has cost you. Look at you now. Look where your freedom and strong will have taken you." He took a single step closer, holding the flask inches from my face. The smell of Trystan's blood was potent, causing my incisors to lengthen. The thirst so intense it nearly knocked me to my knees.

He scowled, drawing another step back. "You will no longer be free, my pet. And now, he will never have you."

He walked toward a small drain at the center of the cell and poured Trystan's blood down it. I collapsed to my knees, watching every drop of hope fade.

When the flask was drained, Prince Roehl screwed the cap back on and tucked it into his pocket.

In another flash, he was on his knees in front of me, inches away. His lip curling above long, sharp incisors. Then his broad frame pressed against mine, fastening me back against the wall as his hands seized my cuffed wrists, forcing them above my head.

"Since you declined to bond with the Carpathian prince, you are now free to claim." In one swift movement, Roehl's teeth punctured my flesh—the area where my neck and shoulder met.

I screamed out in pain, trying to thrust him away, trying to stop him, but he wouldn't budge. When he finally pulled back, my blood dripped from his lips and chin.

His tongue licked the wet crimson on his lips. He closed his eyes. "So unbelievably delicious. Now I see why Trystan couldn't resist you." He leaned forward and ran his tongue across the skin he'd just bitten. "Consider yourself lucky. If I didn't have a better use for you, I would have drained you dry."

I sealed my eyes, not wanting to look at his face. I despised him. He was wrong. His scent, his feel, everything about him. He was vicious and vile, the cause of my mother's murder, and it was simply a matter of time before my father and I were next.

Being in his presence caused me to wonder if Nicolae was really to blame. If Roehl's brother was anything like him, I was glad he had performed a service and rid Talbrinth of him.

I was helpless, tethered to a rock wall, in a dingy, cold cell somewhere in the bowels of Morbeth's dungeon. My chest ached, knowing all hope of sealing the bond with Trystan was gone. I couldn't turn back time. All I could do was figure a means to survive the future and whatever horrors lay ahead.

CHAPTER ELEVEN

With my blood still wet on his lips, Prince Roehl unsheathed a dagger from his side, then slit his left wrist, holding it inches from my face. Bright red blood spilled from the wound, down his forearm and dripped off his elbow onto the ground. The coppery scent, the color, and the fact it was offered to me freely, virtually drove me to the edge of insanity.

Gods, it'd been days since I'd fed, and every cell inside my body urged me to drink. But I knew the consequences of drinking Roehl's blood, and there was no way in hell I'd be bound to that monster for the rest of my immortal life.

"It's simple," he said coolly, his obsidian eyes narrowing on me. "Drink, and all your pain and suffering will cease. Drink, and your father will survive. Drink . . . and you will become a queen."

As his blood spilled, my mind reflected to the site of my mother and the blood pooled around her head. Her lifeless body slaughtered on the deck of their merchant ship, along with Brynna's parents and the rest of the crew. All dead . . . because of this monster.

"Never!" I wailed.

The look in his black, vicious eyes was terrifying, causing my insides to shudder. The crimson rim around his irises were pronounced. A wild look emblazoned within them.

I barely saw him move, but felt a blast to my side, followed by a snap. Crippling pain exploded through my rib cage, doubling me over. He moved again, kicking my legs out from under me. I hit the ground, the back of my head slamming into the solid floor.

Roehl kneeled at my side. His long fingers clasped tightly around my neck, cutting off my air. "Ignorant fool. You've been living as a mortal, under a veil of darkness all your life. You know nothing of our world, or the powers immortals possess." His face appeared within an inch of mine, his breath brushing against my face. "I advise you tread lightly. You will learn who is master in my kingdom. Resist, and you will perish. Submit to my authority," his expression somewhat relaxed, "and you will discover how reasonable I can be."

He then had the audacity to sweep a stray hair from my cheek before rising, gesturing to a figure outside of the cell to enter. "Clean up the mess," he ordered. "Talk some sense into her. Tell her how generous I can be when one surrenders."

Bastard! My body screamed out in agony and fury as he left. I could barely breathe. The pain was agonizing.

A young woman stepped in, bowing her head as he left, then quickly shuffled over to me. She was young and beautiful, around my age, with flawless chocolate skin. Her eyes were almond-brown, bordered within the longest lashes I'd ever seen. But it was the worry etched in her eyes and crumpled on her brow that made me wonder what I truly looked like.

In one hand, she carried a small pail and in the other a rag, like they'd already planned for something like this to happen. She pulled a pouch dangling from her side. Kneeling next to me, she picked up the rag and soaked it into the pail of water, then wrung it out and lightly wiped my forehead.

I couldn't take a full breath, or even half a breath, without shooting pain. I was nauseous, my head throbbing and my eyes a bit blurred. I wondered if the fall caused a fracture to my skull.

"I'm sorry," the girl whispered so softly I could barely hear her.

I lolled my head to the side, which caused pain to shoot through my eyes. "You don't have to be sorry."

She cautiously raised her skirt and under it, belted to her thigh, was a small pocketknife. From her pack she plucked a miniature wooden bowl that fit in the palm of her hand. I watched, bewildered, as she tugged up her sleeve and created a narrow incision right below her bicep.

As her blood started to flow, she placed the dish under her elbow to catch it. When it was filled, she carefully set it down and immediately tied a bandage around the incision and tugged her sleeve down.

"You need to drink," she said quietly, scooting closer with the bowl cupped in her hands. "You're too weak and won't heal unless you do." She slipped her right arm under my head and gently raised it. I gasped as pain shot through my side. But she didn't pause. She set the bowl to my mouth. "Drink," she urged, and I obeyed.

Her blood was heavenly, as sweet as honey, and as soon as it hit my throat, I could already feel it working. By the time I emptied the bowl, I could breathe a little easier, the pain in my skull and chest had dulled. It wasn't gone, but it had become tolerable.

"What's your name?" I exhaled, laying my head back down on the hard floor.

"Sabine," she said, tucking her blade back under her skirt.

"Thank you, Sabine."

"You're brave," she said, plunging the rag back into the pail and wringing it out, continuing to wipe my face, neck, and arms. "If it were anyone else, we'd be dragging a corpse out from this cell. You're lucky."

"Lucky?" I laughed, then grimaced in pain. "Lucky to have been punched and kicked so hard my ribs are broken and I probably have a fractured skull?" My tone had a sting to it, but I was furious. That bastard didn't blink an eye before he struck me.

I'd heard about the cruelty of Morbeth but had now

witnessed it firsthand. There was a hatred for this man that had seeped deep into my core. I wanted him to die.

"I've seen him do much worse," she stated, glancing toward the door. She stood and walked over to it, peering through the few barred slats at the top. When satisfied, she returned to my side.

I groaned, trying to move, but a shooting pain in my side held me still. "I'm surprised he didn't force me to consume his blood."

"He can't force you," Sabine replied, wringing out her rag.

"Why not?"

"Because it wouldn't work. A blood bond must be reciprocal. Each person must agree wholeheartedly for it to be sealed." Her brow crumpled, and that look of worry was back. "If you stop resisting, even if you don't consume his blood, you might be able to get out of this cell."

Looking into her eyes, I saw something . . . maybe pity. But I didn't need anyone's pity. "Why do you care?"

"Because you are the first person who has stood up to the prince and lived." She placed her warm hand over mine. "I respect you for that. But I wouldn't press him. His limits are exceptionally low. But realize this, he does favor those who submit."

Power-hungry, evil prick.

I tried to sit up, but the shooting pain knocked me back down, making me gasp for air.

"I'd rather wither away in this cell than give that bastard my submission."

"You don't have to surrender," she whispered. "Just pretend." She shrugged and didn't say more. I knew what she was trying to say. And maybe what she was saying wasn't so bad. To play the submissive captive until I could find a way out of here, and ultimately . . . out of Morbeth.

Her almond-brown eyes swirled with worry. She stood and untied her smock, then rolled it up and tucked it under my head. "Rest. It might take a few days before you feel better because you're malnourished." She settled her hand on my shoulder and leaned down so her mouth was close to my ear. "Don't tell anybody about the blood I gave you," she whispered. "He'll kill me if he ever found out."

"Why?"

She glanced back toward the exit. "Because I am meddling in his affairs. And all who interfere with the prince end up dead."

"But he ordered you to tend to me."

"Yes," she murmured. "Tend, but not heal. That's why I provided you just enough blood for the healing to be slow, so he won't notice something is amiss."

"Don't worry," I breathed. I could play the injured victim. "Your secret is safe with me."

"Thank you." She bowed her head, then carried the empty bowl to the drain in the floor and poured water inside to rinse it clean. Grabbing a water bucket, she splashed it over

Roehl's blood, and scrubbed it as best she could, pushing the bloody water down the drain. When the floor was as clean as it could be, she reached back into her satchel and drew out a small vial filled with clear liquid and placed it in my hand. "This will help ease the pain. If it becomes intolerable, drink it, and you will fall asleep."

I didn't notice it before, possibly because of the severe pain wracking my body, but I could hear a heartbeat . . . loud and strong.

"You're mortal," I said.

"Yes," she grinned. "All servants in the kingdom are. The prince likes it that way, to be surrounded by the weaker species. If anyone steps out of line, they are punished, and used as an example to keep everyone else in order."

"Sadistic prick," I exhaled, and she nodded in agreement. "Is the king as evil as his son?"

"No. The king reigns with a steady hand, but he is also just. He's never killed without cause, and his people truly respect him. But the king has become ill, and after his brother's death, Prince Roehl has done nothing but instill fear and terror throughout the kingdom. He thinks his people react better to fear than reverence. In that regard, he is not like his father."

"Which makes him more of an ass than I expected." I moaned as sharp pains continued to wrack my insides.

"I heard your friend was brought here too," she whispered, and I gave a slight nod. "Just be prepared. Roehl will use her to try to break you."

I sighed, knowing the one thing that would break me would be the safety of Brynna and my father.

"Sabine," I murmured. "Earlier, Roehl spoke a word and I couldn't move."

She let out a lengthy exhale. "All pureblood vampires are born with a unique ability. Prince Roehl's is magic. When he was mature enough, his father brought in high witches from across Talbrinth to teach him. Although Roehl was powerful, he coveted more, pleading with his father to let him practice dark magic.

"His father forbade the practice of dark magic in the kingdom, but once he became ill, Roehl sought out the dark mages and brought them in. Now, he's even more powerful than before, and I'm not sure there is anyone who can stop him."

"There has to be someone."

"There might be," she muttered. "A few months ago, a Seer on the outskirts of town had a vision. She saw a girl. A young woman with great power who would rise up and defy Morbeth and eventually claim the throne."

I laughed, then groaned in pain as Sabine looked at me with a hopeful expression.

"Wait. If you assume that girl is me, you're dead wrong. First, I am not a noble. Second, I want to get my ass out of Morbeth and stay the hell out. And third, I've been a vampire for less than a week, thanks to Trystan."

"Trystan?" Her eyes expanded. "Do you mean Prince

Trystan Vladu?"

"Yes."

She sighed, her hand settling over her heart. "The Prince of Carpathia was the one who bit you?" I could see it in her eyes. She was smitten by him too.

"Yes." I didn't see why this mattered. "Do you know him?"

"No, but he came to Morbeth once with this father, to speak with the King. I was there. He is—" she batted her lashes.

"Believe me. I know," I sighed.

"But think about it. Why would the Prince of Carpathia bite you? There must be a reason."

"It's not what you think," I sighed. "He was just trying to save me." But as the words escaped my mouth, the truth remained . . . he traveled a considerable distance to claim me, a mortal girl. Then sent his personal cadre to watch over me. Even Kylan said the cadre didn't understand his motives.

What were the real reasons behind his decisions, besides a feeling or connection? Would any normal person risk their life to save someone because they felt a connection?

Roehl must have considered that too, wondering why Trystan claimed me so abruptly. "Does Roehl know about the Seer's vision?"

"I'm sure he does." Sabine gathered her things. "Seers are required to share every vision with Roehl. The last one who failed to share a vision was beheaded in the courtyard."

Good gods. "Do you think he believes I'm that girl?"

"I don't know." Her head angled toward the door. "I've said too much. I should go."

I snatched her hand. "Thank you."

She gave me a smile before she left without turning back.

It was days before the cell door groaned open. I was terribly weak and could barely move my head to see who was entering. With much effort, I managed to peel open one eye. It was one of the guards.

"The prince wanted me to make sure you were still alive," he replied smugly. When I didn't respond, he strode over and booted me in the side. I wailed in agony, folding into myself. He shifted toward the exit and yelled, "She's still alive!" Then he walked out and sealed the door.

Piercing pain radiated through my entire frame. I could hear him and another guard laughing as they made their way down the hallway. When it was silent, I decided to sit up, but couldn't.

My wounds weren't healing, and I was starving. I tried to eat the stale bread, but after ingesting it, I vomited it up minutes later.

I was sure this was hell, and there was no escaping it.

I'd lost count of the days. My wrists were still cuffed, the skin raw and infected beneath them. With each passing day, I became weaker and weaker. Everything, inside and out, throbbed. It was an utterly cruel punishment, and the only thing getting me through was my hatred for the man who put me here.

As minutes bled into hours, the hatred increased.

The moments I slept were dark and just as lonely as my waking hours. The cell was deafeningly quiet, and the seclusion slowly nibbled away at my sanity. The longer I lingered in this hell, the more I could feel the depression and desolation and fear of death from all the past prisoners who stayed here. Maybe I was delusional, but I could nearly hear the stifled sobs and whispered prayers . . . pleading for someone, anyone, to save them. So much pain. So much suffering. So much death.

Rats scattered in and out of my cell, squeezing through small fractures in the walls, stealing the uneaten bread and crumbs from my tray. I normally hated the rodents and would've screamed in horror to have seen one, but here, I accepted them. Hearing them scamper about made me feel not so alone.

I needed to talk to Trystan and let him know where I was. To thank him for attempting to save me and not to blame his cadre for my capture. But every night, those silent prayers went unanswered. Every night, the same darkness and silence gobbled me up.

Why did it suddenly stop? Why couldn't I see Trystan anymore? Was it this place? Or had Roehl's bite erased the blood bond we had?

But as time bled into itself, now and then, I would recall the pictures in Melaina's bowl of water. Of Nicolae, and how, with a flip of his hand, made his entire camp disappear. He had magic. Powerful magic, Melaina had said. I recalled the Wanderer's words to me. *There is magic in you. Dormant and suppressed by even greater magic. Find a way to release it.*

Was there magic inside of me? And was there anyone in this castle who could tell me how to release it? Anyone besides Roehl?

In the following days, I attempted, in every way imaginable, to free my magic. I tried willing it to life, to break free from whatever spell had bound it. But there was nothing, nary a spark nor a glimmer. And the more I tried, the weaker I became.

Maybe they were wrong. Maybe I didn't have magic. Perhaps the magic had disappeared, just like my hope was gradually fading, day by day.

I awoke countless times from pain and hunger. I was freezing yet covered in sweat. My skin beneath the metal cuffs was raw and burned like fire. I knew the infection was getting worse and there was nothing I could do. I was dying, and at times, prayed for death, but my new immortal body wouldn't grant that small wish.

I could scarcely move without suffering. My mouth was parched, my lips dry and cracked, my eyes swollen. I hadn't eaten anything in what seemed like ages. The Prince of Morbeth was forcing me to suffer and feel everything.

CHAPTER TWELVE

"Get up!" A kick against my boot sent a jolt of pain through my body, waking me.

It took every effort to open my swollen eyes, but when I did, *he* was standing above me.

"Hello, pet," Roehl crooned.

I wished I had enough energy to punch him in his smug face, but even at my strongest, it probably wouldn't do a thing except piss him off.

He kneeled at my side, sweeping his icy fingers across my face. I was so weak I couldn't even flinch away. The only thing I could do, with the strength I had left, was close my eyes.

"Look at you, shriveling away into nothing. If you surrender to me, I will take care of you. If you surrender to me, I will keep you, your father, and your lovely friend Brynna, alive."

Bastard.

He picked off a few pieces of hair glued to my face from either perspiration or vomit. "This can all go away if you answer the one question." He lay his palm on my arm, his eyes narrowed. "Will you surrender to me?"

I had nothing left. If I remained here any longer, I'd turn into a living corpse. There was no alternative, other than to continue being starved and abused.

A tear trickled down my cheek as I gave him my answer—a single nod.

With a snap of his fingers, the cuffs around my wrists fell away and I was lifted into his arms. My limbs were limp, my head lolled sideways, resting against his large, sturdy shoulder.

Roehl carried me out of the cell, down a series of torch lit corridors and up a long staircase. The stone walls were dank, and the air smelled musty.

When we arrived at the top, he opened the door and we stepped out into a wide hallway. Curtains blocked the sunlight, but my eyes throbbed, even in the dimmed light. I inhaled the clean, cool air that carried a wonderful floral scent mixed with lavender and vanilla—my mother's favorite smells.

All around us were large flower arrangements and potted trees with beautiful blooms in vibrant hues.

These pieces of beauty were nothing I would relate with Roehl or Morbeth.

I drew in another deep breath, savoring the rich floral essences.

"My mother," Roehl murmured. I didn't want to hear his voice, which was causing my head to pulse, but I was too weak to move, and my tongue too swollen to speak. "My mother loved flowers. If she were still alive, this entire castle would be laden with them. She would set them in places around the castle she related with misery and death. Like right here, outside the dungeon, to conceal the stench. My father's wedding gift to her was a garden. She claimed it was the only gift that truly made her happy."

Why was he telling me this? Did he think I cared, or that it would make this place a bit more tolerable? His mother sounded like a decent woman, and by the tone of his voice, it sounded like he genuinely loved her. So, what happened to him? What made him become a monster?

We finally halted, and I opened both eyes to find us standing in front of a door. A guard opened it with a key—an outside lock—and shoved the door open.

The draperies in the room were drawn, but there were candles everywhere, and a fire crackling in the fireplace.

"This is your new room," Roehl spoke.

New cell.

He carried me through another doorway and inside were three women; one of whom I recognized but didn't acknowledge.

Sabine. Her eyes met mine but displayed no emotion.

Between them was a wide tub filled with water. "Bathe her, feed her, and put her to bed," Roehl ordered.

"Yes, Prince," they answered, bowing in unison. Sabine and another blonde girl received me from him and seated me on an armchair. It took every ounce of strength I had left to remain upright and not topple over.

Roehl gave a swift gesture to the older woman, who had white hair and a stern face, and she followed him outside.

I concentrated on their voices.

"Give her a minimal supply of blood. Not too much," Roehl's deep voice uttered.

"Yes, my prince," she responded.

After a few moments, the elder woman strode back into the washroom and they started undressing me. I would have been embarrassed but was too weak to care. As soon as my shirt came off, Sabine gasped at the bruises all over my body.

The skin around my wrists was gone, the exposed flesh was bright red and oozing yellow from the infection.

They carefully helped me into the tub, and as I slipped under the water it was like a hot blanket being wrapped around me. Sabine and the younger girl carefully washed my hair and body. The soaps, in several floral essences, smelled like heaven. So much better than vomit and excrement that had clung to me for too long.

After I was washed, they applied medicine to my wrists and carefully bandaged them. It stung like hell, but I didn't make a sound. I knew once I had some blood, it would heal me. But Roehl ordered the woman to keep it minimal, which meant he wanted to keep me in a fragile state. Then the blonde girl excused herself and withdrew from the room.

Once I was dried off, they dressed me in a comfortable, white, cotton bedgown and laid me on a bed fit for a queen. The sheets and bedspread were luxurious, feeling like silk against my delicate skin. I sunk into the mattress and let it mold to my frame. After sleeping on a rock floor for so long, this mattress felt like I was floating on a cloud.

The older woman shuffled over to me with a golden goblet caressed in both of her hands. Tired green-gray eyes, obscured behind dark circles and wrinkles, tightened in on me. She looked as if she hadn't slept in days.

"Here," she said, sitting on a chair next to my bed. "Drink."

I hesitated and shook my head when a warm hand clutched mine.

"Don't worry, Calla. It's not the prince's blood," Sabine whispered. Her brown eyes were soft, caring. Raven hair tumbled down her shoulders in perfect curls. "It's from a contributor—a young woman."

The older woman huffed at her, but Sabine extended her hand and the woman reluctantly handed her the goblet. Sabine stood by my side, slipping her other arm under my head to raise me up.

As soon as she brought the goblet close, I could smell the blood. Every cell inside my body went mad. I closed my eyes, my incisors lengthening, and as soon as Sabine pressed the cool rim to my lips, I lost control.

I was starving. The thirst grasped and kept me in its clutches. I snatched it from her and poured it down my throat. But it wasn't enough. I needed more. My body demanded more.

My eyes opened. The room and everything in it had turned a deep shade of crimson. The woman gasped, reaching for the goblet. I seized her arm and yanked it to my mouth. My teeth sunk deep into her flesh.

Her warm blood gushed down my throat, giving me a different kind of high. A high that took over my mind. A high I never wanted to come down from.

I could feel the intensity of her fresh blood coursing through my body, restoring me from the inside out.

"Stop!" I could barely hear Sabine's muffled cries. "Stop, Calla! You're killing her!"

I was killing her.

The words struck me like a hammer. I fought the thirst, fought my carnal urges to feed until this woman was drained and dead. But they were so powerful.

No!

I didn't want to be a monster. I refused to become one.

Pulling on every ounce of strength and sanity I had left, I shoved the woman's arm from my mouth and screamed. She collapsed to the floor, her body limp. I sat, panting, the blood still coursing through my veins. I closed my eyes and focused, hearing Sabine calling to the older woman.

"Ms. Alcott," she cried.

After the high settled, I opened my eyes to see Sabine's body folded over the woman, shaking her, trying to wake her.

"Sabine," I said softly, the world fading back to neutral colors.

"What have you done?" she wailed, her brow furrowed, her eyes brimmed with tears. "You almost killed her!"

The expression on her face was one that would permanently be fixed into my memory. A look I would never forget. A mix of fear and disgust.

I peered down at my white bedgown, and the entire front was stained red. My hands, my legs, the bedding were all sodden with blood.

How could I allow such a thing to happen? I vowed to resist the urge to feed off a mortal being. But I failed. I was too weak to resist the thirst and allowed myself to become the thing I detested most.

Ms. Alcott moaned, but her eyes remained closed. She was alive. *Thank the gods.*

"I'm sorry," I bawled. "I'm so sorry." I was overcome with remorse and sadness. My chest heaved as I launched off the bed and ran into the washroom, slamming the door shut behind me. I pushed my back against the door, slid to the floor, and wept until there were no tears left. Until everyone had gone.

When I had nothing left inside, I picked myself up and moved to the washbasin. Mounted on the wall was a mirror. I stepped back, gazing at the grizzly sight. I didn't recognize the person staring back at me.

The young woman was emaciated and sickly pale, her eyes dimmed and sunken in. Her mouth was glazed in crimson and drips of it trickled down her chin and neck, staining the garment at her front. This wasn't the same girl I'd known all along. No, it wasn't me in the mirror's reflection. It was a monster. A dreadful, vile beast . . . no better than the Prince of Morbeth.

Maybe I did belong with him. Maybe we deserved each other.

I yanked the bloodstained gown off, then went to the tub and turned on the hot water. Once full, I submerged myself and scoured my face, neck, and chest so hard it was practically raw. Until all traces of blood were gone.

I was bare and didn't want to see or deal with anyone. My mind couldn't erase the look on Sabine's face. A look which spoke a thousand words.

Would she ever forgive me? I wasn't sure if I could forgive myself.

When I finally exited the tub, I listened for movement outside, but the place was silent.

Cracking the door open, I peeked outside. The area was empty, so I wrapped a towel around my body and stepped out.

The fire still crackled in the fireplace, and everything had been cleaned. On top of the new bedsheets was a clean bedgown which I'd slid on before I tumbled into bed, dragging the blankets over me.

The blood, even though I had fed a while ago, was still working. I could feel it tingling through my limbs. The aches had subsided, and I was feeling strong. But for what? This lovely room was still a cell, and I wasn't going anywhere.

I wanted to sleep and forget what happened. Maybe it was all a dream. Perhaps I'd wake up in my cozy cottage in Sartha and chalk this up to a terrible nightmare. But reality slapped me in the head.

The buzz was wearing off, and as I stared into the fireplace, watching the flames dance and whirl, my eyes became heavy. I let sleep wrap its arms around me in a strong embrace.

CHAPTER THIRTEEN

I awoke to voices outside my door; whispers that sounded like they were right next to me.

"Please don't make me go in," a sweet female voice pleaded. "She almost killed Ms. Alcott. What if she kills me?"

"Listen, it was a mistake, and I'm positive she's terribly sorry for what happened." The response came from Sabine.

As the doorknob twisted, I shut my eyes, hoping they'd assume I was asleep.

The door opened and shut. Then there was a shuffle of feet against the floor.

"Calla," Sabine whispered, lightly tapping my shoulder. "Calla, it's time to wake up."

I gradually opened my eyes to see Sabine standing next to me with her long, wavy hair and dark-almond eyes. "Why?" I moaned. "It's not like I'm going anywhere."

She chuckled quietly. "You've slept the entire day away.

Come on. We've come to get you up and ready for the Shadow Festival."

"What?" I whined. "What's a Shadow Festival?"

Sabine turned back to me with a glint in her eyes. "It's a great celebration held across Morbeth, marking the end of the harvest season and the beginning of winter. The witches celebrate this day as their new year and hold their own private festivities. Tonight, the veil between the living and the dead is removed, and we can connect with those who've crossed over into the next realm."

"You're kidding, right?" I yawned and stretched my arms into the air.

She stopped what she was doing and shifted to me with a crumpled brow. "Why would I be kidding?"

I shrugged as Sabine nodded to the girl who looked no older than thirteen. She had brilliant green eyes and long blonde hair that was drawn back into a single braid. Her hands twisted around themselves like she was nervous. She had cause to be, and the thought made my chest ache.

The girl nodded back at Sabine and proceeded into the washroom to fill the tub.

Sabine moved toward the changing room and raised an exquisite silk gown, hanging it on a hook. The garment looked like it was created for a princess. Silvery gems sparkled over the bodice, while flowy silver fabric cascaded to the floor. It was the first gown I'd seen in this hue of silver before and knew Brynna would die if she saw it.

"Have you overheard anything about my friend or my father?" I inquired.

Sabine shook her head. "Nothing about your father, but your friend is in another suite in the east wing . . . much like this one. She's well taken care of. At least until . . ." She hesitated, and my chest compressed.

"Until what?"

Her tone softened. "Until you make your decision."

Despite the decision, relief washed over me knowing Brynna was safe and being taken care of. I groaned. "I don't want to attend this stupid festival. Besides, what is Roehl going to do? Lead me around on a leash all night?" I wouldn't put it past him. He referred to me as his "pet" after all.

"I'm sorry, Calla. We're merely following orders." A grin lurked on her lips. "And on a relatively brighter side, with Roehl's capabilities, you won't need a leash."

"Hey, who's side are you on?" I grumbled.

She thumbed toward the door. We all knew the guards—vampires with acute hearing—were probably listening. "I'm a fence-sitter."

"What's that?"

"Someone who remains indifferent." She winked at me, then went about her duties.

"I'm so *sick* of Roehl." I flipped over and yanked the blanket over my head. "Tell him he battered me too severely and it hurts to walk."

Sabine sighed. "He won't believe you and will show up

himself to make sure." I felt the side of my bed sink down. "If you gain his confidence, life here can be better for you."

"He has ulterior motives," I replied under the blanket. "He marked me for a reason."

"With the prince, things are either black or white. He is swift at doling out rewards or punishments. He will offer a choice, and you either accept it or refuse. Once an individual has made their decision, there is no turning back. They remain with the aftereffects . . . good or bad. That's how Prince Roehl runs things here."

I groaned, shoving the blanket off and flipping to look at her. "How is Ms. Alcott?"

Her chest expanded and fell. "She's seen better days, but she'll recover. If you had stayed latched for any longer, she would have died."

I resisted the tears threatening to occupy my eyes. My chest throbbed as I reflected to that dreadful moment when I lost control. "Please tell her I'm sorry. I couldn't help myself. The thirst . . . it was too powerful, and—"

"I know," she said. "We all know the prince is to blame. He left you down in that cell and starved you, trying to crack your will. On top of that, you're a newborn." Her warm, calloused hand covered mine. "But you did fight the thirst, and you won. You broke free. And because of it, Ms. Alcott is alive."

I swallowed hard, fighting the increasing ache inside. "That still doesn't make me feel any better."

"If it's of any comfort, I've never experienced a newborn control their thirst like you did. I know it takes control over everything. Newborns lose themselves and all sensibility until—" A tear crept down her cheek. "It's how my sister died. A newborn latched onto her and drained her to death."

I could feel her despair. "Sabine." I couldn't find the right words to comfort her because there were none. "You must despise us."

Her russet eyes met mine. "No," she exhaled, wiping a tear trailing down her cheek. "Not all vampires are evil. There are those who are good, surviving without torture and bloodshed." She peered deep into my eyes. "Those like Trystan, the Prince of Carpathia."

My heart constricted at the utterance of his name.

She halted, dragging my sheets all the way off. "I overheard some of the guards talking before I arrived." She leaned in closer, her lips a breath from my ear. "They were saying Prince Trystan will be attending the festival tonight."

"What?" I shot up so quick I was dizzy. "Are you positive?"

When she nodded, I found it difficult to breathe, and even harder to think straight. *Could it be?* Could Trystan really be coming?

Sabine pressed her finger to her lips. "Word is, he's sought counsel with Prince Roehl to barter for your freedom."

A surge of adrenaline shot through me, kindling hope deep inside. He was coming for me. Trystan was coming into

Morbeth . . . for me!

If I had to play by Roehl's rules and put on a show for a while longer, I would do it. I just had to make sure Brynna was safe and prayed to the gods that my father was tricky enough to stay hidden and not get caught. He had friends and contacts throughout Sartha, and even in Aquaris, that could help him stay hidden. Hopefully, he could use those connections.

After my bath, while wrapped in a towel, I sat on a chair in front of a desk laden with brushes, pins, and a number of colorful powdery things. Sabine stood behind me, and the green-eyed girl took a seat next to me. Her eyes were large, and I could hear her accelerated heartbeat.

"What kinds of things go on at this festival?" I asked in my most non-scary voice, hoping to ease her fear.

She gulped hard. "You will be in the grand ballroom, dining and dancing with the most affluent and powerful in Morbeth's kingdom. Everyone will be dressed in elegant gowns and fancy suits and they are required to wear a mask," the girl explained, without making eye contact.

"What's your name?" I asked.

"Spring." Her eyes moved to mine, then quickly looked elsewhere.

"It's nice to meet you, Spring." I held out my hand to her. "I'm Calla, and you don't have to be afraid of me."

She hesitated, her eyes flashing to Sabine, who gave her an acknowledging nod. She slowly stretched her hand and shook mine. It was so warm, but she was trembling.

"There, see? We're friends now. And I don't hurt my friends," I said tenderly. "What happened to Ms. Alcott was a mistake. One I will never make again."

She nodded, but her eyes still carried a hint of fear. I hated that. Hated I was the cause of it.

"Are you in charge of doing my hair for the festival, Spring?"

She shook her head. "Sabine will be doing your hair. I will be making up your face."

"Hmm. So, I suppose I need to pucker my lips like this?" I sucked in my cheeks and crossed my eyes.

Spring laughed, covering her mouth. "No. Not yet."

"My best friend, Brynna, made me up a few times, so I know how this works," I closed my eyes and relaxed. "I'll sit here patiently and let you both work your magic."

Spring giggled and when I opened an eye, I noticed some of her fear melt away.

Sabine took a brush to my wild and tangled mane. "Alright, Spring. Let's make Calla look like a princess."

The two of them worked while I sat, eyes closed, recalling the night of my eighteenth birthday celebration. The night Brynna did my makeup, and the night I met Trystan.

I wondered what would have happened if he hadn't come. I would have gone back to my cabin, and the enemy would have captured me. I would probably be dead or sealed up in the cell and left to die as a mortal. But because of Trystan's involvement—his attempt to claim me—it was somehow enough for Roehl to take notice and keep me alive. For now.

I finally understood how much Trystan was risking. Not only his life, but his family and his kingdom as well.

From the start, he never forced me. Everything that transpired that night was because I allowed it . . . except for the bite. But now I realized why he did it. To spare me and my family. But because of Roehl, my mother was dead, and my father was still running somewhere in the Whisper Woods.

"You're done," Spring's gentle voice chimed.

When I opened my eyes, they were both beaming at me with expressions of admiration. Sabine's hands were clasped over her heart, and Spring wore a smile as radiant as the sun.

"Can I see?" I attempted to stand with the towel still wrapped around me.

"Not yet." Sabine held my shoulders in place.

Spring took the silver gown from the hook and brought it over to me. Then, as a team, they proceeded to clothe me. First, they set a corset around my midsection and cinched it so tight I could barely breathe.

The gown was a perfect fit, making my cleavage look halfway decent. The jeweled waist hugged me tightly before the silvery silk fabric cascaded like a waterfall down to the floor. I slid my feet into a pair of sparkling silver heels to finish the look.

"You look like a princess." The fear in Spring's eyes had been replaced with a look of awe.

"Go ahead," Sabine said smoothly, reaching for my hand

and leading me over to the mirror.

I gasped, taken aback by the girl in the mirror. She looked like royalty. Not the same gaunt and pale girl, stained in blood, I saw in the washroom mirror the night before. There was no trace of the monster that remained under my skin. Right now, I was beautiful.

My auburn hair was curled and pinned up with glittery jewels—a few strands were curled and left down to frame each side of my face. The arrangement of the gems somehow made it look as if I were wearing a silver diadem.

The makeup made my face look flawless, not like the corpse girl I looked like before. My lashes appeared twice as long, curled upward, making my golden eyes stand out. My eyelids were dusted with silver that shimmered like the gems on my bodice, and my lips looked full, stained a rich red. Even though I'd lost a significant amount of weight, I couldn't tell. They worked some magic.

Spring picked up a vial of pink liquid. "May I?" she asked, aiming the bottle at my collar.

"What is it?"

"Perfume. It smells like flowers. I like it." The beam on her face caused me to smile.

"Spray away," I said, closing my eyes.

Spring sprayed me all over. "Done," she said while setting the bottle back on the desk. The scent was wonderful. A variety of floral bouquets, delicate and sweet.

"What do you think?" Sabine asked, stepping behind me.

"I—I love it all." I was on the verge of tears, not knowing why I felt so emotional. "I don't even recognize myself."

"That's the whole point of the festival," Spring admitted cheerfully.

In her right hand was a fancy silver mask with black satin ties affixed to it. She passed the mask to Sabine, who carefully put it on my face, then tied it to the back of my head, pinning the ties to my hair to remain in place.

It was a delicate filigree, molded perfectly around my nose and eyes, emphasizing the golden hue in them even further. The bottom half of my face was left untouched.

I looked in the mirror at Sabine. "Aren't you two going to dress up?"

"Yes, but we won't be attending the festivities in the castle."

"What? Why?" I felt my stress level rise. "Where will you be?"

"Mortals within the kingdom are not invited. They, along with citizens outside the kingdom, hold festivities elsewhere, beyond the castle boundaries. The witches have their own private rituals, so we'll attend the mortal festivals first. Bonfires, dancing, food, wine, and maybe a cute boy or two." Sabine accentuated *wine* and *boy* with a widened smile.

"Is there a boy in your life?" I questioned.

She winked. "That, Calla, is a secret."

She grabbed my hand and twirled me around in front of the mirror. The bottom of the dress flared out, and when I stopped, it curled around my ankles. She beamed and bowed at the waist. "You look radiant, Princess Calla."

I groaned. "I'm not a princess."

"Tonight, you definitely look the part," Spring said, peeking over my shoulder.

"Thanks to both of you." I gave each of them a hug. Spring was tense at first, but she loosened up and hugged me back. "I'd much rather be with you two, then with the rigid prudes and pricks I know will be at the festival."

Sabine sighed. "Yeah, we do have a lot more fun. The people are more relaxed outside of the castle. No stuffy attitudes or formal attire."

"The witch celebrations are my favorite," Spring said.

I turned to her. "I thought the witch celebrations were private?"

"They are," Sabine replied, fluffing the bottom of my gown. "Spring's grandmother is the leader of one of the covens, so we don't need an invitation."

Her words bubbled inside my head. Maybe, just maybe, they could find someone who could help me.

I waved them both into the washroom and sealed the door.

"Can I ask you a question?" I whispered.

They both nodded.

"The Wanderer who brought me here said I have magic that is being suppressed by an even stronger magic. That means someone put a spell on me, right?"

Sabine's eyes widened. "A Wanderer? You spoke to a Wanderer?"

I nodded.

"Heavens above. I didn't even think they existed." She shook her head in wonderment. "What was he like?"

"He looked like any other man, except he had white eyes, was magical, and traveled through the wind."

They turned to each other. "Calla," Sabine stepped toward me. "If you have magic, maybe you *are* the girl the Seer saw."

Spring nodded in agreement.

"Absolutely not," I countered. "I told you, I'm not royalty."

Sabine sighed. "If you have magic, it's likely someone in your bloodline is a witch."

"Do you think one of the witches would help release the bind put on my magic? I'm not sure if I really do have magic, but I doubt the Wanderer and a witch would lie to me. They sensed something."

She seized my hand. "Few witches can be trusted here in Morbeth. Many have allegiances to the prince and are unwilling to hold things from him. But we know a few we can depend on."

Spring leaned in close. "I'll ask my mother. She has no ties to the prince. Her magic is pure. Not dark."

A rap on the door had them both moving out of the washroom. Spring made her way to the door and cracked it open. After a brief conversation with the guard, she opened it all the way and made her way over to me.

"Princess Calla, your escorts await," she said with a low curtsey.

"Please don't," I sighed, taking her arm and pulling her back up. "I'm *not* a princess."

"Tonight, you are," Sabine said, tugging the back of my gown. "You look like a princess, so you might as well act like one."

"I wish you were coming with me." I hugged her one last time.

She hugged me back and whispered, "If you run into the handsome Carpathian prince, please extend my best wishes." She winked. "And if there are any steamy details, I demand them *all* the next time I see you . . . unless he slips you away."

"Don't expect any steamy details with Roehl around," I murmured.

"Any detail will do. Good luck." She took my hand and escorted me to the door.

Two guards entered and stood on either side of me. They were young, their hair and features black and menacing, just like their leader.

The thought of Trystan in Morbeth made my entire body tingle with excitement. He was the sole reason I wanted to attend this stupid Shadow Fest. I doubted Prince Roehl would allow him anywhere near me. But even a glimpse from afar would do wonders for my spirit.

I was escorted to the end of the hall where we met a much larger guard. He was dark-skinned, tall, and muscular. He looked like he could have been related to Brone. They were both around the same height and build, with a rugged handsomeness.

The guards escorting me stepped to the side as the larger one stepped forward.

"My name is Markus," he said, his voice sharp and frightening. "I am head of the King's guard. Step out of line, and you will be escorted back to your room. Leave the castle, and you will be sent back to the cell that received you when you first arrived. Do I make myself clear?"

There were a thousand curses I wanted to throw at him, but I bit my tongue, painted on a smile, and responded, "Crystal."

I couldn't believe they had the King's head guard babysitting me tonight. Or maybe I could. But I had a feeling they chose him because Trystan *was* coming. For all I knew, Roehl's entire army could have been dispersed throughout the festival tonight. But I didn't want the night to start off with the head guard mad at me.

Tonight, I would play a different role. Tonight, I would be humble and on my best behavior with the guards, to establish I wasn't a threat. If I could bend them toward my side, even in the slightest bit, I might have an advantage. It was better than no advantage at all, and I needed to break down as many walls as I could.

After strolling down a few hallways and descending some stairs, we took a few more turns before we came to a wide platform made of black marble. Connected to it was a black-and-white marble staircase leading down to a huge ballroom floor. On one side of the dance floor, a few tables were overflowing with every kind of food imaginable. Smells of spices and meats, commingling with freshly baked breads and pastries made my mouth water. There must have been affluent mortals attending this festival with such a spread.

Musicians stood on a stage, elaborately decorated to look like a moonlit night. Violas, flutes, drums, citterns, and lutes played the most wonderful music. The melody, smooth and pleasant, was a complete contradiction of Morbeth. This was the kind of music that made you joyful. Made you want to be whisked out on the dance floor, to be twirled and dipped and then spun again. And perhaps to end in a kiss.

A few hundred guests had already assembled, masked, and clad in their finery. There was no way to tell who-was-who. The masks were so diverse, some monstrous and grim, though others stunningly beautiful.

"Go," was Markus's only word to me as we reached the top of the staircase.

"You're not going to escort me down?" I gave my best pouty look.

His head jerked to me, eyes glaring as if I'd asked him to cut off his finger. "No."

My eyes saddened behind the mask. "I'm wearing

expensive heeled shoes," I said, raising the hem of my dress to show him. "If I slip and tumble down these stairs, it will cause a huge scene and attract unwanted attention."

A growl rumbled deep in his chest. "The railings are there to keep you from falling," he replied.

"Grasping the railing is embarrassing. It cries that I'm single. *Men* will notice and might come to talk to me or maybe even ask me to dance. Then I'll have to tell them I can't dance with them because I'm Roehl's prisoner. And that might lead to other conversations where the fact that their beloved prince senselessly murdered my mother might slip. On accident, of course. It's still a raw subject for me." I forced a smile, even though the bitterness and pain were building inside as I spoke. "However, if *you* escort me, they'll likely avoid me and all that nonsensical chatter."

One of the younger guards nudged him. "She's right. You should escort her down."

After a deep internal growl, Markus turned to me and extended his arm, which felt like a steel bar. This man had zero body fat, and there was no doubt he could do some damage in battle. I didn't mind having him around. He reminded me of Brone, who was even more intimidating on the outside and deadly in battle, but a big softy inside.

I wondered, countless times, if he and the others were okay. I had a feeling they would be. They were probably back in Carpathia right now, safe and sound.

As we slowly descended the fifty or so marbled stairs,

I held tight to Markus, glad I had his support so I wouldn't fall. Heels were not my thing. They were Brynna's. My chest ached, wondering if I would ever see my friend again.

Playing the part, I straightened my back and held my head high while the gown flowed gracefully behind me. Markus was tense and I wondered what he must have been thinking. From the intermittent growls, he wasn't too happy.

Above us, a great crystal chandelier hung, twinkling like thousands of diamonds. Eyes of male and female patrons shifted to us as we reached the bottom. I could feel the weight of their stares as Markus escorted me to the refreshment table. As soon as we arrived, he disconnected from me and took three steps backward.

I swiveled to look at him. "I take it I'm on my own for the remainder of the night?" He ignored me as I poured myself a cup of whatever red liquid was in the punch bowl. Drinks didn't seem to affect me. When I consumed the water in the cell, I'd kept it down. It was solid food that made me sick. "Suit yourself. I am a reasonable dancer."

Markus stayed silent and I knew it was because he was playing his role. *Head guard.*

Tonight, for whatever reason, Prince Roehl had set me free. Free in a sense that I could mingle with guests, and I was going to make the most of it. Tonight, I was an actress playing lead.

I was thankful for the mask. Thankful no one could see the true me behind it. A tortured girl, mourning the loss of her mother and worried sick about her father and best friend.

A throat cleared, and as I turned, a tall, muscular man attired in an all-black suit stood next to me. A black cape, lined in red velvet, was draped over his shoulders. He wore a menacing mask over his face . . . that of a demon. Large fangs painted in red extended over its lips, while red horns spiraled from the top, causing it to look even more frightening. But it was those eyes that gave him away. Those red-rimmed obsidian eyes.

"You look beautiful, Calla," he said gently, lifting his mask to sit atop his head. "I knew the gown would suit you."

Roehl was handsome, his features strong and sharp, his raven hair pulled back and fastened behind his collar. But what he'd done, what he represented, made him repulsive.

"Thanks," I said, taking a step away from him, while warning myself to keep playing the part.

"I'd like you to meet someone," he said, taking my hand and pulling me to his side. I didn't resist. Now wasn't the time to make a scene.

Behind him stood a heavy-set man, wearing a white mask which covered the right side of his face.

"Miss Caldwell," he said, with a deep bow.

I knew who this man was. Lord Mathias—the mortal ruler of Morbeth. He was taller than I expected, thick around the midriff and not muscular by any means. He had dark brown hair, which fell to his shoulders, and a matching full beard. His eyes were forest green, but they had a stern haughtiness to them.

He carried himself like he was untouchable, having Morbeth's vampire kingdom backing him. But I knew he was just a man, like any other, who happened to have pulled the lucky-vampire-card to rule.

I had no doubt that if he stepped out of line—like Markus had so eloquently warned me—things wouldn't end well for him either. He was a puppet, and I could already see how tightly his master's strings were attached.

The way Lord Mathias reverenced Roehl—like he was a god—made my stomach clench. He was undoubtedly playing a game of his own. A game of survival. A game, it seemed, we were all players in.

CHAPTER FOURTEEN

Roehl dismissed his guards and positioned himself at my side.

"Tonight, you will be on my arm and will do as I say to keep your friend from harm." He warned through gritted teeth.

His mask was still resting atop his head so I could see the seriousness on his stone face. Deviltry was his flaw, and his costume was a true representation of the demon that lay within.

"How do I know she's here or that she's safe?" I wanted to put further distance between us, but I stood my ground. "How do I know you haven't already killed her?" The thought caused my chest to press with pain.

He sneered before drawing his mask back over his face. Grabbing my arm, he tugged me past dozens of masked patrons, clear across the room.

In a narrow alcove, resting on a red velvet chair surrounded by four guards, was a young woman in an elegant blue gown wearing a black-feathered mask. Baby-blue eyes stood out underneath the stark black, while long golden hair spilled in curls around her shoulders.

"Brynna?" I swung free from Roehl's grip and rushed toward her. "Brynna," I breathed, falling on my knees in front of her. I immediately examined her exposed arms, but she looked unharmed.

Her eyes met mine, but as she blinked, there was no flicker of recognition.

"Brynna," I repeated, taking hold of her hands. "It's me, Calla."

"Calla?" She echoed my name like it was unfamiliar. "That's a nice name."

"Brynna. It's me. Your best friend." I slipped my mask up to rest on my forehead and took her hands in mine. Her head cocked to the side, giving me a contemplative look.

She didn't recognize me.

"This is a beautiful ball, isn't it, Calla?" she murmured.

She stood and grabbed the sides of her gown, then began swaying side to side to the music.

Standing to my feet, I grabbed her arms and pulled her to face me. "Brynna, what's wrong with you?" But her eyes remained distant. Hollow.

Rage burned inside as I marched over to Roehl. "What did you do to her?"

"She's unharmed. Just under a spell," he said, addressing her with a wave of his hand. "Do you think I'd let her recognize you? The two of you would likely cause a scene. Besides, look at her. She's enjoying herself."

"You bastard," I cursed through gritted teeth. "If you harm her—"

"What?" he said slowly, leaning in inches from my face. His incisors lengthened, the red around his eyes became more pronounced. "What will you do?"

I held my tongue, but my mind answered his question. *I will kill you.*

Another evil grin tugged on the edges of his mouth. "Before I make my speech, I'd like to offer you some helpful advice."

"Advice?" I scowled. "What advice would I take from you?"

"The kind that could save your life and the lives of those you love," he replied.

I glared at him, waiting.

"The Prince of Carpathia has come to offer a trade. You, for half of his kingdom's riches."

"What?" The word barely escaped my lips in a whisper. My world spun at his statement.

He laughed, shaking his head as if it were a joke. But I found myself holding my breath.

Why would Trystan offer so much for me? I wondered what his father had to say about it, or if he even realized he was here making such an unreasonable deal.

"Don't look so aroused by his generosity," he replied smugly. "Here is my advice to you. If for any reason you accept to leave with him, either now or in the future, your friend will be the first to die. I'll take some enjoyment from her first. But when she is dead, I assure you, I will locate your father and command his slow and excruciating execution, right before I proclaim war on Carpathia. I will crush their Kingdom and strip them down to nothing."

"Why? Because of Nicolae?"

"This is *all* because of Nicolae. I will take great delight in listening to him scream as I peel the skin from his flesh. It's the least he deserves for murdering my brother."

I knew I shouldn't press, but I needed answers. And here, in front of all his patrons, I felt a little safer.

"Why did he kill your brother? Why would he, after all these years, break out of hiding to come to Morbeth, slip past the impenetrable Red Wall, and murder someone who is highly guarded and trained?"

Roehl shrugged. "Why would I know his motives, except that he has a death wish? And he is lucky I am an expert at granting such wishes." He stepped closer to me. "Trust me, it will only be a matter of time."

There was something amiss with the murder of his brother. There had to be a motive behind it. And why was the Prince of Morbeth so keen to dole out death sentences to Nicolae and his entire bloodline? Because even now, that order was faltering. Why would he insist on hunting and killing me one moment and claim me the next? What the hell was his twisted plan?

I'd have to discover out the truth before he killed me.

His dark eyes pierced straight through me, causing the hair on my body to stand erect. "And one more piece of advice, Calla. If you mention to anyone that I have your friend captive, both of you will be severely punished."

Reaching out his hand to me, I refused to take it. Instead, I stepped to his side, twisting back to see Brynna twirling in circles to the music, her gown swirling around her. She had a smile on her face, but her blue eyes were still empty. At least, for now, she was content and free. And as much as it killed me, I silently swore I'd find a way to keep her safe.

To open the festival, Roehl gave a long-winded speech about how dominant and prosperous his kingdom was. He indirectly made sure the people were reminded of their places—that without him or his family, they would be nothing, possess little, and would have no protection.

I looked through the crowd and was astounded. His people were buying into his bullshit. How in the hell could they believe him? Because all I heard spouting from his traitorous lips were lies, lies, lies.

He continued, quickly reviewing his father's declining health, which led to another speech on how honored he would be to one day acquire the position of King of Morbeth, taking on the obligation of the crown.

The masked crowd cheered and applauded their prince, and it made me wonder what kind of people they were. Were they genuinely thankful for what the Kingdom of Morbeth had provided them, or were they frightened of the repercussions they would suffer for not showing their thankfulness? Maybe this way of life was all they knew. To be pawns in Roehl's twisted game. Puppets, moving and acting, presuming they were independent while Roehl's hand was above them, tugging their strings, determining their next movements.

But I had one pressing question that I couldn't get out of my mind. If the king was a vampire, why would his health be failing? He was a pureblood immortal, supposedly resilient to illness and disease. He shouldn't be ill unless it was from some invisible force or magic.

Did the king know about Nicolae? Did he know Roehl had issued a death decree to eliminate his entire bloodline?

I filed the queries in the back of my mind as Roehl ended his speech and ordered the musicians to play. His darkened eyes settled on me. As he strode toward me, he presented his hand.

"We must lead the dance," he said leaning in, his lips brushing against my ear. "And that's not a request."

A shiver raced down my spine. I despised him. And every second I spent in his presence, that hatred grew and grew.

Reluctantly, I accepted his hand and let him lead me to the center of the dance floor. As the music built, he set one arm behind my back and the other out to his side. I obliged, allowing him to lead me around the ballroom floor.

I had become the marionette, and my strings were stretched so tight I could scarcely breathe. A few days ago, he had neglected me in the bowels of this dreadful place, battered and starved. Now, he was parading me around like a dog on a leash, and I realized it was all because of Trystan. All I had to do was hold on to whatever strength I had left. Which wasn't much.

As we danced, I heard murmurs from his people as we moved past them. They were wondering who I was, and where I'd come from. The curious visitor who had captured the attention of their handsome prince. I knew he heard them too, because his eyes latched on mine and a twisted smile rose on his lips.

If they only knew the truth.

As the music ebbed and our dance ended, another began. Bodies swarmed onto the dance floor, whirling and twirling all around us. There were so many scents of perfumes and oils, it was making my head throb.

"Loosen up and stop looking so gods damned miserable," Roehl snarled.

I glared at him. "How can I *not* be miserable, Prince, when I'm dancing with the devil?"

A devilish grin exposed his long, gleaming incisors. He spun me, and as I turned back to him, I observed his eyes raking over a voluptuous woman dancing by. Her breasts were so enormous they were virtually spilling out of her gown. It was a mystery how she managed to cram those beasts into the meager amount of fabric she was wearing. She made it clear she wanted him. Her eyes were on Roehl, her tongue sweeping across her full, ruby lips. When her partner twirled her back to face him, she bit the lower edge of her lip.

I gulped down the overpowering impulse to vomit. Good gods.

As the song died down and another started, Lord Mathias tapped Prince Roehl on the shoulder.

"What?" Roehl growled, presenting him a warning glance.

Lord Mathias bowed at his waist, his eyes settling on me. "May I?"

Roehl's brow furrowed, then he glanced at me. I must have had an appalled expression on my face because Roehl's eyes glimmered with amusement.

"Good luck," he declared to Lord Mathias, whacking a strong hand to his back. I scowled as he passed me over to his minion.

Lord Mathias was over six-foot tall and cumbersome, but surprisingly agile on the dance floor. As we moved away from Roehl, he leaned forward and whispered.

"Calla, I don't have much time, so you have to listen carefully."

I shoved back from the disgusting swine, but he held me tight. "Why would I listen to you?"

His eyes found mine, stern and intent. "It's me, Kylan." I

stopped fighting after hearing his voice. A familiar voice.

"Kylan?"

He gave a careful nod and drew me back to him. "I came with Trystan."

We paused, then started dancing again. I gazed deep into those forest green eyes and failed to recognize the handsome assassin, but it was clearly his voice.

I gulped hard. "How?"

"Melaina. It's a glamour, but it won't last long." His head remained upright, his eyes avoiding me.

"Where is Lord Mathias?"

"In a cabinet, unconscious."

"Is Trystan here?"

A slight nod. "He's with Roehl. But don't look," he admonished as I shifted my head to look at him.

It took everything inside of me not to look, to continue playing the part of reluctant dance partner to Lord Mathias. "I haven't been able to connect with him," I exhaled, trying to hold my face expressionless.

"We know," he acknowledged, spinning me as the music began its crescendo. "In my right pocket is a small vial. Take it."

"What is it?"

"A potion to reverse the spell that is barring the connection between you and Trystan."

"Melaina?"

He nodded and moved us closer to the center of the dance

floor. As the bodies concealed us, I slipped my hand into his pocket and clutched the small vial. Quickly, as he twirled me, I tucked it into my cleavage, shoving it down until it was secure.

My corset would keep it from falling, and my cleavage would hold it from going anywhere.

When I peered up, a blond male dancing past was gaping at my breasts.

"Pardon me?" I growled. "Can a lady adjust herself without being ogled?"

He turned away, but not before his female partner noticed and slapped his face, withdrawing from the dance floor in a huff.

"Nice." Kylan grinned.

"Playing the game," I responded.

As the song concluded, he let me go and stepped back, bowing at the waist. "Melaina should be in your room when you return," he whispered.

"Thank you," I replied with a straight face and drab curtsey, still performing. But inside, my gut was flipping over and over on itself.

As he walked away, I wandered toward the area where the guards were assembled, toward Roehl, but my eyes prowled the space for someone else.

Then, everything around me stood still as my eyes settled on him. Those azure eyes found mine, and the expression they gave stole every ounce of breath from my lungs. Trystan was devastatingly beautiful, and it made the hollow ache in my chest expand.

I wasn't the only one he'd stole attention from. Everyone around him, notably the females, were murmuring. *Carpathia. Prince. Handsome. Wealthy.* It wasn't just mortals who were charmed by him.

Trystan was unmasked, attired in a black suit with deep gray tones. His onyx hair was neatly combed back. When he looked at me and smiled, it was like sucking in a deep breath of pure, crisp air amidst the horrid pollution.

Standing behind him, clad in black warrior leathers, were Brone, Feng, and Andrés, with arms crossed over their chests and no weapons in sight.

They had come. *He* had come. For me.

His eyes carefully scanned me, examining me from head to toe, and they spoke clearly. Within them was a mixture of relief and worry, and then a flare of rage. But with a blink, it was gone.

I hadn't had any kind of contact with Trystan for weeks. Maybe even months. I'd lost all record of time down in the gloomy chamber, and I knew he recognized the difference. I was thankful for the mask, the billowing gown, and makeup on my face. I couldn't imagine what I would have looked like if I hadn't nearly drained poor Ms. Alcott. Probably like a corpse.

I wished I had telepathy to know what Trystan was thinking. I wanted to tell him everything that had happened.

But no matter how hard I struggled to open the connection between us, my head remained silent and empty.

I could feel the weight of Roehl's harsh stare, observing every look and every movement that was made between us. Attempting to be non-conspicuous, I casually made my path toward Trystan and felt that invisible cord pull taut between us. The air was charged like it had been the night of my party when his eyes found me hiding in the shadowy corner of Brynna's back patio. I couldn't look away from him, nor did I want to. He was here. My dark knight come to rescue me from the pit of hell.

My hand unconsciously reached out to him, but as he stepped forward to meet me, a powerful arm wrapped securely around my waist, tugging me away.

Roehl.

Trystan growled, his eyes went black and feral, but he stayed put, tethering whatever power he had roiling within him—something I had yet to see released.

"There are rules in my kingdom, Prince of Carpathia," Roehl snarled. But Trystan's eyes remained locked on me. "I knew you would come for her. But I'm amazed you even let her go."

"She was never a prisoner," Trystan replied, the muscles under his suit going taut.

"Then, the bigger question is . . . why claim her?" Roehl's eyes raked over me. "You claimed a mortal, then gave her a choice to complete the bond?"

He was toying with Trystan, trying to force a reaction, but Trystan's face remained calm. "And because she is not bound by a blood bond, I took the liberty of claiming her for myself." Roehl pressed his nose to my neck and inhaled deeply. I snapped my eyes shut and scowled. "Calla is mine, and no one is allowed to touch her. Especially you, Prince Trystan Vladu," he crooned wickedly.

Roehl brushed his hand down my spine, pausing at the small of my back. I felt his eyes on me, but I didn't look at him. My eyes were on Trystan. "Don't fret, Prince. I'll make sure she's thoroughly satisfied." He purred, his hand slipping to my side, dragging me tight against his body. "Soon, she will be my mate."

"Mate?" I choked on the word, stepping back, pushing away from his grasp. But he held me even tighter. "I'll never be yours!" From the side of my eye, I could see movement from Trystan's cadre.

"Oh, my pet," Roehl breathed, unnaturally composed. But I knew there was a madness broiling beneath his calm, and with one wrong move, he could snap. "One day, you'll see things differently."

Everybody in the ballroom was now silent. Even the musicians ceased playing, their attention directed on us.

I would willingly die than be Roehl's. I tugged away from him again, but he clutched my arm and gripped tight.

The fury on Feng, Andrés, and Brone's faces was frightening, but nothing compared to the murderous look in

Trystan's eyes. I knew they could unleash hell, but they were severely outnumbered.

I wouldn't allow them to get injured, not on my account. Not because of what Nicolae had done.

Trystan took a step forward, and so did Roehl's guards. Roehl raised his hand, stopping them. There was no fear in Trystan's eyes as they met Roehl's, but I saw darkness—a fury that flickered within. A burst of wind tore through the ballroom, rattling the windows, causing everyone to gasp and squeal. Brone put a palm on Trystan's shoulder, and he stilled. Immediately, the wind died.

"Have you forgotten Roehl, who claimed her first?" Trystan's tone was even, controlled.

Roehl's rage subsided, like water to a flame. He let go of my arm and took a cautious step to the side, away from me, holding his arms out to his sides. A calculating grin grew on his lips.

"Alright then, Prince Trystan." He spoke loud enough for the entire silent and motionless crowd to hear. "Calla is free to go, and I will also grant her a choice, just as you did. She can remain here with me or leave with you. If she chooses to go, you can take her now and leave unscathed. You have my word." He placed his left hand over his dead heart.

Cunning bastard!

I glanced at Roehl with unmitigated contempt. That's why he warned me earlier. He knew this was going to happen. I was set up. A pawn in his sick and twisted game. He knew I wouldn't go while Brynna was still here. He knew how much she meant to me, and that I wouldn't endanger her life or well-being. That's why he brought her down here. So I could see her, and he could prove he had her . . . and the upper hand.

I couldn't breathe. It was as if the surrounding walls were closing in.

Now. Now, he was offering me freedom in front of Trystan and everyone else in this gods-damned room, to demonstrate where my loyalty lay. Knowing full well what my decision would be.

"Calla," Trystan said, stepping toward me, extending his hand. His eyes had softened, returning to their beautiful azure hue. "Come," he said, his voice so gentle.

My chest ached, and tears filled my eyes. Everything inside me begged to seize his hand. But I had no other option. As long as Brynna was here in Morbeth, I would have to remain here too. I couldn't leave her here alone . . . a helpless mortal in a den of immortal monsters. They'd rip her to shreds.

"Calla," Trystan spoke again, taking another step forward, stretching his hand even further toward me.

Tears spilled down my face. I regretfully and unwillingly took a step backward. Afraid I would reconsider and take his hand.

"Calla, come," Trystan implored, brow furrowed, eyes pleading.

A heavy sob burst from my chest. I couldn't speak. All I could do was shake my head and take one more excruciating step backward.

Brone, Feng, and Andrés stood directly behind him, faces and arms tensed, in case anything should happen. But I wouldn't allow it to get too far. I wouldn't let them get hurt. Not over me.

My chest was caving in, knowing Roehl had held my tongue and tied my hands. Taking another step backward, I watched all hope shatter.

I mouthed the words. "I'm sorry."

Roehl gave a victorious laugh. "She's made her decision, and everyone here has borne witness." Roehl slipped his arm around my waist again, and Trystan's eyes went deadly. "I advise you and your men to leave now. For your own safety."

The heartrending expression in Trystan's eyes made me want to escape from this miserable, gods damned world and fade away into nothingness. My salvation—Prince Trystan Vladu—was a few steps and a hand grasp away. But at this very moment, there could have been a million miles between us.

"Please, go," I breathed, begging him.

I knew Trystan was smart enough to realize this was not the place or time to start a war, especially being outnumbered, with their weapons confiscated.

I couldn't handle it anymore, so I turned to Roehl. "I'd like to return to my room."

With a beam of triumph, Roehl gestured to Markus, who promptly moved to my side.

Roehl then turned his attention back to Trystan. "Like you, Prince, I allowed her a choice. She was able to leave with you but has chosen to remain here with me."

Trystan's eyes were black as midnight, a ferocious growl ripped from his throat. "I have no doubt her decision was made under duress."

"Think what you will," Roehl snapped, and his guards drew their weapons. "She is staying, and if you ever step foot in my kingdom again, I will not be as welcoming."

The look Trystan gave Roehl would cause any mortal to drop dead. The muscles under his jacket flexed, his hands balled into tight fists. "If you are ever in Carpathia, I shall return the favor."

Before Trystan left, he looked at me one last time and bowed his head. Then pivoted and walked away, followed closely by his cadre.

Tears flowed, and my heart shattered over and over as I watched them leave. *Him* leave.

Markus offered me his arm as an act of mercy. I took hold of it and held on tight, watching Trystan, Brone, Feng, and Andrés walk out the doors.

All hope of escaping this evil place vanished with them.

CHAPTER FIFTEEN

Markus remained mute until we arrived at the corridor leading to my bedroom. Reaching my bedroom door, he hesitated.

"If you require anything, let the guards at the door know. I'll make sure you get what you need." His tone was much softer than before. Maybe even sympathetic.

I nodded as he gestured for the guard closest to the door to hold it open while I stepped in. When Markus stepped in behind me, trepidation pricked my skin, wondering if Melaina was inside.

"You don't have to stay," I said, swiveling toward him, wiping away the last tear that had slipped.

He went around, sniffing the air. "I've been ordered to check the room thoroughly at your return."

"Why? Guards are standing right outside. Wouldn't they have known if someone came in?"

He threw me a stern look. "I have orders. I will leave

when they are complete."

"Fine." I sighed and started to pull out the pins holding my mask. Moving out of his way, I headed toward the washroom. "May I? Or do you need to check it first?"

"Just go," he snarled.

Before I headed into the washroom, I casually strolled over to where he stood and turned my back to him. "Could you please unzip my dress?"

"No." His reply was immediate and firm.

"I can't reach the zipper, and I don't want this lovely gown to get ripped." He didn't move or respond. "Please," I pleaded in my sweetest voice, holding up my hair.

After a growl of displeasure, Markus unzipped the dress halfway down my back. I knew he'd seen the bruises that were left because his breath caught. "You can manage the rest," he said, shifting and scanning the room.

"Thank you."

"It's clear." He paused before he exited the room. "Sleep well," he said, then stepped out and sealed the door behind him.

Sleep well? It was a cordial remark. Maybe he felt bad for me after what his asshole prince had done.

Before moving or doing anything else, I retrieved the vial from between my breasts, tugged off the top, and poured its contents down my throat. It was bitter, but I made sure to ingest every drop.

Hurriedly, I made my way to the washroom and latched

the door. There was a narrow window on the far wall, and below it was a magnificent garden blooming with flowers, despite the season. It had to have been magic. I held the vial out the window and let go, watching it drop into the middle of a red rose bush. Perfect. No one would consider poking around in thorns.

My eyes swept the courtyard ahead of me, wishing to catch a glimpse of Trystan and his cadre. But the entire front area was flat, aside from the silhouettes of dark trees stabbing the sky. And beyond that . . . an enormous wall. *The Red Wall.*

Tears welled, but I refused to let them spill. I had to be strong and not selfish. I had no other option but to stay here. Besides, there was still hope if — *Melaina!* Was she here?

The room didn't smell any different, and it was dead quiet. I didn't dare call her name, especially with the vampire guards outside who were on high alert due to Trystan's arrival.

I checked the washroom first, searching for any traces of magic, maybe a swirl or variation in temperature. But there was nothing. I opened the door and scanned the bedroom. It was empty. As I exited the room, I quickly unzipped what remained and slid out of the dress, careful to drape it over a chair to keep it in a good condition.

I proceeded to check under the bed, behind the armchairs, and in the corners of the room. Again, nothing. Something must have happened to her. Maybe she ran into trouble getting past the guards. Once again, all fragments of optimism were being siphoned out.

The corset was constricting my air, so I quickly untied it and flung it to the floor, realizing I was half exposed. If Roehl or one of his guards stepped in — I shivered at the thought.

Heading toward the wardrobe, I opened the door to discover three white cotton bedgowns hanging. Nothing else. I guess I shouldn't have expected anything less from Prince Asshole.

I slipped a gown over my head and as it fell over my fragile frame, a hand flew over my mouth from behind. "Shh! Don't say a word," a voice whispered in my ear.

I nodded and it released.

I turned to meet fiery red hair, freckles, and intense jade-green eyes beaming at me. I'd couldn't have been happier to see the snarky witch.

I flung my arms around Melaina's neck and she hugged me back. Pulling away, she placed a finger to her lips. I nodded and quietly watched her close her eyes and cast a spell. A wall of mist swirled around us, encasing us in a cocoon of air. When it was finished, her eyes snapped open.

"Great goddess. What the hell did they do to you?" she gasped, her hands clutching my arms.

"Is it that awful?" I saw real concern in her eyes.

"Well, no," she exhaled, then shook her head. "Actually, yes. You look like they starved you to near death." Her somber eyes met mine. "What happened to you? You were gone so long without a word, and when Trystan couldn't make contact, we all thought you were dead."

"I was in a cell, shackled to a wall. They fed me nothing but stale bread and water."

"Goddess in heaven." Rage flared in those jade eyes, her hands balled into tight fists. "Those bastards."

I let out a heavy exhale. "How long have I been gone?"

"Fifty-seven days," she said sadly.

The earth beneath me seemed to shift. *Fifty-seven?*

I fell to my knees and burst into tears. I'd truly lost all track of time. I must have been asleep for days at a time. I was grateful for those times of darkness—all the days that eluded me. Because the days I spent awake, starving and in pain, were enough to last me a lifetime.

Melaina's eyes brimmed with sorrow. "I'm so sorry, Calla. I don't know how they broke through my ward. We were scared shitless when Kylan told us he saw a man take you and vanish."

"It was a Wanderer," I said quietly. "He delivered me to Morbeth in a matter of seconds."

Her eyes flew wide. "A Wanderer?"

I nodded and she glanced down. I could practically see the cogs turning in her mind.

"That's how they found us and broke through my ward. There isn't much on Wanderers, except they are sorcerers with great magic who live in seclusion. I wonder what magic Roehl had to conjure to find a Wanderer. It had to have been very powerful." Her eyes met mine again. "Did he speak to you?"

I nodded. "His name was Erro. They bound him under

an oath that he couldn't break. The lives of his family were at risk, so he had no choice."

"Figures." Melaina shook her head. "Trystan received an anonymous tip saying you were in a cell in Morbeth."

"Do you think it was Erro?"

"Possibly, since he was the one who delivered you there." Before I could say another word, Melaina kneeled next to me and wrapped her arms around my neck. "I'm sorry we failed you."

"No. You didn't fail me," I replied, but my tears said otherwise, flowing uncontrollably.

I told Melaina everything. About the cell, about Roehl and his abuse, about him claiming me, what I did to poor Ms. Alcott, about Brynna and his warning, and what happened with Trystan.

She placed both hands on my shoulders, soothing me. "Trystan would have come sooner, but because of Roehl's reputation, he had to plan and make sure I could get in without being detected. He also made it a priority that we didn't threaten your safety. It killed him, Calla. Kylan said he's never seen Trystan so miserable or unhinged, especially when he couldn't contact you."

Hearing her words made me sad. "Kylan gave me the vial, and I drank it as soon as I returned. Will it work? Will I be able to contact him again?"

"It could take a few minutes or a few days. But it should destroy Roehl's spell."

Should wasn't a word I needed to hear. I needed something solid. "What if it doesn't?"

"The only reason it wouldn't is if Roehl finds out and recasts his spell."

"I hate him." Words couldn't describe what I really felt.

She sighed. "We all do."

"Roehl is covering up the truth about Nicolae. Something isn't right. There's more to what he said happened. I know it. I feel it."

"Trystan is sending Brone and Feng to Northfall tonight to try to locate Nicolae. From the description we gave, Brone thinks he knows where he might be."

"I don't think Nicolae will want to be discovered, especially by someone like Brone."

"That's why Trystan also sent Feng," Melaina shrugged. "He's a lot less scary and has a way with words. Perhaps he can persuade him to come back with them."

It was a long shot, but I was grateful they were trying. I needed to talk to Nicolae and find out what really happened. Because I knew I wouldn't get the truth from Roehl.

"I thought you said you'd never set foot in Morbeth," I said, glancing into Melaina's jade eyes.

Melaina's head cocked to the side with a half grin. "I was given an offer I couldn't refuse."

I couldn't help but laugh. "You shouldn't be here. If Roehl finds you, he'll kill you."

"I know," she said. "But it was a risk we were all willing to take."

"Why?" I had to ask. Why would they take that risk?

"Because he's wrong, and we won't let him get away with what he's doing."

Overwhelming emotion filled me. "Will you be able to escape safely?"

"Yes, but once I do, I won't be able to return. Prince Roehl's wards are too powerful. The only way I was able to get in was because he released them temporarily when Trystan arrived." She looked me directly in the eyes. "I have one spell," she said carefully. "It can get you and me out of here, right now."

"Would you be able to take another?" I pleaded, expectantly.

Worry was etched on her brow. "I'm sorry. The spell is only strong enough to hold two. No more."

I knew Melaina came to save me. But they hadn't known about Brynna, or that she'd been captured. And Brynna's safety was much more important than mine.

I took hold of her arms. "Melaina, Roehl has my best friend, Brynna. You must get her out of this place. Please. If she's free, I won't have to carry the burden of knowing if she's safe or alive."

Melaina's eyes shut tight. "I'm sorry she's here, Calla. But I was given strict orders."

"I'm begging you. I won't leave unless Brynna is safe. And the only way that will happen is if you take her." I exhaled, seeing the stress swimming in her eyes. "Look, I realize you made a vow to Trystan, but I feel there are answers here. Answers about Nicolae and my ancestors that I need to discover."

She groaned. "Trystan won't be happy with me."

I took hold of her hand. "If Trystan is at all like the man I think he is, he'll understand. And besides, if your potion works, I'll explain it to him myself."

She pressed her fingers to her temples. "I respect your devotion to your friend, but Roehl will kill you if you stay here."

"I don't think he will anytime soon. He is out to prove something . . . especially to Trystan. Plus, there was a perverse gratification on his face when he rubbed in the fact he's claimed me. So, I'll play along until I find a way out." I took both of her hands in mine. "Melaina, please. Brynna is like a sister to me. Her parents were murdered by Roehl." I swallowed down the massive lump developing in my throat. "She's mortal, just like you, and can't stay here. We've taken care of each other since we were kids, and I owe this to her. Please."

After a few moments, Melaina nodded. "I'll take her."

I threw my arms around her neck and squeezed.

"You don't know how much this means to me. Thank you."

The witch's eyes beamed. "Well, when you get the chance, please explain it to Trystan. He'll be upset when I return with the wrong girl."

"I know he'll accept her." I had no doubt he would.

From the start, Trystan was looking out for me and my family. If he knew Brynna was here, I had no doubt he would have worked out a plan to get us both out.

I gave Melaina a brief description of what Brynna looked like and where Sabine said she was being held. And to look for a door with guards outside.

Melaina stood and drew me to my feet. "Calla, just promise me I'll see you again."

I sighed deeply. Not knowing what the future had in store. "The best I can give you is . . . I'll try."

She exhaled loudly with a snarky grin.

"Thank you, Melaina. I owe you one. And trust me, if there is a way out, I'll find it."

"I have no doubt," she said. Suddenly, her face went pale, and her head shot to the door. "He's coming. I have to go."

"Be safe. Tell Brynna I love her, and I'll see her soon."

She nodded and closed her eyes. With a twist of her hand, she vanished, and the surrounding cocoon dissipated. I felt the chilled air against my skin as I rushed to the bed. Slipping under the blankets, I rolled sideways, away from the door, hoping they'd think I was asleep.

Hearing Roehl's voice, I cringed and prayed to the gods that Melaina would make it to Brynna in time. Roehl asked the guards if I was inside, and after they confirmed it, I heard the doorknob twist and the door swing open. I counted twelve heavy footsteps across the floor in my direction. Then they halted.

I remained still and relaxed, hoping Roehl would think I was asleep. He moved closer until he stood at the edge of my bed.

A firm hand clutched my right forearm and snapped a familiar bond around my wrist. Gasping, I twisted to meet Roehl's bitter, merciless eyes.

"This is assurance. To make sure no one outside of Morbeth tries to free you." He closed his eyes, and when they reopened, they were glowing red, fixed on the wall behind me. Following his gaze, the thick chain connected to my wrist was connected to the wall behind my bed. Where the chain and wall connected, symbols were glowing in a bright red circle. He angled back to me with a vicious smirk. "Like I said . . . assurance."

"Haven't you done enough?" I broke down, looking at the iron cuff around my wrist, which had more symbols glowing in red around it. I could feel the strength of that spell, gripping my wrist, coiling up my arm. "Just leave me alone."

He shifted to leave, but before he walked out the door, he paused. "One day, you will come to love me, and you *will* become my mate."

"Never!" I wailed. "I will *never* love a monster like you."

A growl burst from his throat. The red around his eyes blazed bright, and his lip curled over lengthened incisors. "Then you will rot in this room, shackled and alone."

I fell back onto my pillow and cried.

Never in my life had I felt these emotions. Despair, and a hatred so deep it was eating away at my insides. Eating away at all goodness inside me.

The door clicked shut as he took off. I would rather die here alone than to see his vile face again. I wept until there was nothing left. Until my tears had dried up. Until sleep had finally claimed me.

Voices yelling outside my door yanked me from a deep sleep. The door swung open and heavy feet stomped inside.

My eyes were swollen and blurry, focusing on Markus as he entered the room with three guards behind him. As soon as his eyes met mine, he relaxed. "Tell the prince she's here."

"What the hell is going on? Why are you here?" I demanded.

"Your friend is missing," he declared sternly. "Do you know where she is?"

I stopped breathing. Melaina had done it. She kept her promise and freed Brynna. I wanted to scream with joy, but instead kept my face emotionless.

Lifting my wrist, I yelled at Markus. "Do you think I know where the hell she is? Your prince shackled me to the wall with dark magic and has a gazillion guards outside my door." I tightened my eyes at him and felt something shift inside, like a rubber band expanding so wide, it finally snapped. "I hope she's gone. I hope she found a way out of this shit hole. No one deserves to be kept against their will. Especially when they're innocent!"

Markus stood still, as if weighing my words. "I'm sorry I woke you," he murmured. With a bow of his head, he gestured to the guards, then withdrew out the door, sealing it.

Letting out a sigh, my insides burst.

Brynna was free, and my father was still hiding. Roehl could no longer sway their lives carelessly above my head. I felt that burden lift, and smiled, staring at the ceiling. It was a huge victory. My best friend was safe, hopefully on her way to Trystan. I knew he'd take care of her.

Melaina said it could take a few hours, maybe days, before I could connect with him again. How long had I been asleep? I wasn't even sure what time it was. Glancing out the window behind me, the sky was still dark.

It didn't matter though. My best friend was out of Morbeth, and I now had some clarity to figure out my next move.

CHAPTER SIXTEEN

I couldn't sleep. The thought of Brynna's safety had my stomach twisting in relief and happiness.

Did she and Melaina arrive in Carpathia? Would they inform her about her parents?

My heart ached for her. I hoped she would forgive and not hate me for having a grandfather who dragged her into this chaos. Dragged us all into it. But I wouldn't blame her if she did. At least she was safe. I just had to trust my father was too.

My eyes flickered open to see a welcomed face.

"How are you?" Sabine asked, moving to my side, her eyes examining the long steel chain.

I shook my shackled wrist. "I've had worse days."

"Yeah, I suppose," she breathed. "I heard about what

happened last night. Word has spread like wildfire about the young woman who captured Prince Roehl's heart. The girl the Carpathian prince came to take, but in front of everyone, she turned him down." She frowned. "Sounds like that girl had an overwhelming night."

I moaned, throwing my free arm over my eyes. "You have no idea."

"I also overheard a few guards talking about a missing girl. You wouldn't know anything about that, would you?" Her eyebrows rose, as did her lips.

I shrugged, then finally sat up. I would inform her, but not with the guard's right outside. "Have you heard any news about my father?"

"I haven't. But that's a good thing, right?"

"I hope it is." No word could hopefully mean he was still out there, running and hiding.

I wondered if he knew why those men were after him. Or if he knew I was still alive. Did he see my mother and the rest of his company get murdered?

I couldn't begin to understand what was going through his mind, except for that short glimpse into Melaina's magical water. He was frightened and confused, trying to stay alive.

"Hey, did you hear what I said?" Sabine asked, plopping down on the bed.

"I'm sorry. What did you say?"

"Never mind." She said, but leaned forward and whispered quietly into my ear, "I found a witch who might be able to help you."

"Really?" A spark of hope reignited inside me.

She raised a finger to her lips, her head gesturing to the door. She then mouthed the words, "She'll be here shortly."

"How?" I mouthed back.

"Spring is ill," Sabine said out loud. "Someone else will be coming to help me with the chores today."

I didn't answer but acknowledged her with a nod.

"When was the last time you fed?" she asked.

"Ms. Alcott," I replied, then grimaced as the thought flashed in my mind. "He's going to starve me again, isn't he?"

"We aren't allowed to feed you unless the prince tells us to. I'm sorry." She gave a wink, then withdrew her small bowl and pocketknife from under her dress. I watched as she made a slight incision on her arm, filled the vessel, and offered it to me before dressing her incision.

"You don't have to do this," I whispered, as she pushed the bowl toward me.

I received it and immediately drained its contents, handing it back to her.

"Thank you," I replied quietly, and she nodded.

Sabine disappeared into the washroom to clean away the evidence. While she was gone, I settled back and closed my eyes, letting the limited amount of blood run its course through my veins.

I could have easily let my anger and self-pity overwhelm me, but I was thankful I wasn't back down in that dingy, cold cell.

Sabine had become my friend, the only one who was trying to keep me alive. I knew I could depend on her because she was putting her life at risk for me. I would never forget her kindness and hoped that one day I could repay the favor and free her from this miserable place.

When she returned, she started to clean the room, sweeping, dusting, and humming as she worked. She had a beautiful voice, melodic, and it made the room seem happier and a lot less lonely. She was a bright and beautiful soul amidst Morbeth's gloom. Fate had led her to me. It had placed her in this castle to comfort me through these trying times, and somehow, I felt she would play an important role in my future.

There was a brisk rap on the door before it opened and a tall, slim woman with long golden hair and a pleasant smile walked in. I instantly recognized it was Spring's mother. The resemblance was uncanny.

In her hands was a vase stuffed with a colorful arrangement of flowers mixed with greenery.

"Good day, miss." She spoke with an accent. "I've been down to the gardens and brought this bouquet up for you."

"Thank you," I said giving her a smile. "They're lovely."

She stepped toward me and bowed her head. Her eyes as blue as the sky on a cloudless day.

"You're welcome. I'll set them here on your nightstand." A variety of scents, from sweet to earthy and herbal, hit my nose as she set the vase next to me. "My name is Summer."

I smiled. It was so fitting . . . Spring and Summer—perfect

representations of their natures. "It's nice to meet you."

"I picked these especially for you, thinking you might appreciate some fresh blooms to liven up the room." She winked, picking out a stick from the center of the vase while holding a finger to her lips. "It's okay, dear. Rest. We'll be extra quiet while we clean."

"Thank you," I replied.

Swirling the stick above her head, Summer's mouth started moving, but her words were barely discernible. That's when I realized she wasn't carrying any stick . . . it was a wand. She'd used the arrangement to conceal her magical tool.

When she opened her eyes, she grinned. "There," she said, thumbing toward the door. "Now the ticks can't hear us. But we must be quick, or they'll suspect something is up."

I chuckled. "Ticks?"

"It's what we mortals call the bloodsuckers here in Morbeth," Sabine replied, attending to her duties. Then her eyes flashed to mine. "Sorry. That doesn't apply to you."

I laughed. "It's fine."

Summer sat on the mattress next to me. "I overheard the kitchen help say the prince is leaving tomorrow at noon and taking a third of his army with him."

I sat up. "Where?"

"West, to Northfall," she replied.

I nodded, my thoughts racing. "He's going to look for Nicolae."

Sabine's eyes narrowed on mine. "And you know this because?"

"Before I was brought here, a witch named Melaina performed a locator spell on Nicolae.
Being related, she used my blood and it worked. I saw him, for the first time, in a bowl of water. He was in a grassy area with tall trees filled with lavender blooms. There was also a lake or river nearby."

"Jacaranda," Summer said.

Sabine stopped mid-sweep. "What?"

"There is a large Jacaranda grove in Northfall with beautiful lavender blossoms," she explained. "They are on private land owned by the Lord of Morbeth."

"How do you know this?" I asked.

Summer's eyes sank to the floor. "I used to live in Northfall with my husband, before Talbrinth's Great War. He was one of the many soldiers sent to Morbeth and was captured by their army. Morbeth officials sent messengers to Northfall to deliver letters to the prisoners' families. They were nothing more than demands. Those letters simply declared that our spouses would be executed if we didn't travel to Morbeth to claim them."

Her eyes drifted to the flowers, her fingers lightly grazing over a rose petal. "When we reached Morbeth, we were notified that every soldier had already been executed, and we were now slaves, forced to work in Morbeth as compensation for the bloodshed our men caused. I was six months pregnant with Spring. She was born in Morbeth and hasn't seen anything beyond the Red Wall."

I couldn't begin to imagine what she had to endure. For what Spring had to face being born in this godforsaken place. "I'm so sorry."

She shook her head. "You have nothing to be sorry for. But word is, you may be able to help us." She shifted to Sabine, her lips curving into a radiant smile.

"I wouldn't place any wagers on me," I said.

"Well, there's a reason why two vampire princes are contending to bond with you."

I sighed, still struggling to discover the reason for that. "I'm leaning toward pride and covetousness on Roehl's part. You know . . . one wants what the other has. Or in my case, what the other has claimed."

"I despise being a killjoy, but we should hurry," Sabine said. "Those younger guards outside are skittish."

Summer nodded, her eyes met mine. "Sabine said you have magic blocked inside of you?"

"I'm not certain, but the Wanderer that brought me here said I do. But that it's somehow contained by stronger magic. He said I need to find a way to release it to survive." I grabbed hold of her hand. "Can you help me?"

"I'm going to try," Summer said, patting my hand. She stepped back toward the flower arrangement and started to pluck some foliage. She folded a cluster of green leafy things together in her palm, forming a small square, then held it out to me. "Chew on this," she said, and I did.

The concoction tasted sweet, with hints of citrus and mint. "Do you know where your power came from or who put the bind on it?"

"I'm not sure if it even exists. Neither of my parents were magical. And if they were, they never showed any signs of it. I'm pretty sure it's from Nicolae. I watched him glamour his entire camp with a flick of his wrist."

Her brow rose and so did a grin. "It's safe to say the magic is from him."

I swallowed her concoction and it made me cough. "What are the herbs for?"

She handed me a glass of water. "The mixture will help prepare you for the spell."

I began to feel a little lightheaded and tingly all over. "Have you done this before?"

"No," she answered. "but my mother is a powerful witch and has taught me everything she knows. The herbs will act as both a sedative and pain reliever."

"Pain?" I asked, my tongue feeling numb.

"If you have magic that has been repressed all these years, I don't know how it will react once it's released. I saw something similar performed on a witch who had her powers bound because of a crime she was charged for, but they later found she was innocent. When they released her magic, it almost killed her."

Sabine's eyes jerked in my direction. "Calla, you don't

have to do this right now. We can wait."

"No, I can't wait," I sighed. "Time is my enemy." There was no backing out now. I had to do this, even with the risks. Who knew if we'd ever have another chance like this? "But—" I paused.

"What is it Calla?" Sabine asked.

"If I die, don't bury me in Morbeth. I will come back and haunt the hell out of anyone who allows it. I want to be cremated and my ashes spread in Sartha, along the coast of the Argent Sea, where my mother died."

"Calla," Sabine said. She came and stood next to me. "Have you forgotten you are an immortal? You can't die. And if you do, I'll do my gods-damned best to beat you back to life."

I giggled at her exasperated expression. "Fine. I'll hold you to that."

"Are you ready?" Summer asked.

I wasn't sure what I was getting myself into, or what I was to expect. But I'd already endured excruciating pain and starvation. At least this pain would yield a purpose. Or I hoped it would.

"I'm ready," I exhaled.

Summer instructed me to lie back, making sure I was comfortable. I peered up into her radiant blue eyes. "The magic. How will I know how to control it once it's released?"

"It depends on what type of magic you possess. But, if you like, I can show you a few simple spells while the prince is away," she replied. "Learning to connect with your gift comes with time and practice."

I nodded, feeling a bit woozy. The herbs she'd given me were performing a magic all their own. "I feel sleepy," I slurred, my tongue heavy, my brain numb.

"Then sleep," she whispered, resting her hand on my forehead.

And I did.

I was standing barefoot in a vaguely familiar bedroom, bearing nothing more than a short, silky nightdress. It was revealing, a thin-strapped, biased cut fabric that fell mid-thigh. I felt exposed and had nothing but my hair to pull forward and cover my chest.

A fire cracked in an ornate fireplace to my left. White gossamer curtains fluttered in a wide archway to my right.

Heading toward the archway, I spotted the dark sky and the sea of stars glimmering above. Then, I found a familiar veranda of white marble and two large alabaster columns with dragons carved into them.

I felt a charge in the air, along with that undeniable tug.

"Calla," a familiar voice said from behind me, causing my skin to tingle.

I twisted back and Trystan, who hadn't been there a moment ago, was now sitting in a comfortable, black leather armchair next to the fireplace, a glass half full of amber liquid in one hand, the other raking through his thick, unkempt hair. He was wearing nothing but black slacks, and gods . . . he was perfection.

Across his chest were archaic symbols. Over his shoulder and down his right arm curled a long, barbed tail. A dragon, maybe. Like on his crest and the columns outside.

He slid from his armchair, setting his glass on the mantle before striding toward me. His eyes were fixed on my face, a modest grin lifting the edges of his full mouth.

"You're here." I wanted to run to him, but I remained still. Watching. Waiting.

His scent, that perfect blend of earth and wind and spice, filled the surrounding air. I inhaled deeply, filling my lungs. It was a scent that made me weak and heated my core.

"I'm sorry," he sighed.

"For what?" My gaze met his.

"I failed to save you."

"But you didn't fail." I exhaled and smiled at him, wanting to move closer, but remained in place. "You rescued Brynna."

He tipped his head. His eyes went distant. "She's secure in one of the rooms downstairs. Melaina is watching over her."

Tears brimmed in my eyes. "Thank you, Trystan. I couldn't leave her in that place. Not with Roehl dangling her life in front of me."

Without thought, I strode forward, closing the distance between us and threw my arms around his neck. I wasn't sure what he thought, but I didn't care.

Trystan's powerful arms folded around me, enclosing me in a tight embrace.

Emotions began to simmer, threatening to explode. I rested my head on his chest. I felt so safe in his arms. So secure, I never wanted to leave.

"We knew he wouldn't let you go," he finally spoke, releasing his arms and stepping away, letting cold air seep between us. I could tell he was wrestling with his own emotions. "We were only there as a diversion, so Melaina could sneak up to your room and get you out. I didn't know he'd taken your friend. If I'd known—" Sadness swam in those azure eyes.

"I wanted, more than anything, to leave with you. You don't know how much I wanted to take your hand and run out of that place . . . out of Morbeth, forever."

"I know." He breathed, raking his fingers through his thick, raven hair. "I was worried. Because I couldn't make contact, I thought he might have killed you."

"He almost did." I moved to the archway, staring out into the darkened, starlit sky.

"What happened while you were there?" he asked, his voice tightened. "Tell me everything. I need to know."

I exhaled, dredging up the memory I wanted to lose forever. I told him about the Wanderer and what he spoke, and how they'd stolen my pack. Told him about Roehl, and how he tormented me with the flask and his blood before emptying it down the drain. Thinking back to that time made me nauseous. It sounded so farfetched to be true.

"He bit me," I breathed, the image of Roehl's lips stained with my blood tainted the beautiful starry night. "And then he slit his wrist and offered me his blood." I turned back to Trystan, who remained still with a rage building in his eyes. Every muscle in his arms, chest, abs were tense, his hands balled into tight fists.

"When I refused him, he hit me and shackled me to the wall. I had a few fractured ribs and he broke my leg." I glanced down at my left leg that he'd kicked, splintering the bone in the process. "But a servant girl saved me. Against Roehl's orders, she gave me just enough of her own blood to help, but not heal me."

I swallowed, recalling those long, dark moments of horror and pain. Praying for death but knowing it would never come because I was now an immortal.

"The only food they offered me was stale bread and water, for over a month. But all that pain and suffering didn't hurt as much as thinking I'd never be free. Thinking I'd die in that cell—never seeing the ones I love again." I looked at him through tear-filled eyes. "Or you."

Trystan walked over to me and drew me back into his arms, into a loving embrace. "I will get you out of Morbeth, Calla. And I promise . . . I'll make him pay for what he's done to you." The sincerity in his voice seeped deep into my soul.

"Thank you," I whispered against his chest. "Roehl is leaving tomorrow and heading to Northfall with a third of his army. I think his dark mages located Nicolae."

"Brone and Feng are on their way to Northfall. I sent

them right after we left Morbeth." His hands moved to rest on my hips. "I'll find a way to free you, even if it means taking on the entire Morbeth army myself."

I shifted to meet his beautiful eyes, still unclear of why he was willing to give so much for me.

"I don't want you to go to war or to die for me," I said. "There is a woman with me right now. A witch who is trying to release a spell cast over me—the spell the Wanderer said is suppressing my magic. I'm not sure if it's true, or if magic does exist inside of me, but if it is, it might be my way out."

Trystan took both my hands in his. "Calla, you have no idea how powerful Roehl is."

I loathed the sound of his name. "I don't care. He thinks I'm just a newborn vampire, which he's held on the verge of starvation." A growl rumbled inside his chest. "So, if I do have magic, and can somehow release it, maybe I'll stand a chance of surviving and finding an escape."

"If you have magic, he can never learn about it. If he finds out, who knows what he'll do."

I groaned. "I'll continue to play his game and make him believe I'll agree to be his mate—"

In a split second, my back was fastened against the wall with Trystan's rock-hard body pressed tight against mine. The tendons in his chest were taught, his eyes had gone completely black.

"You will never be his," he growled.

Trystan's lips crashed against mine, eager and unyielding. His lips and tongue were magic, making my entire body tingle and my insides melt with desire. His hands roamed my body. I couldn't get enough. I needed more. I craved all of him.

His hips rocked into mine, causing a moan to burst from my throat. He smiled against my lips.

A sudden punch of pain shot through my center. "Trystan," I exhaled. My body went rigid. Pain and heat consumed every part of me. I clutched his arms, holding on tight, not wanting to leave him or this beautiful place.

"What's wrong?" Trystan asked, his arms folding around me. Anguish filled his face. "Calla? What's wrong?"

"Don't let go of me," I cried.

Trystan's arms curled tighter around me. His breath was ragged, his muscles tense.

Kissing the top of my head, he declared, "I'll find you, Calla. I promise."

Another piercing pain exploded through my body.

I couldn't speak. The pain was excruciating.

I held tight to Trystan, but a blinding light burst around me. Pain pulsed from my chest and radiated through my entire body, causing me to scream out in pain.

I was torn away from Trystan. The beautiful dream ended.

CHAPTER SEVENTEEN

All at once the pain receded and I found myself standing in a long, brilliantly lit tunnel.

"Calla!" I could hear Sabine and Summer calling my name, begging me to rejoin them.

"Sabine!" I bellowed, but their voices were already fading.

Summer said the releasing of power almost killed a witch. What if my magic was too powerful? What if I was dead?

I ran toward their voices, down the endless bright tunnel. But as far as my eyes could see, there was no way out. No doors, no windows. Just an endless path.

"Calla, you don't have to run anymore," a familiar voice spoke, which seemed to be all around me. "Turn around, sweetheart."

I stopped dead in my tracks and twisted back.

My mother stood behind me in a flowing white gown, her face flawless and bright, her long auburn hair spilling like silk around her shoulders. I couldn't believe my eyes. She was here, wherever this was. And she was beautiful and so . . . *alive*.

"Mom!" I ran as fast as I could, straight into her open arms. She hugged me tight, peppering the top of my head and cheeks with kisses. Just like she had when I was a child.

"I'm just fine, darling," she said into my hair. "You don't have to worry about me."

I pulled back and stared at her face, tears pouring down my cheeks. "Mom," I sobbed, my lips trembling, "I miss you so much."

"I know you do. And I miss you, darling," she breathed, her palm tenderly stroking my hair. "Calla, always remember that you are never alone. I will always be with you." She lay her palm in the middle of my chest. "Right here. Forever."

"I'm sorry. I'm sorry I couldn't save you," I sobbed. "It was Nicolae."

"I know," she breathed. "I know. But although my life has ended, yours is just beginning. You must be strong."

Tears pooled, then flowed down my face. "How am I supposed to live without you?"

"I have no doubt you'll be fine," she answered. "You've proven from a young age that you can flourish on your own. I wish I could reverse time. I should have stayed back with you, instead of sailing away on those countless business trips."

I shook my head, drying my tear-stained face. "You raised me to be strong and independent. I wouldn't be here right now if I were any different."

Tears trickled down her fair cheeks. "I'm so proud of you, Calla. I have always been."

She hugged me again while I sobbed. I missed her terribly.

When she finally let me go, I had so many questions. "Where are we?"

"We are in the In-Between. A place that connects life and death."

"Am I dead?"

"No, my darling," she answered, her fingers feathering across my cheek. "You are alive, and there are so many things I would love to sit and talk to you about. But I can't stay. I've come to say goodbye."

"Goodbye?" My chest felt as if it were going to implode. I'd already lost her once. I couldn't lose her again. "You can't leave now. You've just arrived."

"I have to. There are rules here," she replied wistfully. "The veil between realms was removed last night during the solstice. But it's closing." She gently settled her hands on my shoulders. "Calla, there is someone I want to introduce you to. Someone who has been waiting a long time to meet you."

Meet me? "Who?"

She looked to her side and my eyes followed. Standing a few yards away was one of the most beautiful women I'd ever seen. She was tall and slender, wearing a fitted gold gown. A golden filigree crown sat atop her shimmering blonde hair. Royalty. She had to be royalty.

But there was something about her eyes. She had the most striking golden eyes with flecks of auburn. Just like mine.

"Calla," my mother said warmly. "I have to leave now."

"No!" I wailed, wrapping my arms around her. "You can't go. You can't leave me again."

She hugged me for a moment, then drew back, cupping my face in her soft, warm hands. "You stole my heart, Calla, from the moment you were born. From the moment they placed you in my arms you became my world and owned my entire heart. There are choices I wish I made differently—"

"I never doubted your love," I wept.

"Please take care of your father for me," she said, drawing me back into her embrace. "He's strong, but he'll need you."

"I will." I promised.

My body trembled as she stepped backward and smiled. "Mom, wait!" The only words I could speak were, "I love you."

"I know, darling. And I will always love you." She blew me a kiss, and just like the wind, she vanished.

Pain slammed through my chest, making it hard to breathe. She was gone. And I would never see her again.

"She'll be fine," the woman spoke. I'd forgotten she was there.

She folded her delicate hands in front of her and smiled.

233

"You don't know how long I've waited to meet you, Calla."

I wiped the tears soaking my cheeks. "Who are you?"

"You do not know me. But I've known you your entire life." Her face was glowing in an ethereal light. "I am Leora, Princess of Incendia." She took a few steps closer until we were a foot apart.

A princess? How did she know me, and why would she be waiting to meet me?

"I know how confusing this must be. But I am not only a princess, Calla," she spoke, her smile as radiant as the sun. "I am also your great-grandmother."

My thoughts became a whirlwind. "Great-grandmother?" I breathed and she nodded. "I've heard of Incendia, but it was destroyed centuries ago."

Her eyes saddened as if she flashed back to a memory. "Yes. Our entire existence was wiped out by a strong and evil force." She reached out and took my hand, and a tingling sensation from where her skin touched mine sent goosebumps up my arm. Then she led me down the tunnel. "There were a few who escaped the massacre, and Nicolae, my only child, was one of them."

Gods. This was a lot of information to take in. "Nicolae?" I repeated, trying to piece the puzzle together.

So many emotions swirled within her golden eyes. "Yes." She paused. "I met Nicolae's father at a royal ball. He was a handsome young prince, so full of life. As soon as our eyes connected, we both felt an undeniable connection."

Her eyes went distant, glancing elsewhere, down that bright corridor with no end. "We fell hard and fast in love, and had a bond so powerful, it went beyond the stars. But fate had another agenda. As a prince, he had been betrothed to another—an arranged marriage from birth. Because we realized we could never be together, we loved without inhibition or abandon. When we finally separated—days before his marriage to the princess—I learned I was pregnant with his child.

"My prince attempted to contravene his father's order and break the engagement, but the king became furious. He sent his son to the flogging post, then secretly had spies trail him. Those spies found us and reported back to the king of our affair and the child growing in my belly.

"The king blamed me for his son's betrayal and insubordination, but he also knew of the great power I possessed as an Incendian Royal. He knew that I alone could ruin him and his entire kingdom. So, he remained silent.

"Instead, the king devised a terrible and wicked plan. First, he sent me a demand. In exchange for my safety, he wanted the child growing inside me." A lone tear trailed down her cheek. "There was no way I could let that cruel, vicious man near my child.

"Month's later, Nicolae was born, and I knew his life would be in constant danger. So, I made the most painful decision any mother could make. I gave my only son to my chambermaid and ordered her to leave Incendia and never return. She was to take him far, far away—to a place even I was unaware of. She vowed to instruct him in our ways and remind him of where he came from." Her eyes went distant again, a great sorrow filled them. "When they left, I fell into misery. A sadness greater and deeper than I'd ever known."

I swallowed, demanding to know the answer. "Who was Nicolae's father?"

She peered deeply into my eyes. "His name is Romulus Tynan."

"No," I exhaled, my entire body trembling. "The King of Morbeth is my great–grandfather?"

She nodded.

Good gods. "Wait, wait, wait." I was on the verge of hyperventilating. "So, Roehl is Nicolae's brother?"

"Half-brother," she corrected. "Roehl was born from the king's wife." She gave a mournful smile. But I wanted to vomit after hearing this news. "Because Nicolae is a son of Morbeth and Incendian Royalty, he is rightful heir to the throne." There was a glimmer in her eyes. She inclined her head to the side. "Why do you think Roehl was so eager to give an order to dispose of his entire bloodline?"

This knowledge was like a blast to the gut. No wonder he wanted us dead. We were a threat. And that voice I'd heard in the Whisper Woods, through Nyx's eyes, was clearly his.

I had so many questions, and maybe . . . maybe she had the answers.

"Does King Romulus know Nicolae is alive?"

Her eyes went cold. "Everyone thought the child had died with me, even Romulus. But when Roehl found out about Nicolae, and came back and told the king his story, giving him the name Nicolae Corvus, he knew then that he was alive. He knew, because I'd told Romulus, while I was carrying his child inside me, that if I ever bore a son, I would name him Nicolae. I had also teased that I'd give him the second name Corvus, after Romulus's favorite bird—a raven he'd had since it first hatched."

Heaven's above. My mind was a whirlwind that kept growing stronger. But I needed more answers.

"Did Nicolae kill Roehl's brother?"

She nodded. "Yes, he did. Defending himself."

I knew something wasn't right. "Do you know what happened?"

Leora let out a heavy and painful sigh. "Before the Queen of Morbeth passed, she told her sons about their father's affair and the illegitimate son born from it. She didn't trust the king and sought out mages in the enveloping forest who practiced black magic. They told her Romulus had a child, a firstborn son who was still alive and incredibly powerful. She shared the news and made them vow to never tell the king.

"The Queen had a mental illness. And for years, she grew more and more paranoid. Then one day, she took her own life, not being able to live with the fact that her husband's heart was never hers.

"After her death, Roehl became obsessed with finding

Nicolae. His mother's fears had fed his own, and he wanted nothing more than to capture him and dispose of any threat to his legacy—his throne.

"Using the dark and powerful mages who resided in the Forest of Murk to locate him, Roehl and his brother Rurik set out one day, telling the king they were leaving on a hunting trip. They traveled for days on horseback to the place where the witches had located Nicolae—in a cabin near Blue Lake in northern Belfast.

"They plotted to arrive at the cabin while Nicolae was sleeping, stick a blade in his chest, and leave. But Nicolae, through magic of his own, discovered they were coming. The night of the attack, he'd planted a decoy in his bed.

"When Rurik stood above Nicolae's bed with a dagger aimed at the decoy's chest, Nicolae snuck up from behind, with a sword, and beheaded him. Roehl bore witness to his brother's murder, and when he tried to avenge him, Nicolae vanished like the wind.

"Mad with hatred, Roehl brought Rurik's body back to Morbeth and spread lies throughout the kingdom. He told his father that while they were hunting, a man named Nicolae Corvus murdered his brother and tried to rob them. The very next day, the king fell gravely ill."

My thoughts were spiraling out of control. It wasn't Nicolae's fault. This entire mess was because of Roehl. *The bastard.*

Knowing Roehl had considerable power, I had to ask.

"Do you think Roehl has something to do with his father's illness?"

"What do you think?" Her eyes narrowed on me.

"I think the king saw through Roehl's lies, and maybe even confronted him. Knowing Roehl and his temper, he probably cast an evil spell on his father out of spite, likely because he tried to defend Nicolae—the rightful heir to the throne of Morbeth."

"You are wise beyond your years, Calla." Leora smiled. "Your great-grandfather would be proud."

"I want to see the king, but I'm not sure how. Roehl has me chained in a room, and the chain is enchanted with powerful magic."

Her smile brightened as she took a step closer to me. "Roehl's magic is no match against yours."

I shook my head. "I don't understand how that's possible. I've never felt or displayed any kind of magic growing up."

"That's because there is a very powerful concealment and repression spell upon your magic."

"Who would cast such a spell?"

She grabbed hold of my hands. "I did."

"I—" I didn't know how to respond. "Why?"

"I placed a spell on Nicolae's entire bloodline, knowing that if anyone found out you were heir to Incendia's throne, you would be hunted and killed. They destroyed our kingdom because they were envious and frightened of our power. They attacked us when we least expected it—when we were most vulnerable."

"I'm so sorry," I breathed.

"You are the sole female heir in my lineage, Calla." Her fingers brushed gently against my cheek. "And to you, I will bestow the power of Incendia and the Fire Goddess."

I wasn't sure what that meant, but it seemed like a lot more than I could handle. "Why me? Why not give it to Nicolae or my father?"

"Because the power of Incendia can only be given from a female predecessor to her *female* heir."

"But Nicolae has magic. I've watched him use it."

"All Incendians of royal blood are born with magic. And as powerful as the males are, their abilities are not as great as those of the females. In Incendia, the women royals were the defenders."

"If Incendia was so dominant, then how could it have all been destroyed?"

She sighed and pulled me along as she began walking again. "It happened the night of the solstice and the great Fire Festival. It was our biggest celebration and most sacred day of the year. A night we welcomed summer and celebrated the fire goddess for blessing and bestowing her power upon us. It was a night filled with festivities, feasts, and peace. The only night we let our guard down."

Tears slid from her eyes. "They attacked us in the hours before dawn, while everyone was asleep, worn from the night's festivities. Morbeth's mages had cast powerful spells over the entire kingdom, keeping us in a deep slumber while their army moved in and massacred everyone . . . men, women, and children. They destroyed the palace and the surrounding village, setting everything on fire."

I didn't understand. "How could anyone, especially a king, commit such a heinous crime? To eliminate an entire kingdom knowing his grandson was among them."

Leora shook her head. "When a wicked heart remains in the darkness too long, it begins to crave that darkness, until there is no light that can drive it out. When Romulus learned of his father's murderous rampage, he was enraged. The hate for what his father had done grew with each passing day, driving him mad. A few months later, when the king set out on a hunting trip with a half-dozen of his guard, Romulus followed in secret. And while they slept, he crept into their encampment and executed them all, keeping his father for last. The man who killed his one true love and his child, so he thought. He let his father see his face and feel his rage as he slit his throat and let him drown in his own blood.

"No one found out who murdered the king. And soon after, Romulus assumed the throne." Her eyes went distant again. "As king, he banished all those who practiced dark magic and executed those who conspired with his father against Incendia. Romulus became a great ruler. He was fair and noble, but strict."

Hearing this story . . . a story of lies, deceit, and murder was one thing. But knowing it was taking place within one kingdom, one family—part of my lineage—was reprehensible and heart shattering. Morbeth had a very dark past, so it was no wonder Roehl was a monster. He was raised by a spiteful mother who wanted to eliminate Romulus's firstborn son and his offspring, so her son could be king.

There was a question pressing on my mind. "If King Romulus is my great-grandfather and he is a vampire, wouldn't the vampire gene be passed down to me?"

"Yes," she replied.

"Then why haven't I shown signs of being a vampire? Why did I go through the transition when Trystan bit me?"

"The spell I cast was extremely old and immensely powerful. It suppressed *all* magic inside of you, erasing all traces of immortality and power, making you an ordinary mortal. That's why, when the handsome Carpathian prince bit you, your body reacted as if you were a newborn."

I sucked in a heavy breath and exhaled. "Does Trystan know about Nicolae? That he is Romulus's heir, and a son of Incendia?"

Leora shook her head. "He doesn't. But he is searching for the truth as we speak. A truth Romulus's father covered up all too well."

I let out another long breath. At least I knew Trystan's motives were pure. That he hadn't sought me out and claimed me because he knew of my lineage. But . . . "Why would Roehl, after sending out a decree to have Nicolae's entire bloodline eliminated, claim me instead of killing me?"

Leora turned to me and took both of my hands in hers.

"What Roehl ultimately seeks is power. If he claims you and makes you his mate, the threat to his throne will be eliminated. And whether he realizes it or not, he'll also possess the most powerful Incendian heir." Her eyes were gleaming as if she'd just revealed a deep mystery. "But don't think for one moment that he won't reconsider his decision if he finds out how powerful you truly are. He will kill you in an instant. Or worse . . . make you a servant to his sinister plans."

I had no doubt he would either enslave or kill me. I'd tasted his rage and knew he'd have no remorse or regret either. He was a monster. A scary and savage monster with great power.

I'd just have to play his game better than he did. To remain the ignorant, defenseless victim until he dropped his guard.

But the truth was . . . Roehl already knew about Nicolae. That he was his half-brother. If he knew that, then his mother must have told him about Leora and Incendia. The thought of him knowing sent a chill through my bones. But what was even more disconcerting was that he'd known we were relatives, yet he chose to claim me and make me his mate. There was no doubt he was using me to get to Nicolae; to draw him out so he could capture and kill him.

I looked deep into Leora's familiar golden eyes and asked, "Does Nicolae know I exist?"

"No," she breathed. "Nicolae kept to himself for most of his life and had few relationships, aside from my chambermaid. But," she hesitated and smiled, "there was one young woman, one beautiful, charming girl who happened to steal his heart. She was a farmer's daughter who lived in Northfall. One summer, Nicolae went to work for her father on their farm.

"The farmer's daughter was captivated by Nicolae's good looks and strong work ethics and fell for him. They were friends at first, but as the days drew on, they became inseparable. It was the first time Nicolae had felt true happiness.

"Near the end of the season, the young woman discovered she was pregnant with Nicolae's child. When her father—a devout follower of the church—found out about the pregnancy, he fired Nicolae and banished him.

"Despite the girl's pleas, her father refused to let his daughter keep the baby. And during her entire pregnancy, kept her out of the community's eye. When the child was delivered, the young woman's father took the baby while she was sleeping and boarded a boat to Sartha. When he arrived, he took the baby to a nearby parish and left him in a basket on the doorstep. The clergy's wife found him and brought him to her husband. They took him in, raised, and cherished him as if he was their own."

My grandparents.

"Your father was blessed by the gods to have been raised by such a loving couple."

Leora knew everything about my family's life. All this time, even after death, she'd been watching over us.

"So, the answer to your question is no," she continued. "Nicolae left before he knew the girl was pregnant. He does not know he bore a son, or that he has a granddaughter. If he did, I have no doubt he would be fighting to protect you both."

My chest ached for blaming Nicolae before I knew anything about him. I'd despised him because of what he'd done, and wrongfully judged him before I knew the truth.

"I need to find Nicolae." There was an urgency now. Especially after learning the truth. "A friend said Roehl located him in Northfall and is leaving tomorrow to capture him."

"He is in Northfall, but Nicolae is much wiser than they realize. He can only be found if he wants to be."

"How is he able to use his power with your repression spell?"

"When he came of age, I released the spell on his power alone. My chambermaid raised Nicolae well, and he'd mastered the art of becoming invisible. I also knew it would be a matter of time when Romulus's wife—the Queen of Morbeth—would find out he was alive and come after him."

It was impossible not to become emotional after hearing the truth about who I was and where I came from. I still couldn't believe I was here, standing in front of my deceased great-grandmother, an Incendian Royal, who was slain by my great-great-grandfather, the former King of Morbeth.

Leora's fingers grazed my cheek.

"Calla, always know that your mother and I love you, as we have, from the moment you were born. I've been watching over you and will continue to do so until we are reunited once more, on that day you cross through the In-Between. But our time here has come to an end, sweet child."

"Wait! There is a lot more I need to know."

"The rest, you will need to learn for yourself. If you seek the answers, you will find them. And you will find that most of what you seek can be found in Incendia—the home of your ancestors. And yours, Calla. And once you arrive, you will find that the heart of Incendia is not dead." She pressed a kiss to my forehead. "May the power of Incendia protect and guide you." She took two steps backward and extended her arms. "Give me your hands, Calla."

My insides twisted, realizing she was about to impart her power to me.

"Will it hurt?" I asked.

"It is nothing you won't be able to handle." A sincere smile shone on her face. "This gift is extremely powerful. Be careful to whom you present it, and even more careful to whom you wield it."

"Will my father also gain power once the spell is released?"

"He will, but it won't be as strong as Nicolae's, or yours. He probably won't know he possesses it. But rest assured. Your father is safe for now. He's managed to dodge Roehl's men and it appears as if he's heading to Aquaris."

Good. Aquaris was where my mother's parents had lived. He had friends and places he could hide.

"I'm scared," I declared, mostly to myself.

Leora took a few loose strands of my hair and tucked it behind my ear. Her warm hands settled on my shoulders. "I know you're frightened, but don't be. Power flows through the very fibers of your being. As you learn your abilities and exercise them, they will grow stronger and become easier to call. I have no doubt that you will be the greatest Incendian Royal that has ever lived. You are my heir, after all. Embrace the power and it will protect you."

Although her words were meant to reassure and encourage me, I was still doubtful.

What power would I truly possess that could make me that powerful? Was I ready for that kind of power? Would I be able to conceal it from Roehl?

It seemed like a great responsibility. But I was ready. I had to be. I had no other option, especially if I was going to escape Morbeth and Roehl.

I straightened my back and stretched out my arms, offering my hands to Leora.

Before her hands touched mine, she steadied her gaze on me and said, "I love you, Calla. Please tell your father and grandfather I will be watching over them."

"I will."

Leora leaned forward and placed her hand in the middle of my chest, her eyes meeting mine. A tender smile rose on her lips. "Above all else, guard your heart." A warmth radiated from her palms, heating my chest.

Then she lay her palms over mine.

A surge of tremendous power slammed into me, thrusting me backward, causing everything around me to shatter.

CHAPTER EIGHTEEN

My back slammed into the mattress. My eyes opened and Sabine and Summer were on either side of me, mouths agape, eyes wide with terror and panic.

"What happened?" I coughed, my entire body throbbing.

Sabine's lips moved to speak, but nothing came out. Her finger aimed at me.

"Y-you were on fire. A-and levitating." She finally exhaled. "You incinerated your sheets."

Rolling my head to the side, I noticed all the bedding was charred and still smoldering.

Summer pinched her eyes shut. "If Roehl finds out—"

"He won't," Sabine said, already stripping the bedding. "We need to clean this up."

"You were unconscious," Summer added. Her hand hovered above my forehead like she was afraid to touch me. "What happened?"

"I was in the In-Between. Inside of a bright tunnel that bridges our world and the afterworld."

"The veil still must have been open," Summer said to herself, helping me up while she and Sabine stripped the rest of the charred linen, replacing them with new ones.

"What was it like?" Sabine asked. "The In-Between?"

I steadied my trembling limbs. "It was quiet and peaceful there. I was visited by my mother and—" My eyes shifted to Summer, who was wiping ash from the side table. "Have you heard of Incendia?"

"Yes. The island." She pulled out a bandage from a small pouch around her waist and stood next to me. Carefully, she moved the steel cuff up as high as she could and wrapped it around my wrist. "They say it's nothing but ruins now. But I've heard many tales of its people. The Incendian royals were some of the most powerful beings in this world, born with the magic of the fire goddess in their blood. They were able to control the elements, but fire was their dominant force." When Summer was finished wrapping my wrists, she grabbed a broom, quickly sweeping up ash near the bed and disposing of it in a nearby dustbin. "They were slaughtered, though. An entire kingdom wiped out in a single night. If the tales are true, I can't imagine what it must have been like."

"The tales *are* true," I said. "I met Incendia's princess in the In-Between."

Summer paused. "The Incendian Princess came to you?"

"Yes."

Her eyes widened. "Why?"

"Because she's my great-grandmother."

I glanced down and noticed my palms. Each of them bore a tattoo, a twin of the other. They were circles, with triangles inside them. On my right palm, the triangle was facing upward with what looked like an image of fire in it. On my left palm, the triangle was facing downward, with the symbol of water in it. And around the circle were symbols I didn't recognize.

"Goddess above," Summer exhaled. "Calla, do you know what these mean?"

I shrugged. "That I could get killed if they are discovered?"

"Yes. That and—" her finger traced the markings on my right palm. "Only those of Incendian Royalty bore these marks. Magic branded on their palms from the fire goddess herself. These markings around the circles are symbols of the zodiac."

I grabbed hold of her wrists. "How do you know?"

"I've heard and read stories, but I've also seen these exact tattoos before."

"Where?" I asked. She hesitated, and I sensed trepidation. "Summer, where?"

She looked directly at me. "In the king's chamber. They were engraved on his side table, and I think he did it himself."

My limbs felt weighted, my breath burdensome. It was as if all the air in Summer's magic bubble was being siphoned out.

"What is it, Calla?" Summer asked.

I gazed deep into her bright blue eyes. "Romulus Tynan—the King of Morbeth—is my great-grandfather."

Sabine cursed and dropped her broom mid-sweep. Her hands cupped over her mouth. "Gods, no. Tell me you're mistaken."

I shook my head. "I can't. It's the truth."

"Does Roehl know?" Summer asked. Her face was contorted with a mix of shock and maybe dread.

"He knows. He also knows about his father's affair with the Incendian Princess, which produced Nicolae. But I don't think he knows about my powers. Especially since they've been repressed . . . until now."

"Goddess help us." Summer exhaled. "That's why he wants you all dead. You're a risk to his throne." Her eyes first narrowed on Sabine, then on mine. "You *are* an heir of Morbeth's throne."

"I knew it," Sabine said, throwing a finger at me. "I knew you were the one the Seer spoke of."

Maybe she was right. But, "I don't want anything to do with Morbeth or its throne. Roehl can have this shithole. I just want to get out of here and never return."

I didn't want to be associated with Morbeth—the kingdom known for its devastation and death.

I shifted my attention to Sabine. "I think Roehl put a spell on the king to make him sick. I must find a way to see him. I need to speak to him."

"There is no way," Sabine breathed. "There are a half

dozen guards outside his door, and even more inside. No one can enter or leave the king's chamber without Roehl's approval."

"There has to be a way." I exhaled in frustration. "If Roehl finds Nicolae and murders him, he'll return to Morbeth and kill his father. I have no doubt that's his plan. Then he'll assume the throne, become king, and force me to be his mate."

Both Sabine and Summer remained silent. I could see the cogs in their minds spinning.

As soon as Sabine finished sweeping, there were two sharp taps on the door. I quickly plunged back into bed and drew the fresh blankets over me.

Summer released her magic barrier with a quick swish of her hand, and a gust of wind seemed to carry all odor of smoke away with it.

"Enter," Sabine hollered.

My attendants scurried off to perform other duties as a young guard with short blond hair and sky-blue eyes stepped in. "I'm sorry to disturb you, but it was quiet, and we've been ordered to make sure you don't disappear."

Glaring at him, I shook the heavy manacle clamped around my wrist. The weight of the chain clanked loudly against the floor. "I'm shackled to this room with a dark spell. I couldn't leave if I wanted to." I dramatically threw my head back onto the pillows and covered my eyes with my free arm.

It wasn't the guard's fault. He was simply carrying out his duty. But being chained and underfed put me in a rotten mood.

"I'm sorry," he whispered. "And by the way, Prince Roehl is coming for you."

"What?" My head shot back up, and both Sabine and Summer stopped what they were doing. "Why?"

His shoulders shrugged. "I believe he's taking you to lunch." He quickly bowed his head, then reversed out the door and shut it.

I plopped my head back on the pillow and stared at the ceiling. "Where in this gods-forsaken place would he be taking me to lunch?"

Because the barrier was down, Summer and Sabine remained quiet but wore troubled expressions on their faces as they quickly finished their chores. Summer carried the vase of flowers to the washroom, and when she returned a few moments later, some of the flora were missing. She then placed the arrangement in the middle of the mantle above the fireplace and did quick work, using her wand to put a barrier back around us so we could talk again.

"You'll have to hide those tattoos," she said, inspecting my palms.

"I think these tattoos are the least of my worries." I grabbed hold of her hand. "Do you think Roehl will sense my power now that it's released?"

"Let me see what I can do." Her eyes landed back onto my tattoos. "I can put a glamour over these, but it won't last long. A day or two at most."

"I just need a day. Roehl will be on his way to Northfall

this evening."

She nodded, then took her wand. With a few swishes and magical words over my tattoos, they faded until there was nothing left but smooth skin. But Summer didn't stop there. "I'm also going to put a temporary glamour over your magic, to dampen the power. Hopefully, Roehl won't be able to sense it." She spoke a few words in another tongue, which made me tingly all over. Then she stepped away.

"Is that it?" It seemed too simple.

"Yes," she replied. "Just be cautious at all times. Now that you have this untapped power, make sure no one sees it. If Roehl finds out about it, there is no telling what he would do."

My stomach roiled. "I don't know if I can be civil around him. I don't trust myself with whatever is inside me. I already want to kill him." I had no idea how to call upon the power, or what would happen if I accidentally released it. Roehl brought out emotions in me I couldn't control and knowing I had magic that was supposedly more powerful than his . . . I couldn't let my emotions get the best of me. I had to reign them in, keep them in control, even though every cell in my body wanted to see him dead.

Sabine gathered her supplies and made her way over to me. "You'll be fine, Calla," she said in a gentle tone.

The air in the room became heavy, knowing Roehl was on his way. Summer released the surrounding ward before she hurriedly gathered their things and headed for the door.

"We'll return this afternoon," Sabine said with a wink. I

nodded and smiled.

When they left, I didn't feel alone like I usually did. Now, I knew my mother and Princess Leora were watching over me. And Leora had given me something to hope for . . . to fight with. A gift I could use to defend myself.

The thought sent a surge through my veins.

I felt Roehl before he entered, thanks to the wretched partial bond. I would die before I was fully bound to him.

There was no knock before the door rudely swung open and Roehl stepped in.

"What do you want?" I demanded, hoping, and praying he wouldn't detect any hint of my power.

As he prowled toward my bed, my body stiffened. He stopped a few feet away. "I've come to take you to lunch."

"If you're serving stale bread and water, I'll pass. I've vomited enough of my guts to last a lifetime."

His smile, now feline, appeared amused. "Do you think I would offer my future mate prison fare?"

It didn't matter how handsome or young Roehl looked on the outside. He was freaking insane. A demon who could snap at the flip of a coin. Not only that, but he was my grandfather's half-brother.

"How could I not feel like a prisoner? You've chained me to the wall, and I can't even use the washroom if I need to."

Roehl casually folded his hands behind his back and inclined his head toward the washroom door. "You are free to roam anywhere within this room," he remarked casually.

"What?" I scowled at him.

"See for yourself." He presented me with his hand, but I refused, rising without touching him. I walked toward the fireplace, and just when I expected the chain to go taut, it didn't. It stretched somehow. Or grew longer.

What the hell?

"It would've been nice to have known this sooner," I grumbled.

He waved it off. "I was preoccupied with more pressing matters."

My face remained hard as stone while my insides twisted, knowing those pressing matters were the arrival of Trystan and his cadre, along with Brynna vanishing.

As if he could read my thoughts he added, "I'll deal with the Carpathian prince later. It is no coincidence that his leaving and your friend's disappearance are related."

His smirk stretched. *The bond.* Could he hear my thoughts? "You saw him leave. How could he have taken her? They didn't know she was being held captive here."

"You'll soon find out that I always discover the truth. I know they used a witch. And that witch will pay greatly for entering into my kingdom and stealing from me."

"You," I seethed but stopped to quell my emotions. Heat roiled under my skin, so I shut my eyes, calming myself. When I opened them again, I continued, "Remember, you stole her first."

Roehl took a few steps forward until he was inches away.

"Don't," he said with a cold calm that sent a shiver down my spine. He then grabbed hold of my shackled wrist and the manacle instantly fell away. That easy. He didn't blink or utter a word.

"I need to change," I said, tugging my hand from his grasp.

Still in my bedgown, I walked toward the wardrobe and found more bedgowns and a red dress inside. I removed the dress from the hanger and held it up. It was short and fitted and revealing. How the hell did it get in there? Sabine and Summer didn't bring it.

I groaned, considering wearing my bedgown to lunch.

"You have five minutes to fix yourself," Roehl ordered as he headed for the door.

Bastard.

Inside the washroom, I removed my bedgown before brushing my teeth and hair. Grasping the scanty red fabric in my hand, my contempt for Roehl grew.

I just had to remind myself I was still playing a game. A careful game where I needed to remain impassive, with a straight face, and portray my part of the powerless, fragile, new vampire. Most importantly, I was to *never* let him assume I had powers.

Reluctantly, I dragged the red dress over my head. It was a thin-strapped V-neck, but it was loose on my frail frame. Then, by some magic, the dress started to shrink, hugging my body like a glove, and squishing my breasts together until I had cleavage.

This was outrageous. Damn him. Perverted bastard.

It was impossible not to see how much weight I'd lost. The small amounts of blood Sabine had given me worked just a bit, giving my skin a dewy glow, concealing the pallid prisoner beneath.

I pulled sections of my auburn hair over my shoulders, then pivoted, and headed out. As I exited my bedroom, Roehl was standing outside in the hallway. His eyes seductively swept over my body, from head to toe, making me shudder inside.

Play the game.

"Shall we?" he asked, offering me his arm. I linked my arm around his, keeping my palms fisted, praying Summer's glamour would work.

We walked down the hallway followed by at least four guards. Two stayed behind, watching my empty room. For what? I had no idea.

Markus was standing at the end of the hall, and as we neared him, he bowed and led us down the stairs.

"Where are we going?" I dared to ask.

Roehl gave me a sidelong glance. "I wouldn't want to spoil the surprise."

I let out a deep, annoyed sigh. "I hate surprises."

"Well, this surprise will be worth it."

After multiple hallways and stairwells, we stepped into a great open room. The floors were made of obsidian marble, and the décor was ornate mostly in blacks, reds and golds. Atop a dais at the back of the room, were two golden thrones seated side by side. But there were no tables set up and no food. It was just Roehl, me, and his guards.

"Why are we here?" I asked. A sense of dread pricked at my skin. "What about lunch?"

"Oh, pet. You should know by now that vampires don't dine traditionally. And the throne room adds to the overall effect. Don't you agree?" He extended his arms out to his sides.

Something bad was about to happen. I could sense it.

"Come," Roehl said, walking toward the dais.

Roehl took a seat on one of the thrones and ordered me to sit next to him. I hesitated, knowing his evil mother once sat there. A wicked woman who played a part in Leora's death and Incendia's demise. And a huge reason I was here.

"Your father is still king," I said with a little too much sting.

A growl rumbled deep inside his chest; his eyes narrowed on me. "This throne is mine. It's merely a matter of time."

I felt sick and unsettled knowing what he meant. But I wasn't going to push it. I'd been on the receiving end of one of his outbursts. Besides, I was in no condition to take him on. Not while I was still weak because he barely kept me fed.

I heard a whisper—a still small voice inside my head that said, "*Sit, Calla. You are heir to this kingdom too.*" It was Leora.

I took a seat on the throne next to Roehl and participated in his game. I straightened my back, trying to act as nobly as possible . . . as much as I could in a skimpy red dress.

The guards bowed to Roehl, no doubt. I knew their allegiance to him was based on keeping their positions and their heads. Little did they know they were also bowing to me—great-granddaughter of their king and heir to this very throne. And sitting next to me was my half great-uncle, and it made me wonder. Would their allegiance turn if they were given an option?

One thing was certain. I didn't want to be part of this kingdom. I needed to find a way to heal the king so he could rule again. But the only way that could ever happen would be to defeat Roehl. And not only beat him. I'd have to kill him.

"Markus," Roehl called out. The towering, intimidating man strode forward.

"Yes, my prince," he said, bowing deeply.

"Bring our lunch."

"Yes, prince." He bowed again, his unreadable dark eyes flashed to me, pausing for a half-breath before he pivoted on his heel and departed the room.

When he entered a few moments later, I felt as if I'd been punched in the gut.

CHAPTER NINETEEN

Bound and gagged, two bodies were yanked into the room. The first was Lord Mathias, the mortal ruler of Morbeth, and the second — *No!*

My stomach sickened and my veins turned molten as I looked at Spring's terrified face. She was in a white bedgown, just like the ones I wore, which told me they must have taken her from bed.

"You bastard!" I cursed, glaring at Roehl.

He didn't answer. Just crossed his arms over his chest and watched as the guards halted a few feet before the dais, forcing Spring and Lord Mathias to their knees.

Spring's face was red and splotchy like she'd been crying for hours. Lord Mathias looked no better. He was pale, his expression one of sheer terror. His forest green eyes were bloodshot, like he'd had no sleep at all.

"Why are they here?" I demanded. I could feel the heat

of my rage smoldering under my skin. *Breathe. Breathe. Breathe.*

He smirked. "They are here because they were with you the night of your friend's disappearance," Roehl replied casually. "Lord Mathias was found in a broom cupboard, bound and muzzled, while the girl was sighted last night at a witch ceremony. It could have been her or my dark-haired servant." He was talking about Sabine. "But she's been with me for a lengthy time and knows my wrath. Still, anyone could betray me. None are within my grace."

"You have *no* evidence that they were part of Brynna's disappearance," I growled, rising from the throne. Gasps echoed throughout the room.

Apparently, no one ever opposed their prince.

Roehl's eyes went completely black at my outburst. His incisors lengthened—long and pointed. He was a demon. A blood demon.

In a blur, he stood in front of Lord Mathias, clutching a handful of his hair, and shoving his head backward to expose his throat. The Lord struggled against Roehl's solid grasp, an anguished scream burst from his nose, as his mouth was gagged.

Roehl twisted his head to me, his crimson rimmed eyes brazen with evil. In a split second, his teeth sunk deep into Lord Mathias's neck and the room fell silent, except for the sickening sound of Roehl feeding.

Spring's eyes rolled back, her body fell limp to the floor.

She'd fainted, and at that moment I was thankful she wasn't conscious to witness the grisly scene.

The sounds of Lord Mathias gurgling, drowning in his own blood, as Roehl clamped tight to his throat made me ill. The large man's body thrashed and convulsed as Roehl continued to drain the life from him.

Every guard in the room stood still and silent like the brick walls behind them. Their faces impassive.

How could they ignore this? Were they all as evil as Roehl?

Lord Mathias finally stopped struggling; his body went rigid, then limp. Roehl unlatched from his neck and shoved his chest with a finger, sending his large frame backward. It hit the floor with a thud, lifeless—his throat ripped out.

"Take him away," Roehl ordered. No remorse could be found in those red-rimmed obsidian eyes.

Two guards rushed to the body, each taking two limbs before lifting the man out of the room. Reaching into his pocket, Roehl pulled out a red handkerchief and gingerly wiped the blood from his lips and chin, but it did nothing to mask the blood on his white collared tunic.

Heat erupted deep in my core—a mix of fury and disgust. My power flickered against my skin, urging to be set free. But I had to hold it in.

I glanced at Spring's body on the floor and made a silent vow. I wouldn't let him get away with this. She was innocent. I knew she was. And Roehl knew it, too.

"I will not participate in whatever wicked game this is," I said, fisting my hands, squelching the rising heat in my palms, drawing slow and steady breaths.

Calm and collected, Roehl turned to me and said, "If you don't partake, then I shall dine on that sweet child myself."

"She is innocent, and you know it!" I roared.

In a flash, Roehl was inches away from me, his fingers wrapped securely around my throat. "Then tell me. If she is innocent, who is responsible of aiding your friends escape, Calla? Tell me now and I'll set her free."

I couldn't let Spring die. I would never, ever forgive myself. "You already know the answer to that question," I answered through gritted teeth.

His fingers relaxed a bit. "I know the Carpathian prince and his cadre are in on it. But there had to have been someone who helped from inside Morbeth. And I will drain every mortal here until I get answers."

"Why would you think anyone here would aid Carpathia? No one here has ties to my friend. I was the only one who knew Brynna was here."

His fingers tightened around my throat, practically cutting off my air. "Was it you, Calla?"

I clutched his hand and pushed out from his grasp. "Me?" The rage was now thundering in my ears. "How the hell could *I* take her? You had me tethered to the gods damned wall with a million guards outside my door!"

Spring moved. Her eyes flickered open to view the

pool of blood where Lord Mathias had taken his last breath. Gasping, she scurried backward on hands and knees, but a guard grabbed hold of her arm, halting her.

Her eyes. The fear in those big, green eyes was the same as I'd seen in my father's. The kind of fear that knows death is lurking nearby.

Roehl aimed his finger at Spring, but his bloodthirsty eyes remained locked on mine. "Feed. Or I will."

This was a test. A test he bet on me failing.

I didn't trust myself latching onto another human, and he knew it. He knew I was starving and wouldn't be strong enough to let go. Just like what had happened with Ms. Alcott. But that's what he wanted. That's why he brought me here. Not only to teach me a lesson, but he hoped I *would* kill her. If I did, it would prove to everyone in the palace that I was no better than he was. That I was a blood sucking murderer.

That was his intention. To make them hate me, to despise and fear me so deeply that no one would help me.

"Well?" he rumbled.

I stepped toward Spring. I wouldn't let him touch her.

Her breath quickened, and her body started trembling. She was already frightened of what I'd done to Ms. Alcott.

I stepped closer to her and stared into those wide, green eyes. "Spring. I promise I won't hurt you."

Roehl barked out in laughter behind me. "Just get it over with and make it quick. I have business to take care of."

Heat slithered around my chest and coiled up my neck.

265

This was my only chance to strike a bargain with him. "Do you think I'll kill her?" I asked, shooting a glare at him.

A casual shrug. "Why do you think I brought you to lunch? You're weak and starving, and it's been a while since I've reminded my guards what happens when their loyalty falters. Besides, I found out what happened to the poor old woman who tried to help you. If not for the others prying you off, she would be dead."

Prying me off? That was a lie. I let go of her myself.

I was about to snap a remark but bit my tongue.

"How about we make a deal?" I said. "If the girl lives, you set her free and don't ever get to use her as an example again."

With a tilt of his head, he considered my offer. "If you are capable of feeding and keeping her alive, I will set her free."

"I want your word," I said out loud so everyone in the throne room could hear.

He gave a sneer. "You have my word." Reading his expression, I knew he didn't expect I could do it. "And if you kill her—" he started.

I spun and glared at him. "Don't you realize that murdering an innocent and seeing her blood on my hands for the rest of my immortal life is punishment enough?"

He shrugged and stalked forward a few steps, getting into a better position to watch. "She won't be your first. You'll come to understand that it takes human blood for you to survive. Fatalities are bound to arise."

"There are other ways."

"Like what?" he spat in disgust. "Like sipping on donated blood out of a plastic container?" He let out an evil laugh, and the rest of the guards followed suit.

"It's humane," I growled.

"Mortals are nothing more than livestock that keep us fed. The fresher the blood, the stronger we become. Which is why *he* will never defeat me or my army."

Gods, Roehl was worse than I could have imagined. I despised him with every fragment of my being.

I looked into Spring's eyes, which reminded me of fresh grass on a warm spring day.

"Trust me," I uttered softly, plucking a wet strand of her golden hair from her cheek, and tucking it behind her ear.

Through bloodshot, tear-filled eyes, Spring nodded and inclined her head to the side, offering me her fair and flawless neck. She trusted me. This girl who was afraid of me. I had to save her. I couldn't let her down.

So much was riding on this one event. It would prove to everyone bearing witness just how weak or how strong I truly was. It would also prove to me if I was someone who could hold my word. Or would my loyalty be demolished because of the thirst?

I said a silent prayer to the gods, to my mother, and to Leora, to give me strength. Strength to save this beautiful girl who had a full life ahead of her, even if it was in this gods-forsaken country. Strength to help me unlatch before I killed her.

I was just about to bite Spring when Roehl spoke. "I'll make you an even better deal."

I stood strong and faced him, revealing my interest.

"To save this human from becoming food, you have the option to sire her."

"Never!" I said through gritted teeth. "I would never put anyone in that position. Especially her."

"Why? You'll save her from sickness and aging. She'll make a beautiful immortal."

"That's not my decision to make. I am not a god, nor do I wish to play one."

He threw me a villainous grin. "But you don't seem to mind that Prince Trystan sired you, without your consent. Am I right?"

Oh, this prick. He knew he was pushing the right buttons. I had to breathe to keep my sanity and my head straight. My hands were fisted so tight, I could feel my nails digging into my palms.

"Thought so." Roehl casually shrugged, crossing his arms over his chest. "I was simply proposing a way to give this child a better life, since it seems you care so much for her."

"A better life? By killing her and changing her into a monster? Her life is of no less importance than mine . . . or yours. I refuse to make that decision for her." There was no way I would sire her. Every mortal in the castle would despise me, especially Summer and Sabine.

"Pathetic," he spat. His face a mask of revulsion and frustration. "A bleeding heart makes you weak and will get you killed."

I stood firm, scowling at him. "I'd rather possess a bleeding heart than no heart at all."

He let out a devilish laugh. "My time and patience are waning, pet. Feed or sire. Make a choice, or I will."

I knew if I didn't do something soon, he'd make a move. I shifted my attention back to Spring and gave her a look of reassurance. "You'll be okay," I confided.

Tears pooled in her eyes as she gave me a nod. That simple act added to the fuel inside me. To fight to keep her alive.

I leaned forward, and as I watched her pulse thrumming in her neck, my incisors lengthened. I heard Spring's heart beating strong and fast and could literally taste her fear. Sweat beaded across her forehead and dribbled down the sides of her face.

I wouldn't hurt her. I couldn't. I would feed enough to heal myself and pull away.

Inches away, I could already feel the weight of the thirst drawing me tighter, urging me to consume.

I am stronger than the thirst. I can conquer it. I will keep her alive.

The words resonated through my mind as the room fell dead silent. I could feel the weight of their stares.

Watching.

Waiting.

Waging.

Spring sucked in a heavy breath and let it out, her eyes bloodshot and glazed, her quivering, sweet voice cracked the silence. "It's okay, Calla. I forgive you, no matter what happens."

My tears dripped onto the floor as I stared at this brave, young girl. She'd already forgiven me—the monster who was about to feed on her.

CHAPTER TWENTY

"Tick. Tick. Tick," Roehl growled. "Feed now or I'll have Markus escort you back to your chamber. Anyone else here would be more than eager to take your place. The thirst never ends."

No. I would do this. For her. And for her mother.

I decided to bite her in the same area Trystan bit me. The tender area where the neck and shoulder met.

I said another prayer as I held her arms steady. Then, I sank my teeth into her butter-soft flesh.

Spring whimpered as her fresh blood burst into my mouth. A swell of greed and power blasted through my cells. It was regenerating. Strengthening. Healing.

Everything around me became subdued and numb . . . fading into the background. The hunger had seized hold of me and was yanking me further, deeper into its bloodthirsty

I heard a voice above the thirst. Quiet, yet powerful.

Stop, Calla.

But I couldn't stop.

Her blood was like a drug, dominating every part of me. It didn't want me to stop. My weak body had given in much too quickly to the bloodlust. It needed it. Craved it. Demanded it.

Calla. The voice cried out again, this time louder. But my body resisted.

Calla! Stop. You're killing her!

Killing. I was killing Spring. The innocent girl I'd made a promise to.

Against my body's will, I fought. Fought through the numbness and the high and the ruthless strength of the thirst, and pushed away from Spring, screaming at the top of my lungs.

In slow motion, I watched her limp body fall to the floor. I collapsed to my knees, blood dripping from my chin onto the obsidian marble.

No one moved. Their stares were latched on me with expressions I couldn't interpret.

A soft moan escaped Spring's lips.

Alive. She was still alive.

"How did you release in the middle of feeding, when every guard in this castle has failed?" Roehl roared, his expression cold as ice. "Even when ordered to feed on those dearest them."

This was my chance, with his royal guards surrounding him. I rose and faced Roehl, my legs strong and steady, my body still humming as the blood coursed through my veins, restoring, reviving, working its magic.

"You are an evil narcissist, and I would never want to live in a place with you as king."

"You have no choice, pet," he stated with a deadly calm. "It's only a matter of time when the only family you'll have left is me."

"I hate you," I said, my words slow and sure.

He laughed and stalked over to me, his eyes moving to Spring. "Take her away."

One of the guards approached her. "Where do I take her?"

Roehl waved him off. "I don't give a damn. Finish her off and dispose of the body."

"What?" I roared. "You promised! You promised if I let go, you'd set her free."

His head dipped, his crimson glare narrowed on me. "I am keeping my word. She *will* be free and never be fed upon again."

"You lying bastard!" I made a fist and swung at Roehl's face, but he caught my wrist and twisted my arm behind my back.

Applying pressure, my wrist snapped. I wailed in agony, twisting out of his grasp.

The pain. The rage. It was overwhelming. The heat inside my bones grew until I could no longer contain what was writhing beneath my skin.

Before Roehl could react, I slammed my fist against his chest. Power and flame burst from me, sending him hurtling backwards. His body crashed against the brick wall, blasting shards of cinder and mortar dust across the room.

His guards didn't move, nor did they utter a word. Their mouths were wide in either dismay or awe. I couldn't tell.

Roehl's face contorted with fury. I prepared for him to charge toward me with a bone-crushing blow, but he rose, laughed, and casually dusted himself off. If this was a tactic for me to drop my guard, it wasn't working. I raised my hands in front of me. Hands that were consumed in flame. Blue and orange and red flames danced in my palms and through my fingers. The magic of Incendia was alive and wanted to play.

I felt that immense power when I struck him, and I felt it was only the tip of the iceberg.

Roehl waved a finger at me. "You were hiding power from me and protected it well. I knew there was something more to you. I could sense it."

I didn't have time to ponder the consequences. He'd seen my power, but he had no idea what more I could do, because even I didn't know the full extent of my power.

He took a step toward me. "You can't harm me here, pet. I'm always prepared."

Before I could voice a word, three black-hooded figures stepped into the throne room, immediately suppressing the fire from my palms. I tried to call it back, to will it back, but it died. No heat, no spark, nothing. My power was snuffed out, just like that.

I could feel the tendrils of their shadowy, dark magic crawling through the room, coiling around my frame, strangling whatever magic I had inside. I struggled to move, but every muscle was locked. Frozen.

"Are you afraid of me, Roehl?" I hissed.

His eyes went fire red. "Never afraid, pet. This is simply a safeguard until I learn the full extent of your power."

Lies. I knew my power rocked him, and he didn't like it. I'd given him a taste of his own medicine, and it pissed him off.

Markus took a step toward Roehl, his eyes latched on me. "What is she?" he asked.

"The last of her kind," he declared, indicating he already knew. Bastard. "I want Nicolae to meet his granddaughter, my future mate, before I rip his head from his shoulders."

Markus shifted his attention to Roehl. "Is she—"

"Incendian royalty." He casually stalked toward me with his arms folded behind his back, moving so close I could feel his breath against my cheek. Then Roehl froze, his gaze narrowing, before he pressed his ear to the middle of my chest.

Swine.

His eyes lifted to meet mine with a vicious glare that sent a chill deep in my bones.

"You are something. A vampire with a beating heart," he announced coolly. Gasps erupted from the surrounding guards.

A beating heart? "What the hell are you talking about?" I growled.

He slowly stalked around me, sniffing me like a dog. "After Lord Mathias was expelled and the girl was left, I heard an extra heartbeat in the room. The question is, my pet . . how is that possible?"

"You expect me to know the reason?" I replied through gritted teeth. Was it true? Was my heart still beating?

Leora's words sounded in my head. *Above all else, guard your heart.*

She knew. Maybe it was her magic that had protected my heart.

"Can you imagine how powerful our offspring will be?" Roehl spoke. "Hybrids of the most potent blood."

Bile rose in my throat. "You're disgusting. I will never bond with you or bear offspring for you . . . grand uncle." I addressed him with contempt.

Markus's face contorted, his eyes scanning between Roehl and me. "Grand Uncle?"

Roehl's lip curled above razor-sharp incisors. "It seems my father managed to sink his pole into foreign waters before he married my mother. Incendian waters."

Markus's brow furrowed deeply as if he was trying to piece together the puzzle laid out before him.

Roehl exhaled. "The elusive, Nicolae Corvus, is my bastard half-brother. The man who murdered Rurik."

"You're a liar!" I yelled, the words shooting out of my mouth. "You plotted to murder Nicolae—to eliminate any threat to your throne. But Nicolae found out you were coming and defended himself. I know the truth. What he did was done in self-defense."

"You know nothing!" The room rattled with Roehl's rage. Instantly, he was in front of me, his fingers wrapped around my neck like a vice.

"I know more than you realize," I choked. "And it didn't require dark mages to inform me."

The mages hissed, and I felt their power squeeze tighter, compressing my rib cage, making it harder to breathe.

"Who told you?" He roared.

I smiled, knowing it ticked him off. "The dead."

"Don't lie to me," he squeezed, cutting off my air. Darkness edged my eyes, and right before I passed out, he let go. I dropped to the floor, gasping for air before glaring up at him.

"I didn't lie." My voice was gravelly.

A guard clad in Morbeth's black and red fighting leathers walked in and murmured in Roehl's ear.

Roehl growled then stalked over, taking a knee beside me. "I have to leave, but I'll deal with you when I return." He snatched my face with his fingers and pressed his lips against mine.

I bit his lip, and he pushed me back, then licked the blood dripping from the minor wound I left. His crimson eyes flickered. "Oh, we're going to have fun, pet. I prefer a fiery girl."

I didn't respond. I didn't even look at him.

He turned to Markus. "Take her and the girl to the dungeon. To the *special* chamber." His gaze moved to the mages. "I demand you accompany them and make certain no one enters or exits that cell without the pain of death."

The mages bowed their heads.

"What about a healer for the girl?" Markus asked, nodding to Spring's limp body lying on the floor.

The sight caused bile to rise in my throat. I hated myself for taking it that far. For nearly killing her. If she died, I would never forgive myself. I made her a promise. A promise I nearly broke, if not for the voice in my head.

"She's lucky to be alive," Roehl replied with no regard. "No one is allowed in the cell until I return. The guards can slide them some bread and water, nothing else."

"And what about Calla?" Markus asked. That was the first time he'd used my name.

Roehl glanced at me with distaste. "If she needs to feed, the girl's body is at her disposal."

"You bastard," I growled. I knew they'd be gone for weeks, at least. Unless Roehl had a company of Wanderers to whisk them to Northfall and back in seconds, which I doubted.

He didn't reply or even cast a glance in my direction. Roehl laid his hand on Markus's shoulder. "You're in charge while I'm gone. You realize what will happen if anything goes wrong."

Markus placed his fisted hand in the center of his chest and bowed deeply. "Yes, my prince."

"Tell the men I'll meet them at the front gate in a half hour," Roehl commanded the guard that came in. Then he marched out of the room without another word.

Markus took Spring in his arms. He then made a gesture with his head, and two guards flanked my sides. They both hesitated, as if they were afraid to touch me.

"I'm not the cruel one here," I said, folding my hands behind my back. "And I won't do anything to get you in trouble." Their brows furrowed as they glanced at each other. As did Markus's.

I didn't want them to think I was a tyrant like their prince. They should know there were decent and respectable people beyond their Red Wall. Beyond their huge prison called Morbeth. Leaders who cared for their people and about their well-being, who didn't make them submit out of fear.

The hallways were eerily quiet as we made our way to the door that led down into the dungeon. "How are Roehl's guards able to travel in daylight if they aren't pureblood?" I inquired.

It was Markus who replied. "Magic. Roehl puts a cover of obscurity over them, which protects them from the light."

Of course.

I drew in a deep breath, savoring the smells of the blossoming flowers and fresh air around us, knowing that once we were on the other side of that wretched door, the stench of misery and death would be awaiting.

Sadness and fear enveloped me as Markus opened the door and we descended back into the dark and suffocating bowels of hell. We seemed to walk even further than before, to an area no guards were posted, and then down another unusually long, dark corridor. There were no cells along these walls, just one solitary door at the end. *The special cell.*

One of the guards unlocked the door and tugged on the handle. Even with his vampire strength, it took some prying before the door cracked open. It was obvious this cell wasn't used in an exceptionally long time. It must have been for those who were left and forgotten.

Inside the cell, there were no windows or light. Just a boundless darkness lying in wait, ready for the doors to shut before it swallowed us whole.

Another guard from behind us, bearing a torch, entered first. The cell was the same size as my former one, with another crude toilet—a board with a hole in it lying over a pail, and a musty pile of hay against the far wall.

"Fetch them clean water," Markus ordered one of the guards. He carried Spring's limp body into the cell and set her gently on the bundle of hay. A couple of rats scattered from within and ran out the exit.

The guard returned with a bucket of water and set it in a corner, then hustled out.

Markus turned his dark eyes to me, and he didn't need to speak. His eyes told me what he was feeling. A mix of sadness and concern, maybe even regret. "You will have to remain here until the prince returns."

"I know." I wasn't worried about me. I was concerned about Spring, wondering if she would survive until he came back.

As Markus stepped outside of the cell, the three mages stepped up to the threshold. They raised their arms and started chanting in an unfamiliar tongue—words that sent a shudder down my spine and caused all the hair on my body to stand erect.

Red veins stretched along the walls inside the cell until the entire room was pulsing, as if it were alive.

"What is that?" I asked.

"A spell to keep you in and everyone else out," was Markus's terse response.

When the mages were finished, they turned around and shuffled away under cover of their large dark cowls. Then Markus began to close the door.

"Wait," I pleaded, and he halted. "Please tell Sabine what happened to Spring. Her mother needs to know."

Without responding, Markus closed the door, sealing Spring and I in that suffocating darkness.

I didn't expect him to respond. He was captain of the guard and had orders to follow. I just hoped he'd at least grant me that one favor and tell Sabine what happened.

In the darkness, with my arms extended in front of me, I slowly shuffled forward, feeling for the bed of hay. When I finally bumped into it, I reached down and felt Spring's warm arm. Kneeling next to her, I found her neck and pressed my fingers against one side. Her pulse was weak, but she was still alive.

"Spring, please hold on. I'm so sorry. I won't let you die."

It was a hollow promise but keeping her alive was now my main priority.

CHAPTER TWENTY–ONE

It could have been days, but I wouldn't know. Time was nonexistent in the pitch-black cell. I was afraid to sleep, wondering if Spring's frail life would slip away if I shut my eyes, even for a moment. The thought of being alone in the asphyxiating darkness was frightening enough.

The question remained.

Would Markus let Sabine know? Did anyone, besides Roehl and his guards, know we were down here?

I had a sinking feeling no one would come for us, especially with the mage's spell on the cell. No one was foolish enough to risk death.

Spring was still unconscious, but her even breaths were a welcome sound.

I felt for the bucket of water and pulled it closer. Tearing off a portion of the bottom of my dress, I made a small washcloth. Although I couldn't see, I spent time wiping down her face and arms, dropping water on her lips. I knew it wasn't enough to keep her alive. If she ever woke up, she would need food and a healer.

As time ticked on, the darkness was getting to me. But the longer I remained in this silent isolation, I started to hear a gentle, familiar voice in the recesses of my mind.

Your gift has never left you, Calla. Neither has it weakened. The mages have masked it, a trick to cause you to doubt. They want you to think it's gone, but they cannot stop or suppress it. Push through their wicked veil. The power of Incendia is much stronger than any dark magic. You must believe in it. Believe in yourself.

Light. I possessed a light inside that could cut through this endless darkness.

I reflected to my visit with Leora, the Princess of Incendia, and how much she believed in me. I was her heir, a royal with the power of the fire goddess inside of me. I couldn't doubt it, because if I did, I wouldn't only be letting her down, but would allow the dark mages of Morbeth to win again. And I wouldn't let that happen.

I let the hope and belief of who I was seep deep down into my bones, flooding the doubt and fear, replacing it with a warming heat. Out loud, I called to the power of Incendia and the fire goddess and ordered it to come to me—the new wielder of its flame.

My hands started to heat, and as I held my palms up in front of me, they burst into flame. The brilliant light gobbled up the darkness, and with that light, I could breathe again.

I held my hands over Spring, illuminating her frail body, but she was still asleep and unresponsive. I had to do something. I had to find a way to help her.

Scurrying noises on the far wall diverted my attention. I aimed my palms toward the movement. There, at the bottom of the stone wall, was a slight hole. It didn't surprise me that the rats had a way in and out. They were probably the same ones who had run out when we came in and were trying to get back to their beds within the hay.

Silently, I observed a large rodent poke its snout out of the hole. The reddish veins in the cell's wall began to pulse as if it was waking from slumber.

As the rat stepped further into the cell, the veins turned dark crimson. Then, those pulsing red capillaries started to move like slithering snakes toward the rat. They seemed to be alive, trailing the movement of the rodent attempting to breach the cell.

The rat stepped halfway into the cell when those red veins moved off the wall and coiled around it. The sound of bones crunching filled the chamber before the rat let out a tortured scream. Its limbs and tail twitched before it finally stilled, blood oozed from its orifices.

Heavens above.

The curse. *No one enters or exits the cell without the pain of death.* I guess that included the vermin. We were stuck here until Roehl returned.

I needed sleep—craved it. Not only because I was exhausted, but because the thought of seeing Trystan again offered me hope. Yet falling asleep was virtually impossible. I had too many distractions keeping me wide awake. The biggest of which was making sure Spring stayed alive and breathing.

Sighing, I sat down on the ground, my back resting against the stack of hay. During the following hours, I called my flame over and over, and each time I did, it came to me, faster and easier. After some time, I found I could shape the fire into a ball between my palms. And if I concentrated enough, I could make it expand, growing wider and brighter, or smaller and dimmer.

I wondered what would happen if I tossed that fiery ball against the cursed cell wall. Could I kill it? Leora said my power was stronger than any dark magic. I wanted to test it out and see if it was true.

I rose to my feet and aimed for the wall that had taken the poor rat's life. I called a flame and drew my arm backward. Thrusting it forward, the flame shot from my palm and slammed into the wall, exploding in a burst of blinding light.

The red veins in the walls pulsed brightly, revealing the curse was still intact.

Dammit.

I tried again and again, but every time I threw my flame, those red veins would respond. They weren't fading. But I had to admit, the sight of it pulsing did bring some satisfaction. I considered that with each blast; I was weakening, or maybe even hurting that curse.

In between practicing, I gathered some hay, bundling it securely together with a piece of fabric from my dress and made a small torch. It helped free up my hands so I could tend to Spring. The light kept me sane but also revealed how frail and pale Spring had become. She was dying. Her breath and pulse were slowing, and there was nothing I could do.

I promised myself I wouldn't change her into a blood-sucking monster that had to survive off the blood of others. And I would keep that promise, even if her life was dangling by a thread.

Time crept on and on. Countless seconds, minutes, hours, days. I couldn't tell. It had all fused together.

As I lay back, humming a song my mother used to sing, Spring screamed. I shot up off the floor, aiming my flaming palms toward her face, discovering she was still unconscious.

"Spring," I said, dousing the flame in my left palm. I touched her forehead, and she was burning up. Or was it me? Maybe my hands were heated from countless hours of calling the flames.

Beads of perspiration streaked down her face. I lowered my flame to her shoulder and saw the bite marks I'd left. They were red and inflamed. They weren't healing, and possibly the cause of an infection.

"Please," I begged the air, anything, or anyone who could hear me. "Please don't let her die."

I curled up next to her on the hay, a small flame burning in the palm of my hand, watching her chest rise and fall, listening to her constant but shallow breaths exit from her lips. Each breath meant hope.

But after a while, my eyes grew heavy. I didn't want to sleep and leave Spring unattended, but knew it'd been days.

When my eyelids became too heavy, I extinguished the flame from my palm, wrapped my arm around Spring's waist, and closed my eyes. I wasn't sure if I was sleeping because the darkness was still there. But then, I heard a familiar voice within the blackness.

"I was wondering when you'd fall asleep, my pet."

No. No. No.

"You were expecting someone else?"

"No," I lied. "Get the hell out of my mind."

"You have no say in the matter. When I return from Northfall with Nicolae, we'll have a lot to discuss. Especially after witnessing the power you possess. You will be a great benefit to my Kingdom."

We were still in darkness, and I was glad for that. I didn't want to see his face.

"Morbeth is not my kingdom, and I will never become your pawn."

"But, pet. You already are."

I didn't respond. He didn't deserve my words. Not after what he made me do to Spring.

"You offer me silence? Well, we'll talk soon enough."

"Wait!" I exclaimed. "Spring needs a healer. She'll die if she doesn't get help."

"You think you can bargain with me now? If she dies, it's on you."

"You bastard."

He laughed. "You are weak because of her."

"I know your weakness, Roehl. You have no heart. And if you did, it would be black and calloused all the way through."

"Ah, but have you not heard that when placed under severe pressure, the blackest, hardest stone turns into a precious gem? A gem greatly desired by all, and stronger than all others."

"I've never desired precious gems," I said.

He laughed, and I wished I could meet him in the dream, just for a moment, so I could send a fireball to his face.

I heard him growl, low and guttural. "You'll learn not to contend with me, pet."

Then, just like that, his presence dissipated.

I smiled to myself, knowing I'd won this match against him.

Continuing to search through the darkness, I hoped to see a light—a path that would lead me to Trystan.

"Trystan," I called out. "Trystan?"

"Calla?" I could hear him, but his voice was distant. Muffled.

"Trystan, where are you?" I was desperate to find him. Desperate to meet him again. To tell him what happened when

I was ripped from his arms in my last dream.

"Calla, there's a block. I can't get through." Trystan's voice was fading.

Then I heard another voice. The voice of the wicked snake Roehl, strong and clear. "You can't hide anything from me, pet." There was an evil bite to his words.

"I hate you!" I shouted. "Just leave me alone." There was a pause before I heard Roehl's laughter. "What do you want from me?"

"I was wondering what the Prince of Carpathia thought, hearing you shout that you hated him and wanted him to leave you alone."

My chest felt like it had been struck with a sledgehammer. "I never said those words to him."

"Yes, but he doesn't realize that. Only you can hear my voice, and after you yelled those awful words, I cut off the connection between you. Treacherous girl. I don't know how you managed to restore the bond, but you'll learn that I know everything. I know where you are, when you're awake, and when you're asleep."

"Leave. Me. Alone!" I snapped out each word, spiked with bitterness and hate. And then, I felt Roehl's presence leave like a frigid wind.

But now Trystan was gone too. Blocked again by that bastard.

I was crushed. The thought of Trystan thinking I shouted that I hated and never wanted to see him again . . . I couldn't bear it. I could only believe he knew those words weren't meant for him.

I needed to get out of this nightmare and wake up. *Wake up!*

My eyes opened to see the walls glowing and pulsing in a deep crimson. Then it stopped. Something was wrong. Was I still sleeping?

"Calla!" a voice called from beyond the door.

"Sabine?" Fear surged through me at the thought of her coming in and being bound and crushed to death by the veined curse. "Don't open the door! You'll die."

"I know," she responded.

But how was she here? Was I still dreaming?

The lock clanked and the entrance to the cell swung open. But it wasn't Sabine who walked in. It was Markus.

"Hurry. You must come at once," he said, holding his hand out to me.

"Markus? How did you get in?"

"They'll explain." He pulled me up to my feet, then headed for Spring and lifted her swiftly into his arms.

As I moved toward the exit, Sabine and Summer were just beyond the doorway.

Behind them, standing against the walls, were six others in white robes holding wands in their hands, aimed at the three dark mages who had cursed the cell.

Sabine ran over and grasped my wrist, pulling me out. "You have to leave now."

"What about Spring?"

"We'll take care of her," Summer replied. "This is your only chance, Calla."

Markus exited with Spring in his arms. "Put the mages inside and spell it," he ordered, and the white witches moved, forcing the dark mages into the cell.

"You will all perish," one of the mages roared, her voice gravelly.

"Like we haven't heard that before," a white witch snapped, slamming the door shut. Then, the six white witches faced the cell, wands up, casting a spell over it.

"It won't last long. A few hours at most," the oldest of them said when the spell was completed.

Summer came over to me and took my hand, drawing me out of the hallway and toward the stairs.

"Markus told us what happened. I know you were forced to do it, and I don't blame you."

I didn't know what to say. Emotions bubbled inside and began to spill over. "I'm so sorry."

"Don't be." Summer hugged me. "You're already forgiven."

I wiped the tears from my eyes as we moved up the dank stairwell. Then, I glanced back at Markus, carrying Spring, who had just risked his life to save us. "Why?"

"Because what he did was wrong," is all he said.

That was enough of an answer for me. Markus, the head of the king's guard, had confirmed there was good in this wicked country.

When we made it to the top and exited into the bright flowery hall, Markus gently laid Spring's body on the floor. Summer and the rest of the white witches kneeled around her. They held their wands over her body and recited a spell in unison. In moments, Spring's eyelids fluttered open.

"Spring," I breathed, dropping to my knees at her side

She sat up and took my hand. "Calla. You saved my life. You kept your promise."

I tried to hold my tears in, but they spilled uncontrollably. "You were hurt and sent to the cell because of me."

"We must leave," one of the white witches said. "We could be captured at any moment."

"Go," the oldest one spoke. Five of them stood and hurried away.

"Wait," I responded. "I need to see the king. I have to speak to him."

Markus stepped beside me, offering me a hand. "Come with me. I'll take you."

I grabbed his hand and he pulled me up. "What about the guards attending him?"

He gave a half-grin. "They've been relieved of their duties. Indefinitely."

"You killed them?"

"I had help," he stated, shifting his gaze to the oldest witch.

"Spring can't stay here," I urged. "Roehl will kill her."

"I'm taking her to Northfall," Summer said, "back to

our home and our family. We're already packed and ready to leave. We'll detour through Havendale to avoid Roehl and his men."

I exhaled in relief. I didn't want any more lives in danger because of me. I stepped toward Spring and gave her a hug. "Be safe. I hope our paths cross again."

"I'm counting on it," she replied, hugging me back.

Summer came to me next, holding both of my hands in hers. "May the goddess be with you. And may the light of Incendia defeat all darkness."

"Thank you," I said. "For everything." She bowed and took her daughters hand, then moved to stand near the oldest witch. "Calla, this is my mother, Aurelia. She is one of the most powerful white witches in Morbeth."

I bowed my head to her. "Thank you for rescuing us. I wish we had more time, but we don't."

"Yes," Aurelia agreed. "We must hurry if you are to speak to the king and make your escape. Once the dark mages break free from the cell, their vengeance will be great."

We said our last goodbyes before parting ways with Spring and Summer. Aurelia came with us as Markus swiftly led the way to the king's chamber. Three headless bodies were sprawled on the floor outside the door.

"Don't ask," Markus said, rushing past them. "The king is inside."

I followed closely to discover more dead bodies sprawled out on the ground. Did Markus do this to his own guards? If he did, there was no way Roehl would let him live. And I was certain he would make it slow and painful, especially if I was missing.

Markus stopped in front of two broad wooden doors, embellished with gold.

"Go. Our time is running out," he said.

I moved past him, swinging the doors wide, stepping into a great, lavish bedroom. Thick velvet draperies were drawn over the windows, the room illuminated by candles and a crackling fire in the fireplace. Against the far wall was a huge bed. And lying in that bed was a man.

I moved closer, my heart racing.

The figure lying there wasn't just the King of Morbeth, Romulus Tynan.

He was my great-grandfather.

CHAPTER TWENTY–TWO

As I walked to the side of the bed, my breath hitched at the sight of the king's gaunt face. He had shoulder-length chestnut hair, graying on the sides, with a full mustache and beard. His body was still, eyes closed.

Upon closer inspection, I watched his chest rise and fall with steady, heavy breaths.

"Your majesty." I spoke softly, reaching my right hand toward him, gently nudging his shoulder. "Majesty?"

He didn't move.

"He's under a sleeping spell," Aurelia said.

"Can you help him? Can you remove the spell?"

She stepped forward, lifting her wand, and kept it hovering an inch above the king's body, moving it from head to toe while reciting a spell. I didn't pay much attention because my eyes were fastened to his face. A face with an unmistakable resemblance to the face I saw in Melaina's water bowl. The face of his son, Nicolae.

But what was I going to say to him when he woke? Would he believe who I was, or anything I said?

Aurelia went silent, stepping back behind me. When I shifted my attention back to the king, I noticed his arm twitch, and then saw movement under his eyelids.

His eyes popped open. They were a rich chestnut brown but horribly bloodshot.

"Go ahead, dear," Aurelia said quietly over my shoulder. "Say what you must but make it quick."

I nodded, taking a step closer. The king's head lolled to the side, meeting my gaze.

My heart was thundering inside my chest, and I knew if I didn't speak now, I'd lose all train of thought.

"Your majesty, I'm sorry to barge in like this, but we don't have much time."

The king's tired eyes fixed on mine, broadening. His trembling fingers reached for my face.

"Leora?" His voice was weak and hoarse; a tear seeped from the corner of his eye. "Leora?"

I glanced back to Aurelia, and she gave me a slight nod.

Taking another step closer, I reached for his hand. It was ice cold. "No, sir. My name is Calla Caldwell." I paused, gathering my courage. "I am Leora's great-granddaughter. *Your* great-granddaughter."

The king's expression was unreadable. His eyes shifted to Aurelia, and then to Markus, who both confirmed it was true. Then, his weak, shaky hand gripped mine. Tears slipped from his tired eyes before his trembling lips uttered, "Great-granddaughter?"

I nodded. "Yes. My grandfather is Nicolae Corvus, your firstborn son from Princess Leora of Incendia."

The king pressed his fingers to the bridge of his nose and closed his eyes. "What happened to me?" he asked.

Markus came to his bedside, on the opposite side of me, and bowed his head. "My king, Roehl put a spell on you after Rurik's death. Then, he issued a death decree for Nicolae Corvus and his entire bloodline."

The king struggled to sit up but couldn't. He was still too weak. "Treacherous son," he declared through gritted teeth. "How did he happen to learn of Nicolae?"

I sat on his bedside, his hand still in mine. "The late Queen told Roehl about Nicolae and cautioned him of the threat to the throne and his future as king. After hearing this, Roehl plotted to murder Nicolae and convinced Rurik to join him. But somehow, Nicolae found out about their plan, and when they came to murder him, Rurik happened to be in the wrong place at the wrong time."

The king's expression was one of complete bewilderment. "How do you know all of this?"

I shook my head, realizing how hard it was to believe. "It's a long story. But in short, I participated in a séance during the Shadow Fest, and in the In-Between, I met Princess Leora. She's the one who told me everything." I grasped both of his hands. "She wanted me to tell you that she still loves you and has been watching over you all these years."

"Leora," he murmured to himself. "I've never ceased loving her." He closed his eyes, then opened them again, this time with a stern look. "Where is Roehl?"

Markus bowed again. "Majesty, he's on his way to Northfall in hopes to capture Nicolae. We don't have much time, my king. The guards loyal to Roehl will arrive soon."

I gazed deep into the king's eyes. "I'm leaving Morbeth, and I want you to come with me."

"No," he replied. "I won't leave my kingdom."

"Roehl will come back. He wants your throne, and I have no doubt that he'll kill you to get it."

The king slowly sat up and stood from the bed, his strength steadily returning. "Don't fret, child. When Roehl returns, I will be ready for him. I am King of Morbeth, and I will make sure my kingdom survives his betrayal." He took hold of my hand. "Do you have a place to go?"

I nodded. "I'm going to Incendia."

The king's eyes swam with sadness. "All of Incendia lies in ruins. I'm afraid you won't find much there."

I squeezed his hand. "Princess Leora said that most of my answers are there, and I feel a call. I have to go."

The king slowly nodded before gesturing to Markus. Markus stepped to the side of me, then bowed deeply. "Your Majesty?"

The king placed his palms on Markus's shoulders. "I want

you to leave Morbeth and travel with my great-granddaughter. Guard her. Keep her safe. This is my decree."

Markus looked at the king, and then at me with widened eyes. I was just as shocked as he was.

"Yes, your Majesty," he responded with another bow.

"Behind the tapestry," the king spoke. Raising his arm, he pointed at a specific one hanging against the far wall of him on a great black stallion that reminded me of my horse Shadow. "There is a loose stone. Remove it and take whatever sacks of gold skrag are inside." Markus did as he said and drew out six small sacks. "Head to the docks at Crimson Cove," the king continued, "and seek out Captain Sebastian Salloway. Tell him I sent you. If he doesn't believe you, tell him I should have believed the story he told me at the Mermaid's Tavern. He'll understand."

"I want you to come with us," I pleaded. "Who knows what Roehl will do once he returns and finds out what happened. He's powerful and dangerous."

"I will not deny that my son has great power, but that power is also his weakness and blinds him to a great many things surrounding him. I have lived a much longer life than he, and trust me, this time, I won't be easily deceived. I have powerful witches in my kingdom, like Aurelia, who can protect me." Aurelia bowed before Romulus, confirming her loyalty. "Now that I am aware of his treachery, I will prepare. I will be ready."

I could only hope he was right.

I swung my attention to Aurelia. "Roehl said he is able to find me no matter where I am because of the partial blood bond. Is there any way to remove it?"

"Yes," she answered. "I can remove it."

"Can it remove the bond with Roehl, while allowing another bond to remain?"

She shook her head. "I'm afraid not. The spell is not specific."

That meant the bond with Trystan would be severed and he would never know the truth. But I had no choice. "It has to be done," I said. "Remove it."

Aurelia nodded and aimed her wand at my chest. As she closed her eyes and murmured a spell, a wave of power slammed into me, causing my body to jolt back, setting my veins on fire. But before my knees buckled, Markus caught me from behind and steadied me on my feet.

"It's done," Aurelia finally said. Her vivid green eyes, just like Spring's, glimmered. "You're free."

"That fast?" I breathed.

She smiled and bowed her head. "That fast."

"Calla," the king spoke. "I wish I had more time with you, but I do believe our paths will cross again in the future." He clutched both of my hands in his. "I pray the gods offer you safe passage to Incendia, and that you find whatever it is you are seeking. Remember, you will always have a home here. You are an heir to Morbeth's throne."

"Thank you." I wasn't sure if it was appropriate, but I

threw my arms around the King's waist and pressed him in a hug. "Please be safe," I breathed. He hugged me back and kissed the top of my forehead.

"Don't worry about me, dear child," he countered, stepping backward. "Without the spell, I will steadily regain my strength." He then gave me a look of adoration. "I'm deeply sorry for what you've suffered. Roehl will pay for what he has done." He cupped my face in his large hands and gave a melancholy smile. "You have her eyes."

I wanted to spend more time with him but knew those devoted to Roehl would soon come for us. And now that the bond was severed, Roehl would know something was amiss, and likely return.

"Go," Aurelia urged. "The spell won't keep the dark mages much longer."

"Will you be safe?" I asked her.

"Yes. After you leave, I'll put a protection spell around the king and his chamber. Summer has made the other witches aware of what has taken place. We won't let the dark mages take control of the king or his castle anymore."

"I will have the mages who served with Roehl executed," the king declared. "I'll also seek to locate your father and assure his safety."

"Calla," Markus urged.

I turned back to the King, thankful he was back in command, knowing he could keep my father alive. "Thank you. I'll see you again." I gave him one last bow, but he took my arms and drew me back into a strong embrace.

"Thank you for freeing me, Calla. I'm sorry it was under these circumstances to have finally met you, but I am grateful the gods allowed us this time. And I assure you, I won't let you down."

A tear trickled down my cheek. I could feel his words down to my core. They were true and sincere. I drew out of his embrace and turned to Aurelia.

"Please, take care of him."

"I will, princess," she said, bowing her head.

I didn't have time to debate the title she'd flung at me, because Markus grabbed my wrist and hauled me out of the room.

"Stay silent," he said, unsheathing his sword. Someone was coming.

A figure appeared from around a corner, and just before Markus swung, Sabine threw up her hands.

"No! Wait! I'm with you."

"Sabine?" I choked.

She nodded, out of breath, then shuffled next to me with a large sack slung over her shoulder. "I had to grab a few things. Did you think I'd let you leave on an adventure without me?" A mischievous grin rose on her lips.

I snatched her arm and linked mine around it. "You're really coming?"

"Do you think I would stay in Morbeth after what Roehl did to Spring? It would only be a matter of time before I was next. Besides, I have supplies. And extra clothes. I don't think running around Morbeth in a torn, skimpy red dress will keep you hidden for long."

I swear I heard Markus chuckle, but when I glanced at him, his face was expressionless.

"You're right," I exhaled, hugging her arm. "I'm glad you're coming with us."

She returned a radiant smile. "Let's hope the gods and goddesses can bring us out of this in one piece."

"You won't need them today," Markus noted, his voice low and serious.

"Why not?" Sabine grumbled.

He gave a sidelong glance. "Because the captain of the king's guard is with you."

"Even better," Sabine chimed, making Markus smile.

We traversed down a few corridors and down a lengthy flight of stairs, nearing the castle's exit. Through the windows, I noticed the sun had set, and a crescent-moon hung in the dusky sky.

As we moved down the last set of stairs, at least a dozen guards were standing at the exit.

CHAPTER TWENTY–THREE

"Remain silent, and stay close," Markus said before marching us right up to them. Sabine and I remained close behind.

Two guards stepped forward in our path, barring the exit. Their hands clutching the shafts of their swords.

"Where are you taking the prisoner, captain?" The shorter of the two asked.

Markus quickly side-eyed me. "I am working under direct orders, none of which concern you."

The most massive guard in the bunch stepped forward, withdrawing his sword. The sound sent a shiver up my spine. "Well, captain. Per *our* prince's request, we are to make sure the girl doesn't leave the castle, under any circumstance. What I'd like to know is how she managed to escape a heavily spelled cell?" We were suddenly surrounded by all twelve guards, swords drawn and pointed directly at us. "Give us the girl, and you'll be spared until Prince Roehl returns."

Heat tingled under my skin. I could take out a few of these guards and I was sure Markus could too, but we were still heavily outnumbered. Besides, unless we decapitated them, they'd keep coming.

I had to do something. Markus was obeying orders from the King. I wouldn't let him die because of me. I called a flame to the palm of my hand, and they all halted. Their eyes widened, fixed on the flame.

"I'll go quietly, and no one will get hurt if you let them both go," I said, the flames growing larger.

"No, Calla," Sabine said, gripping my arm.

"We don't make bargains with prisoners," another guard spoke.

Another dozen guards rushed toward us, completely circling us in. Archers appeared on the staircases with razor sharp arrows nocked and aimed at our heads. We were trapped. There was no way out of this. If we resisted, we would die.

I could hear Sabine's heart hammering hard and fast. There was only one option. I had to keep her safe. To surrender and let them take me. I wouldn't fight. I wouldn't endanger her.

The guards moved toward us and bound our hands.

"Take the captain to the block," the largest guard ordered. "Let the girl watch and see what takes place when a guard disobeys an order."

"No!" I cried. "You said you'd wait until Roehl returns."

"I've changed my mind," he said with too much bite.

Oh, if my hands weren't bound. There were more than a few who deserved a fireball to the face.

I thrashed as the guards took all three of us and dragged us outside. We were forced around the side of the castle, to a smaller cobbled courtyard hemmed in by a large rock wall. In the center of the yard was a large rectangular stone. It was about six feet long by three feet high and wide, and stained with the blood of its countless victims.

The block.

"Strap the captain down," the largest guard hollered, and the men obeyed.

Who was this bastard? Probably Roehl's second in command.

It took four guards to force Markus to his knees. His arms and legs were bound, his head pulled tight against the stone with a large strap.

Behind them, a black-hooded executioner exited a worn, brick cottage, clutching a massive, two-handed ax. He was a nightmarish giant. Nearly ten feet tall.

The eyes beneath the hood appeared hollow and lifeless. I wondered if this death dealer was haunted by the lives he'd taken. His was no doubt a cursed life.

On the side of the cottage, near the door, was a table and whetstone.

What sort of life did this monster have? Dealing death and whetting his blade over and over again.

Markus struggled against the binds, his cheek pressed

tight against the rough stone. His eyes were on me and Sabine. "I was given direct orders from King Romulus himself."

"The King?" The head guard sneered. "We all know the king is incapacitated and hasn't been able to speak for months."

"He was under a spell," Markus growled, still straining to free himself.

"The prince told us to be on the lookout for traitors. We never expected it to be you, Captain," another guard exclaimed. The rest of the guards yelled out in agreement.

"You can't do this!" I screamed, wishing I had the power to stop them. But I was powerless, my hands bound behind my back.

Roehl's head guard glared at me with contempt before lifting his arm to the executioner.

"No! He's innocent," I wailed.

The hooded giant raised his huge steel ax in the air, directly over Markus's neck.

"Please," I pleaded. "He's telling you the truth!"

But they wouldn't hear it from me. I was an outsider. A prisoner whose grandfather killed their prince.

The executioner's dark eyes locked onto the guard, his fingers tightening around the shaft of his ax, awaiting the signal.

The guard's arm dropped, and I screamed as the executioner swung his ax down.

But the ax never reached Markus.

It was torn from the executioner's hands and flung clear across the courtyard, beheading a guard instead.

What the hell happened?

The executioner roared. His mouth opened unnaturally wide, like some nightmarish monster.

"Stop!" A powerful voice thundered from above. Three stories up, looking over the execution courtyard, stood the true King of Morbeth. King Romulus's face was pale, but he stood firmly on his feet.

Gasps and murmurs echoed through the gathering crowd, faces in astonishment as if they'd seen a ghost. Every guard dropped to their knees, their heads bowing in reverence.

Behind the crowd, Aurelia, along with a group of witches dressed in white, entered with wands of pale wood gripped securely in their hands.

"Release them," The king demanded, his finger aimed at me. "The captain of *my* guard has spoken the truth. I ordered him to take my great-granddaughter around the grounds."

Dozens of wide eyes shifted to me. It was out now. They all knew who I was.

The guards immediately untied our bonds. Then King Romulus pointed to the head guard who ordered Markus's execution. "You." Fear swam in the guard's eyes, his limbs quivering.

"Yes, your majesty," the guard said, bowing so low his head scraped the ground.

"Gather every guard in the palace and bring them to the

throne room. Immediately!" The king's voice was becoming stronger with each moment, more powerful, filled with regal authority.

"Yes, your majesty." The guard stood, ordering the others to follow him.

The king's eyes found mine, and he winked. Leora was right. I could sense he was a good man, and I hoped I'd have the chance to experience it in the future.

"Thank you," I said, bowing my head.

"Leave now," Aurelia urged. "We'll take care of this."

The king spoke to the still gathering crowd. "I am your king. The ruler of Morbeth. Anyone who thinks otherwise can line up behind the block."

I took hold of Aurelia's hand. "One day I will repay you."

She squeezed mine and shook her head. "You kept my granddaughter alive. There is no debt to repay." She wrapped her arms around me in an embrace. "Now go."

As the king continued to address his people, Markus, Sabine, and I left the grounds.

I smiled at the girl who had become my friend and ally. "Sabine, you're still coming?"

She flung her pack back over her shoulder. "Does it look like I'm staying?"

I laughed as the three of us rushed through the courtyard.

"How will we get past the wall?" I panted.

"We aren't going past the wall," Markus said, pointing toward the coast.

We were heading to Crimson Cove. A place named after a battle during Talbrinth's Great War, where hundreds of bodies had washed up on the shores, staining the rocks and water with blood.

Now it was where notorious pirates and crooked merchants of the north were known to dock and commingle. It was a place no common citizen would want to find themselves. Especially a young woman, scantily clad in a torn, revealing red dress.

We followed Markus into the woods, where the oak trees were towering and dense, and the ground was damp and spongy from the countless fallen leaves. The air was brisk and smelled of wet moss and earth. I watched puffs of mist exit from Sabine's lips.

When dusk became night and it was too dark to see, I called a flame into my hand to light the path.

Sabine grinned. "Well, that's helpful."

"I had a lot of free time down in the cell," I quipped.

Pulling the flame between the palms of my hands, it grew, making the area brighter.

Sabine's eyes grew wider and I even caught Markus gawking, but he quickly turned away.

"We don't want to draw any unwanted attention," he grumbled.

Sabine and I gave each other exasperated looks, and I toned down the flame.

We snaked through the woods, the Red Wall becoming

a monstrous boundary before us. My legs were scratched and red from being flogged by the surrounding brush. But I pressed on, not stopping until I could hear gulls and water. The sea was near.

"Wait!" I halted, breathing heavily. "Before we go any further, I have to change."

Sabine was already digging through her pack. "You're right. A noble cannot be seen in," she waved her hand at me, "*that.*"

Markus sighed and turned his back to us. "Make it quick. We still have to find Captain Salloway."

I didn't notice how weak I was until I stopped. My limbs were visibly shaking. I just had to hold myself together a little longer until we reached the docks and secured our ride.

"Here," Sabine said, handing me a set of clothes. They were the same ones I'd arrived in—the black pants and tunic left in my cottage by Trystan. I quickly slipped them on and instantly felt better. Warmer. She then handed me some wool socks and my black boots. "Give me your dress and shoes. Who knows when these will come in handy again?"

"Hopefully, never," I groaned. "How did you get my things? I thought they were long gone."

"Roehl told me to burn them, but I couldn't. They are well made, so I had them washed and pressed. And . . . I managed to find these." She held out a cloth and carefully unwrapped it. Inside of it was the necklace Brynna gave me for my birthday—the silver amulet with the azure stone—

Trystan's flask, and his dagger still in its sheathe.

"Heavens above." I gaped at her. "Where? How?"

She gave a broad, toothy smile. "I was cleaning Roehl's chamber this afternoon and just happened to find them. In a sealed wooden box. Under his bed."

"Sabine!" I gasped.

She shrugged her shoulders. "What? He'd already left for Northfall. I wasn't in any danger."

I took the necklace and fastened it around my neck, then strapped Trystan's dagger to my side.

Sabine pulled out my old pack and put the flask, dress, and shoes into it. "I'll hold on to these until we get to the ship."

"Thank you, Sabine." I wrapped my arms around her neck, and she hugged me back.

"I also had this made for you," she added. She held up a hooded black cloak and handed it to me. The material was thick and warm. The interior of the cloak was lined with a dark red fabric. And onto that fabric, large flames were stitched in a golden thread.

I ran my fingers over the stitching and glanced up at her. "Flames?"

Sabine grinned. "The day Summer and I found out about your power, I had a friend who happens to be the royal seamstress, make it. It was going to be a gift, but she just finished it night before last. I guess it was fate."

"I guess it was." I threw the cloak over my shoulders,

attaching it at the chest. It was a warm and thoughtful gift. A perfect gift, especially for the approaching winter weather. And, a perfect fit, falling mid-calf.

"Thank you, Sabine." I spun in a circle. "So, what do you think, Markus?"

He raised a brow. "I think you'll blend in just fine with the cove's riffraff."

"I'll take that as a compliment," I huffed, walking past him.

A low growl rumbled in his chest. "Just keep your head down, hood up, and leave the speaking to me."

"Yes, sir," I said, shifting to salute him.

He gave me a firm look. "Don't ever do that again."

Sabine and I laughed, but he didn't seem to find it amusing.

"Then how shall we address you, sir?" I asked.

"By my name."

I nodded. "Then, let's move, Markus. Time waits for no man . . . or woman."

Markus sighed loudly and plodded ahead. I glanced at Sabine and gave her a wink. She covered her mouth, stifling a laugh.

We'd made it to Crimson Cove. We were free. We were finally free.

Now, we just had to leave Morbeth. And put some major distance between us and Roehl.

CHAPTER TWENTY–FOUR

I tried to hold my breath as we wandered through the cobbled walkways saturated with the stench of urine. Places like this scared the hell out of me. It reminded me of a town in Sartha everyone called the Bogs, an area where the drunk and troubled seemed to congregate. I passed through the area once with my parents, but my father had hired men to escort us through, so we were protected.

But there was a time when my father traveled through the Bogs alone, on business. When he returned, he had a swollen face, a fractured arm, and severely bruised ribs. My father was unable to work for weeks. Whoever beat him, also stole his money, wedding ring, and the pocket watch given to him by his father. After that, we never went near the Bogs again.

Markus took the lead as we entered the heart of Crimson Cove.

Sabine hooked her elbow in mine and leaned in. "These

people scare me just as much as the ticks do."

Markus twisted his head to her and growled, revealing an elongated fang, making Sabine's eyes widen.

"Sorry. Except you two," she murmured, averting our eyes. "You two are friends. I hope."

I nudged her with my elbow. "Me, for sure. Markus is still on probation."

He threw us a glare. "If you two want to make it out of here alive, I suggest you keep quiet."

A couple of men wearing seaman's garb rounded a corner, drunk as hell. One held an amber bottle in his hand and raised it in the air as they neared us.

"Cheers, my friends," he hollered much too loudly.

Markus tipped his head. "Good evening, gentlemen. Would you happen to know where I could find Captain Salloway?"

The man holding the bottle shoved his partner and let out a boisterous laugh. "Did you hear that? He called us gentlemen."

The other man, not as drunk as the other and dressed in finer clothes replied, "As luck would have it, we're on our way to see the good ole Capt'n Salloway now." He waved for us to follow, then threw his arm around the other man's shoulder as they stumbled past us. "Right this way."

I looked at Markus wide-eyed, but he pivoted and followed the drunken riffraff. Keeping my word to remain quiet, I pulled Sabine along with me.

Ship. Ocean. Seasickness.

I didn't like being on the water. I'd heard one too many horrifying stories—mostly real—of what had happened to countless vessels that sailed on the Sangerian Sea. Storms, monsters, disappearances of ships, never to be seen again—no bodies, no wreckage . . . nothing. They said the sea was cursed, which is why when I was old enough, I never traveled with my parents to Merchant Port. Besides, water was an enemy to fire. Maybe I'd felt that all along.

But it seemed fate had a sense of humor. For now, I would be traveling way beyond the safe area of Talbrinth, into the Sangerian Sea, with drunken sailors and a captain I didn't know, to a distant island that lay in ruins.

The only reason keeping me from ditching this plan was that I had to get out of Morbeth and away from Roehl. That, and the overpowering pull I had toward Incendia.

We passed dozens of ships docked at the cove, each bobbing up and down as the waves lapped at their sides. Beyond the vessels was the sea—vast and daunting and beautiful as the moon's silvery glow shimmered across its surface.

The wind was gentle, carrying a briny aroma which was pleasant compared to the sewage smell that tainted the town. The sky overhead was crystal clear, making the stars shine brighter than ever. A lovely evening, aside from the voices of raucous men in nearby taverns.

We proceeded to follow the two bumbling men, now

singing loudly, clanking their drinks now and then, until they boarded a large ship. The name painted on the side was *The Damned*. As my eyes traveled upward, I spotted a flag at half-mast. It was black, with a half-skull sitting above two crossbones.

Heavens above. This wasn't a merchant ship. It was a pirate ship.

"Markus," I rumbled through gritted teeth. He ignored me, following the men onto the deck.

Markus was broad and muscular and captain of the king's guard. There was a reason why he was appointed for that position. Because he was the best at what he did. But even knowing that, the feeling of uneasiness had settled in my gut and wasn't going to leave anytime soon. For the duration of our trip, we would be in the company of pirates, and I'd never heard anything good about pirates. They were drunken troublemakers known to rape and pillage with no regret. They were the Roehl's of the sea.

"Calla, I don't think we should be here," Sabine whispered, tugging on my arm.

"No, we shouldn't," I breathed. "Just keep your head down and stay close to Markus and me. We'll make sure you're safe."

Markus tilted his head to us as if he agreed. A subtle yet reassuring movement that must have worked because Sabine's vise grip somewhat relaxed.

I pulled my hood down even further, obscuring my entire

face. I wondered how many of *The Damned*'s crew were still out partying in the taverns and how many had already staggered back to the ship.

"The capt'n is through dem doors," the drunkest sailor spat, his finger aimed in a different direction than his bloodshot eyes.

"Thank you," Markus said, his head giving a sharp whip for us to follow.

We walked down a narrow hallway and halted in front of a door marked with a large red X.

I elbowed Sabine and whispered, "Do you think there's treasure hidden inside?"

She giggled but stopped when Markus turned back and gave me a narrowed glare.

As Markus knocked thrice on the door, I could hear Sabine's heart hammering inside her chest. I took hold of her hand and squeezed, hoping to reassure her.

"Enter!" a voice beckoned from beyond the door.

Markus pushed the door open and stepped inside. We followed closely behind.

"Captain Salloway?" Markus asked.

"Yep," the man replied, his back turned toward us.

The man spun in his chair, and hazel cataract eyes glared at each one of us. Captain Salloway was old and wrinkly, with a mustache that connected to a long white beard. In one hand he held a pipe, and in the other, a glass of amber liquor. He took a good look at Markus and said, "Looks like the dogs brought in a few ticks."

"Father!" a younger voice chided. A young man stepped out from an adjacent room. "Please forgive him. My father is old and has misplaced his manners some time ago." He held his hand out to Markus. "*I* am the present Captain Salloway, but please, call me Sebastian." He had a slight accent. An accent befitting of a pirate.

"Sebastian Salloway. Serpent of the Seas," the old man blurted.

"Father, why don't you roam the deck and see who's returned. We've but a few hours before we set sail."

The old man set his drained glass on the desk, then slowly pushed off his wooden chair and patted Sebastian on the cheek. "As you wish, sonny."

The captain sighed. He was tall and handsome with sea-blue eyes and shoulder-length, light-brown hair—tousled like he'd run his fingers through it one too many times. His skin was sun-kissed, likely from spending long days on deck. His clothes were made of fine fabrics—a white collared shirt under a black waistcoat with burnished brass buttons. On his legs were fitted black trousers and long brown boots which matched a knee length leather coat. Around his waist, a glimmer revealed the golden hilt of a sword.

Sabine and I lowered our hoods. The captain didn't seem like a threat.

"What brings you to Morbeth's pig sty?" The captain chuckled, clutching a glass and a half bottle supplied with gin.

His eyes narrowed on me, making me suddenly feel flustered.

Markus took a step forward and withdrew a pouch from his pocket, causing the gold skrag to clink inside. "King Romulus sent us. He instructed us to seek you out for help."

"The king?" Captain Salloway's eyes expanded. "I thought he was—"

"He was placed under a dark spell by his son Roehl," I blurted. "But the spell has been broken."

His brow rose even higher, but his eyes were suspicious. I continued, despite Markus's glare. "He wanted us to tell you that he should have believed the story you told him at the Mermaid's Tavern."

The captain paused, then a broad smile adorned his full lips. "Aye. He should have." He backed up to the desk and leaned against it. I wondered if he was going to tell us what he said, but he didn't.

"I haven't seen King Romulus in some years. We had our days in the sun." His eyes went distant as if he were rewinding to the past. Then his eyes caught Markus's. "How is the king?"

"He's seen better days, but he's on the mend."

"Ahh, yes. The benefits of immortality," Sebastian said with a roguish smirk.

"Are *you* immortal?" I inquired.

Captain Salloway gave a dimpled grin. "I, love, am one hundred percent human, with a real ticker." He tapped his chest. "However, a few years back, while in a drunken stupor, I asked the king to sire me."

"You did?" Sabine gasped.

"I did," he responded, shaking his head, draining the glass of gin he'd just poured. "Thank the gods he was in his right mind and refused. He's a decent fellow, despite what people think, and I have yet to discover this *Monster of Morbeth* they keep referring to him as."

"Have you met Roehl?" I asked.

Sebastian belly laughed. "I haven't had the pleasure of meeting the prince but have learned of his father's many concerns regarding him." His eyes narrowed on each of us, then paused on me. "Which makes me wonder why the king sent you to me, along with his personal guard." His eyes then darted between Sabine and me before speaking ever so slowly. "Who are you?"

Sabine stepped out from behind me. "I'm not the one he sent. It's her," she said, pointing to me. Sebastian's eyes widened and met mine. "She is the king's great-granddaughter, and if we don't get her out of Morbeth soon, Prince Roehl is going to kill her."

"Now why would the prince want to kill you?" he asked, those sea-blue eyes piercing straight through me.

"It's complicated," I replied with a shrug.

He inclined his head slightly. "Well, I'm a very complicated fellow, and before I decide to save you, I'd like to know why."

Markus glanced at me and gave me a nod. So, I gave the captain the short, undetailed version of my story. I didn't know or trust him enough to share everything. I wanted to get the hell out of Morbeth.

"You are not merely a vampire, but an Incendian Royal?" Sebastian questioned. His eyes were boring into mine.

He wanted confirmation.

I raised my right hand, palm facing upward. A bluish-orange flame danced above it.

"Pirates be damned," Sebastian exhaled, his eyes entranced on the flame. I curled my fingers into a fist, instantly extinguishing it.

"I need to get to Incendia," I said. "Can you take us there?"

"Yes," he answered. "Although, the island is a bit off our scheduled course. We will need to acquire further supplies for the extra week's journey."

Swindler.

Markus reached in his pouch and withdrew another sack of gold skrag, then tossed the two bags toward Sebastian. The pirate caught both quickly, opened each one and peeked inside. Satisfied, he sealed and tucked the sacks into his pocket.

We still had four bags left unless we were swindled out of it. But I knew Markus wouldn't let the remaining skrag leave his side. Not when our future depended on it.

"That'll do," Sebastian said, hopping off the desk. "We shall set sail shortly to the Isle of Incendia."

"Thank you," Markus said with a bend of his head.

"My pleasure. I have one cabin to spare, so you'll have

to share," he said. "It'll be cramped quarters with three of you, but—"

"We'll take it," I said quickly.

I could almost read Markus's mind as he gave me another of his familiar glares. The amount of skrag we'd given, we should have had the captain's cabin. But I wasn't about to strike a deal with a pirate. And by his silence, Markus wasn't either.

I just wanted to go to the room as quickly as possible and become invisible again. To lie low until we reached Incendia. Exhaustion had settled heavily in my bones, and I was glad when the captain was about to lead us to our room.

"Oh, captain," a woman's voice sang from behind the door he'd first exited. "I'm ready to walk the plank." The door swung open, and a half-naked girl stood there, draped in a white bedsheet, wearing a patch over her right eye, leaving not much to the imagination.

I bit back a laugh and lowered my head.

"Pardon me for a moment," Sebastian murmured, holding up a finger to us. He pivoted and strode toward the door, blocking the woman.

Clearing his throat, he spoke to her in a commanding tone. "I'm attending to business, woman. Please gather your things and disembark my ship promptly. I am no longer in need of your services."

"What?" The woman's voice turned ferocious. "How dare you? I will make sure you—"

"Enough! Show some decency." He pushed the door shut and swiveled back to us. "I apologize," he said, placing a hand over his heart.

"It's fine," I whispered, and he gave another dimpled grin.

Trouble. The captain was trouble.

"We'll set sail in a few hours. While you can roam the ship, I suggest that the two of you," he pointed to me and Sabine, "remain hidden. Most of my crewmen are superstitious. They believe having a female on board is bad luck. I, however, don't believe in superstitions, but should they find out there are two beautiful women aboard my ship? Well, let's just say it is bound to produce a lot of unnecessary tension.

"My men have specific duties that must be fulfilled to keep this ship running smoothly. The sea and the ocean beyond can be dangerous, and I require their complete cooperation." His eyes shifted to Markus. "The less they know about our little arrangement, the better."

"You don't have to worry about us," I said. "Once you take us to our room, we'll become invisible."

Another devilish grin. "Right this way then," the captain said, leading us out of his quarters and down a dingy hallway. He swung open the first door on his left and stepped to the side.

"I apologize for not having anything a little more . . . accommodating."

"We'll be fine," Markus said, stepping in, his huge frame gobbling up half the space.

It was cramped quarters—a small desk with a wooden chair sat in one corner, and a hammock suspended from large bolts in the ceiling on the other. That was it. The floor was filthy, stained and covered with soil and dust.

"Thank you, captain," Sabine said, setting her pack on the desk, her eyes taking in the unkempt floor.

As I stepped into the room, the captain's hand gripped my shoulder. The warmth from his chest seeped through my clothing as he pressed his body against my back. His scent was spicy with a hint of salt breeze. "My cabin has room for one more," he whispered, his warm breath brushed against my ear, his voice low and seductive.

I angled my head slightly to the side. "Then maybe you should invite Markus. I think he would appreciate the extra space. And so would we."

Captain Sebastian chuckled; his breath sent tingles down my spine. "You wicked woman. Then, how about I take you on a tour, when time warrants, to stretch your legs and take in some fresh air?"

I twisted around and faced him. "I just might take you up on that offer."

"Aye," he responded. "I thought you would. Being on the sea, under the vast sky with the endless stars above . . . it's truly magical."

"You sound like a romantic, captain."

Lust glinted in those sea-blue eyes. "I have my moments, love."

"I'm sure you do." I took a few steps back into the room and said, "We thank you for your kindness and hospitality." Then I shut the door in his face.

"Calla," Sabine gasped.

"What?" I swung to her with wide eyes.

Sabine's eyes averted to the floor. "That was . . . rude."

"Rude? Me?" I gasped, throwing my hand over my heart. "I wasn't rude. I was helping him. The captain has a ship to run and we have important matters to discuss. Like sleeping arrangements. Right, Markus?"

"Right," he replied, plunging into the hammock, claiming it. The boards above creaked and groaned, straining under his weight.

"You are going to bring the ceiling down on top of us," I grumbled. He closed his eyes. "You have no problem knowing your two female companions will be sleeping on the hard, filthy floor?"

One of Markus's eyes opened and darted between me and Sabine before he held up his hand . . . his thumb and finger an inch apart. "Maybe this much."

Sabine huffed.

"I think it's fair. Neither of you would want to sleep next to me. I roll." Markus gave a grand smile. "It's a win-win situation all the way around."

I exhaled and nodded. "Well, since you are our official bodyguard on this expedition, we'll *let* you take the hammock."

"Thank you, princess," he said with a bend of his head.

"Don't call me that," I groaned.

"Why? It's fact." He re-closed his eyes and tucked his arms behind his head.

"Just call me, Calla. I've always been Calla, and I'd like to keep it that way."

"Fine, princess," Markus snickered.

Ever since we'd left Morbeth, Markus's temperament had altered. I could sense a different man beneath the façade, a softer edge beneath the rough surface, hidden by the Captain of the Guard's mask for countless years.

Sabine picked up her bag and mumbled. "I don't think this floor has ever been cleaned. It's dreadful." She took out a small rag, and on hands and knees, started sweeping the dirt into a corner.

I coughed as she stirred up dust plumes. "Sabine, you don't have to do that."

She paused and looked up at me. "I've been a servant all my life. This comes naturally to me. So please, let me do this by myself, or I won't be able to breathe in this room, let alone sleep."

"Okay," I said softly, backing away while she worked swiftly and efficiently.

In no time, the floor was as clean as it could get. Sabine even managed to collect the dirt into her rag and toss it out the small porthole window.

"There," she announced. "Now, we can lay out our bedding.

After the bedding was down, I sat, leaning my back against the wall. The bobbing of the ship was making me nauseous, and we hadn't even sailed out of the port yet.

"You look pale," Sabine said, kneeling in front of me. "When was the last time you fed?"

I had to think about it. I hadn't fed since . . . "Spring."

"Spring? That was five days ago. No wonder you look pasty. You need to feed." She searched through her pack, withdrawing her small blade and bowl.

I rubbed my cheeks. "I look pasty?"

Markus glanced over at me. "Pasty is a *nice* way of putting it."

"Gods." I whined and hunched over, hugging my knees "I look like a pasty vampire girl."

"Well, you technically are," Sabine stated. "But it obviously doesn't matter. Pasty or not, the captain still hit on you."

"Like that means anything," I murmured. "He's a pirate. I'm quite sure the peg between his legs has no prejudice."

Sabine let out a boisterous laugh, then covered her mouth, while Markus's face showed no emotion. "When did you feed last, captain?" Sabine questioned.

"Mid-afternoon," he answered before adding, "from a willing contributor. And call me Markus."

She gave him a nod and quickly looked away. "Then you should be fine for a few days."

"Don't concern yourself with me," Markus said drably.

"I have no problem feeding."

I cleared my throat. "Markus, remember what the captain said. He needs all hands on deck to sail this ship. *All* hands. Please don't make any of those hands disappear."

"Don't fret, princess. I've been doing this for an awfully long time and haven't killed anyone yet. Except on purpose." He peeked at me with one eye, cracking a devilish grin.

"Fine, Captain of the Guard," I replied. He shut his eyes.

He was right, though. He'd learned to manage his bloodlust well before I was born, and I knew he wouldn't kill unnecessarily. Even though he was the king's captain, I sensed there was good inside of him. Just like the king. Maybe that's why Romulus chose him. Because they shared similar spirits.

Markus tried his hardest to hold his hard-as-nails façade, but Sabine and I were wearing him down. Now and then he'd reveal a gentler, friendlier side, and then catch himself and fling his barrier right back up.

But his kindness had set off a chain of events. Without him, I wouldn't have escaped, and Spring might not have survived. Not to mention the fact he risked his life to bring Sabine and Summer down to us in the dungeon.

Now we were free, and the king's curse was broken. All because of him. Because Markus did what was right, and not what he had been ordered to do. Even under penalty of death.

It must have been rough being under Roehl's command. Who knows what lengths Markus had to go through to prove his loyalty? I could tell there were things eating at him.

As I reflected, Markus did attempt to console me as he escorted me back to my room after the confrontation between Roehl and Trystan the night of the Shadow Fest. I never acknowledged it at the time because I'd been so wrapped up in my own misery.

I peered up at his broad, muscular frame. His eyes were closed, his breathing long and steady. One day I'd get a chance to thank him.

Sabine also glanced at Markus, and I thought they'd make a beautiful couple. They looked like they could have come from the same region, with their beautiful tanned skin, raven colored hair, and dark features. But even if they did share feelings for each other, it wouldn't work. Not if she remained human.

CHAPTER TWENTY–FIVE

While Sabine filled the small bowl with her blood, I stood and made my way to the porthole, peeking outside. "How long will it take for us to get to Incendia?" I asked no one in particular.

"Fifteen days, depending on the wind," Markus answered, his eyes still shut. "If the wind is on our side, we could arrive in nine."

I groaned. "Right now, I'd exchange my gift of fire for wind."

"That would be helpful." He grunted. "Too bad the Carpathian Prince isn't around to help us with that."

My head jerked to him. He had to be referring to Trystan. "Why would you say that?"

Markus turned to me with a bemused expression. "You don't know?"

"Know what?"

He smirked. "I guess he hasn't told you about his gift?"

"No," I exhaled. "It hasn't been a topic of discussion in between running for my life and being imprisoned." When Markus didn't respond I shifted to him with hands on my hips. "Well? Are you going to tell me?"

Markus opened his eyes. "Prince Trystan is a pureblood, born with the gift of air manipulation."

"Air?" I turned to Sabine but was looking right through her.

I'd never thought about it before, but it made sense. It was the reason he could sail across the Sangerian Sea—what usually took four or five days—in one.

"The Carpathian prince is an elemental like you, which is probably why he felt an attachment to you," Sabine said. "Air can either give life to fire or extinguish it."

She stood and walked toward me, handing me a small bowl of fresh blood. "Drink," she implored. And I did. In one gulp, the bowl was empty. I closed my eyes and let the tingling sensation work its course through my body, instantly feeling better.

"Thank you," I exhaled, returning the bowl to her.

"You're welcome." She took the bowl and set it on the desk, before returning to me. Taking my hands, she turned them over, revealing the tattoos on my palms. "Incendian royals could manipulate more than one element. Especially the females. My grandmother told me a story once of an Incendian Queen who could manipulate all four of the elements."

If I hadn't met Leora, or experienced the gift she gave me, the story would have been hard to believe. Fire was an incredible gift. But to manipulate all the elements? That must have been some incredible power.

Sabine looked closer at my tattoos. "Although fire is dominant, it looks like your secondary element is water." She pointed to the triangle on my left palm, which looked like it had waves within it. "But look. All the element symbols are around the circle."

I hadn't looked at the tattoos in detail, because Summer had placed the glamour over them. But water? I hadn't been able to summon water. In the throne room and cell, the only element that appeared to me was fire. There was no sign that water was part of my arsenal.

"Don't worry, Calla. I'm confident we'll figure it all out when we get to Incendia," Sabine said.

I pushed my back against the wall. "I hope so. I hope I'm not chasing after some insane intuition and dragging you both with me."

"I'm glad to do it. Pursuing a dream is far greater than living a life without one. Incendia is where your ancestors lived and received their magic. Maybe it's where you'll find all your answers. And maybe, just maybe, the fire goddess will give them to you directly."

I laughed. "The fire goddess?"

Sabine's face was serious, so I cut my laugh short. "Yes. It is said that the volcano on Incendia is home to the fire goddess. And if an Incendian royal stands on the edge of the volcano and summons her, she will appear to them."

It was hard to believe. But I was finding most myths we grew up hearing were true, and now I was a part of them. An immortal. An Incendian royal, about to sail through the treacherous sea to reach the homeland of my ancestors. A place I'd never been. A place where the magic of its people made others envious, and because of that envy, it lay in ruins.

I took a better look at Sabine. Her eyes were bloodshot and encased with dark circles. Stretching her arms over her head, she yawned, confirming she was tired.

"How are *you* feeling?" I asked her. "We need to get you some food."

"I'll make sure she's fed," Markus blurted. "They have a cook onboard and with what we paid, she should eat well."

"Don't worry about me," Sabine said gently. "I packed a few things that could last a week if I ration properly."

I sighed. "You can't ration food when you're donating blood. You'll need a lot more than a few bites a day." I rested my palms on her shoulders. "Let Markus get you some proper food, or I won't accept any more of your blood."

She stilled and after a moment tears brimmed in her eyes.

"What's wrong?" I felt horrible for making her cry.

She shook her head and dried the tears trailing down her cheeks with the back of her hand.

"Sabine, I'm so sorry. If I said something to upset you—"

"No." She shook her head. "It was the nicest thing anyone

has ever said to me." Her lips quivered as she looked at me. "No one has ever *cared* about me before."

It was then I realized this orphaned girl probably had no real friends growing up in Morbeth. She'd likely been used and abused—a servant for as long as she could remember—being forced to do as her masters commanded or be punished.

But not anymore. Once we sailed away from Crimson Cove, she'd be free, and I'd make sure she remained free.

As Sabine lay down and Markus remained still and silent, my thoughts traveled to my father.

Was he safe? Did he have powers released when Leora broke the spell? He was also a descendant of Incendia, and if his father, Nicolae, was born with magic, then maybe he had some too. And perhaps that magic would keep him alive.

My father was a respectable man. He'd built up his wealth through arduous work, never flaunting it because he knew there were so many less fortunate. Not only in Sartha, but in Talbrinth as a whole. There were many, barely getting by, struggling to survive day by day, especially after the Great War.

My father lived by example and helped feed the hungry in Sartha. Once a week he'd donate ten percent of his earnings to hire cooks in the town. And each week, they prepared large kettles of soup and freshly baked bread for those in need. There were hundreds, many of whom were children, who lined the cobbled streets. For some, it was the only meal they would receive that week, so we made sure everyone left with a little extra to get them by.

From time to time, my mother and I would help serve them. It kept us grounded and aware of how many were struggling right in our own town.

I could only hope my father would find a place of safety to hide until I could figure out how to save him from Roehl's jealous wrath.

A small amount of relief came from knowing King Romulus was back in power. And as long as he remained king, I knew he wouldn't allow my father to be killed.

Three quick raps at the door and Markus was up in a flash. I did not understand how his sizeable frame, cocooned in the hammock, could move that fast.

He stood at the door and cracked it open.

"Sorry to bother you, mate."

It was Sebastian.

"How can we help you?" Markus asked in a non-grumpy but deep voice.

"There's a storm brewing overseas so we'll be leaving shortly in hopes to outrun it. I've sent my father to gather the few remaining crew members. I just thought I'd let you know." He handed Markus an armful of blankets, pillows, and a basket of provisions. "Small conveniences to make your journey a little more bearable."

"Thank you," Markus said.

Sabine and I also thanked him, even though we couldn't see him. But the captain managed to poke his head inside and smile, his sea-blue eyes landing on mine.

"It's the least I could do."

Thank heavens Markus was with us. He stood like a brick wall, blocking the door from letting the captain enter any further.

"Alright then, I'll leave you be. You know where my door is if you need anything. Just knock thrice." He turned to leave but paused. "And please don't mind my father if you happen to run into him. He's an old, muddled jackass on his good days."

Markus tipped his head, then shut the door.

"Well, well. Look who's being the rude one now." I giggled.

Setting the basket down on the table, he threw Sabine and I each an extra pillow and an extra blanket before settling back into his hammock.

"He interrupted my rest," he replied. Closing his eyes and didn't say another word.

Sabine lit a small lamp hanging in the corner of the room before walking over to the porthole and covering it with her rag. After living with vampires, she knew the protocol.

I hadn't attempted to touch the sunlight since my hand caught fire in my cottage. That day would be forever burned in my memory.

"We should get some sleep," Sabine whispered after eating some biscuits and cheese she'd packed.

"Yes," I said, settling down on my pillow. It smelled like

Sebastian. I wondered if he'd done it on purpose. Wily pirate.

Time seemed to slow as I waited for the ship to disembark Crimson Cove. Sabine and Markus fell asleep, so I quietly stood and tiptoed to the porthole. I could hear the voices of sailors outside and felt a slight jerk. The ship moved and I watched the dock slowly slip into the darkness.

We were leaving Morbeth. And the extra weight pressing on my shoulders suddenly lifted.

Ahead, the sea was vast and dark, and I hoped we wouldn't become another tale . . . a ship lost, trapped in the clutches of the Sangerian Sea or its monsters, never to be seen again. We were now in the hands of Captain Sebastian Salloway and the crew of *The Damned*.

I remained at the window until the only thing I could recognize were the moon and the stars in the sky. Holding my hands up in the dim light, I stared at the tattoos on my palms and traced the one on my left. Water. Could I manipulate water?

I held my right hand out to my side and watched a flame coil through my fingers and dance in my palm. But as much as I tried, I couldn't summon water. Not a drop.

How was I expected to figure out my abilities when I had no instruction or someone to train me?

I called to the water again and again, but there was no response.

In frustration, I slapped my hand against the porthole window.

The ship rocked and I tottered.

What the hell?

Was that a coincidence? Or was it me?

I glanced back to my left palm. Stepping back up to the porthole, I sucked in a deep breath, then thrust my palm against the small round window.

A line of whitewater shot in front of me, across the sea, as far as the darkness would allow me to see.

Good gods. Was this really happening? I had to see it again. Just to make sure.

Once again, I shoved my palm against the porthole. Whitewater blasted out in front of me, rocking the ship. Stumbling back, realization hit me. This was no coincidence. It was raw elemental power.

I couldn't summon water like I could fire because water was secondary. It was something I could manipulate. Incendians were known to wield fire. It was their primary element. So water wouldn't come from within.

This awareness made me want to find some water and see my new gift up close.

I paced back and forth, knowing the only place I could go without being seen would be the toilet room a few doors down. But there was a reason I avoided that disgusting hole in the wall. So that was out of the question. I'd have to wait.

Heading back to my bedding on the floor, Markus's snoring became loud and rather scary. At least he would be rested for the approaching days. We needed him to be.

Sabine's slow and steady breaths told me she was in a deep sleep. I settled down next to her, thinking about all that had ensued over the last few months. Too much to make sense of it all, and it still had my mind in a spiral. I needed sleep. And knowing the distance was growing between me and Roehl afforded me some peace.

As I settled down in the dark, the ship gently rocking back and forth, my thoughts moved to Trystan. The bond between us had been severed. He no longer had ties to me, and for some reason the thought made me sad. I wished I could have spoken with him, at least once, before it happened. To let him know how grateful I was for all he'd done for me.

I had a feeling our paths would cross again, especially while Brynna was in his care. The thought of meeting him again, in person, made butterflies flutter in my belly.

CHAPTER TWENTY—SIX

We'd survived four long days on the Sangerian Sea. While the sun was up, Markus and I slept, while Sabine cleaned and probably read the books I'd seen tucked in her pack. During the nights, Sabine slept, and Markus left us to feed.

I was terribly seasick and suffering from cabin fever. I felt like I was a prisoner in this new cell out in the middle of the sea. I needed to breathe fresh air. I was suffocating in this tiny room.

As night fell, I became stir-crazy. I moved to the porthole and cracked it open, thankful it was even possible. I needed to get out of the room. Every day, the walls seemed to shrink.

Maybe I could sneak out, get some air without anyone seeing me, and come right back.

The ship seemed silent and the water calmer than it had been the past few nights.

I tiptoed over to the door and pushed my ear against it,

listening for any outside noise. But it was quiet.

I wasn't a prisoner. I could leave. I just had to face the consequences if any of those superstitious sailors spotted me. They'd probably make me walk the plank. And I wasn't a strong swimmer.

I quietly twisted the doorknob and cracked it open to peek. The hallway was empty, so I swung the door fully open.

"Evening, love," Sebastian cooed, striding out into the hall.

How the hell?

I froze, not expecting to meet him, deciding whether to slink back into the cabin and shut the door.

His sea-blue eyes surveyed my face. "Are you all right?" he asked, striding toward me. "You look pale and in need of fresh air. The deck is free. I can escort you if you'd like?" He extended his hand to me.

I inhaled and pulled myself together. The captain was a single man who lived on the sea, traveling for weeks and even months at a time before seeing the shore. There were two females onboard, and right now he was flirting with me.

Sebastian took a step closer, his hand still extended. "Being on the sea can be unpleasant, especially when being held up in a box. Come with me," he said. A smile grew on his full lips. "I promise, love. I won't bite. Unless you want me to."

Oh, he was good. Tall. Tanned. Handsome. Charming. He had it all, and I was sure that most women went weak at the knees whenever he was around. But as charming as the pirate captain was, I wasn't interested in any kind of romance. Not right now.

"I'm fine," I replied. "I just need to stretch my legs."

"Well, you're in luck. I've sent the crew to bed, and my father is at the helm."

Was all that just a coincidence too? I cleared my throat. "You mentioned there was a storm coming?"

"Aye. It's northwest, but if the wind continues to push us forward, we could very well outrun it."

I nodded, still terrified of being on a ship in the middle of the sea.

"Don't fret, love. The ship is my home, and the sea is my yard." His arm was still stretched out toward me. "Come, let me give you a tour. A bit of fresh air will do you wonders."

His offer was too good to pass up. I needed to get out of this room . . . this cage. I glanced at Sabine, wondering if I should tell her I'd gone. But she was sound asleep, and Markus was gone. If he could roam the ship, why couldn't I? I had the captain's permission and was being escorted by him. Besides, this was a ship. There was nowhere I could go that they couldn't find me.

"Let's go." I grabbed hold of Sebastian's hand, and with a brilliant smile, he led me out.

The swaying of the ship was throwing me off balance and making me sick. But Sebastian kept walking like he was on solid ground.

"It takes time to get sea legs," he said, folding his arm

around my waist, steadying me. I allowed him, because I knew I'd probably fall or bump the walls on the way out to the deck.

"My parents used to sail to Merchant Port in Hale every month, but I'd stay back. I was always frightened of the sea," I said, trying to make conversation.

"Why?" I felt his eyes on me but kept mine on the exit.

"I don't know. I guess it's because the sea is so enormous and filled with all kinds of scary creatures. I've heard the horror stories."

"Ahh, yes," he exaggerated. "I've lived on the sea for over twenty years. I've been in the heart of hurricanes, wrecked on rocky coasts, and have even seen a few monsters of the deep. And yet . . . I'm still alive."

"The gods must favor you," I said.

He hesitated, his eyes finding mine with a feline grin on his face. "Maybe they kept me safe for this very moment."

Oh, yeah. He was good. I wondered how many times he used that line on other girls.

We exited the hall and a crisp breeze curled around me. I paused and drank it in, relishing the feel and briny smell of it. The sky above was clear, and the stars were shimmering.

Sebastian's arm tightened around my waist. "Come," he said, his eyes on me, as if he were enthralled by my moment of freedom.

I let him lead me to the deck which was considerably larger than the one on my father's ship. The wooden floorboards were worn, but the ship was in good shape.

"How did you become a sailor?" I asked.

He led me to the railing, where I grabbed hold. "I suppose you could say it was destiny. My father was a fisherman, and when he was old enough, he became captain of Morbeth's fleet. He met my mother on shore, not in a tavern, but in a small shop that sold bread and pastries. She was a baker. It was the smell that lured him in, but her looks and charm held him there." There was a glimmer in his eye. "It wasn't long before they were wed, and not long after, I was conceived onboard his ship. I was born on one too." He chuckled, his eyes went distant. "My father was a seaman, so it was natural I became one. I spent most of my life on the sea. It's a different world out here."

He grabbed my hand and led me to the forecastle—the deck just above the bow of the ship—where I clutched the edge tightly, making sure I wouldn't fall. Sebastian stood next to me, with the endless sea before us. "All this," he declared. "It's all mine." I studied him as he gazed out into the dark waters, the wind whipping through his hair, and I saw a glow in those eyes. He truly cherished the sea and loved his life on it. "I wouldn't trade this for the world."

"You're extremely fortunate, captain. To be living a life you love," I said, shifting away.

"Aye. That I am," he replied, his intense gaze settled on me, warming my cheeks. "And what about you, Calla?"

I sighed deeply. "My life is in shambles. But not long

ago, I'd had a simple and mostly quiet life. A life I was content with. A life I could have loved for a long time." I peered back at him, and there was a deep furrow in his brow. "That life is gone, vanished as if it were all just a wonderful dream and has been replaced with horror and nightmares."

His warm hand covered mine. "I don't know the details of what you've been through, love, but I am sorry. You've weathered many storms, and I trust that one day, you will live a life you truly love."

"I hope so. If I can survive this seasickness first."

He laughed, and I relished the sound. A sound of joy with no care. It seemed like a lifetime ago when I felt true happiness.

Sebastian stepped behind me, his strong fingers kneading my shoulders. "You carry such heavy burdens."

His fingers were magic and felt so good. Amazingly good. I moaned as he hit all the right spots, his warm chest pressed against my back. With swift hands, he twirled me around, his hands grasping the railing on either side of me, locking me in place.

I swallowed, my insides knotting. I just needed to come out for a breath of fresh air, and now, I was fastened against the bow of the ship by the young and handsome captain.

"You're beautiful, Calla." He was close. So close. His lips, a breath away, was making it hard to breathe. The warmth of his mortal body seeped through my clothes, straight to my core. *Trouble. He was so much trouble.*

"Sebastian," I responded softly, my body and mind melting.

Lust darkened in those dangerous, sea-blue eyes. "We are but two lonely souls adrift in the midst of a dark and endless sea."

I planted my palms on his chest. "Captain, please." If circumstances were different, I would have given in. But I couldn't. Especially with Markus somewhere on this ship. If he discovered us, he'd probably take off Sebastian's head.

Sebastian paused, then his eyes softened. Taking a step back, he shook his head, an almost embarrassed grin on his lips. "Well, that's quite an unusual feeling."

His expression caused me to laugh. "I guess you've never been turned down before."

The dimpled grin was back on his handsome face, his fingers combing through his hair. "I can't say that I have."

"Believe me, you are tempting, captain. But the timing . . . it's all wrong."

He nodded this time, taking another step back. "I understand. The deck is yours to roam for the next few hours. Use this freedom wisely." He bowed his head and shifted to walk away.

"Where are you going?" I called after him.

He paused and gave me a look that would make any woman strip bare. "To douse myself in cold water. You wicked, wicked woman."

CHAPTER TWENTY–SEVEN

I waited until Sebastian disappeared and then waited a few more minutes after that before I moved. This was the perfect chance to test my ability of water manipulation. Glancing around the deck, I made sure it was empty before I stepped closer to the railing, looking over the bow of the ship.

Holding up my left palm—the one with the water tattoo on it—I heaved my hand forward, willing the water to move.

The black waters ahead of me exploded, like something enormous had fallen into it from above. Water shot high into the heavens. The ship plunged forward into the void I'd created, dropping down before snapping back up again. The entire boat creaked and cracked as it leveled off.

The water that had burst into the sky showered down on the deck, soaking me completely.

Gods above!

I looked at my palm, confounded by the power that

existed within. It seemed to be just as potent as the flame.

Voices started shouting below. I had probably woken the entire crew.

I sprinted as fast as I could across the deck and down the hallway. When I came to our door, I threw it open and lunged inside, slamming it shut behind me. I froze, hearing voices shouting outside. Pressing my ear against the door, I listened to what they were saying. They thought they were under attack.

I was so concerned about what was going on outside the door; I didn't notice Markus and Sabine standing behind me. I turned to find both pairs of eyes fixed on me and my wet, trembling frame.

"What the hell did you do?" Markus growled, his black eyes tightened.

"I—I went for a walk, and . . . well—"

Three sharp raps on our door made my body tense. I closed my eyes and sighed before slowly turning the doorknob and opening it.

Sebastian was standing at the doorway in knickers and a half-buttoned tunic, exposing a tanned, muscled chest. He pressed one hand on the doorframe and leaned toward me, examining my soaked frame from head to toe.

"Love, I leave you for one minute—one—and my ship feels like it's being split apart. What happened?"

I gulped and offered him my best innocent look. "I—was just enjoying the fresh air."

"Mm-hmm," he hummed, lifting a brow. "I don't know what you did, or how you did it, but you woke my entire crew and scared the shite out of them." After a strained moment, his laughter permeated the cabin.

Had he cracked? "Are you okay?" I asked.

"Yes." He reached out and seized my hand, still chuckling, with a smile on his face. "Thank you. I've been wanting to give my crew a surprise exercise but didn't know how to go about it. You've managed to do it and assured me they are still worthy of working on *The Damned*."

I gave a half-witted smile. "You're welcome?" I opened my mouth to say something else, but snapped it shut and kept quiet.

Sebastian's eyes softened, a crooked grin on his mouth. "Please, love. Promise there will be no more surprises in the dead of night."

I freed my hand from his and placed it over my chest. "I promise."

He winked and stepped away, his eyes still on me as he strolled down the hallway. "Sleep well, Calla," he called, before disappearing into his quarters.

I didn't want to close the door, because I knew I'd be sealing myself in with Markus. If Sabine weren't here, I would have probably taken the captain up on his offer to share his room for the night.

Sucking in another deep breath, I closed the door and faced him. His eyes narrowed with pressing questions, his arms crossed firmly over his burly chest.

"I—I." I was bumbling. But it wasn't my fault. I'd just found out I possessed this new and untamed power and had to find out what it could do. But I guess curiosity got the best of me . . . and everyone else on *The Damned*. "I just needed to get out of this room and breathe some fresh air. But—"

"What happened to the ship?" he asked. "I nearly fell out of my hammock." He turned and aimed a finger at Sabine. "And she rolled halfway across the floor."

How could I explain this? "Well . . . I needed to know if what Sabine said was true. I had to test out the theory I can manipulate water. And . . ." I shrugged and gave him a toothy grin. "I can."

Markus's brow furrowed again. He and Sabine glanced at each other, then back at me.

"What did you do?" Markus asked, this time with a deep sigh.

"I didn't break the ship. I just . . ." I began to tell them what happened. Seeing the water outside of the porthole. Meeting the captain in the hallway, and when I was finally alone, I tested my new ability.

They remained silent, taking in my words.

"I wish I was there to witness it," Sabine finally exhaled, with a look of amazement. "Your gift is incredibly powerful, and you haven't even begun to tap into its full potential."

A growl erupted from Markus. "You are forbidden to use your powers on this ship," he ordered, using his deep and commanding voice. "It's too dangerous. Too raw and untamed. You cannot throw it around without knowing what it can do. You need to bridal it until we find someone who can train you."

I nodded. "Which is why we are heading to Incendia. Maybe there is someone still there, or a book, or something that can help me?"

Markus stopped me on my way back to my bed. "You shouldn't be alone with the captain either," he murmured.

I grinned at him. He was worried. "Don't worry about me. I can handle the captain," was all I said.

That was that.

The next few days were spent cooped up in the stifling room. Sebastian made sure to deliver hot food from the kitchen for Sabine each night, and I was happy to watch her eat.

She and Markus played cards every night before bed and their laughter and snarky banter were welcome sounds. They tried to get me to play, but I couldn't focus. The magic inside my bones wanted to be set free. It warred against me, making it hard to concentrate on anything.

And being stuck in the cramped room only made it worse. I felt like a caged animal. The heat was smothering, the air suffocating, and the boat—rocking back and forth—was nauseating. I felt like I was slowly going mad.

We'd been sailing for a week, and the days were dragging. We had outrun the storm, but there was another brewing, even closer. And, as luck would have it, the wind died.

"I suggest you prepare for a rough night," Sebastian spoke, having turned up at our cabin. "The sea might get a little choppy." He turned his eyes to me before narrowing them. "You don't look well. Is everything okay, love?"

"Since I've walked onto this ship, I've been nauseous," I admitted.

Sebastian extended his arm and I hesitated. "I have something that can help you." His eyes went to Markus. "I'd like to take her to get something for her sickness. She'll be safe and I vow to have her back momentarily."

Markus growled and shot me a narrowed glare. I could tell he didn't want me to be with Sebastian alone. He knew his type. Handsome, flirtatious, and promiscuous. And our first impression of him confirmed it.

"You have my word," Sebastian added.

I smirked at Markus, thumbing back to Sebastian. "You have his word."

With Markus's wary nod of approval, Sebastian led me back down the hallway, into his quarters. We walked past the small office and into his bedroom. When I entered, I no longer felt like I was on a ship.

His room was spacious. Three times the size of ours with wide windows that looked over the rear of the ship, and a view of the sea beyond. Windows that were cracked open with fresh air circulating freely.

His king-sized bed was neatly made and covered with extravagant, plush bedding.

"Go ahead. Lie down," he said, gesturing toward his large, welcoming bed. "I'll just be a moment."

"Where are you going?"

"To whip you up a special tonic for sea sickness."

"But I can't—"

"Don't worry, love." He winked. "I'm not ignorant of what you are."

Of what I was. No longer a simple mortal.

Sebastian paused at the door. "The bed is yours until you feel better. I won't get in it . . . unless you want me to." Another wink and he was gone.

I chuckled to myself and sat on the edge of the bed. It was soft, molding to my form. So much more comfortable than the hard floor I'd been laying on. I leaned back, just on the edge, and gods, it felt like heaven. I turned to my side and realized the bed was large enough to fit four men.

So not fair.

At this point, I would take anything he gave me. The King of Morbeth trusted him. So why wouldn't I? I had nothing left behind in my guts to throw up, and the days and nights of dry heaving were wearing on me.

Sebastian returned a few minutes later carrying a drink. "Here." He offered it to me. "Trust me, it'll make you feel better."

I sat up and took it from him. It was warm and forced my incisors to lengthen. It was blood, a tall glass, but there was a hint of something else.

355

"Whose blood is this?" I dared to ask. Then I caught him putting pressure on his right forearm.

"It's the least I can do." His brow rose, a smile brightened his handsome face. "Now you'll get to say you've tasted the one and only Captain Sebastian Salloway."

"Ahh," I breathed. "And this is a good thing?"

"A rare thing."

"Rare?" I questioned, thinking back to the woman who was in this very chamber when we arrived.

"Aye. You, Miss Caldwell, are the *only* person I have—or will ever—incise myself for," he claimed with a devilish smile. "Not even the King of Morbeth was given such an offer."

"Then I humbly accept this *rare* and selfless gift," I said, raising the glass. "Cheers."

He winked. "Cheers, love." His smile remained, his eyes intently watching my every move.

I put the rim to my lips and sipped. Gods, it was delicious. So wonderfully rich. I hadn't realized how weak or on the brink of starvation I was. Although I appreciated Sabine's blood, it was never enough.

The thirst grabbed hold of me, but I was aware of it, and kept it at bay. I wasn't about to embarrass myself in front of the captain.

In no time, I'd emptied the entire glass.

This blood—Sebastian's blood—felt different from Sabine's. It was somewhat magical. My breath quickened as the fluid slithered through my body, instantly strengthening my limbs, and taking away the nauseous feeling.

"Give it a few minutes, love," he said, peeling the glass from my clenched hand, his fingers brushing against mine.

I couldn't respond because I was riding an incredible high. I closed my eyes and laid back on his billowy pillows, letting the overwhelming buzz of the fresh blood run its course. My body felt heavy. My mind numb.

Soft. The bed was so soft.

My eyes snapped open. I was disoriented, wondering where the hell I was. Glancing around, I tried to get my bearings.

"Well, well. Look who's back from the dead," Sebastian cooed from the side of the bed. "You've been asleep for nearly two days, love." He was relaxing in a lounging chair, flipping the page of a book. He was wearing long black trousers and a white, cuffed tunic. The drapes were drawn, blocking the brilliant sun from frying me to a crisp.

"Wait. Two days?"

"You slept like the dead," he replied, uncrossing his legs.

I stretched my limbs and they felt strong and refreshed. I wasn't nauseated for the first time. I gasped, suddenly wondering what Markus would think.

"Your friends know you're here," he added casually, that dimpled grin widening. "The burly guard has been in and out.

Probably making sure I'm not ravaging you." He winked, and I laughed.

"What about the storm?" I yawned.

"It wasn't very rough. You slept right through it."

I leaned back into the pillow and turned to him. "Thank you, Sebastian. I guess I really needed that."

He placed his book on the desk. "Aye. You were so exhausted you were snoring."

I gasped. "I was not!"

"You were, and it was quite unpleasant." He kept a serious expression for a few moments before bursting out in laughter.

I growled at him. "And where did you sleep those two nights?"

He pointed to the opposite side of the bed. "But don't fret, love. Between cold baths and your rather large friend popping in, nothing transpired. Though, watching you sleep was rather tempting."

"Mmm," I hummed.

Sebastian chuckled, rising from his chair. "I'll be back momentarily."

Minutes later he walked back in with another glass filled with crimson liquid.

"Breakfast in bed," he announced. "Fresh, with nothing but my exceptional, high-quality, blood." He handed it to me, his fingers skimming over mine. This man was a master of seduction and he knew it. He knew the right words, where to touch, how to touch . . . subtly, yet effectively.

I sat up and took the warm glass. Closing my eyes, I inhaled, savoring the smell. His blood had my body tingling. My incisors lengthened, knowing I was about to feed.

When I opened my eyes, Sebastian's sea-blue eyes were attentively set on my face.

"What?" I breathed. Heat filled my cheeks.

"It's so gods damned sexy, watching you crave my blood."

"I crave *all* human blood."

"Yes, love. But right now, you *want* mine." He smiled widely. "Hell, woman, I'd even let you bite me right now."

"No," I said, holding a hand up.

"Why not? I thought if it comes straight from the source, it makes you stronger."

"It does. But I'm still new at this. It's difficult for me to let go." The image of Spring made my stomach churn. "Besides, I can't let this fine glass of your exceptional blood go to waste." I held the glass up to my nose and inhaled again. Gods above. My body craved it. Yearned for it. I tilted the glass to my lips and drank. Consumed until every drop was gone.

His blood was rich—sweet and savory at the same time. Much different from Sabine's. Hers was pleasant, but Sebastian had something distinct. Maybe it was his overpowering male essence, but when I was done, it caused me to moan.

His blood coursed through my veins, restoring my cells . . . and my libido.

"Hell, woman. You're not allowed to moan in my bed when I'm not in it," Sebastian exhaled.

I opened my eyes and licked the traces of blood off my lips. Lust filled his eyes as he watched every movement.

"Mmm," I hummed. "Delicious."

"Wicked," he breathed. "Simply wicked."

I rose from the bed and walked up to Sebastian, pressing so close I could feel the warmth radiating through his flesh.

I put the empty glass in his hand. "I should get back to the others."

His head dipped forward, his face inches away. "Or, you could stay."

"I would," I whispered, buttoning the top of his tunic. "But you're much too tempting, captain."

He groaned, a mischievous grin played on his lips.

This game between us could go far fast, but we both knew a relationship could never happen. Yet despite knowing what I was, he'd been nothing but kind to me, helping keep me alive and strong. . . just like Sabine had. I really liked Sebastian and had come to realize why my great-grandfather trusted us in his care.

I lay both hands on either side of his face and kissed him. Lips and tongues and teeth swirled and danced until my mind became numb. Sebastian's arms folded around me, pushing me tight against his warm frame.

I was losing control, but Sebastian was the first to pull away, leaning his forehead against mine, his breath ragged.

"Thank you, Sebastian," I murmured against his lips. "For everything."

"Aye, love. Anytime," he said, giving me a handsome dimpled grin.

I gave him one last kiss before I left his embrace and walked out of his bedroom. My legs still weak.

"You're going to sink me, you wicked woman," he hollered after me.

I smiled and turned around. He was leaning against the doorframe, a hand combing through his golden-brown hair.

Maybe, if circumstances were different and I wasn't running for my life, I would be open to a relationship. Or perhaps not. Not with Sebastian, anyway.

Sebastian was a man of the sea. A pirate. And he would die a pirate. He would never settle. Not when he probably had women at every port, awaiting to satisfy him.

Besides, I hated sailing and couldn't wait to set my feet on solid land. I would be glad never to set foot on a ship again. And my life, at the moment, was way too complicated and still filled with too much danger.

No. We were two passing souls who found and comforted each other in a time of need.

Walking back to my room, I couldn't help but smile. I felt incredible. Stronger than I had since I'd transformed. And without guilt. Sebastian had willingly given me generous amounts of blood, enough to heal me completely.

When I opened the door to my cabin, Sabine and Markus were in the middle of a game of cards, both laughing. It was nice to see their friendly faces.

"Calla!" Sabine squeaked. She jumped up and ran over, throwing her arms around me. When she released, she examined my face. "Wow! You look so much better."

"I feel amazing. Captain Salloway gave me some of his blood." I glanced at Markus who had a scowl on his face. "Served in a glass."

"Sure," he rumbled. "But you do look better. Not so . . . pasty." I saw a slight smile play on his lips.

"Thanks," I chimed. "I'll take that as a compliment."

His gaze drifted to Sabine. "Are we going to finish this game?"

"Yes!" She plopped back down across from him.

As they wrapped up their game, I didn't know what to do with myself. The sun was out so I couldn't open the porthole, even though I wanted to. I wished I could feel the sunlight on my face and soak my body in its warm rays. But I was now a creature of the night. Darkness was my life. And I wasn't sure if I could deal with that for the remainder of my new immortal life.

"You are made of fire and magic. The light of day cannot harm you." That voice.

It was Leora's, and it was so strong, as if she were speaking directly into my ear.

Could it be true? Could I live like the purebloods?

But I saw what the sunlight could do. It turned my hand into a fiery torch.

"The spell has been released, and you are no longer bound by darkness." The voice spoke again.

I had to find out.

I walked up to the porthole. I could feel my heart racing. My heart. The heart that should have been dead . . . not beating. The heart Leora's spell protected. So—I gripped the rag Sabine put over the porthole window and tugged it off.

"Calla!" Sabine wailed, scrambling to her feet.

Before she could get to me, I stuck my arm directly in the sunlight.

Sabine froze and so did Markus, who was on his feet. Their eyes were fastened to my arm. All of us watching, waiting for it to burst into fire.

After almost a minute, I still *wasn't* burning. I realized then that my life had changed.

I dared to step further until the sunlight touched my face. Warmth kissed my cheeks, nose, eyelids. Closing my eyes, I savored the feeling. A feeling I thought I would never experience again.

The sun was life. I'd been a drained battery, but standing in its rays, I felt like it was recharging my cells.

Tears poured down my face as I looked back at my friends.

"I can't believe it. It's a dream come true."

I was standing in the sunlight, like the rest of the purebloods. Only I wasn't like them. I was something entirely different.

Markus's expression was riddled with confusion. "How is this possible?"

I shrugged my shoulders and gazed into his eyes. "I don't know. I just thought about how amazing it would be to feel the sunlight on my face again. Then I heard a voice in my head. It told me I am made of fire and light and that the sun cannot harm me."

"Calla. This gives you an incredible advantage," Sabine breathed.

"We can't tell anyone about this," Markus warned. "Enemies of Incendia will be after you. And vampire clans will seek you out. There is no one like you. A merging of Vampire and Incendian Royalty."

He didn't need to tell me how dangerous my powers were, especially to those who already despised the Incendians for their abilities. A power beyond all others, snuffed out because of envy and hate. And now, here I was, a half-breed.

Because I'd been kept on the verge of starving, I still hadn't confirmed the vampire powers. But I knew, when fed properly, I could probably be just as strong and fast as the others. I also possessed their heightened senses, so I literally had the best of both races.

A wave of hope struck me. I had a beating heart and now I could live in the sunlight. There was one person I wanted to share this incredible news with, more than anyone. And that was Trystan.

I wondered where he was, or what he was doing right now. I wondered if he'd met Brynna and tried to explain everything that had happened. But most of all I wondered—even if I shouldn't have since our bond was severed—if he still thought about me.

Between Markus and Sabine's endless questions and theories—most that went unanswered—night fell swiftly upon us. As we were about to settle down for the night, a powerful boom rocked the ship.

"What was that?" Sabine gasped.

We waited in silence.

Boom! The ship lurched again, this time to the starboard side.

Sabine and I bellowed, desperate to gain purchase on anything to keep us from tumbling across the room.

Something big hit us. Or maybe we'd hit it.

When the ship evened out, we heard Captain Salloway's voice echo down the hallway. "All hands on deck!"

We stood by and listened as footsteps pounded down the hall toward the deck, but in the minutes that pursued, the shouting of the crewmen suddenly shifted into screams of terror.

Markus shot up and was at the door. "Stay here. I'll be right back," he ordered, his face tight.

Sabine and I nodded.

"Do you think its other pirates?" she asked, her eyes wide with panic.

"I don't know." I wasn't sure what it was.

Another hit, and the ship rocked again, tipping port side. Sabine wailed, sliding across the floor.

This wasn't pirates. This was something else.

Maybe the sea had finally awakened, and *The Damned* was its prey.

There was no way I was going to stay in this room and die. I was given a powerful gift—to call fire and manipulate water. Maybe I could help, even if I was still learning how to use those gifts.

"Sabine, get in the hammock," I implored. It would protect her from rolling around and getting hurt. She was coiled up on the floor, sobbing and trembling. I picked her up in my arms, rather effortlessly, and put her in the belly of the hammock. "You'll be safe here," I said, folding the sides around her. "I'll be back shortly."

"Calla," she sobbed, tears rolling down her cheeks. "I don't want to die."

Burying my own fear, I clasped her hands and gave her my bravest smile, hoping I could inject the same hope she'd offered me countless times.

"You're not going to die, Sabine. Not while I'm on board.

Even if I have to swim to Incendia with you on my back. Or," I said, tapping my chin, "we can both ride on Markus's back." Her slight smile warmed my heart. "Don't leave the hammock. It's the safest place to be. I'll be back. I just have to see what's out there."

She nodded and settled into the hammock, gripping the rungs as if they were lifelines.

Seeing she was secure, I made my way out the door.

The ship rocked again, throwing me off balance, but my legs were sturdier with Sebastian's blood in me.

As soon as I exited the hallway, I saw chaos. Sebastian's crew were running and hollering with horrified expressions on their faces. Then, my gaze caught sight of what they were running from.

Fear seized every part of me.

CHAPTER TWENTY–EIGHT

It was something right out of hell's abyss. A dark nightmare brought to life. A sea serpent.

Its head looked like a dragon, horned and vicious. Its eyes were glowing yellow. Its mouth filled with rows of razor-sharp teeth.

The creature didn't roar, but let out a painful, high-pitched screech that knocked the crew to their knees, covering their ears. The monster's muscles stretched and shifted. Thick onyx scales rippled down its long neck. A neck which seemed unending, vanishing into the murky sea. In the distance, approximately thirty feet away, a tail raised and slammed down into the water.

Gods, it was enormous.

The sea serpent slithered up the side of the ship, plucking men off the deck. I watched it crush a man between its jaws, then swallow him whole.

Tortured screams echoed as the monster thrashed, tossing men into the sea. The crew tried to fight it off with swords, sticks, and torches—anything they could get their hands on. But their weapons did nothing against the monster's thick scales.

Strong, muscular arms wrapped around my waist and tugged me backward into the shadows and out of immediate danger.

Markus.

"What is that thing?" I exhaled, my body trembling.

His eyes focused beyond me. "A sea serpent."

"Where's Sebastian?" I questioned, praying he wasn't one of those that had been tossed over the side or swallowed whole by the monster.

The serpent thrashed, taking out a mast, tipping the boat port side. Wood and splinters rained down as men wailed, slipping across the deck, struggling to grab hold of anything to keep them from plummeting off the side. Markus held me up, steadying us both in the corridor.

I couldn't remain in the shadows any longer. I'd been given a gift that could help these men. I couldn't stand by and watch them die. Because they *were* dying.

My parents and ancestors would have wanted me to try.

I could feel the magic inside answer my challenge, ready and eager to do my bidding. Markus's arms gripped tighter around my waist, holding me back. He was trying to protect me. A vow he'd made to the King. And I knew he would do everything in his power to keep that promise. But I had my own path to take, and I knew my great-grandfather would understand.

"Let me go," I demanded through gritted teeth, unable to move under his steel grip.

"I will not," he replied. "It's too dangerous out there."

There was no reasoning with him. He would die protecting me.

"Markus, I *have* to go," I said, this time with authority.

Markus's grip tightened to the point I had trouble breathing. "You know I can't let you."

"I know," I panted. "And I'm sorry."

"For what?" My hands heated, and as they did, I touched his arms. Markus cursed, his arms recoiling from the burns I'd given him. Burns I knew would be fully healed in no time.

Using my temporary freedom, I sprinted forward, only to be captured by the arm and dragged back down the hallway.

"Let go of me, Markus!" I howled, tugging against him.

"I was ordered to protect you," he snarled, dragging me with him. "You're going back to the room with Sabine."

"No, I'm not!" I shoved my palms into his back.

The power blasted Markus down the hallway. He sailed through the air and struck the wall at the end of the corridor. Before he could recover, I dashed toward the deck.

As I exited the hall, two of the crewmen spotted me.

"A girl!" one shrieked. "There's a girl on the ship!"

I ignored him, charging forward.

"She brought this curse!" the second yelled, but I continued advancing across the deck.

"Calla!" It was Sebastian's voice. I turned to catch him charging toward me with a sword grasped in his hand. Relief washed over me knowing he was alive.

But with my attention on him, I didn't notice the serpent's yellow eyes fixed on me.

In a split second . . . it struck.

Sebastian dove forward, shoving me out of the way. I hit the deck and rolled. Turning back, I watched in sheer horror as the serpent's jaws clamp down on Sebastian's leg.

"No!" I cried.

It would've been me. It should have been me.

The monster raised Sebastian into the air. His agonizing cries echoed straight through my soul.

He'd saved my life. I couldn't let him die.

Rage filled me. Heat roiled under my skin until steam billowed from my flesh and curled around me. Then, my palms burst into flames—bright yellow, orange, and red.

The remaining crew gazed on me with horror in their eyes and backed away.

I stalked toward the sea serpent, the power growing inside, leaving no room for fear. I thrust my arms toward it, like I did in the cell, one after another. But the monster's scales were indestructible, and I was barely inflicting injury.

I called another flame, this time aiming for its eye.

With all my might I shoved that power forward and it

struck its mark. Screeching in agony, lashing its head, the sea monster finally unlocked its jaws. Sebastian fell to the deck, his body limp, unconscious.

"Take him off the deck!" I wailed at the closest crew members. They rushed over to Sebastian, grabbed his arms, and dragged him to safety.

The serpent was focused solely on me—the one who'd blinded its left eye. It struck, but I dove to the side, its head crashing through the deck's floorboards. I quickly produced another fireball between my palms, and as it grew, hurled it toward its head.

The serpent let out a shriek so loud it knocked me to my knees.

It was hurt, but not dying. Its scales were too thick for my flames to penetrate.

Water was my only other option. But that power was so new, I didn't know how to control it.

Strike after strike, the sea serpent targeted me, and each time, even with my new vampire speed, I barely managed to escape.

The sky was black, the water an inky abyss that would become our grave if I didn't stop it.

Another strike barely missed me. As the serpent's head smashed through the deck, I raced to the edge of the ship and drove my palms out. A wall of sea water blasted forward, striking the creature's body, thrusting it backward. It let out a screech before plunging back into the water.

I knew it wasn't done.

Water rippled near the edge of the ship, and I caught a glint of yellow. The creature broke surface, jaw unhinged, razor-sharp teeth aimed at me.

The creature struck, breaking the top part of the bow. He was tearing Sebastian's boat apart. His life. His home.

Again, I thrust my palms over the water and begged, pleaded, demanded it serve me. I sent my fury, along with every ounce of strength I could muster, and channeled it into the water. The water swirled faster and faster. Then, like a cyclone, it shot skyward, forming a water cocoon around the entire serpent's frame.

The creature struck against the funnel, but it held.

Temporarily.

I could feel that great energy coursing through every part of me. The power was strong. Much stronger than I was. And it was weakening my body. The tattoos on my palms throbbed, my arms shook under the tremendous stress. I couldn't let this monster free. If I did, we'd all die.

This monster must have been the reason so many ships and crews had disappeared without a trace.

The serpent thrashed and struck at the water cocoon, and each time he did my power waned. I didn't know how much longer I could hold it.

"Calla." Markus was at my side, but this time he wasn't ordering me back. Instead, he slapped a fist to his heart, "What can I do to help?"

I looked at him, not sure if he could do anything. All I wanted was to end this nightmare. I needed the sea serpent, wrecking Sebastian's ship, to die.

The serpent's head struck repeatedly, making me weaker and weaker. As my power faltered, the creature's head burst through the funnel of water. It wouldn't be long until it would entirely break through.

I watched water rush down the serpent's head, down its neck. *Water.* Water I was able to manipulate.

I dropped my arms, letting the funnel dissipate. The serpent plunged back into the sea, but I knew it wouldn't be long before it returned with a vengeance.

Any more damage to the ship and the sea would swallow us whole. Either that, or our flesh and bones would be digested in the belly of the monster.

Weakened to the edge of exhaustion, I gathered whatever strength I had left inside me.

Terrified screams of the crewmen pierced the blackened sky as the creature broke surface. It was a hundred yards away, barreling toward the ship. It was going to sink us.

I faced the serpent and punched both arms out over the water. It shot up like a dam in front of me. I forced that water and all my energy outward.

The wall of water charged forward, slamming into the creature, slowing its course. But it shook its head and continued its path of devastation.

As it closed in, I focused on the water rushing down

the serpent's body. I directed my energy to its neck, which I assumed was its most vulnerable part, and drove my palms forward.

With a loud shout, I threw out every ounce of energy I had left, pushing further. A piercing and indescribable scream was accompanied by a sickening snap. The creature's head twisted unnaturally. Its body went limp, its upper body crashed onto the deck.

It was dead.

I'd killed the monster. Broke its neck.

The crew rushed forward with blades and sticks in their hands, chopping and hacking until they'd decapitated it. When the head was severed, I watched them cheer, their faces beaming and bloodied, with weapons grasped in their raised arms.

The cool, briny breeze felt refreshing against my heated flesh. Gripping the side of the rail, my body was failing. Every part of me was spent—weak and trembling. But watching them, so happy to be alive, was worth it. My power had proved itself, not only to the crew members, but to me.

Markus headed toward me from across the deck, eyes narrowed, a smirk on his face. But that smirk instantly turned into an expression of dread.

"Calla!" he howled, hurtling toward me, his arm reaching out.

But his gaze was beyond me.

The serpent's body flailed out of impulse, thrashing

across the deck. Before I could blink, it slammed against me.

I was weightless, thrust over the side of the ship. Falling. Falling. Falling.

My back slammed into the icy water, punching the air out of my lungs. My vision dimmed as I watched the ship sail away from me.

I could hear Markus hollering my name. Torches lit the edge of the ship, the crew searching for me. But I'd drifted too far, too fast. The night and the shadowy water concealed me, immersing me in an icy embrace.

The serpent was dead and the ship intact because I'd used my power to save them. But it came with a price. My life. And I would go to my watery grave, thankful that Sebastian and Markus and Sabine and the crew of *The Damned* were still alive.

My eyes were heavy. Exhaustion gripped me in tight clutches, drawing me down into the dark, watery abyss.

CHAPTER TWENTY–NINE

I woke to see a pitch-black sky. No, it wasn't the sky. It was a cave where the air was stagnant and smelled of brine and rotted seaweed.

I was lying on a bed of sand. And there was sand on the entire floor around me.

Was this purgatory?

"Ah, the Sea Star awakens," a rich voice spoke off to my side.

I rolled my head to the side and watched a young man, perhaps early twenties, step out of the shadows. He was over six feet, but his eyes . . . they were lambent, a mesmerizing icy blue. He was handsome, with a sharp nose and jaw, with full lips that were curled slightly upward. Light silvery-blue hair fell to his shoulders. He was shirtless, muscular abs, pecks, and biceps glistened on sun-kissed skin in the light of a nearby

"Who are you?" I questioned, my voice a bit hoarse.

He stepped closer, muscular arms crossing over his tanned chest. "I'm Kai. And you are lucky I happened to be passing by. I sensed your energy and by chance, saw your body splash into the sea."

I scanned the area and realized we weren't in a cave. The walls surrounding us were transparent. They were made of *water*. It was a dome, maybe twenty feet in height and width. And if I looked hard enough, I could see things—sea creatures—swimming around us.

Good gods. I sat up, my breath quickening. I suddenly felt claustrophobic, like I was in a watery coffin waiting for the air to run out or crash down and drown us. And drowning was one of my greatest fears.

"Where are we?" I asked, my eyes scouring the entire dome.

"Somewhere under the Sangerian Sea," he responded, a gleam in those luminous eyes.

"How long have I been here?"

His head inclined slightly, his eyes calculating. "I'd say about two days."

Two days? Sabine. Markus. Incendia.

"I have to return to the ship." I rose to my feet, but when I tried to take a step, my knees buckled. In a split second, the man captured and drew me tight against his broad, athletic frame. His scent was unique. Not sweet or spicy, but it reminded me of fresh rain.

"You're still weak. You should sit down." His body was

pressed tightly against mine, his warmth seeped through my clothes . . . which were completely dry. "Your ship is still sailing, but with the lack of winds, I'd say they still have a few days before they spot land." I sighed, wondering if they thought I was dead. "You don't need to be afraid of me, Incendian."

I looked into his icy-blue eyes with the unnatural glow. Eyes that appeared sincere.

"How do you know I'm Incendian?"

His head gestured toward my hand. "I saw the symbols on your palms. I also felt your power pulse through the water. I'm an Aquarian," he stated, reaching out and taking my wrist, twisting my palm upright. "You are an elemental, like me, with the ability to manipulate water. Aquarians also possess that power, which is how I formed this water cave." He raised his arm and casually swept his hand above him. Water rippled across the ceiling, mimicking his movement. It was magic. Powerful magic that appeared so easily manipulated by him.

I was in awe of him and his power.

"I once heard a story about an Aquarian," I breathed.

"And?" Kai's gaze narrowed on mine.

"My grandfather told me the story. He was a fisherman who lived in Aquaris," I explained. "He spoke of encountering a man who lived in the sea. No. Not in the sea . . . *under* the sea," I amended. "No one believed him. They all assumed he'd gone crazy in his old age, but he swore it was true, up until the day he died.

"He said, while on one of his fishing rounds, he'd discovered a man, unconscious and barely alive, lying on a stretch of rocks in a deserted cove. He carried the man onto the shore, where he made a fire and tended to his wounds. Because the man was unconscious, my grandfather built a small shelter, and for three days, remained with him until he finally woke up.

"My grandfather fed him fish and crustaceans he'd caught and nursed the man back to health. During that time, the man told him wondrous stories of his home and of his people who resided beneath the sea, in a place called Aquaria.

"When the man was strong enough, he thanked my grandfather and vowed that one day he would return his kindness. My grandfather said he watched the man walk into the water, and with one glance back, waved before he sunk under the waves, never to be seen again."

Kai's expression altered. He looked addled, or maybe even shocked.

"What was your grandfather's name?" He spoke evenly, his eyes locked on me.

"Marinus," I replied. "Marinus Thorne."

Kai released my wrist and took a step backward, eyes expanding, his hand fisting on his chest. "Marinus Thorne was the man who saved my father."

"Really?" I was shocked. For one, my grandfather's story about the undersea man was real. And two, I just met the man's son. "What a small world." I smiled and held out my hand to him. "My name is Calla. Thank you for saving my life. And since it seems my grandfather saved your father . . . I suppose we can call it even."

"No," he said, his voice as gentle as a soft breeze, taking my hand. "My family is forever in your debt."

"Not me," I corrected. "It was my grandfather who saved him, and now he's gone. So, there is no longer a debt to pay."

He gave a melancholy smile. "You don't understand. My father is irreplaceable. If he died, the weight he bore would be on my shoulders. What your grandfather did cannot simply be paid off."

"Just tell your father that you saved Marinus Thorne's granddaughter. To him, you'll be a hero."

A twisted grin raised on his lips. "Not a hero. Just someone who was in the right place at the right time." His expression shifted. "I'm saddened I'll never get the chance to meet the man who rescued my father. Your grandfather is a hero in my kingdom."

Kai fisted his right hand and slapped it against his chest, directly over his heart. His eyes met mine, this time with a veracity I could not dismiss. "If you *ever* require my assistance, Calla, just call, and I will come to you. No matter where. No matter when."

I was taken back by his gesture, and knowing the danger I was in with Roehl, having allies would be advantageous.

"If I ever needed to call you, how would I do it?"

Kai stepped forward and held my left hand, placing my

palm flat against his. Threading his fingers through mine, he closed his eyes. Warmth radiated through my hand, tingling through my fingers, up my arm, and throughout my entire body. When his eyes opened again, he smiled.

"What did you do?" I look at my palm, the tattoo glowing bright blue.

"I've connected our elements," he replied. "Don't worry, it has nothing to do with our power. Consider it a means of reaching me. Should the need ever arise."

I examined my hand closer, the glowing blue diminishing. "How does it work?"

Kai took hold of my left wrist, his eyes serious, latching onto mine.

"To call me, just hold your palm up to your mouth and speak my name."

He let go, and took a step back, his eyes anticipating me to do as he instructed.

I hesitated before raising my palm to my mouth.

"Kai? Can you hear me?"

"Of course I can hear you. You're two feet away." He let out a barking laugh before bowing dramatically. "But I'm here and willingly at your service."

My face heated with embarrassment and anger. I fisted my palm and crossed my arms over my chest. "You tricked me."

"No," he said, his expression softening. "I just wanted to hear you say my name."

Good gods.

Kai took a step closer. "In all earnestness, Calla. If you should ever need help, just make a fist, and call out to me in your mind. It's as simple as that."

"Can you do the same?" I asked, my arms still crossed. "Can you call me too?"

He gave a smirk, then closed his eyes. The surrounding water rippled as he fisted his hands. Then I heard his voice, loud and clear, reverberating off the watery walls even though his mouth wasn't moving. "I am here, Calla. And promise to come if you should ever call."

One of his eyes slid open, a slightly darker shade of blue, but still illuminated. Then both eyes snapped wide.

"No!" Kai roared. Suddenly, his arms were enclosed around me, twisting me around, shielding me from a blast of water behind us.

Kai quickly let go of me and moved toward three men who literally vaulted into our water cave. They looked like soldiers, or guards, but not like the soldiers I'd seen. These men wore helmets that were pearlescent, their armor in gradient from dark blue to light and scalloped like fish scales. Across their breasts were crisscross straps with a pearlescent circle in the middle that bore a symbol—two tridents in an X shape with a seahorse in the middle. In their fists, they grasped long, silver spears.

They must have been Aquarians.

The guard in the center, tanned with silver hair and aqua

eyes, took a knee in front of Kai, placing a fisted hand over his chest.

"Your father sent us when your escorts returned, stating you'd evaded them." The man paused, his eyes finally glancing in my direction.

"Come on, Torrent," Kai chuckled, slapping a hand to his shoulder. "You know those escorts can't keep up with me."

"We were given orders to accompany you to your destination, Highness."

Highness?

I swore I heard a growl from Kai as he grabbed the guard's arm and yanked him up to his feet. "Tell my father I'll make the meeting. And I don't need escorts."

"But, highness—"

Another growl. "I told you to refer to me as Kai," he said through gritted teeth, his back to me.

Little did he realize, with my heightened vampire senses, I could hear every word they were saying, even while whispering.

The man bowed his head. "Yes, hi—I mean . . . Kai."

Kai exhaled noisily and shifted to me, frustration crumpling his face. "I'm sorry, Calla. I would have got you something to eat, but if you're ready to leave, I will take you to your ship."

I removed the smile from my face and nodded. "I'm ready."

I wondered why he was trying to hide the fact he was

Aquarian royalty. The guards made it obvious he was.

Kai walked up to me and took my hand, but I didn't move.

"How are we going to travel?" I asked. Being an Aquarian and living underwater, I was sure they had a way to breathe in it. But I couldn't.

Kai led me to the edge of the watery dome and tugged me against his rock-hard frame, making me gasp. "Do you trust me?" His luminous eyes tightened.

I angled my head to the side. "I don't know you well enough."

He took my wrists in his hands and raised my arms, interlocking them around his neck. His right hand moved to the small of my back, pressing me even tighter against him. *Good gods.* We were so close I could see the veins pulsing in his neck.

Before the thirst slammed me and my incisors elongated, I turned my face away from his neck and held it against his shoulder. I was weak and hungry but wasn't going to bite my only ride out of here.

"Hold on tight or you might drown," he said flatly, making my heart race with fear.

I looked over at the guard's and their faces were like stone. Void of expression. Kai turned his head to them with a smirk. "I hope you three can keep up." With me in his arms, he leaped into the wall of water.

I held my breath, tightening my grip around his neck. I was going to die. I couldn't hold my breath much longer. Then, in a split second, an air bubble formed around our heads, to our shoulders, allowing me to suck in a heavy breath.

"I advise you wrap your legs around my waist for added grip," he said, his eyes ahead.

"Is that what you say to all the girls?"

"No, it's great advice. A matter of life or death, Sea Star."

"Sea Star?"

"That's my nickname for you, because this ride will have your limbs suctioned to me." His broad smile made me growl, but I obeyed his request, securing my legs around his waist. Because the thought of drowning was far worse. As soon as I fastened my ankles together, Kai straightened his back, jettisoning us through the water. I screamed as the force caused my body to slip. My legs and arms gripped tighter. So tight, they started to ache.

Kai's laughter filled our little air bubble. "Told you so."

I finally managed to yank myself back up, locking my limbs securely around him. Looking around, all I could see was whitewater and bubbles. We must have been traveling fast. Really fast. I shifted my head backward and saw nothing but darkness ahead. How could he see where he was going? Maybe his lambent eyes were like underwater headlights? I had no idea. And really didn't care. I just wanted to get out of the water, alive.

"How are we moving so fast?" I dared to ask.

We suddenly slowed, then Kai raised his right hand and wiggled his fingers. "We use our energy to drive us through the water."

"Wow," I exhaled, then peered behind us. "Where are the guards?"

He snickered. "Like I said before, *no one* can keep up with me." He shoved his hand back down to his side and we blasted through the water.

I examined his neck and didn't see any traces of gills and wondered if he could breathe underwater. "You don't need an air bubble, do you?" I asked.

He turned his attention to me for a moment. "No."

Before I could ask another question, he spoke, "So, Sea Star, why were you on a pirate ship in the middle of the Sangerian Sea?"

I blinked. "What?" He'd thrown my line of thought completely off. My grip was slipping, so I readjusted and clamped down tight, my muscles starting to ache.

"I hope you know I would never let you drown," Kai murmured, as if he could read my mind. "You don't have to squeeze so tightly. Unless you want to. And in that case . . . I really don't mind." A devilish smirk.

I rolled my eyes and loosened up a bit. He was right. He did save me, so why would he go through all the trouble and let me drown?

"So?" he questioned, his eyes fixed on the darkness ahead.

"So, what?"

"Why were you on a pirate ship in the middle of the Sangerian Sea?"

I sighed, thinking about the bizarre tale that brought me to Captain Sebastian Salloway and *The Damned*. "It's a really long and complicated story."

"We have about an hour," he said. "And I happen to like stories."

"Wait. The ship has been sailing for two days. Can you really catch up to it in an hour?"

There was a glint in those lambent eyes. "I could do it in a fraction of the time, but . . . I have a passenger to consider."

Heavens above.

I couldn't imagine traveling any faster. Especially underwater.

CHAPTER THIRTY

Since Kai *had* saved my life, and because our families were connected, I felt I could trust him. And since we had an hour to kill, I told him the story that had brought me to this point.

It seemed I was doing a lot of that lately. Before Trystan, my life was private, and the only person who knew anything about me was Brynna. But life had changed. I wasn't that same girl. If I were to survive, maybe sharing my story with the right people would help keep me alive.

The truth needed to be told. Especially about Roehl, who was spreading his lies.

When I finished, my head was throbbing, having relived the horrific ordeal all over again.

But spilling my guts to Kai was also freeing. Like a fragment of the heavy weight I'd carried on my shoulders had been unfettered and set free.

"So," I sniffed, "That's why I was on a pirate ship in the

midst of the Sangerian Sea."

Kai's eyes remained ahead, his expression unreadable. He gave a slow nod, staring ahead like he was deep in thought. "Gods, you weren't joking when you said it was long and complicated."

"I warned you."

His eyes softened as he glanced down at me. "I'm sorry for your loss, and all the horrors you experienced. But I can tell, just from the short time we've been together, that there is a strength in you. You wouldn't be here if it weren't true." He gave a smile that melted my insides before looking ahead into the dark waters. "And you have achieved what no mortal man has ever done before. You single-handedly defeated the Sangerian sea serpent." His eyes met mine again, with an expression I could only interpret as pride. "And that alone, Sea Star, is a feat of greatness."

Greatness. It didn't seem like greatness. There was so much death and destruction that monster did before it died. But the fact did remain, that I, Calla Caldwell, had killed a sea monster. One of which terrible tales were told. Tales of a monster who crushed ships and devoured men whole.

The power entrusted to me was great, but it also came with a cost. It exhausted me and I wondered if using it for too long would eventually drain my life.

There were so many unanswered questions battering my mind. Questions about my father and if he were safe, my abilities, Incendia, and what would be waiting for me there.

Everyone said it was in ruins, but Leora told me my answers would be there. I had to follow. I had to find out.

But it was all so draining, and I was tired and didn't want to talk about my complicated life anymore.

"So, what about you, Highness?" I chimed, trying to flip the conversation.

"Please, don't," he exasperated. "The word vexes me."

"Highness? Why should it? If your father is king of Aquaria, then you are a prince, and they should honor you as such."

A smirk. "Then, how shall I address you, lady? Princess? Majesty? Or will your highness suffice?"

The words made me shudder. "Fine. You win," I blurted. "First names only."

Kai's eyes saddened. "But Sea Star is so befitting. A double meaning. Not only because you are suctioned to my body like one, but you literally fell from above and landed in my watery realm, adding sparkle to my life."

I let out a bellowing laugh. "Great. But if I have a nickname, you should have one too."

His luminous icy-blue eyes twinkled, and a single brow lifted. "By all means. Let's hear it."

"Hmmm." I thought about it, and the first thing that popped into my mind was —

"What about Sea Horse?"

Kai choked on his next breath. "Sea horse?"

"Well, I am riding you—" I paused, not liking my

judgment of words or where this topic was going. "Fine," I grumbled. "No nickname for you. Kai it is."

Kai let out a boisterous laugh. "Well, Kai is a befitting name with numerous meanings." His smile was so wide I could see his straight, pearly whites.

"Meanings like?"

"Like, unbreakable and triumphant," he gloated, before his words and expression turned solemn. "But it also means ocean, a safe harbor, and . . ." he glanced at me, his smile turned soft and sweet, "friend."

My heart swelled inside my chest.

Friend. If there was one thing my life had taught me, was that I could find a friend in the most unlikely of places. A cell in Morbeth, a pirate ship, or even under the sea.

"So," I continued. "Since we've become friends, I think it's only fair that you tell me a little about your life. We should have more than enough time left, right?"

"I suppose," he agreed. "I don't share details of my life. I'm a very private man and like to keep my affairs private. But since we've become *friends*, I'll share a bit with you."

I could tell he was speaking sincerely, and I felt extremely fortunate he was going to share even a small part of his life with me. Since my grandfather's death, I'd wanted to know if Aquaria was real. If its people were real. And now, the truth was literally in my grasp—a handsome Prince of Aquaria.

"Unlike your story," he began, "mine is rather boring and not nearly as complicated. I was born in the Kingdom of

Aquaria, where my father is king and my mother, queen. I've lived a sheltered, highly guarded life, as you've witnessed." His head gestured to the three men, lost somewhere in the darkness behind us. "They try. But no one can tether a free spirit."

Kai's arms suddenly wrapped around me, the air bubble disappearing. Holding my breath, we spun through the black water, making a sharp dive before rising and leveling off.

Suddenly, the air bubble was back, making me gasp and cough.

"I'm sorry about that," Kai apologized, his concerned eyes scanning my face. "Are you alright?"

I blew out a sharp breath. "Yes, I'm fine. What happened?"

"We dodged a shark," he declared flatly.

"Oh," I panted. "Well, that's good." I glanced at him, and a smile was back on his face. "How can you see in the dark?"

He smirked. "I've lived all my life under the water. I can see everything as clear as you do on land."

"You can? How?"

He shrugged. "Maybe it's the awesome glowing eyes." Those eyes shifted to mine, accompanied by another roll of laughter. "You know, with a little practice, you could move through the water like this on your own."

I shook my head. "No thanks. I don't have special glowing eyes, and the ocean and I seem to have a lethal relationship."

Kai let out a long sigh. Disappointment swam in those icy-blue eyes. "Water is a part of you. It is an element branded into the palm of your hand. A gift given to you—to us—for a reason. Remember, *you* are the one who has control over it. The water cannot control you, Sea Star," he replied, his gaze quickly meeting mine again. "Especially not your fears."

His words were reassuring, disburdening my heavy-laden shoulders a bit more. Because he was right. I wasn't truly afraid of the water—well, maybe drowning in it—but the fear grew from the frightening things that existed within. But there were good qualities about water. Comforting things, like hearing the waves crash against a rocky coast, watching the light dance across its mirrored surface, or lapping against a sandy shore or even a pirate ship. Not only that, it's where I met Kai and Sebastian . . . who both found comfort living on and under the water.

"Your ship is just ahead," Kai murmured, slowing ever so slightly.

I saw a narrow track of whitewater trailing from *The Damned* and sighed, a bit sad our visit was about to end. There was so much more I wanted to learn about Aquaria and its people. "We arrived much sooner than I expected."

Kai grinned. "Good company makes time slip by."

"It certainly does," I agreed. "So, have you taken many others on rides like this?"

"No," he replied. "And never like this."

Hmm. "What do you mean?"

"The only other individual I've given a ride to was my little sister, but she was on my back." He thumbed behind him, a grin from ear to ear.

My eyes narrowed. "You mean to tell me that you've never carried a beautiful Aquarian girl through the sea who was attached to you like this?"

"No," he replied. "Aquarian's don't need rides. And it's inappropriate for a prince to carry any girl . . . *especially* like this," his eyes drifted down to my body glued securely to his.

"Well, you don't seem like the type who would care whether something is appropriate or not."

A snicker. "You read me well, Sea Star. My sister was an exception because she's a lot like me. She loves to move fast."

Hmmm. "Then what about me? If it's improper . . ."

"You are the granddaughter of Marinus Thorne. My father would have me whipped on a post in the middle of Aquaria if I didn't take care of you. So, I suppose you are also an exception."

"I don't think your guards see it that way."

"That's because I haven't mentioned who you are . . . yet."

"And you expect that will make a difference?"

"You'll see," he chuckled, and it made me wonder just how much of a hero my grandfather really was. I could understand him being regarded in Kai's immediate family and those around him. "I hope you will come to Aquaria and meet my family one day. It would be an honor, especially if you allow me to be your guide around our kingdom." His arm tightened around me. "I'm sure it will cause a stir."

I laughed, sensing Kai was a bit of a rebel. But I liked

him. He was real, and not a bore to be around. And he was handsome. But he was a prince and he lived underwater. The most I would do is drop in for a friendly visit. Even now, I was still trying to calm my anxiety about being in the water.

"If I ever do come to Aquaria, I would be honored to be accompanied by you."

"Good then," he said, with the widest smile yet.

In a few moments we were at the ship, our heads breaking surface. I inhaled the crisp air, my body soaked to the bone. The three guards were still nowhere in sight.

The sun was on the horizon, the sky darkening, and the breeze was picking up. My eyes searched the rear of the ship for anything I could use to climb aboard. But there was not a ladder or rope in sight.

"How am I supposed to get back onto the ship?"

Kai's arm wrapped around me, drawing me back against his warm body. "Hold on, Sea Star."

I folded my arms around his neck and gasped as I looked into his eyes. They were focused and glowing an even brighter blue. Gently resting a hand on top of the water, it started to whirl around us. So fast, it lifted us right out of the water, up toward the ship's deck. Kai shifted his hand and the water bent, carrying us over the railing and setting us gently onboard. With another motion of his hand, the water instantly withdrew into the sea.

"Wow," I breathed, my lips and body quivering.

Kai held out both of his palms toward me. Thousands

of droplets of water dispelled from my soaked clothing and hovered in the surrounding air. The fading sunlight made those droplets illuminate, like tiny fireflies suspended in the air by his magic. My hair, once wet, was now dry, the wind whipping through it.

"*This* is incredible."

Kai stared at me and smiled. "This? It's nothing. It's something Aquarian children can do."

"Well," I sighed, poking one of the droplets with my finger, mesmerized as it gently glided away from me. "I'm not an Aquarian, so this is magical."

I heard him exhale loudly. "There is so much more to show you, but sadly, time is not on my side. Meetings. I detest the congregating of pompous men who sit around trying to sound wise, passing out orders." He raked his fingers through his silvery-blue hair. "Well, Sea Star, you've been delivered safely, as promised."

"Thank you, Kai, for saving me."

He gave a pleasant smile. "The pleasure was mine." He thumbed over the railing and I peered down to discover the three Aquarian soldiers bobbing in the water, their faces still hard.

I waved to them, but they didn't wave back. And I guess I didn't expect them too.

Kai's laughter resounded through my tired and achy bones. "I'll talk to them about their manners."

"No, please don't," I begged. "I don't want to be on the

Aquarian guard's hate list."

There was a gleam in his narrowed eyes. "Oh, trust me. You will never be on such a list." He chuckled, then bowed at the waist. "It's been a pleasure, Calla Caldwell. Sea Star." Taking my hand, he placed a tender kiss to the back of my fingers. "Till we meet again."

In a flash, he spun and dove off the back of the ship. I gasped, rushing to the edge, and leaning over to watch his head pop up out of the water.

Kai waved and I waved back. "Remember Sea Star, I'm only a fist and a thought away."

I made a fist and held it to my heart. "I promise to call you if the need arises. And I'm holding you to your promise of a tour of your kingdom."

"I'll be looking forward to that day," he said with a broad smile. "Until then!" With a final wave, all four men disappeared under the dark watery surface.

I gazed up at the night sky which seemed to ooze into the shadowy sea, and for the first time, since I'd stepped on board, felt a sense of peace. But my bones, down to the marrow, were tired and throbbing. I hadn't fed in days and everything that had transpired was still weighing heavily on me. I had to make it back to the room to feed and sleep.

Making my path toward the front of the ship, my entire body shuddered. I'd exerted every bit of energy I had on the sea serpent, and whatever was left, to hold on to Kai during the ride over. I struggled to stand straight. Holding onto the railing as I shuffled toward the faint sound of voices. Halfway there, I nearly buckled. The fatigue and weakness were terrifying. I had to stay strong until I reached Sabine.

With the corner of my eyes dimming, I dragged myself along the railing, one hand over the other. But the breeze picked up and caught a sail, making the ship rock. I lost my footing and tumbled onto the deck.

I didn't want to move. I couldn't move. I didn't have the strength to pull myself up, let alone walk across the deck and down the hallway. Right now, all I wanted to do was close my eyes and take a nap, and hope that Markus would find me and carry me back to the room. So that's what I did. I curled up into a fetal position and embraced the darkness.

CHAPTER THIRTY-ONE

Peeling my eyelids open, I found myself back in Captain Salloway's bedroom, under his blankets. This time, the windows were wide open, the heat of the sun was streaming in and caressing my face, and it felt wonderful.

I lifted the bedding covering me and saw I was in a bedgown I had no memory of putting on.

"You are a riddle, love," Sebastian's weak voice spoke.

Whipping my head to the opposite side of the bed, where the captain lay, his head lolled to me with a feeble grin. He looked pale, his face crumpled in pain.

"Sebastian? How are you?" The last time I'd seen him, he'd been bitten by the sea serpent and was knocked unconscious.

"I'm fine, love. But how on earth, after plunging into the sea and disappearing for nearly three days, did you arrive back on my ship?" His eyes were studying me like I was a mystery to be solved.

"Well," I exhaled. "I was rescued by an Aquarian. Luckily, he was swimming by and saw me drop into the water. He took care of me in a water cave until I woke up and then returned me to the ship. How long have I been here?"

"Your burly friend brought you in this morning, and the girl changed your clothes." Sebastian shook his head, his brow furrowed. "You are fascinating. Utterly fascinating."

"I should have been dead countless times, but for some bizarre reason, fate has chosen to keep me alive."

"I think there are greater things at play here, love. Life is an adventure, full of ups and downs and twists and turns. Quite like being on the sea. But it's molding and developing you into the woman you are destined to become. Like it or not, you are at its mercy, and you can only hold on until you arrive at your destination."

I pushed myself to a sitting position, my head pulsing, my body sluggish. "It's nice to have such wonderful friends along this journey." Sebastian smiled warmly. "How are you?"

"Alive. Thanks to you." His sea-blue eyes were terribly bloodshot.

"It was you who saved me, captain."

"I thought it was quite valiant. I had no other choice, given that your attention had wavered. You were smitten by the sight of me, weren't you? I couldn't let the beast eat you for that." He tried to laugh but winced in pain.

"You were valiant indeed. And I might have been a tad

smitten at the sight of you dashing toward me with a sword in hand, being a hero." He smiled and closed his eyes, pain etched his face. "Can I get you something? Medicine? A doctor?"

"No, love. The fellow just left. I must wait until the tonic kicks in. It takes us mortals a while longer to heal, you know." A smirk.

"How bad is it?" I felt horrible that he was suffering.

Behind thick lashes, lust glinted in those bright sea-blue eyes. "Would you care to have a peek?"

I grinned and shook my head. "I saw where the beast clamped down. I just hope it didn't damage any *vital* limb."

"Love, my vital limb is stronger than ever, especially with you tucked in my bed."

I gulped, speechless.

He laughed, then groaned.

"I must add, I would have rather had you bite me than that dreadful creature." His gaze turned back to me, extending his arm. "The offer still stands."

"You're injured, captain," I playfully gasped, throwing a hand to my heart.

"Woman, I'd let you bite me if I was on my death bed."

I shook my head and sighed. "Sebastian, you are a wicked, wicked man."

"Aye, love. Wicked and damned." His eyes turned toward the ceiling. "My crew is rather taken with you. They think you are a great and beautiful sorceress."

"What about the superstition? They don't think I was the

cause of the sea serpent attacking us?"

His head swiveled back to me. "Quite the contrary. They are calling you the Savior of *The Damned*. There was even word they want your face to be carved as our new ship's figurehead."

"Oh, gods no," I exhaled.

He laughed. "You saved most of my crew and my ship. You are powerful, love. Unlike any other I've laid eyes on, and I've seen a great many things on my travels. We will be eternally in your debt."

"You don't owe me anything," I replied. "Besides, you did save me first. So we're even."

Sebastian rolled to his side. "How about *I* bite you? Or nibble. Whatever fancies you. And then we can call it even."

"You, sir," I said, sliding closer to him, taking hold of his warm hand. "I will never, ever forget you or your witty charm."

"Aye. And I the same." His expression turned somber. "I hope you realize my advances are merely play. But if you ever gave in . . ." A mischievous grin. "I wouldn't dare hesitate."

"Oh, believe me, captain . . . I know."

"Although, the King of Morbeth might have me flogged."

I couldn't help but laugh at the thought. I now had the King of Morbeth looking after my wellbeing.

"In the future, if you ever need to procure a ship, my crew and I shall be at your service," he added.

I smiled and lay my head on his shoulder. "Thank you, Sebastian," I breathed.

"Wicked woman. Don't speak my name that way, specially being so close. I might not be able to restrain myself, even with an injury."

"We're about two days from Incendia," Markus stated from his hammock, hands locked behind his head. "Unless the wind picks up. With one mast down, it'll take longer."

Sabine was sound asleep. "How is she?" I whispered. I'd just returned to our cabin, finally able to stand and walk around.

"She was shaken up and a little bruised. She couldn't stop trembling and crying, thinking we'd lost you, so I compelled her to sleep."

I focused my gaze on him. "You *compelled* her?"

"Yes," he said casually.

"I thought compelling was a myth. Then again, I thought vampires were too." He chuckled. "Could you compel me?"

Markus gave me a side-eyed glance. "No. It only works on mortals. Their minds are fragile and easily persuaded."

"Could you teach me to compel?" Maybe it could come in useful one day.

"When I'm rested," he yawned.

I sighed, crossing my arms over my chest. "When will that be?"

"When we reach Incendia."

I growled at his response. He wasn't going to budge. Big, grumpy brute.

CHAPTER THIRTY-TWO

The next afternoon, there was a knock at the door. Sabine was still sleeping, and when Markus didn't move, I went and opened the door. Sebastian stood there with a gold cane in his hand. He was pale but looked dashing dressed in his full captain garb. His hair brushed and drawn back behind his collar.

"I would love for you to accompany me on deck," he said offering me his free hand. "The crew has worked round the clock to repair the damage left by the sea serpent. They would like you to join them in celebration."

"Oh," was all that squeaked out of me.

I wasn't sure if I was ready to meet his crew. I would have been content to have stayed in the cabin for the remainder of our journey and disembark in Incendia with minimal contact from anyone else. I wasn't comfortable mingling with others. Especially people I didn't know. Especially, pirates.

I glanced at Markus, hoping he would forbid me to leave the cabin without his supervision. But he shrugged and said, "It's up to you."

Gods damn him! He was no help.

I knew he couldn't be out in the sunlight but was shocked he would allow me to roam the ship alone with pirates.

I looked back to Sebastian. "I don't have anything to wear." I'd just tied my hair into a loose braid, and was still wearing my black pants, tunic, and boots. At least they were clean after being jettisoned through the water the other night and magically dried by Kai. And there was no way in hell I was going to wear that skimpy red dress.

"Love, you're exquisite just as you are," Sebastian purred.

I internally groaned, hating to be put on the spot. But didn't want to be rude.

"Sure. I'll come," I finally responded.

"Good then." Sebastian reached forward and took hold of my hand, dragging me out.

Before I shut the door behind us, I caught a glance of Markus wiggling his large fingers at me with an immense, toothy smile I wanted to smack off his face.

"Have fun, princess," he piped, making me growl. Before I slammed the door, I heard his laughter. *Big ass brute.*

As we made our way down the hallway, I asked, "So where did you get all the lumber to fix the deck?"

Sebastian inclined his head to me. "After many years and wrecks, we are wiser and have learned to carry extra supplies below. That, and half the crew I employ are artisans."

"Well that's convenient." Sebastian seemed to have a good crew, and they had a great captain.

"Tis," he replied.

My stomach knotted as we neared the end of the hallway. Sebastian paused, gesturing for me to exit first.

I gave him a concerned glance and he offered me a smile and a reassuring nod. "It's alright, love. I'm right behind you."

I straightened my back and held my head high as I strode out of the exit and onto the deck.

Cheers broke out from approximately forty crew members. I suddenly wanted to slink back down the hallway and into my room.

"Sebastian," I growled, feeling uncomfortable with all the unwanted attention.

He laughed and took hold of my hand, leading me forward. "They are fortunate to be alive and wish to celebrate with you."

I was speechless as I peered out on the men's beaming faces, all aimed at me.

They weren't drunk or babbling, and there were no traces of anger, nor any disgruntled faces at my arrival. Instead, they wore wide and cheerful smiles, and seemed genuinely delighted to be alive with their ship intact. Even though a few of their members were taken by the Sangerian sea serpent.

The breeze shifted and an acrid odor drifted to my nose, causing me to gag. "What is that smell?" I choked.

One of the men—an older gentleman with stringy white hair and a long silvery beard—ambled over and extended his arm to me. I joined mine around his and flung a glance back at Sebastian, who hobbled after us, his smile still bright.

"I'm Skip," the man said, his voice sharp-pitched and raspy. "Sorry about the smell. A few drunk men thought it was a great idea to use the serpent's head as a temporary figurehead. But with the blazing sun and heat, they now realize it was a terrible idea."

I laughed, then he led me around the ship and introduced me to the rest of the crew. Each of the men seemed genuinely happy to see me, but I felt uncomfortable watching them bow and address me as princess, serpent slayer, and the most powerful sorceress they'd ever witnessed.

I wanted to stop them, but I didn't. Instead, I smiled and thanked each one. Even Sebastian's father kissed my cheek before leaving, claiming he was in charge of steering the ship for the evening.

To my surprise, they had a banquet of food set up: meat, fish, cheese, bread, and veggies. Nothing I could eat. When they offered me some, Sebastian told them I'd dined in his quarters, which wasn't a lie.

After everyone ate, the celebration commenced. A few of the crew members played instruments: a mandolin, fiddle, lute, and even a concertina, while a shantyman sang his lively tunes.

They carried out a few barrels of gin and rum and everyone danced and laughed and ate and drank until their hearts were content and their stomachs full.

The festivities carried on into the evening, and that was when I finally chose to let go. Let go this once and not feel or think or stress about the future.

After being in Morbeth all those nightmarish nights, I'd forgotten how to live.

All I experienced. All the suffering and horrors and nightmares, being starved and held captive. Despite it all . . . I somehow endured and was now *free*.

I knew my mother was at peace, and now I could only pray that my father and Nicolae were safe and that one day soon we'd meet again. I had a sense, deep in my gut, that we would be together again. Someday. Somehow. But for now, I'd set my fears and worries aside and focus on celebrating our survival and life.

As Sebastian sat on the side, clapping, regarding us with a broad smile, I danced and twirled with his crew. Laughter and music permeated the ship's deck, causing my dark and hollow insides to swell and swirl with all the wonderful and magical colors of life and new beginnings.

As the sun melted on the horizon, Markus and Sabine appeared. I was overjoyed to see them. My heroes. My co-conspirators. My friends.

I ran over to Sabine and grabbed her hands, swinging her round and round until we were in the middle of the deck. We danced and whirled and laughed, drunk on life. Drunk on the fact we were still alive and no longer slaves or captives.

We were free. Amid the beautiful vast sea.

I'd never seen Sabine so happy or carefree, and it warmed my heart. My living, beating heart. Another blessing and a gift given to me. And another thing to celebrate.

There was a raucous shriek from above. Looking up, I watched a black bird circling the ship.

Nyx?

As if the bird heard me, it descended, landing on the railing closest to me. My insides twisted as I made my way over to Trystan's magical crow.

"Nyx," I said, and she cocked her head to the side as if she understood.

I was breathless, gazing into the bird's midnight eyes, knowing Trystan had to have been looking back at me through those same eyes.

This was the first time I'd seen Nyx. The last few times, I was looking out from her eyes. But I *knew* it was her. I had no doubt.

I took a step closer, my heart hammering, my stomach twisting in knots. "Trystan?" I spoke.

The crow screeched again as if Trystan were answering.

In a flash, Markus was at my side. A rumbling growl exited his lips. The crow flapped its wings and let out a loud screech, then tried to nip at the imposing man standing next to me.

"It's okay," I reassured the bird—reassured Trystan. I put a hand on Markus's arm. "This is Markus, and he's made a vow to protect me. He's a friend."

The bird cocked its head to the side again, then squawked, and another growl erupted in Markus's chest. I gave him a narrowed glare, then turned back to Nyx.

"Markus helped me escape from Morbeth. He also helped release the king from a dark spell Roehl placed over him." I sucked in a heavy breath, my head reeling. "I have so much to tell you, and one day I'll share it in greater detail. But the reason I cannot see you anymore is that the witches broke the blood bond I had with Roehl, and in the process, our bond was severed too."

"Calla," Markus roared, stepping closer to me. His voice low and restrained.

I shifted my attention to him. "Markus, you aren't the only one who vowed to protect me."

His jet-black eyes fastened on mine. "But I'm the one who is with you now."

I sighed. "You are. And I appreciate that. But you're going to have to loosen the reins. I think I've more than proven I can take care of myself." He shot me an exasperated look.

I turned my attention back to the crow. "How is this even possible?" I breathed. "We've been sailing for nearly two weeks. How could she fly that far?"

"The crow is magic, and its master is a manipulator of air," Markus responded. "As long as he can see, he can manipulate the air wherever the bird is."

So, Trystan manipulated the wind to help Nyx travel here.

I faced Markus. "How do you know this?"

Markus snickered. "There are a great many things I know, princess."

I glared at him.

Sabine came to my rescue and grabbed Markus's large hand in hers. "Dance with me, Markus," she chimed, tugging his arm.

"I don't dance," he grumbled.

"Then sway with me."

To my surprise, the Captain of the Guard obeyed. Sabine's beautiful brown eyes flickered over to me and winked.

"Thank you," I mouthed.

Her smile widened as she lugged the big brute away.

I turned back to Nyx, not knowing how much time I had left. The bird lurched forward and started pecking at my chest. No, not my chest. The necklace Brynna had given me for my birthday.

I raised the amulet in my fingers and showed the bird. "You like this?"

Nyx screeched and started hopping on the railing. "It was a present from Brynna for my eighteenth birthday. She found it in an antique shop in Sartha." I smiled, looking at the gem. "The color reminds me of Trystan's eyes."

The bird squawked, and my cheeks heated. For a moment I'd forgotten that Trystan could see and hear me.

Nyx pecked at the necklace repeatedly, so I took a step back. What was up with her?

I wasn't about to lose my necklace to a crow. I held the amulet in my hand and swore the azure stone glowed. Tucking it into my tunic, it felt warm against my chest.

"We're on our way to Incendia," I said to Nyx. The bird inclined her head.

I lifted my palms toward the crow to show the tattoos on them. "Leora, the Princess of Incendia, was my great-grandmother. I need to find answers about who I am, and I believe they are there."

The bird flapped its wings, then bowed its head.

"Be safe, Trystan," I said. "And even though the words seem insignificant . . . *thank you*. Thank you for everything. I know the risks you've taken to protect me and my family, and one day, I hope to return your kindness." I blinked away the tears pooling in my eyes. "There are stories I want to tell you, and things I really want to share, *but*," I smiled, knowing Trystan would be happy to hear about my beating heart and immunity to sunlight. "*but* those things I'd rather show you in person."

The crow screeched, flapping its wings, and hopping on the railing. I smiled, guessing that meant he approved.

"Please thank your cadre. Tell them I'm fine and I'll see them again. And tell Brynna I'm so sorry. And I hope she'll forgive me. Tell her I love her, and I'll see her soon."

The bird hopped and flapped and squawked. Then, with a few strong flaps, she lifted into the night sky. I waved and smiled as she circled around the ship before flying away.

As if by magic, the breeze picked up and caught the sail, pushing the ship forward. The crew of *The Damned* cheered, and the music increased. There was so much to celebrate, and now, with the wind in our favor, we'd reach our destination in no time.

I sucked in a deep breath and it hit me. That wonderful scent. That perfect blend of earth and wind and spice mixed with the briny sea air. It swirled around me and tousled my hair. Tears slid down my face as emotions bubbled inside me—everything that had transpired since the night of my eighteenth birthday until this moment.

I closed my eyes and smiled, feeling a tender brush of warm air against my cheek. Perhaps it was a kiss from Trystan.

I imagined it was.

Trystan, manipulator of air, promised he'd find me, and he kept that promise. He'd sent Nyx across the sea to look for me, and now, he knew exactly where I was headed and was helping me reach my destination.

At this moment I felt peace, despite knowing Roehl would eventually come for me.

I stood on the forecastle of *The Damned* with the vast sea ahead of me. The wind steadfast and sure, the moon and stars dancing above in the night sky. My heart was beating and my blood stirring. I felt a tug inside. A firm and persistent pull.

Whatever was out there, beyond the sea, beckoned to me.

I could almost hear it. Calling me home.

To Incendia.

For more information on Cameo Renae, visit her website:

www.cameorenae.com

Join Cameo's newsletter:

https://bit.ly/35hLBGM

Never miss a release. Join Cameo's VIP Text Club.

Text: reads

To: 31996

ACKNOWLEDGEMENTS

A huge thanks to my beta readers: Courtney Smith, Kimberly Belden, Ewelina Rutyna, Cheree Castellanos, Jaci Chaney, Karla Bostic and Kirstie McPherson, for always give me great feedback and catching the little things my eyes didn't.

And of course, to my husband, for keeping me fed, caffeinated, and for being my number one fan and my rock. I love you. Always.

ABOUT THE AUTHOR

 USA Today Bestselling author, Cameo Renae, was born in San Francisco, raised in Maui, Hawaii, and now resides with her husband and children in Alaska.

She's a daydreamer, caffeine and peppermint addict, who loves to laugh, and loves to read to escape reality.

One of her greatest joys is creating fantasy worlds filled with adventure and romance and sharing it with others. It is the love of her family and amazing support of her fans that keeps her going.

One day she hopes to find her own magic wardrobe and ride away on her magical unicorn. Until then...she'll keep writing!

Printed in Poland
by Amazon Fulfillment
Poland Sp. z o.o., Wrocław